IN THIS TOGETHER

LAURA CARTER

Boldwood

First published in 2020 as *Girlfriends*. This edition published in Great Britain in 2025 by Boldwood Books Ltd.

Copyright © Laura Carter, 2020

Cover Design by Rachel Lawston

Cover Illustration: Rachel Lawston

The moral right of Laura Carter to be identified as the author of this work has been asserted in accordance with the Copyright, Designs and Patents Act 1988.

All rights reserved. No part of this book may be reproduced in any form or by any electronic or mechanical means, including information storage and retrieval systems, without written permission from the author, except for the use of brief quotations in a book review. This book is a work of fiction and, except in the case of historical fact, any resemblance to actual persons, living or dead, is purely coincidental.

Every effort has been made to obtain the necessary permissions with reference to copyright material, both illustrative and quoted. We apologise for any omissions in this respect and will be pleased to make the appropriate acknowledgements in any future edition.

A CIP catalogue record for this book is available from the British Library.

Paperback ISBN 978-1-83678-827-0

Large Print ISBN 978-1-83678-826-3

Hardback ISBN 978-1-83678-825-6

Ebook ISBN 978-1-83678-828-7

Kindle ISBN 978-1-83678-829-4

Audio CD ISBN 978-1-83678-820-1

MP3 CD ISBN 978-1-83678-821-8

Digital audio download ISBN 978-1-83678-824-9

This book is printed on certified sustainable paper. Boldwood Books is dedicated to putting sustainability at the heart of our business. For more information please visit https://www.boldwoodbooks.com/about-us/sustainability/

Boldwood Books Ltd, 23 Bowerdean Street, London, SW6 3TN

www.boldwoodbooks.com

For Rocky

1

HANNAH

'...I baptise you in the name of the Father, and of the Son, and of the Holy Spirit. Amen.'

Right on cue, TJ's wide eyes filled with horror, and he started to scream bloody murder in the vicar's arms.

Hannah thought she would cry too if someone threw cold water over her head when she was trying to nap. She smiled, pretending all eyes in the congregation weren't on her as she accepted her baby beside the church font, whispering to him as she bounced him in her arms. The drenched, already thick and unruly mass of black hair on his head served as confirmation that he was now a blessed soul.

She wasn't sure she believed in God and the bible, but she believed in something. And she had many blessings to be thankful for. Luke, her eldest son, who was going through the hormones of a late teenage boy but was a talented, smart kid. Jackson, her middle boy, who was straddling the age of innocence and pre-pubescence – one minute playing tag with friends and the next sneaking glances at the magazines Luke kept under his bed that Hannah pretended not to know about.

And she had Rod, whom she sometimes referred to as the biggest kid of them all, more affectionately known as her husband. When they got pregnant in college, it was as if Rod had frozen in time, forever throwing his clothes on the floor to be laundered by someone else, addicted to all sports – watching, playing, talking about them – but the same guy she'd fallen in love with and was still very much in love with. He was her very good-looking, menace-in-the-bedroom, lazy-ass best friend.

For all their imperfections, including her own, Hannah's family was her world and it was important to her to have them blessed – just in case.

'Can I take him?'

'Sure,' Hannah said, handing off TJ to the waiting arms of Sofia.

Hannah's family didn't stop at her kids and husband. It extended to the three most important ladies in her life – best friends, Andrea and Rosalie, and Sofia, who was biologically Andrea's kid sister but who felt like a sibling to Hannah, too.

Sofia held the baby's soaked head of hair against her chest, and her eyes shone as she made faces to TJ. It had been a while since Hannah had seen the sparkle in those beautiful eyes.

The cause of that spark going out was standing right next to her – Jay, Sofia's husband, whom everyone could see was a waster, except Sofia.

'It looks good on you,' Hannah told her, receiving a soft smile in return, but one that didn't quite reach her cheeks.

'I'm going to be the best god-mommy you've ever had, baby boy,' Sofia told him, miraculously turning his tears to giggles.

'I don't think so. You'll be second best.' The voice belonged to Rosalie, who appeared next to them, tickling TJ's stomach with her perfectly manicured fingers.

Rosalie always looked the part and today was no exception.

Her long hair fell in salon-styled curls across her shoulders. Though she was willing to tickle TJ's tummy, she was standing a safe distance from him in her tailored cream coat, which probably cost more than Hannah earned in a month.

Together, the three women and a baby led the christening party out of the church in New Jersey.

'I don't understand why I'm not a godparent. I'm a godparent to Luke and Jackson,' said Andrea, following behind them.

Andrea was Hannah's oldest and most loyal friend. She and Sofia had moved with their dad from Nashville to New Jersey when Andrea was a young girl and Sofia a baby. They'd moved into a house on the same street as Hannah's parents and Andrea had been in Hannah's class at school.

Their friendship had been formed quickly, when Hannah had shown Andrea the answers to their math homework because Andrea had forgotten to do it. The reality had been that Andrea hadn't just forgotten, she hadn't had time. She was a young girl with too much responsibility at home.

'I thought you said you didn't want to be TJ's godmother?' Rod said, sidling up to Andrea.

'That's not at all accurate,' Andrea quipped, stone-faced. 'I said, if something happened to you and Hannah, wouldn't I have to take the kids anyway?'

'Therefore, you don't need the title,' Sofia said across her shoulder. 'Whereas Rosalie and I haven't been godmothers before and we *need* this.'

Secretly, Hannah secretly hoped that asking Sofia to be a godmother to TJ would give the sisters something new to connect over because recently, there'd been tensions between them.

They reached the churchyard, where Rod called to their group to bunch together for photographs.

Hannah, Rosalie, Andrea and Sofia stood in front of the church, with the remaining friends and family gathered behind them. Luke and Jackson stood to Hannah's left, already looking dishevelled in their school trousers, shirts now partly untucked with skewed ties.

'Plus,' Rosalie said, already smiling as Rod handed his camera to another churchgoer and offered instructions on focusing the lens, 'I buy the best gifts.'

'That isn't true,' Andrea said through her own tight smile, her eyes squinting against the sun's rays as Rod slipped into the row between her and Hannah. 'What about the drum kit I bought Jackson for Christmas? He said that was the best gift anyone has *ever* bought him.'

Rod held out his hands from his side and turned to Andrea. 'And she wonders why we didn't make her godmother?'

Just as Andrea retorted, pointing a finger at Rod, TJ started to cry, Luke pushed Jackson and the stranger sent the camera flashing.

Hannah laughed. A perfect picture of her family.

Her oldest boys fighting. Her baby crying. Rod bickering with Andrea. Rosalie posing as if she was on a red carpet at a movie premiere, oblivious to the world around her. Sofia trying to appease TJ.

If this *were* Hollywood, the four women might be referred to as the ditzy rich one, Rosalie, the bitchy promiscuous one, Andrea, the three-times mom (one accidental) who married the college jock, Hannah, and the slightly quirky, quietly bitter younger sister, Sofia.

On the face of it, Hannah, Andrea and Rosalie might have seemed unlikely friends, and heck, they could drive one another up the wall at times, but they shared a bond as strong as any family.

* * *

Hannah's small yard wasn't really big enough to host twenty adults and countless kids after the christening, but the other options had been expensive. She and Rod were far from flush at the best of times but things were tighter than usual whilst she had been on maternity leave. When she'd go back to work next week, they would get abundantly worse, thanks to childcare bills.

That was the thing about three kids with large age gaps between them. Just when she thought they could start to get on track financially, another kid would come along. Her boys were the loves of her life, but they weren't cheap.

So they had a questionably safe bouncy castle in the yard, Hannah had made party food, Rosalie had generously decorated the place with blue bunting and balloons, and Andrea had supplied a bar load of alcohol.

Happily, the sun was shining. Though it wasn't the warmest of spring days, sitting directly in the sunlight with a sweater, it was warm enough to have the party between the kitchen and outside.

As people started to arrive from the church – kids making a dash straight to the bouncy castle and adults making a dash directly to the drinks table – Hannah fussed around her kitchen, uncovering bowls of dips and chips and laying them out on the bunting-trimmed kitchen table.

'What can I do to help?' Sofia asked, appearing at the kitchen door.

'There're a few pizzas in the freezer in the garage, if you wouldn't mind grabbing them and popping them in the oven?'

'Sure thing,' Sofia said, knowing her way around Hannah's house well enough to get on with the task.

Hannah took a stack of three trays of sandwiches she'd prepared the night before from the fridge.

'Can I help?' Hannah's mom lifted the top two trays from Hannah and set them down on the countertop.

'Thanks.'

She had a strained relationship with her parents.

They'd never approved of Hannah dropping out of college to have Luke. After his birth, everything they said had felt like 'We told you so.'

Whilst Rod was away playing football and finishing college, Hannah had struggled to bring up Luke alone. Night after night and all day long, he screamed through colic. Then one night, when Luke was only weeks old, she heard her parents having a blazing row. Her father – her *own* father – gave her mother an ultimatum. Either he left, or Hannah left with Luke.

Though they'd all agreed to move on from what had happened after Luke was born, things had never been the same between them. Hannah would always invite them to birthdays, christenings and her annual Christmas gathering, and they would spend too much money on gifts for the kids as a way of making amends for the past, but she would never be able to get past the fact that the people who were supposed to love her unconditionally had kicked her out of their home with her newborn baby.

One thing it had taught Hannah though was that unlike her own mom, she would always put her kids first.

'You look pretty,' Hannah said, nodding to her mom's peach dress and jacket combo.

'Thank you. You, too.' She gestured to Hannah's blue fitted dress, which she'd bought for a friend's wedding about five years ago and that she had only just managed to squeeze into. She still had a few pounds of post-baby weight to move before she would be back at her happy weight.

'She always looks pretty,' Rod said, swooping into the kitchen and planting a kiss on Hannah's cheek as he snuck his arms around her waist, stole a sandwich, then left again.

'A little help might be appreciated, Rod,' Hannah called after him.

'I'm entertaining, babes,' he replied through a mouthful of ham and cheese sandwich as he headed back out to the yard. 'Have we got any more ice?'

Rolling her eyes, Hannah left her mom needlessly rearranging things she had already placed on the kitchen table and headed to the garage.

The door was already open and she could hear Sofia and Jay talking inside.

'Soph, come on. It's a kids' party. There're a million better places to be. You used to be fun.'

She leaned against the wall and listened, instantly rattled by Jay. Since he and Sofia had been together, he'd slowly changed her. From convincing her to change her signature edgy haircut, to stopping her from seeing her friends. Jay was manipulative and sly. Increasingly so, Hannah thought.

'Jay, I'm godmother. My dad is here. Plus, I told Hannah I'd help out.'

'Are you telling me you'd rather cook pizzas and listen to kids screaming than be with me, huh?' Then his tone changed and Hannah could imagine him schmoozing up to Sofia, the way he did.

Whatever happened next, Sofia started to giggle. 'Stop it. Not here. Let me help sort the food, then we'll leave.'

Hannah heard the freezer door shut.

'Whatever, Soph. Go cook your pizzas.'

Hannah tiptoed a few feet away from the door, making a mental note to share the latest of Jay's shitty behaviour with Andrea, then called out... 'Soph? Would you be able to bring some ice, too, please?'

'Sure, will do!' Sofia called back.

In the kitchen, Hannah looked up from the quiche she was cutting and watched Jay sulkily traipse outside. Sofia planted a fake smile on her face and set the pizzas and ice down on the counter.

'Listen, Hannah, I'm really sorry but Jay isn't feeling too good. We might have to take off earlier than I wanted to.' She gave Hannah an apologetic look and added quickly, 'Not yet, though, not for a while.'

'Really? It's so great to have you here, though.'

'I know.' Sofia looked glum.

Like Hannah had told Andrea countless times, it was up to Sofia to finally see the truth about Jay, in her own time. Hannah putting guilt on her from both sides wouldn't do anyone any good.

She turned her lips into a smile. 'But there's nothing you can do if Jay isn't well.'

She busied herself with the quiche rather than seeing Sofia's sadness because it broke her heart. The sooner Sofia saw through Jay's act, the better.

Who knew, maybe it was everyone else who had it wrong. Hannah would willingly be proven wrong if it meant Sofia was happy.

When she stepped outside, Hannah saw Rosalie holding on to her latest boyfriend's shoulder as she leant down and fiddled with the heel of her stiletto shoes.

'Shoe trouble, Ros?' she asked.

'Oh, no, Dior doesn't cause shoe trouble.' Rosalie wafted a

hand dismissively as she spoke without a trace of irony. 'I'm just clipping on these protectors.' She held up a translucent plastic thingy in demonstration. 'You clip these on to the heels and they stop you sinking into the lawn, you see?'

'Genius,' Hannah said, chuckling. Only Rosalie would come to someone's house prepared with anti-sinking heel protectors.

Rosalie was aspirationally glamorous. In fact, Rosalie's glamour was essentially what had brought her into the lives of Hannah and Andrea. Back when Andrea had been running her family's indie music label, Hannah had been her assistant and Rosalie had been making headlines as a socialite. She'd been dating one of Andrea's clients, a frontman of a rock band that had since won multiple awards and had numerous platinum albums.

Rosalie, being somewhere between unemployed and self-employed – also known as living off a trust fund and charitably working if she felt like it – used to tag along to the band's recording sessions. She would always bring coffees or food, and she'd sit in the sound booth with Andrea, Hannah and latterly Sofia, as the band laid down their music.

Beneath all the clothes and bags, Rosalie was a genuinely kind and funny woman. Her life was unreal. The money, the cliquey, gold-digging friends, the electronically revolving wardrobe. And the fact she seemed destined to forever search for but never find the Prince Charming to her princess. Knowing Rosalie was like having a free subscription to a television series the others just could not get enough of. Hannah strongly suspected that for their part, Hannah and Andrea brought a sense of realism to Rosalie's otherwise surreal world.

* * *

Hours later, almost everyone had left Hannah's place. Luke had gone to a friend's house to stay over, having had enough of 'kids' – his words. Jackson had crashed from a sugar high and gone to bed earlier than usual. TJ had taken a full bottle of milk and was currently sleeping. Hannah, Rod, Andrea, Rosalie and her boyfriend, George, were sitting around a firepit in the yard as the last of the wood burned. Christmas lights, which Rosalie had incorporated into the decorations for the day, cast a low glow around the lawn.

'Let's go and do something, George,' Rosalie said. 'The night is young. We could go for cocktails when we get back to the city, or—'

'Rosalie, some of us have to work tomorrow.'

It was clear to Hannah that Rosalie wanted to take the huff with George, but then she must have thought better of it. For now, at least. To Rosalie, Sunday night was no different to Friday, Saturday or any other day of the week.

When Rosalie and George left, Rod announced he was going to take a shower. He kissed Hannah on the head where she sat in a garden chair and asked Andrea, 'Will you still be here when I'm done?'

Andrea checked her watch. 'I should be getting back to the city. I'll babysit Hannah whilst you're upstairs, then leave you guys to it.'

'All right,' Rod said, resting a hand on Andrea's shoulder and patting her once. 'See you when I see you. Let's not make it too soon.'

Andrea looked to the sky but amusement teased the half-moons on the sides of her mouth. 'Sweet dreams, pumpkin,' she called after Rod, whose laugh they heard from inside the house.

The nice thing about Andrea and Rod was that, as much as they bickered about Rod's constant tales of when he was very briefly a pro-footballer, and Andrea always thinking she had better taste in music than *everyone*, Hannah knew they would do anything for each other. And the nicest thing was that they would do anything for each other because they both loved Hannah. For her sins, Hannah just didn't exist without Rod *and* Andrea in her life.

Hannah leaned into her garden chair and reclined as far as it would go, closing her eyes. Andrea did the same, so that they were both lying back, staring at the stars.

'How are you feeling about coming back to work next week?' Andrea asked.

Hannah was still Andrea's personal assistant, which sounded like it shouldn't work but for the most part, it did. Hannah had always worked with (or technically *for*) Andrea. When she'd been a new mom and Rod was on the cusp of turning pro but not yet earning any real money, Andrea had given Hannah a job at Sanfia Records. She had allowed Hannah to work flexible hours and bring Luke into the studio whenever she'd needed to.

Seventeen years on, Hannah had never left Andrea. When Andrea moved on from Sanfia Records, it seemed a given that Hannah would go with her. Of course, neither of them had planned for Hannah having TJ and being off work for the last four months.

'Mixed,' she confessed. 'I'm *so* ready for adult company and I've missed the water-cooler chat. But I don't know how I'm going to work out the logistics of travelling to Brooklyn every day and putting TJ in nursery. I was a lot younger the last two times around. Now, the sleepless nights are extra painful.'

'You're only thirty-eight, Han.'

'Believe me, when it comes to screaming babies, there's a big difference between twenty-one and thirty-eight.'

They fell into companionable silence.

'I'm glad you're coming back,' Andrea said in a rare display of affection.

Hannah had the sense there was more to come and remained silent, waiting.

'I've missed you,' Andrea continued, turning to look at Hannah. 'You kind of keep my life together. Don't ever repeat this, but you stop me from... making bad decisions.'

Hannah felt her eyes narrow and her brow furrow. 'Have you been making bad decisions recently?'

Andrea stared at her and Hannah could almost see the thoughts whirring behind her eyes. But in true Andrea fashion, she turned back to looking at the heavens without saying another word. The brief moment of openness was gone.

Andrea pushed her legs down, forcing her garden chair upright. 'I should get going. I have a meeting tomorrow about the CEO position.'

She was on the cusp of a significant promotion. If she got it, it would be an incredible achievement, but she had a long list of successes in her career history as a music producer and she deserved the position. Still, thirty-eight years old was young to attain a role like CEO of a label at a music industry giant *and* Andrea was female, which meant the promotion, if she got it, would be a huge deal.

They both stood, Hannah making the first move to hug her friend. 'You'll smash it.'

As the women separated, Andrea's cell phone started to ring. She rifled through her purse to find the phone and cancelled the call.

'It's late for a call on a Sunday night,' Hannah said, her voice betraying her intrigue. 'Are you seeing someone?' She was almost singing the question, desperate for some adult gossip.

But Andrea wasn't in the mood to play, apparently. Scowling, she put the phone back in her purse and hoisted the bag onto her shoulder. 'I'm a little busy to be seeing anyone right now.'

In Andrea-speak, that was a blatant *yes*, but there was no need for Hannah to call her out on it just yet. The fun could start when she got back to work next week.

Andrea was subtly promiscuous. She quite often had a man on the go but, with the exception of Hannah, most people didn't know that.

Hannah wondered who it was this time. The chances were, she wouldn't know them anyway. The only person Andrea tended to go back to was 'rock god' Tommy Dawson, and it had been a while since their last fling.

Once Andrea left, Hannah brought the last of the glasses and plates inside and started to tidy the kitchen. As she began filling the sink with soapy water, two strong arms wrapped around her waist. Rod smelled of soap and manly deodorant. She breathed him in as he kissed her neck with his big lips.

'This can wait, let's go to bed,' he mumbled against her skin.

What he really meant by that was *Let's leave it for you to do on your own tomorrow.* But it'd been a long day and the thought of curling up on Rod's chest was too tempting to resist. Hannah turned out the lights, leaving the messy kitchen in darkness, and let Rod lead her upstairs to bed.

2

ANDREA

The sound of a champagne cork popping was music to Andrea's ears. She rarely drank champagne – her drink of choice was whiskey on the rocks – and that sound was one she always associated with good things, like her younger sister Sofia's independent music award for Best Producer last year. Like Christmas when she was a child, before her mom died. Like Hannah's baby's christening. But mostly, it was the sound of her own success. It was one beat in a score that had become the soundtrack to her life. Above all else these days, Andrea strived for success, to be the best at her job.

She poured the pink bubbles into a flute and walked to the window of her new office. She closed her eyes as the first hit of effervescence danced in her mouth, and opened them to her upgraded view across Williamsburg, East River and out to the big old city of New York.

The lights of the city's skyscrapers shone out against the black backdrop of the sky. *Not bad for a girl from Nashville, Tennessee*, she thought. She scanned the view, closer to her office, and her eyes landed five blocks away on the old building that had started it all for her. The lights were still on at Sanfia Records – the indie recording label that her father had started twenty-five years ago. Two short years ago, she had been heading up the label when she was poached by XM Music Group to come over to one of their fastest-growing labels. She had never planned on leaving Sanfia Records but circumstances, plus the fact that XM Music Group's offer had been too good to turn down, had forced her hand. Now, being promoted to chief executive officer of the group's Stellar label proved she had made the right decision.

It had been a difficult transition at first and she still had doubts sometimes. Every now and then she would feel a wave of guilt for having left her sister to take over the family business, but now that she was CEO of Stellar, she could help her sister by throwing work her way.

She raised her glass, wondering whether her sister was still working inside Sanfia Records. In that move, she toasted her own success. She wished her sister and Sanfia Records the best of luck. She silently thanked her father for everything he had done for her for thirty-eight years because telling him to his face was not something she would do.

'Knock-knock.'

She hadn't heard him come in, but Hunter's familiar voice was welcome. She watched him close the office door behind him, taking in his latest slick-cut suit. Hunter always dressed to impress. He was a man in his late fifties who looked barely a day over forty-five. He was tall and deadly attractive. The creases that decorated his eyes served only to add charm to his face and fiercely blue eyes.

'Mind if I come in to toast my newest executive?' he asked, holding up a bottle of Dom Pérignon and two glasses.

Andrea felt her lips curve up slightly. 'Sure.' After all, he had been the first person she had wanted to tell when her promotion was approved by the leadership board.

Hunter clocked the bottle of fizz Andrea was already enjoying and flashed her a devilishly handsome smile. 'Great minds think alike.'

He poured himself a glass and as Andrea came to stand by him in front of her unnecessarily large desk, he clinked his drink against hers.

'You deserve it,' he said.

'That means a lot coming from you, Hunter.'

He was, without doubt, an industry great. Like a lot of execs at the top of the music giants, Hunter's background was actually Wall Street, rather than the music industry. He was cut-throat and sharp and helped XM Music Group – its artists, producers, sound engineers and the business in general – achieve more accolades and awards than the world's other two largest recording labels. He had an eye for the market and trends, for lean financials and tight management. With Hunter at the helm, XM Music Group was capable of causing ripples that could result in wholescale waves in the global music industry.

He moved around the office, sensually running his fingertips along the black leather sofa at one side, the windowsill that ran the length of the full wall of windows, the table and chairs that took up one corner of the room. Power and control oozed from him.

'Do you know what I like most about this office?' he asked, running the back of his hand along the vertical blinds that hung on the interior windows. 'That you can do this.'

He tugged on the line that drew the blinds closed, then he turned the lock on the door, shielding them from any prying eyes that might still be in the office.

Andrea's heart thumped in her chest and her mouth was

suddenly dry. No matter how many times they had been together, each time still felt exciting, outrageous, sinfully sexy. He was not hers. He belonged to another woman. She hated the truth – that knowing it was so wrong caused her body to hum with anticipation.

'Hunter.' Her voice was so heavily drenched in lust that his name left her as a hoarse whisper.

He crossed the room, his eyes on her. She licked her lips as her breathing quickened. Then he was pressed against her, and all she knew was pleasure. The kind of pleasure that made her forget all the sensible questions she should have been asking herself – *How did I let this happen? How did I fall for the one man I absolutely cannot have?*

She had lost count of how many times they had done this, how many nights they had shared countless orgasms over recent months, but she now knew the feel of him, the shape of him, the undertone of every noise he made.

When she was once again presentable, her tailored suit in place and the rogue hairs from her chignon smoothed, she topped off her glass of champagne.

'Another?' she asked Hunter.

'Afraid not. I have a dinner tonight,' he said casually as he unclicked the lock to the door and moved to open the blinds.

Andrea checked her watch. 'It's already eight thirty. Where is your dinner?'

He paused by the blinds, gave her a look of pity, and said, 'Let's not become those people, Andrea.'

Which she took to mean he would be having dinner with his wife and possibly his daughter. She shook it off. 'You're right,' she said, waving a hand vacantly. 'I have a few things to sort out here so you best leave me to it.'

He smiled condescendingly. 'That's my girl. You know my

advice – new posts demand a stamp of authority. You should be working on your first big move.'

Hunter flipped open the blinds and standing right outside the office was Bryant Matthews, talking with another senior member of staff. Both men looked into the office; first at Hunter, then Andrea. Andrea jumped up from her position on her leather sofa, uneasy, but Hunter took it in his stride, dipping his head in acknowledgement to the men.

If someone could have freeze-framed the look on their faces at that very moment, Andrea's would have said *I'm guilty*. Bryant's would have said *I finally understand her promotion*. He had been second-in-line for the role of CEO of Stellar but he had believed himself to be ahead of Andrea and now there was no doubt he would be harbouring a grudge the size of Canada.

'Fuck,' Andrea whispered.

'We're two colleagues enjoying a celebratory drink, Andrea,' Hunter reasoned.

'With the blinds drawn?'

He picked up his suit jacket and drained what was left of his drink. 'That, I admit, was unfortunate timing. I'm late so I'll be seeing you. I'm proud of you, kiddo.'

She watched the door close behind him, waiting for it... Sure enough, the guilt came. She wished she could put an end to it. But he had become an addiction to her. She was always waiting for her next fix. And they both knew that if he was a *happily* married man, he wouldn't come to her. What they were doing was wrong, dirty but sensationally erotic. Just one more time, that was what she would promise herself after every romp.

But her promotion to CEO had brought with it a stark realisation... When she had first found out, she hadn't wanted to tell her best friend and executive assistant, Hannah. Nor had she wanted to run to her sister, Sofia, and tell her how she'd been promoted two short years after ditching the family label. She *definitely* hadn't wanted to tell Rosalie. No, the first thing she had wanted to do was celebrate her new role with Hunter.

That thought terrified her.

3

ROSALIE

'I told him to go screw himself. Or her. But definitely not me.'

Rosalie bit out the words as she stomped her foot into a one-size-too-big Christian Louboutin shoe. She was a familiar face to the staff of the glamorous Upper East Side store. They were always willing to listen to her troubles in return for a swipe of her trusty Amex. They were Rosalie's CBT.

'Good for you,' one of the staff said, whose name Rosalie really ought to remember just one time.

'Amen,' said another as she handed Rosalie a freshly topped-up glass of Laurent-Perrier.

The first woman, a petite blonde in a white shirt with silk neck scarf and a tight French braid, massaged Rosalie's ankle and smoothed the skin of her foot that was exposed in the pointed shoe. 'How does it feel?'

Rosalie smiled. 'As painful as a divine shoe should feel.' She assessed the way the crystal-encrusted heels looked with her royal-blue silk wrap dress. 'I'm not sure about it with this outfit, though.'

'Too much sparkle?' the second woman asked.

Rosalie looked to her and told her, 'A lady can never have too much sparkle. But let's try that pretty leopard print – print is so in right now.'

As the women fussed around her, Rosalie sipped her champagne and picked up where she had left off – the break-up.

'Do you know what he said to me? He said I'm not responsible enough for him. He said he wants someone less *frivolous*. Frivolous! Oh, and that he wants a woman who is capable of looking after him. Can you believe that?'

She lifted one foot out of the sparkling stiletto and slipped it into the leopard-print sandal, so that she had a different design on each foot. Pouting and adjusting her stance, she assessed the get-up.

'You know, I cooked for him on more than one occasion. One time, I actually chopped things and made a sauce from scratch. Does that count for nothing?'

She turned her back on the mirror and looked across her shoulder at her reflection. 'The heels of the leopard print are just so cute.'

'How long were you seeing each other?' the blonde woman asked.

'Who? Oh, George and me? A while. Eight weeks, in fact!' Rosalie sighed. 'I just can't decide.' She took another sip of champagne. 'Hell, I'll just take them both. I deserve the endorphins, right, ladies?'

* * *

Pooped. Feet red and sore. Dehydrated. Rosalie settled herself and her shopping bags onto the padded sofa of her favourite Italian restaurant. She was anti-carb 99 per cent of the time but when it came to her one-quarter Italian heritage – Mommy's side

– she made an exception. Good al dente pasta, perhaps brightened with a little shaved truffle, was worth missing two meals either side. And that was exactly what she felt like today.

Mauricio, the owner of the restaurant, which was a gem, tucked away down a side street off Central Park, hip-swayed his way flamboyantly to her table.

'Bella, you look as perfect as ever.'

Rosalie tried to look bashful but she knew she looked well. She had been on a juice diet since the break-up and her Dior dress hugged her slender frame perfectly, not to mention the salon blow-dry she had prescribed herself this morning, for medicinal purposes. She flicked her long brown waves across her shoulder as she thanked Mauricio.

'Your daddy's assistant called just a moment ago and said he would be a few minutes late. Perhaps some wine while you wait?'

Rosalie rolled her eyes. 'Poor Daddy. He's so hard-working. The usual would be fabulous.'

Though family run, the restaurant was not traditionally Italian in feel. It was bright and airy, with a wall of windows looking onto the street, white furniture and table-tops decorated with succulents in ceramic planters. The glasses and cutlery always gleamed under the overhead lights. The kitchen was exposed to the eyes of diners, meaning it was immaculately clean.

Rosalie slipped her heels out of her shoes under the table so that they hung loosely on her pinched toes, and she leaned back against the padded seat to enjoy her first sip of wine.

How had she been dumped, again? She was a catch, wasn't she?

She was beautiful and slim. She had great taste in music, décor and clothes. Food and beverages were something she was expert in. And she did run her own design business, kind of –

was it a business if she never asked for payment for her services? True, it had also been some months since she had designed the interior of a property, but she had to be careful with the projects she chose. Any interior designer was only worth the reputation of her last client, and they had to be big names. She had not got into the business to design just any old room for just any ordinary person. She designed perfect homes for her friends and nothing gave her more pleasure than to see them and their families happy in beautiful surrounds.

The effort she had put into Stella's mansion in the Hamptons had even earned the home a feature on *Cribs!*

See, she wasn't irresponsible. She sort of worked. A lot of wealthy women didn't work at all. Most of her friends didn't. Other than a few years of modelling, Mommy hadn't worked a day in her life, but Rosalie had. It might not be traditional hours, but not everyone had the great eye for colours and placement that she had.

And frivolous? How could she be guilty of throwing away money if it was her own money?

She never asked any of the men she was dating for a dime. The trust fund she'd gained access to fifteen years ago, when she was twenty-one, had been invested and earned a small fortune. She didn't need to be supported; it would just be nice if someone *wanted* to support her, that was all.

She didn't wait much longer before her father came through the door to the restaurant, dapper as ever in a sharp blue suit and crisp white shirt.

'Sorry, kiddo,' he said, kissing Rosalie on both cheeks.

She beamed. 'It's no problem, Daddy. Is work busy?'

'When is it not? It might have been nice for you to cross the river into Brooklyn just one time,' he said without malice.

'But this is our favourite and, well, Daddy, I've been dumped.'

Mauricio topped off Rosalie's glass and poured one for her father, who audibly appreciated his first mouthful. 'By the man you brought to dinner the other night?'

She nodded. 'Mmm hmm. What's wrong with me, Daddy?'

'There's nothing wrong with you, kiddo. You just know what you like and it intimidates men, that's all.'

She smiled. 'You think so?'

'I know so. What are you ordering?'

'The usual.'

'See. A woman who knows what she likes,' he added with a wink.

Rosalie chuckled. Her father always knew exactly the right thing to say. 'I got a new dress today for the memorial concert for Sir Presley John next week.'

'You did?'

'Yes. I think you'll like it. It's blue, your favourite.'

'Kiddo, anything is my favourite on you. Just make sure you coordinate with your mother this time. We don't need a fall-out.'

They ordered food and talked about the usual things – *his* work, *her* social calendar. They ate their food and drank their wine. Rosalie loved their lunch catch-ups. Her father had so many stories and even the ones he repeated she never got tired of hearing. He was intelligent and funny, not at all the shark CEO the media portrayed him to be. He was gentle and kind, a real family man. He was the kind of man Rosalie wanted by her side but just couldn't seem to get, or keep.

As their plates were cleared and after they had turned down the offer of the dessert menu, Rosalie asked, 'Daddy, do you think I'm irresponsible?'

'Irresponsible? Why would you ask that?'

'Well, George basically said that's why he was breaking up

with me. And, you know, some of my friends have busy jobs, like Andrea, or have kids, like Hannah.'

Her father dabbed the side of his lips with his napkin then set it down on the table, all the while seeming to think of his next words. 'You have plenty of friends who don't have full-time jobs or kids, Rosalie.'

She rolled her eyes. 'All they want to talk about is clothes and shoes and who's screwing who. Do you think I'm like them, Daddy? Do you think George is right?'

'Not at all.'

She sighed. 'He is, isn't he? I mean, Hannah has just had a third baby and you just promoted Andrea to CEO of her own label. I mean, she's a woman, I'm a woman. We're practically the same age. Am I not as capable as someone like that?'

He paused for a moment and shuffled awkwardly in his seat. 'Andrea has had a very different upbringing to yours, Ros. She works hard but she's doing something she loves and she hasn't ever known anything different.'

It was true. Andrea had lost her mother when she was just a girl. Her dad had started the Sanfia Records label when he moved home to New Jersey after her mom, who had been a singer-songwriter, had died months after giving birth to Andrea's younger sister, Sofia. Her father was always at the record label he had founded and by all accounts Andrea and Sofia's education had been sitting in a production booth, eating takeout and hanging with budding rock stars. Rosalie had actually met Andrea, Hannah and Sofia six years ago when she was briefly dating one of their artists, who had gone on to make the big time with his band. They had split but she got to keep the friendships, so in all, she won. She had loved how refreshing Andrea and Hannah, who had worked at Sanfia Records as an administration assistant back then, were. Even Sofia and her quirkiness, though she was more the younger sister of the group with her own friends. They were just so 'down-to-earth' and different from her usual girlfriends. But...

'That doesn't exactly answer my question, Daddy.'

Her father rubbed his chin and said, 'I think that not having an awful lot of responsibility doesn't make you irresponsible. How's that?'

Rosalie scowled. 'You don't think I could do it, do you? You don't think I could run a business like Andrea.' And for the first time ever, Rosalie felt bitter with envy.

Her father shook his head. 'I think you could do absolutely anything you set your mind to, Rosalie.'

She watched him, her head speeding through a thousand thoughts as she sipped her wine. Then she set the glass down on the table, folded her arms across her chest and sat up straighter in her seat. 'Prove it,' she challenged.

Her father chuckled. 'Waiter, can we get the check, please?'

'Daddy! I mean it. Give me a label at XM.'

He coughed into his napkin and she knew he was attempting to disguise laughter, which made her endlessly more determined. 'I'm serious. I've been around the music industry for years. I love music.'

'Rosalie, you have no experience of running a business.'

'Not true. I run design projects.'

'You decorate your friends' homes very occasionally and when you feel like it.'

She blew breath from her nostrils. 'I manage my investments.'

Her father dropped his napkin to the table in a move that reflected Rosalie's own exasperation. No one ever took her seriously. Well, no more.

'You have no experience in music production, Ros. Designing

interiors based on Elvis Presley's jungle room and dating rock stars really doesn't count.'

She gasped. 'You came from Wall Street!'

'Rosalie, I can't just gift you a record label. You have to earn a position like that.' His tone softened. 'Look at Andrea. She has been a producer as long as she's been adult. She's won countless awards. That's experience.'

'But you think I could do it if I had experience, don't you, Daddy?' she asked sweetly.

He reached out and took her hand atop the table. 'Sure I do, kiddo.'

Rosalie snatched her hand back petulantly. 'Fine.'

'Fine?'

'Yes, fine. I'll get experience, then you can give me a label.' She stood from the table and gathered her bags excitedly. 'I know exactly what to do.' She bent and kissed her father's cheek. 'Thank you for always believing in me, Daddy. I won't let you down.'

And she turned on her heels and strutted out of the restaurant, leaving her father to pick up the check and his bottom jaw.

4

HANNAH

'It's fucking four in the morning,' Rod grumbled, rolling over and slamming his pillow down across his ears.

'I guess it's my turn again then, huh?'

Hannah tossed back the bedsheets and staggered to TJ's nursery, feeling her way rather than opening her eyes. He was four months old and had been sleeping in a cot in his own room for two, very long, weeks. They had originally moved him from their bedroom and into Jackson's room, but their eleven-year-old had tried to silence the baby on their second night together by throwing Buzz Lightyear at him as he wailed. So Jackson was now in the 'big boy bedroom' with their eldest, seventeen-year-old, Luke, who basically wanted to kill him all the time – a little to do with personal space and a lot to do with raging hormones, she figured.

Opening her eyes as far as was strictly necessary, Hannah picked TJ from his crib and held him to her chest.

'Are you hungry, little fella? Shhh. Mommy's here. There now. There now.'

The ear-piercing, satanic screaming relented to more of a

painful, body-chugging sob as they made their way downstairs to the kitchen. Hannah warmed milk as she tried to convince TJ to be quiet for just a second, before he made himself sick again. Minutes later, she sat down on a kitchen chair and turned TJ onto his back in the crook of her arm. He latched onto the bottle teat and gulped down milk.

And there it was, the best sound in the world. *Silence.*

Her eyes opened wider as the sky outside became lighter. Her baby boy pinned her with his big teddy bear brown eyes that were a match with his dark skin, like his daddy's. Her exhaustion was momentarily forgotten as she stroked his tight black curls and smiled at her boy.

'You're a pest. Do you know that? But I wouldn't change you.'

TJ had been almost as unexpected as Luke. You might have thought she'd have learned her lesson when the star of the college football team knocked her up at twenty-one. Or again, six years later, after that same football star had recovered from his broken back enough to walk but never play again and gone through a phase of needing to have a second child to reaffirm he was a man. But no, despite having no space for a third child, no money to buy enough space for a third child and both parents working their butts off to make ends meet, Hannah had fallen pregnant for a third time – not quite an accident, since she and Rod were being sporadically lackadaisical when it came to protection, but far from planned.

TJ drained his bottle and gave her an almighty belch across her shoulder before she took him back to bed. It was now four forty-five and she would have to be up in a little over an hour to sort out the kids and commute into New York, where she had, barely two weeks ago, resumed work post-maternity leave as Andrea's executive assistant at XM Music Group.

Rod had told her to find another job after her short maternity leave, to lessen her commute, but the fact was she couldn't earn as much with her experience and skillset as she could in the city. Plus, she liked working in the city. It made her feel like there was more to her life than just being a mom.

Lately, she had felt increasingly like she did need *more*. And, truth be told, she wasn't sure she could ever leave Andrea to her own devices. Her friend liked to play tough but Hannah might be the only person in the world who knew that sometimes, being called a cold-hearted bitch by asshole men in the industry who were jealous of her success could actually pierce that harsh exterior Andrea showed to everyone else.

With her slippers scraping the carpet as she dragged her feet along the hallway, Hannah let her eyes begin to close again and felt her way to the bathroom. Half-asleep, she lowered herself to the toilet and...

Her butt sank into the toilet. Water sloshed up her cheeks and thighs. 'Mother effer! How many times have I told you to leave the goddamn seat down, Rod?'

She wiped off her skin with a towel, which she threw into the wash basket as she attempted again to take a pee. She sank down, this time onto the toilet seat, and from nowhere, tears pricked her eyes. As water came out of her down below, it poured out of her up top too. She covered her face in her hands and sobbed. 'I just want to sleep.'

Going back to work was already proving harder with child number three than it had been with either of the others.

* * *

Coffee. Just one strong coffee and she was sure she would feel human again.

Hannah dumped her purse in a drawer underneath her desk

outside Andrea's office, one of a pod of four connected desks where she sat with the other assistants.

A number of XM Music Group's labels were housed in the Williamsburg high-rise across various floors of the building, but all of the executives had offices on the twelfth floor, ergo, so did their assistants.

Since Andrea's promotion to CEO of Stellar label, she and Hannah had been relocated. Andrea now had a large plush office and Hannah had a shitty desk with no view to the outside world except via the glass walls of Andrea's office. Still, it was the prestigious twelfth floor and no one was crying, or sticking putty in her hair or chocolate fingerprints on her blouse, or leaving up the toilet seat when she had repeatedly asked them not to. Plus, the twelfth floor came with a pay rise and she could certainly use one of those.

Hannah was shortly followed into the office by the three other assistants.

'Ladies, I'm going to make coffee, anybody want one?' she asked.

She received three resounding yeses and was handed three mugs, which she popped on a tray to take to the kitchenette. Sanctuary was near.

'Oh, good, you're here.' She turned to see Andrea coming out of her office toward her and in a split second was able to read the look on her friend's face that said *I'm in a take-no-prisoners kind of mood*.

'I need you to bring me the sales figures for every artist at the label. I also want to see a list of the best-performing artists for XM in Europe who aren't currently being pushed in the US. Rock only. Preferably country rock. Oh, and I need you to find me a dress for the Presley John commemoration concert at Madison Square Gardens on Thursday. Something sophisticated with an air of sexy but nothing revealing. I'm happy to try on up to three outfits. I don't have time for more. Can you bring my schedule for the rest of the week, too?'

Hannah raised one brow. 'Morning, Hannah. How was your weekend? The family okay?'

Andrea smiled. 'Morning, Hannah, and please and thank you.' Then she turned and walked right back into her office in her perfectly tailored and expensive-looking pantsuit.

Hannah took a breath. Andrea had become very different to work for since they moved to XM Music Group two years ago, increasingly so since Hannah had returned from maternity leave. It was as if she had more to prove than ever before. She smiled less, snapped more, and often forgot that she and Hannah were friends first and colleagues second. Hannah wasn't sure if she was simply noticing it more since returning to work, if her tiredness meant she was less willing to overlook it, or if the promotion to CEO had gone to Andrea's head. Regardless, it certainly felt like something was more off than usual.

Hannah looked to the other assistants. 'Anyone else want to get those coffees?'

She handed off the tray of empty mugs and pulled her blonde hair – dark roots starting to show – into a messy knot on top of her head. There really had been no point spending time straightening her hair this morning. Humidity had made it frizzy and there was little chance she was leaving the office today in any event.

* * *

An hour and two sips of coffee after taking instructions, Hannah walked into Andrea's office with a bundle of papers. She found her boss staring out of the swanky wall of windows she'd inherited with her promotion.

'Hey. I have everything you asked for.'

Andrea let out a short shriek as she spun quickly to face Hannah, spilling coffee from the mug in her hands. 'Jesus, Han, you scared the life right out of me.'

'Sorry, I'll just leave everything here.'

Andrea crossed the room to her desk to grab a tissue and rubbed the coffee from her blouse. 'Thanks.'

Nothing like sincere and high praise, Hannah thought. From anyone else, she might have struggled to hold her tongue, but Andrea was her friend and, despite her quirks, their years of friendship meant a lot to Hannah. Andrea had been there for her in her darkest hours.

Hannah had been in her penultimate year of college when she'd fallen pregnant with Luke. Everyone, her own parents included, told her to get rid of the baby. But she and Rod hadn't wanted to. They knew it would be hard but they'd decided to marry anyway.

She hadn't anticipated her own father kicking her out with a newborn baby because he just couldn't stand the crying. Hannah was alone, penniless and homeless, whilst Rod was still trying to make it at college.

For the next six months, it was Andrea who took in Hannah and Luke. She had a one-bedroom rental in Brooklyn where the three of them lived, plus Rod, when he was home.

So people could see Andrea however they wanted to but Hannah would only ever see her as her very best friend and she was certain nothing could ever change that.

'Andi, are you okay? I know you hate heart-to-hearts but you seem your worst combination of cranky and on edge since I came back from mat leave.'

Andrea stopped fussing her blouse and paused long enough for Hannah to know there was something up with her friend. But Andrea's mouth opened and closed without words. Taking a document from the top of the pile in front of her, she turned her back on Hannah.

'It's just the new role. There's a lot to be done.'

Hannah waited but Andrea offered no more explanation. 'Okay, well, you know where I am if you want to talk or drown in tequila. God knows I wouldn't mind a few child-free drinks.'

She made to leave and had reached the office door before Andrea said, 'Hey, do you want to come to the concert on Thursday?'

Hannah's lips curved into a smile. 'Honour the legend that was Sir Presley John? Hell, yeah, I'm in.'

Andrea smiled. 'My closet is yours, if you want to borrow something.'

Hannah nodded. 'That'd be great.' Though Andrea was slimmer than Hannah, her shoulders were broader than Hannah's and Hannah was taller, which meant they averaged at around the same size eight. 'While we're on the topic, any specific requests for your dress?'

'I trust you, and the women in Saks.'

* * *

Hannah always thought Saks had a certain smell about it. As she walked in the main entrance, she inhaled deeply and was struck by rich, clean scents like sandalwood and lemongrass, which could be summed up neatly by the word 'money'. Hannah sometimes enjoyed shopping for Andrea when she was busy. Other times, it reminded her of what she didn't have.

Once upon a time, Rod had been destined to be a professional footballer. He was one of the top three players in college. There were times Hannah would fantasise about what life would have been like for them if he hadn't broken his back so early in his career – she would have walked into a place like Saks and picked out anything she wanted, paying a cursory glance to the price tag at best.

Stopping briefly to indulge in squirts of new scents from the perfume counter girls, Hannah made her way to women's wear. Andrea had closets packed full of shoes and bags, so she needn't worry about picking a dress to match particular accessories. Hannah went right to the evening dress collections.

Sir Presley John's remembrance-cum-charity concert would be a star-studded event. The music industry would be out in force, not to mention the A-list movie stars that would turn up to an event like this, who had no doubt either never met, or had merely met in passing, Presley John. Any event that was big enough to take on Madison Square Gardens was always one of air-kisses, faux compliments and people blowing smoke up each other's ass for no good reason.

Still, Andrea would need to look incredible and suitably like the newly appointed CEO of the Stellar label. Many faces in the music industry would now be blowing smoke up *her* ass, following years of it being the other way around.

Hannah came to a stop in the middle of the Escada concession and began her search for the perfect dress.

There had always been something about Andrea, even at school, that made Hannah believe she would be a successful woman. Of course, back then, they both used to talk about being successful. But Andrea's mom had once been beautiful and an incredible singer-songwriter. Her father had set up his own recording label. And Andrea was strong, sometimes too fierce, especially when it came to protecting her younger sister, Sofia.

Hannah and Andrea had spent hours hanging out in New Jersey, talking about all the things they wanted to be when they grew up. Hannah had wanted to be a singer, an actress, a fashion designer and, at one time, an exotic dancer – before she understood that the profession was not very exotic at all. Andrea, though, she had always said she wanted to be able to stand on her own two feet. She never wanted to *need* anyone.

Of course, she did need people. Everyone did. Andrea would never concede that, but Hannah would always have her best friend's back.

She ran her fingers across the fine fabrics on display – silk, velour, satin – pushing hangers along the sparse rails to get a better look at the detail of the dresses.

She was thinking black. Floor-length. Maybe...

'Hannah?'

She turned on the spot to see Rosalie. 'Ros! I'm just looking for something for Andi to wear to the Presley John concert at MSG. What are you doing here?'

They hugged and kissed each other's cheeks. 'Oh, just looking for a little pick-me-up.'

'Is everything okay?'

Rosalie wafted a hand flippantly. 'Same old. George ditched me last week. Can you believe that? Another one bites the dust.'

'Oh, Ros, I'm sorry. He seemed quite nice at the christening. Did you really like him?'

Picking out a sequinned gold top and holding it against her chest, Rosalie twisted her face in a way that suggested she was either thinking or breaking wind. 'You know, I thought I really liked him but I'm realising he was just... I don't know, plugging a hole for a while.'

Hannah started working through hanging dresses. 'How do you mean?'

'I think I need more in my life. I mean, I have my hobbies and family and friends, but sometimes I feel like all I do is shop and eat out or work out. I look at you, with the kids, and Andrea, with her own label now, and I think, I could do those things, you know?'

Hannah chose in that moment to exercise a lesson she tried to teach her kids – when you don't have anything nice to say...

And in the same amount of time it took Hannah to restrain herself, Rosalie lost – or changed – her train of thought. 'Say, we should grab lunch. Maybe a Bellini?'

She couldn't hold it any longer... Hannah bit down on her lip but couldn't stop her laughter from escaping. 'Ros, I love you.'

It took a second for Rosalie's moody pout to turn to a laugh too. 'Okay, so I'm not saying it's going to be an overnight transition or anything.'

The sound of Abba's 'Dancing Queen' coming from Hannah's purse stole her attention. For a fleeting moment, as it always did, it reminded her of the days when her long blonde hair flowed down her back, ten inches longer than it was now. When her blue eyes weren't buried in black bags. Before she had wrinkles and cellulite and dry skin on her hands from domestic cleaning products.

She fumbled in her bag, not able to find her cell. Still, it rang. 'All right, all right. I hear ya. Where the hell is it?'

She was about to dump her mom-bag on the ground when Rosalie's perfectly manicured hands held it up. In that moment, with that small act, Hannah appreciated her friend more than ever.

Thank you, she mouthed as she finally located the cell.

'Hello, Hannah speaking.'

'Hello, Mrs Washington, it's Ms Hellisham here, from TJ's

nursery. I'm afraid he's been vomiting and he needs to be collected.'

It was one of those phone calls that Hannah could really do without *any* day, but especially any day this week.

When she got these phone calls with the first kid, she would panic. Her heart would race and her mind would immediately go into overdrive thinking about all the horrific scenarios she had read about online – brain tumours, stomach cancer, internal haemorrhage.

With the second kid, she would have at least led with, *Is he okay?*

But TJ was number three. She was a pro at this mommy business now.

'How much vomit are we talking about here? Does he have a temperature?' she asked the very pretty, twenty-something-year-old with naturally pert boobs, Ms Hellisham.

'He doesn't have a temperature but he's been sick three times. One was, well, projectile.'

Hannah laughed. 'Rod and I sometimes call him the exorcist. He has real bad acid reflux, Ms Hellisham. He's fine.'

'I'm sorry, Mrs Washington, but TJ can't stay here today.'

And there it was, her old friend, *panic*. She did *not* have time for this. She had a dress to pick out, documents to finalise, emails to send, talent agents to contend with.

'This is ridiculous. I can assure you he's fine.'

'Nevertheless, he's going to have to stay home for forty-eight hours. I'm sorry.'

'Two days! Are you kidding me?' Hannah checked her watch. There was no way she could end the day at this hour. 'I can't come back to Jersey, I'm at work.' She sighed. 'I'll call my husband and see if he can do the pick-up.'

She hung up the call and immediately called Rod. And called. And called.

On the third attempt, he picked up.

'Hey, babe. What's up? I'm kinda in the middle of somethin'.'

'Well, me too, but TJ's acid reflux is playing up. He's been sick and we have to collect him from nursery.'

'Yeah, okay. Let me know how he is later, babe.'

'W-wait. Rod? Rod, I have too much on. You have to go.'

'Babe, I can't, I'm seeing a guy about another coaching job. I told you about this. Head coach, babe, more money.'

Had he even told her about this? 'Okay, so what time *can* you get there?'

'Babe, I'm in Queens. Oh, he's here, gotta go.'

'Rod? Rod? Are you there…?' The line went dead.

In her mind, she threw herself on the floor of Saks and screamed *MOTHERFUCKER!*

In reality, Rosalie set a jacket she had been considering back on the hanging rack and said, 'I could pick up TJ for you.'

In that moment, Hannah wished she was in her bathroom at home because that was the only place she allowed herself to cry.

'Are you sure?'

Rosalie shrugged and gave the kind of smile that suited her angelic soul. 'Of course. I can pick him up and if he's really not sick we can come back into the city and pick out a dress for Andi to wear to the concert, then you can get on with whatever else you need to do.'

'Ros, I could kiss you,' Hannah said, meaning every word.

5

ROSALIE

As it turned out, Hannah's five-months-old son hadn't been suffering from acid reflux when the nursery had called her yesterday and Rosalie had agreed to come to her friend's rescue. Almost as soon as she had picked him up from daycare and got him safely buckled into the mind-puzzle that was his car seat, TJ had proceeded to throw up all over the back seat of Rosalie's top-spec Porsche Cayenne.

Her plans of heading back into the city and choosing a dress for Andrea to wear to the Presley John tribute concert had been thwarted by the thought of TJ potentially vomiting on Oscar de la Renta's finest evening wear in Saks.

So she had tied up her long locks of glossy brown hair, rolled up the sleeves of her jacket and dropped her car at the nearest valet service. Then she had caught a cab to Hannah and Rod's home in New Jersey.

TJ slept most of the afternoon, which was incredibly dull. So dull, in fact, that once she had exhausted the two men's fitness magazines that were lying around the modest lounge – the photography skills were *excellent* – and made herself a mug of coffee, she had decided to tidy a few things that looked out of place.

Hannah and Rod's home was nothing like Rosalie's modern, on-trend-styled space in the city. They had an old town house with three bedrooms that they had spent years improving. Where Rosalie thought solid rose-wood floors would have been wonderful, they had a light grey rug that was getting worn from three kids wreaking havoc on the threads.

Where Rosalie would have placed succulents on floating shelves around the walls, they had family pictures in mismatched frames. Their sofas had lost their shape from being jumped on and lain across. The soft furnishings were decorated with what looked like chocolate fingerprints.

As TJ had started snoring – she hadn't known kids snored – she had looked around the space and decided she could take it no more. Then she did something she never did… She found one of Rod's hooded sweaters, pulled it over her own clothes, and cleaned and tidied Hannah's home from top to bottom.

She was pooped by the time the older kids had come home from school, barely keeping her eyes open as she snuggled TJ on the sofa. They had hardly registered her presence as they headed straight to the kitchen, banging and needlessly shouting as they raided the food cupboards, leaving boxes and wrappers on every surface that she had slaved away cleaning hours before.

She had stayed in place of their usual sitter until Hannah and Rod had come home from work, having counted down the minutes until she could go back to her clean, noise-free life. She had done her good deed and was ready to leave the circus.

Until Hannah walked through the door into the lounge and stood on one spot as she turned her head around the house, her jaw dropping loose.

'Ros, you… you cleaned my house?'

Maybe it was the tiredness or something, but Rosalie had looked at her friend's full eyes and felt her own eyes cloud over as she nodded and gathered up TJ from the sofa, hugging him to her chest. 'I hope you don't mind. TJ has slept a lot and—'

'Ros, we don't mind at all. Man, you must have been at this all day,' Rod said, hanging his thick, muscly arm around his wife's shoulder.

Rosalie had shrugged, uncommonly bashful, and handed TJ to his mom. 'I'll get going. The valet guys returned my car not long ago.'

In response to the questioning looks she'd received, Rosalie explained, 'TJ threw up again.'

Hannah had covered her gasp with her hands. 'Shit, I'm sorry, Ros. We'll pay for the cleaning.'

She'd waved off the offer. 'I'm just glad I could help.' And, she'd thought in her car as she drove back into the city, she really was grateful. She had achieved something good with her day. She hadn't just lunched and shopped; she'd made someone she cared about happy, and that made her feel... fulfilled, in return.

That thought had prompted her to call Hannah and tell her she would sit for TJ again today. Except she fully intended to have the day out with TJ today that she'd hoped for yesterday.

'How about the Plaza, TJ?' Rosalie asked, watching the baby in his car seat as he chewed a rubber donut in the back of her Porsche.

'I agree. The Plaza it is. Do you like babyccinos? I'll bet you do.'

* * *

A short while and Manhattan's traffic later, Rosalie pulled up outside the Plaza.

'Well, aren't you just adorable?' the concierge asked as he helped Rosalie inside, taking the adaptable car seat harbouring TJ from her.

As they headed inside, the hotel valet climbed into the Porsche behind them and drove away.

'Thank you,' Rosalie replied to the concierge with pride.

'Is he yours?'

For a moment, Rosalie felt affronted – didn't she look responsible enough to have a child?

Then she realised, TJ had much darker skin than hers – somewhere between Hannah's pasty white and Rod's black – and he had Rod's wide nose and Hannah's bright blue eyes.

'He's my godson,' she said with pride – Hannah clearly thought she was responsible.

She tickled the baby's tummy as he swung happily in his seat, which was hooked over the arm of the concierge. When he giggled, the sweetness of the sound made Rosalie's heart swell in such a peculiar way it caused her to falter in her stride.

What *was* that feeling?

She swallowed to loosen her tightening throat and adjusted her leopard-print wrap dress.

They were settled at a table – TJ in a highchair, which Hannah had proudly informed Rosalie was very impressive at TJ's age – under the rose-pink stained-glass roof of The Palm Court room and promptly served a latte, a babyccino and a plate of macarons. It was Rosalie's favourite dining room at the hotel. The ornately decorated Venetian-style walls oozed opulence. The gold chairs with their fancy upholstery signified money. The bright green palm trees allowed diners to feel like they could have stepped off the bustling streets of Manhattan into a tropical paradise. There was controlled chatter throughout the room, everyone respectful enough of one another's space. Music played at a low level in the background and, crucially, staff were always on hand should one need anything particular.

She nibbled a raspberry macaron, just enough to get the taste, then set it to the edge of her plate and dabbed her mouth with the linen napkin that a waiter had kindly laid across her lap.

'So, Teej... Can I call you Teej? We'll have our drinks and snacks, then we'll go pick out a dress for Aunty Andrea to wear to the commemoration concert for Sir Presley John on Thursday. Your mom was in the middle of doing that when you had your bout of puking yesterday.'

Rosalie pulled a face that said *Yucky*, making TJ chuckle loudly. That alien feeling came back to her with the sound. Was it just that this kid's cuteness factor was off the charts? No matter what she did, he was unconditionally happy with her.

'You know how the whole aunty thing works, don't you, baby boy? See, technically Andrea and me, we aren't your *actual* aunties, but we love you better than any blood relative anyway, right?'

TJ gurgled, which Rosalie took as confirmation that he understood.

'Has your mommy told you how we all met?'

She paused to lift him onto her lap and slipped the rubber teat of his bottled babyccino into his mouth. The warmth she felt holding him was more than just his body leaning into hers. It was mutual contentedness. Rosalie was not simply sipping coffee and eating macarons today; she was babysitting. Suddenly, her standard shopping break had purpose. She made sure TJ was happily guzzling, then set about her story.

'I suppose we're unlikely friends, really. See, Andrea and your other god-mommy Sofia took over their daddy's recording studio. Of course, Andrea made some great signings and with her production and management, those signings hit the charts. You won't have heard of the band Leverage and their frontman, Tommy Dawson. Well, they're huge now and it was Aunty Andrea who found them. Successes like that are the reason Aunty Andrea is at XM Music Group now. Anyway, because I seem incapable of finding the right man for me, I was dating a guy that Andrea was producing… what… maybe five years ago now. Gosh, time flies.'

She looked down to TJ, who was still happily attached to his bottle, propped up by her arm, milky saliva running from the corners of his mouth.

'Dang, I should have put you in a bib, huh? Sorry, I'm learning. Have you had enough? Do you, like, need to burp or something?'

She settled his near-empty bottle on the table in front of her and sipped her own drink.

'So, Keith… that's the name of the guy I was seeing… Hardly a rock star name, if you ask me. I don't know why Andrea didn't encourage him to use a stage name. Well, there I was, dating the anti-rock star, and I used to go to the studio when he and his band were recording their first full-length album, which is how I first met your mommy, Aunty Andrea and Aunty Sofia. I saw them nearly every day for three – no, four weeks. I liked them, you know. They weren't like my usual group of gossipy, bitchy friends. Daddy thought they'd be good for me too – diversifying, I think he called it. And I think your mommy and Andrea liked me being around, too. I always brought treats to the studio. It was nice to be able to help out, I suppose.'

She laughed as a memory came to her. 'One day, your mommy said to me, "Do you know why I love you, Ros?" She said exactly these words: "Because your mom is a supermodel, your dad is a music industry giant, you are beautiful and you're dating a budding rock star. You have every reason in the world to be fake, but you're real."

'She meant it as a compliment. Oh, and my momma *was* a supermodel, that's how she met my dad, at an awards bash. But she's had so many injections now her face doesn't move any more. Let me tell you, Teej, there's a fine line between growing old gracefully with a little tinkering and turning your face into a distorted Barbie doll.

'Oh, but I do love her, and Daddy adores her.'

Rosalie finished her latte and beckoned over a waitress with the universal sign for 'Check, please'.

'Right, little man, we need to leave, we have people counting on us today. Should we go buy Aunty Andrea something fabulous to wear to the concert? We might find something cute for a handsome baby, too,' she said, winking at TJ.

He giggled and hiccupped simultaneously, making Rosalie laugh. Hanging with TJ was really a heck of a lot more fun than taking coffee alone.

* * *

Hours later, Rosalie dropped TJ and Hannah back home in New Jersey.

'Are you sure you won't come in?' Hannah asked, holding TJ on her hip as Rod carried his car seat from Rosalie's car into their now clean home.

'I'm good – thanks, though,' Rosalie said. 'Oh, don't forget Andrea's dress. She's going to look fierce in that, I promise.'

'Thanks, Ros, for everything. You've been a lifesaver these last two days.'

Rosalie shrugged. 'My pleasure.' And it really was. Her days had seemed to fly by looking after the baby. 'Goodbye, Teej. Have fun at nursery tomorrow, buddy.'

As she drove away, Rosalie watched Hannah and TJ in her rearview mirror. Hannah kissed his brow then held him high in the air. Rosalie knew he'd be laughing that hearty man-baby laugh of his.

That strange feeling came over her again but this time, she knew what it was. *Jealousy.* Unconditional love and that whole life in her hands, depending on her every day. Rosalie was totally, completely jealous of Hannah. She wanted what Hannah had – only with more money in her savings account and a better zip code. She wanted to be needed like a baby needed its mommy. She wanted a family, love, like her parents had.

But finding a good man like her daddy was proving impossible. *That* she was going to fix with a recording label of her own, where people would look up to her, admire her and take her seriously. It was about time she started implementing her plan.

* * *

It had been a while since her last visit, but Rosalie left New Jersey and found her way through the streets of Williamsburg to Sanfia Records with ease. She killed the engine of her Porsche, slung this season's signature Gucci purse over her wrist, and twisted elegantly out of the car.

She tended not to double-brand but today she had teamed her Gucci purse with a Gucci red belted crepe dress that came to the top of her knee – sophisticated business length – and a painfully stylish pair of Valentino rockstud sandals.

As the car beeped to lock behind her, Rosalie pinned her shoulders back and strode up to the door of Sanfia Records, where she used a tissue over her fingertip to press the door buzzer.

'Come in,' Sofia's voice called over the intercom. 'We're in the sound booth.'

Rosalie remembered her way along the bland corridor that looked magnolia, as opposed to white, more due to years without a refresh than by design.

She wasn't surprised as she approached the sound booth to hear country music – a male voice singing soft rock. Sanfia Records took on a range of artists, but there had always been a preference for country music, which Rosalie suspected came from Andrea and Sofia's father and the fact their mother, God rest her soul, had been a country musician of the Eva Cassidy ilk.

Whilst Rosalie preferred to put her feet up on a pouffe with a glass of something chilled and effervescent with smooth jazz playing on her home speakers, she would happily listen to the dulcet tones of Brett Eldredge or the soothing lyrics of Carolyn Dawn Johnson.

Using her tissue, she pressed down on the handle of the door to the sound booth, which stuck as she pushed, pushed and pushed again, eventually stumbling into the room on her high heels.

'Ros, are you okay?' Sofia asked, standing from her leather stool in front of the room-width mixing board.

Rosalie waved away her blushes. 'You need to give this place a facelift, sweetie.'

'Top of my list when we strike gold, Ros,' Sofia said in good humour, though Rosalie had been entirely serious.

Everything from the dark wood old-style mixing board to the chipped laminate flooring that screamed 1990s, to the tatty leather sofa that wasn't helped by beer bottles sitting in holsters on the arm rests, to a lingering smell of cigarette smoke – it all needed a refresh. Nevertheless, Rosalie wasn't here in her capacity as an interior designer; she was here to learn.

She kissed Sofia on the cheek and held up a hand to Sofia's father, Jimmy, who she wasn't surprised to see. Despite retiring six years earlier, Jimmy had music in his blood, like his daughters.

'How're you doing, darling?'

'I'm good, thanks, Jimmy,' Rosalie said, looking around between the sofa and the spare stool between Sofia's and Jimmy's, wondering which would be least likely to leave a stain on her two-thousand-dollar dress.

Through the glass wall of the room, Rosalie saw the source of the country music she was hearing as three men played, one of them singing, in the studio beyond.

'So, you said you had a favour to ask?' Sofia said, returning to her stool and pulling one knee into her chest.

'Oh, mmm, yes,' Rosalie said, forgetting the state of the worn leather in her excitement and taking a seat on the sofa. 'It's very exciting. So, Daddy is giving me my own label at XM.'

She tried not to be irritated by the scrunching of Sofia's brow, followed by the raising of her eyebrow in the direction of Jimmy, choosing to believe it was confusion.

She wafted a hand. 'Let me take a step back. I'm going to be in the music business now. You know, I have experience, what with running my design projects and things, and I'm ready for a new life challenge, you know? So Daddy said I could have my own label, but there's a catch. First, I have to get a little more experience in the industry, behind the scenes stuff.'

'Ah, and that's where I come in?' Sofia asked.

Rosalie smiled. 'If you'll have me, I would like to be, like, your apprentice, or understudy even, for, maybe a couple of months, until I really get the hang of all the' – she gestured to the mixing board and the hundreds of nodules and flashing lights – 'digits and gadgets.'

Jimmy chuckled, stealing Rosalie's attention. 'Darling, it's going to take longer than two months to crack music production. It's not just something you do with these,' he said, holding up his hands and wiggling his fingers. 'It's what you hear with these.' He tugged his ear lobes. 'And what you feel in here.' He held a closed fist to his chest.

'Sure,' Rosalie said. 'I totally get that. But will you show me a few things, Soph?'

Sofia shrugged. 'Ah, yeah, sure.'

At that moment, the music coming from the studio stopped. Sofia turned on her stool, pushed a button and said, 'Great job, guys. Come on out and we'll listen back to it.'

Moments later, two session players Rosalie recognised and a tall, buffer than average, scruffier than average man with the bluest eyes she had ever seen stepped into the sound booth.

'You smashed it, guys,' Sofia told them, giving each of them an unladylike fist bump.

Jimmy stood and went to the scruffy blue-eyed guy and said, 'My daughter told me you were good, son. She wasn't wrong.'

As the men did variations of fist bumps, back slaps and handshakes, Rosalie stood from the sofa, straightening her dress, and subtly cleared her throat.

'Guys, this is Rosalie,' Sofia said. 'Billy, Frankie, you might remember Ros, she used to come here a lot when—'

'Yeah, I do. The cupcake lady,' Frankie said, winking distastefully.

Rosalie smiled. 'Well, cupcakes were very on trend a few years back. We're really in more of a veggie phase now but I'm sure I can find some treats for you guys over the next couple of months. I'm going to be hanging out here, whilst Sofia shows me the ropes.'

The exchanges of questioning looks didn't escape Rosalie's attention, but Billy said, 'Well, nice to have you onboard, Ros. I, personally, am a carnivore, though I can make an exception for waffles.'

Rosalie giggled. 'I'll remember that.' As she did, she looked around the five other people in the room and it occurred to her that every one of them wore some variation of ripped stonewash jeans – some intentionally ripped, others not – dirty boots or sneakers and flannel shirts. 'This, erm, isn't a compulsory uniform, is it?'

As the others laughed, Rosalie's panic was alleviated because she had been truly concerned that she might have to dress like them to 'fit in'.

'Phew,' she said, wiping her brow.

Then Scruffy Blue-Eyes stepped forward and surprised her with a southern twang as he said, 'Just stay away from the kick drum in those weapons,' he said, gesturing to her sandals. 'If your foot slips off the pedal, you'll pierce the head.'

His lips curved at one side into what could have been a deadly half-smile, if it weren't for his snide remark and the fact he looked like he hadn't showered... ever. Who was *he* to talk about fashion, in his scuffed suede boots, shaggy jeans, open farmer's shirt, that tight white T-shirt and hanging dog tags that were soooo ten years ago?

'I'm Seth, by the way,' he said, holding out a hand and wafting what was surprisingly a musk of soap and outdoors under Rosalie's nose.

'Grab a seat,' Sofia said generally to the room, adjusting the right faders to bring Seth's recording over the speakers.

As they listened to Seth sing, Sofia tweaked the sound,

making the bass more pronounced in some places, enhancing the melody in others. Her foot tapped and her shoulders swayed of their own volition as she worked. It was a pleasure to watch and reminded Rosalie why she was here.

She reached into her purse and took out her leatherbound notebook and Montblanc pen. 'Can you talk me through the buttons as you push them?' she asked, and Sofia briefly did as Rosalie made notes, oblivious to the eyes in the room that were focused on her.

When the track finished, Sofia turned on her stool to face Seth, who was now perched uncomfortably close to Rosalie on the arm of the sofa. 'So, I was thinking the opening riff is just so pretty, maybe you should let it run completely and bring in the lyrics on the repeat.'

Seth's response was to hook his guitar strap over his shoulder and play the riff. Sofia leaned back against the studio wall and let her head move with the beat, her eyes on the ground as she listened. Rosalie, on the other hand, was fixated on the ease with which Seth's fingers commanded the strings.

On the repeat, he began to sing:

> I can still see your smile,
> Right before you closed the door,
> For the last time.

'Keep going,' Sofia instructed.

Sofia listened to verse and chorus, verse. Then she said, 'Instead of picking up the beat for the second chorus, bring it down.'

But Rosalie had stopped taking notes because just inches from her, she heard a voice that surprised her, chilled her and made the hairs on her arms stand on end.

She followed as the group moved into the studio, Billy offering her a hand down the few steps inside.

'Go again from the second verse,' Sofia said.

As the others played, Sofia walked across the room to the upright piano and quickly lifted the lid then slipped onto the stool in front.

At the end of the verse, Frankie killed the bass, Billy dropped the drums and Seth slowed the melody. Sofia flexed her fingers then closed her eyes and began to play. Taking her lead from Seth's tempo, she improvised. Seth's lyrics ended but he stayed with Sofia on guitar, then she built the melody to a crescendo and the others took her lead – Frankie struck a chord on bass, Billy brought back the drums, Seth strummed his acoustic – and at the right moment, Seth let rip on notes Rosalie hadn't heard from a country rock singer before.

They played until the end of the track and Frankie closed on one heavy strum on the bass guitar.

After a moment's pause, the others all shared a smile, ignoring Rosalie's presence in the room entirely. 'That's your first single,' Sofia said, and Seth simply nodded.

Rosalie clapped excitedly, drawing all eyes in the room to her. 'That was super pretty.'

And she found herself looking forward to the day she signed her first Seth-type singer to her own label. Of course, at her label, his image would be less homeless person who's been living under Brooklyn bridge for a decade and more smooth, clean, lust-worthy.

She imagined herself at the Grammys in floor-length silk, cameras flashing around her as she linked arms with her rock stars. The headlines would read:

ADORED BY HER ARTISTS AND AN INCREDIBLE MOTHER: IS THERE NOTHING THIS WOMAN CANNOT DO?

And her life would be filled with love, admiration, success and her very own Prince Charming.

But Rosalie's thoughts were brought to an abrupt end when the studio door was pushed open so hard that it slammed against the wall.

Jay, Sofia's husband, appeared. 'Fuck,' he said as he stumbled and slid down the door, stopping himself from falling by gripping onto the door handle.

'Christ, Jay. It's after ten and you've been out since brunch,' Sofia said, moving to him and helping him stand. 'Have you even been home?'

'Nope. But lishten, Sophs, you schgot to hear this.'

With Sofia's help, Jay made it to a stool, barely acknowledging the others in the room. 'Lishten.' He hit play on his cell phone and an electric pop track played into the room.

As he drunkenly wagged his head and pumped the air in time to the tuneless track, Rosalie risked a glance at Sofia, whose jaw was hard set.

'All right, Jay, let's get you home and we can talk about this later, yeah?' Sofia attempted.

'Ishn't it great? Shay it. Shay it's... it's banging.'

'We'll listen to it properly later. Do you want coffee or do you want to go home?'

'Fucking lishten to it!'

'No, Jay. Let's go home.'

'What isss your problem? Always sho uptight. You used to be fun.'

'Jay, I don't have a problem. Let's just go home, okay?'

'I don't want to go home, I want you to lishten.' He staggered up from the stool, stumbling into Sofia, forcing her back against the open door.

'And I will. But right now, you're embarrassing us in front of clients. You need to go home and sober up.'

Jay laughed sardonically as Jimmy grabbed his arm roughly, hoisting it over his shoulder and all but dragging Jay from the studio.

In the silence he left behind, Rosalie asked, 'Does that happen a lot?'

Sofia lifted her head sharply and snapped, 'He's had a boozy lunch. It happens.'

Rosalie watched her best friend's baby sister follow her drunken husband out of the studio.

6

ANDREA

Paperwork. There was so much paperwork. Andrea still had a say – in fact, a bigger say than ever – in which musicians and songwriters were contracted to the Stellar label, but she had no hands-on role in producing any more. What had once taken 90 per cent of her time had been replaced with management meetings, budgeting and smoothing things out when the proverbial shit hit the fan.

Tonight was Sir Presley John's remembrance concert and at the current time – 4 p.m. – it was looking like there was no end in sight. She had told Hannah they could get ready together at her apartment, but she was starting to think she wouldn't have time.

She hated to let Hannah down when she was sure her oldest friend could do with a night of glamour away from all the kids, but... 'Hannah?' Andrea called from her desk, through the open door of her office.

Hannah had a spring in her step today, which Andrea was sure was down to the thought of dressing up and letting her hair down. She came to a stop on the threshold of Andrea's office, almost with a bounce.

'Hannah, I'm so sorry,' she said, genuinely apologetic.

Hannah interrupted. 'You're not going to make it later, are you?'

'No, I am, I promise. Plus, Tommy Dawson' – she rolled her eyes then, knowing her friend would understand the reference – 'is playing part of the main tribute tonight. Despite his flaws and our... history, he and the band were my first breakout and I feel like I should be there, especially when he's performing on my doorstep.'

She knew as she said the words how shitty they sounded – she couldn't let down one of her artists but she could let down Hannah. 'I don't want to let anybody down,' she corrected. 'It's just that I have to finish then run through my presentation to the board tomorrow.'

'It's fine. I get it.'

'Look, you have a key to my place. There's a bottle of fizz in the refrigerator that I planned for us to share whilst getting ready. Pour yourself a glass, take whatever you want from my closet and I'll be there as soon as I can.'

* * *

It was gone five before Andrea even turned to the slides to support her board presentation. Tomorrow morning, she intended to give the board of Stellar her vision for the future. The problem was, she wasn't even convincing herself with the ideas she had. There was nothing standout or inspirational. She needed something – or someone – new, screaming potential.

Had she lost her touch? She had gotten to this position by being able to spot new talent and though she scoured YouTube and the indie charts, no artist or group was grabbing her. She couldn't remember the last time a voice had made the hairs on her skin stand on end, given her chill bumps, made her breath hitch or her heart soar.

She had considered acquiring a new, thriving label and there were a couple of contenders, but there was only one label that really stood out and that particular label hadn't made it into her presentation for one reason: she couldn't, wouldn't, poach Sanfia Records from her sister, and she knew not all the money in the world would convince Sofia to sell the family label to a giant like the Stellar label of XM Music Group.

She admired Sofia's strength of will. Her devotion to the label their father had founded. Hell, she was almost jealous of the way nothing meant more to Sofia than the people she loved. But Andrea had chosen over the last couple of years – and for the first time in her life – to focus on herself and her career. Things that didn't fight back. Things that didn't misunderstand her and threaten to break her heart. But Sofia's best interests were her kryptonite and damn if that wasn't causing her a headache for her presentation.

She tapped her manicured nail on her desk as she waited impatiently for her PowerPoint presentation to load.

'Come on,' she muttered, checking the small clock on her desk again.

She hadn't even seen the dress Hannah – or Rosalie, as it transpired – had recently bought for her to wear.

'Finally!' she said, as the presentation Hannah had typed, following Andrea's lengthy notes, opened on her screen.

She reviewed the first of twenty slides. *Perfect.* Exactly as she had instructed.

She moved to the next slide. She recognised it but... 'That's number three.' She scrolled on and realised that only ten of her twenty slides had been compiled.

'What the hell?'

She stormed out of her office to Hannah's desk. *Empty,* like every other desk in the secretary pool. Finding her notes amongst the piles of documents on Hannah's desk, she flicked through her hand-drawn slide deck.

'For fuck's sake, Hannah!' she yelled as she realised what had happened. Back in her office, she tossed the pages in temper. Hannah had missed the reverse side of every page. She had missed *every other slide.*

Now Andrea had ten slides to make before she could even rehearse her presentation, which was at nine-thirty in the morning.

Almost on reflex, she dialled Hannah's cell, which went straight to voicemail.

'Hannah, for God's sake! This presentation has to be done first thing and I need to check it before relying on it. How could you miss every other page?'

'Problem?'

She would have gone on an endless rant to Hannah's voicemail but Hunter's appearance at her doorway stole her thoughts, her heartbeat and her breath, all at once.

He strode toward her as she dropped her landline into its holster. His navy dinner suit was trimmed with black lapels and cuffs. The line down the leg of the pants was black and his bowtie hung untied and loose down the sides of his open shirt collar.

Hunter sure did know how to wear a suit – he was as knockout as Sinatra or Martin.

'Shouldn't you be getting dressed?' he asked with a familiar hunger in his eyes that was a match for her own feelings.

'I should,' she replied, gathering herself before she could form a coherent sentence that wasn't a lust-fuelled torrent of rubbish.

Hunter nodded, his gaze growing heavier and the focus moving down to the bottom-most unbuttoned fastening of Andrea's blouse.

'The presentation tomorrow?' he asked.

'A catastrophic fuck-up by Hannah.'

He turned his back on her and she watched him cross the room toward her vinyl player. He ran a finger along the LPs neatly lining her shelf stack and pulled out John Coltrane – *a classic.*

She didn't have time for this, but suddenly time had no meaning. She had forgotten why she was mad and at whom. As Hunter set the music to play, Andrea drew her office blinds and locked the door.

* * *

Whilst they dressed, the infamous post-coital vulnerability that attacked all women – stoics and home-wreckers included – began to creep into Andrea's mind. As if he knew, intuitively, Hunter unprecedentedly approached her from behind and pressed his lips to her neck, running his hands down her arms.

'Hunter? Do you think we'll ever...?'

How did she ask if he thought they could ever be a couple? How did she ask him to leave his wife for her? How did she do anything without becoming what she promised she wouldn't become?

'Shhh... Don't spoil it.' He kissed her temple and backed away, ending the conversation that never got started.

Andrea hated herself for allowing melancholy to come over her. She couldn't. She wouldn't. The whole point was that Hunter was never going to be hers. He couldn't let her down or hurt her.

Could he? A quick, very wrong fling was all they were supposed to have.

She faked nonchalance, waving a hand. 'I guess I'll see you later.'

'Later, kiddo.'

Hunter winked, shrugged on his jacket and left.

Now she was *really* running late and her earlier annoyance at Hannah was mixed with irritation at herself because Hunter was well and truly where he was never supposed to be – under her skin.

She had walked briskly, as fast as her heels would allow, back to her apartment, feeling, and no doubt looking, dishevelled – aka *just screwed*.

Outside her door, Andrea ran her fingers through her hair, rubbed around her lips in case of smudged lipstick – not that she and Hunter ever kissed much – and prepared to face Hannah, who had probably listened to her voicemail by now.

She took a deep breath and entered her apartment to see Hannah, looking beautiful and refined in one of Andrea's dresses. The royal-blue garment had a Bardot neckline, finished just above the knee, and hugged Hannah exactly where it should. She had teamed it with a pair of Andrea's strappy gold scandals and, for a moment, Andrea felt only happiness for her friend.

Hannah came toward her, holding out a full flute of what looked like champagne.

'I'm sorry and I'm going to fix the presentation first thing in the morning, but let's not spoil tonight.'

Andrea pouted and gave her friend a frosty stare, then took the glass of champagne, acknowledging the apology with a curt nod.

It had never felt like a challenge having Hannah as a friend and an assistant when they had been working at Sanfia together. It had felt more collaborative then. Sofia, Andrea and Hannah had been a family, doing what they enjoyed. But it was tricky at Stellar. Andrea had more responsibility, especially since her promotion. That brought with it more scope for screwing up. She needed Hannah not to dip her nose in above her station but to remain within the remit of her job description. Andrea needed an assistant.

She also needed her friend. If Hannah hadn't been on maternity leave, Andrea was sure the mess she was in with Hunter would never have happened. Hannah would have called Andrea out on her bad decisions. And maybe... maybe she had been lonely without Hannah every day.

Trying to keep her office and home life distinct, she clinked her glass against Hannah's and sipped the champagne.

'You look great,' Andrea said, suddenly desperate to spend a real girls' night with her friend and reveal everything – Hunter, the affair, that she was sleeping with a married man who just happened to be Rosalie's dad.

'Take that and go get yourself dressed,' Hannah said, as ever, the only person who dared to order Andrea around.

'Okay,' Andrea said, trying to push thoughts of Hunter from her mind and failing miserably.

Instead, she drained her glass, put it down on the breakfast bar in her open-plan lounge-kitchen-diner and followed the low-level floor lighting toward her bedroom.

Good save, she thought. No one should know about Hunter.

But as she walked away, Hannah said, 'It's true, isn't it?'

If dread could emanate as a physical feeling, Andrea's stomach would have dropped right out of her and hit the floor. She stopped still, her back to her friend. Her affair with Hunter had gone unnoticed for the four months Hannah had been on maternity leave and, though she knew tongues had been wagging with rumours in the office in the weeks Hannah had been back, Andrea had hoped it would all blow over. Bitterness at her promotion and nothing more.

But here she was, faced with the reality that the woman who knew her better than anyone else in the world, who not only knew but diarised her every move, suspected her affair.

'I overheard people talking in the office,' Hannah continued sheepishly. 'They said you were seeing one of the execs. They said you slept your way to the top... I told them exactly where they could shove their Chinese whispers, that you earned your position and deserved their respect.'

Andrea turned to face her friend across the room. She said nothing but could feel heat rising on her neck where Hunter's lips had been less than an hour ago.

'I believe that, Andi. We both know it's true,' Hannah reassured her.

Andrea nodded her thanks because her mouth was too dry to form words, but she didn't feel assured.

'The thing is, you left me a voicemail more than an hour and a half ago, saying I'd fucked up and you desperately needed those slides to be fixed. Yet, when you walked in here and I told you that I'd fix the presentation first thing in the morning, you didn't say you'd already done it.'

Andrea heard herself swallow and wondered if Hannah could hear the deep gulp too, as she stood motionless.

'You're irritable and sheepish,' Hannah continued. 'You're a big girl, Andi, but be careful. Whoever he is, I'm going to guess you're not his number one and that's only going to end one way. He'll break your heart.'

Fuck you, Hannah. Fuck you and your self-righteousness and your forever romance with the guy who knocked you up in college.

Biting down on her lips, her jaw set, Andrea turned her back on her friend and strode to the shower room.

When she was stood under the uncommonly cold spray, letting the water soothe her stinging eyes, her hot skin, her palpitating heart, Andrea tried to work through the torrent of thoughts surging her hectic mind.

Hannah knew she was seeing someone on the executive board, but Hannah didn't know *who*, and it was best that she never did. It was best that *no one* ever knew that she had been seeing Hunter.

Was she seeing Hunter? Was that what was happening? Had she resigned herself to being that other woman? For how long? Would she ever be more than just the other woman? Had she really been foolish enough to risk a heartbreak?

God, she shouldn't be that person. She shouldn't *want* to be that person.

She needed to end *this*, whatever it was, with Hunter. And she needed to do it before anyone got hurt.

She massaged shower oil into her skin.

It wasn't like she hadn't tried to end it with Hunter.

About three months ago, they had gone two weeks without sleeping together. True, Hunter had been travelling for work for one of those weeks, but for the week after his return she had avoided him at all costs – going so far as to dart into the ladies' restroom, behind walls, under her desk if she saw him heading in her direction.

But it hadn't stuck. He was like sugar, caffeine, endorphins to her mind. A fix she needed.

It had to end now. She knew that.

Yet her hand moved to cover her heart unconsciously as she thought about seeing him day after day in the office and not having a claim to him.

What if he wanted her, too? What if he wanted her to be his number one, not just the other woman?

The one person she could ask for advice was currently in her lounge, dressed in her clothes and sipping on champagne.

But Hannah could never know the truth. Never. Knowing the truth would put her in a terrible position. No one could know the truth because the stakes were too high. If Rosalie found out that Andrea had been having an affair with her dad, she would never forgive her.

Andrea had to make a choice between being a friend and being the other woman.

7

HANNAH

'Hannah! Are you kidding me?'

She ran from Andrea's lounge into the master bedroom, where she found Andrea standing in front of her floor-length mirror. And she thought, *Oh, Jesus!*

Rosalie had picked out a stunning dress for Andrea to wear to the concert. The problem was, it was Rosalie-style stunning and very *definitely not* Andrea-style stunning.

The black gown clung to Andrea's incredible figure. The thigh-high slit displayed her slim, long leg almost up to her panties. The neckline plunged to mid-torso, displaying her knock-out cleavage. The long sleeves and high back added a touch of sophistication and the crystal necklace that draped between her breasts added a classy finish.

'Andi, you look a million,' Hannah reasoned with honesty, but knowing she was about to cop it *Andrea*-style.

'I look like... like *Rosalie*.'

'Admittedly, you are a little more exposed than usual but you really do look—'

'Like I'm gagging for it from every rock star going to the concert tonight. For God's sake, look at the time, the limo will be downstairs. I don't even have time to change! Hannah, how could you do this to me?'

'I—'

'Forget it,' Andrea snapped. 'Let's just go.'

Hannah rolled her eyes as she followed Andrea out of the apartment, all the while thinking, *So now she has standards?*

* * *

After a painfully silent ride to Madison Square Gardens, Hannah was relieved to arrive at the side entrance to the arena – the red carpet being reserved for A-listers, and even Andrea, much to her obvious annoyance, was a nobody when it came to the front pages of glossy magazines.

The rear door of the limo was opened by the driver.

'Let's get some of this frosty air out of here,' Hannah said, smiling to herself as she stepped onto the much smaller and significantly less bright carpet to that which would have been rolled out at the main entrance.

Andrea finally put down her cell phone and walked with Hannah into the backstage entrance to MSG.

The grey corridors, though usually dull and chill, were brightened with poster prints of Sir Presley John with his arm around the shoulders of stars that spanned decades – Cher, Michael Jackson, Dina Carrol, Elton John, Tom Jones, Alicia Keyes. There were images of him performing on stage in the elaborate rock star jackets he was renowned for, sitting at a piano, rocking out with an electric guitar, singing that famous duet with Dolly Parton.

Stars had started to arrive and reporters interviewed them in the corridors. It was just past 8 p.m. now, which meant the celebrity guests – the Pitts, Clooneys and Gagas of the world – would be pulling up in their chauffeur-driven rides, coming into the arena one by one in order of status, under the bright flashes of cameras.

The concert was being televised live so, right now, support acts would be playing in the main hall, setting the mood and tone, getting the crowd ready for the main event. Ensuring the room was in great spirits and high with anticipation by the time the TV cameras started to roll.

Hannah and Andrea twisted and bumped their way through the hustle and bustle of suits, fine dresses, stage gowns and, by contrast, jeans and leather jackets of the rock guys. They headed in the direction of the common area where nibbles and drinks had been laid out, and the nearby dressing areas, where Andrea would be able to check on her artists. When she wasn't calming the nerves of some stars and taming the egos of others, she would be saying all the right things to fellow industry professionals and Hannah would be by her side the entire time, reminding her of the names that matched faces.

'Annndi, Annndi, Annndi,' came a familiar drawl, followed by the man himself, Tommy 'Rock God' Dawson.

He stepped into their path, his staple attire of worn jeans, cowboy boots (which emphasised his *extremely* large feet) and a leather jacket in place, his hair as shaggy and purposefully unkempt as ever. In a nutshell, his usual, country-slick, hot self. And, for the record, that was the objective view. The more subjective tended to fall at his feet – literally.

He ran greedy eyes up and down Andrea. 'Mmm hmm, you don't know how to disappoint. It's been too long, Andi. You know where I am.' He mumble-slurred his words, the way guys tended to do after a whiskey or two. It was that mumble-slur in his singing voice that earned him – and consequently Andrea – the big bucks.

Nevertheless, the content of this mumble-slur, Hannah knew, would lead to her hearing another rant from Andrea about the inappropriateness of that dress later.

Andrea pulled on a subtle yet obviously (to Hannah) intentional smirk and flashed the flirtatious glint in her eyes that she reserved only for the botchiest of her male clients.

'Chance would be a fine thing,' she said. 'Are you set for tonight's performance?'

'You know I am.'

He pulled a plectrum from the butt pocket of his jeans and used it to pick his front teeth – something he always seemed to do when he was flirting. Something Hannah couldn't fathom – frankly, it seemed unhygienic. But it worked because Tommy Dawson was always, *always* with another girl – usually of the long-blonde-hair and heavily busted variety. Including, she knew, a number of flings he and Andrea had enjoyed in the past.

He stared openly at Andrea's breasts, then her thigh-high slit. 'Baby, where did we go wrong, huh?'

Andrea laughed. 'A bottle of Scotch and a new woman every night. Just try to keep it clean until after the show.'

He flicked his plec in his teeth again and grinned. 'You always were too good for me, Andi.'

'If I were better, I'd have never gone there in the first place.'

'Or back here as many times as you have.'

He laughed and Hannah watched as the pair shared a familiar and warm smile – they had cared about each other once, deep down, whether Andrea had been willing to admit it or not.

Ironically, Tommy Dawson would be a better option than a fling with a taken man.

Shaking her head, Andrea walked further along the corridor toward the communal area, calling back a reminder. 'Keep it clean, Tommy.'

Tommy shook his head with another laugh, then ran his eyes up and down Hannah's body.

'Hannah, Hannah, Hannah.'

Hannah laughed – God loved a trier. 'Toooommy, Toooommy, Toooommy.'

She followed Andrea and Tommy called after her. 'There's no breakin' you, girl, is there?'

'Not in a million,' she said across her shoulder. And she meant it. Though he drove her half insane, Hannah had never done more than second-glance at a man who wasn't Rod.

As she reached Andrea, she received the kind of side-eye look that told her a dress-related comment was coming. She zoned out entirely because, for one thing, Andrea looked good, and for another, who was she to talk about appropriate or inappropriate? For a third thing, Hannah was trying her damned best to be a mother, a wife, a friend, her own person and Andrea's PA. She had so many faces it was making her dizzy. If Andrea wanted to be a dick, it could fall on Hannah's selective hearing tonight.

The common area was packed full of musicians – established and budding – producers, agents, managers, press and VIPs with backstage passes.

Hannah and Andrea worked the room, slowly, one air-kiss at a time. Since Hannah had worked with Andrea for practically her whole career, her face was just as familiar to most people as Andrea's. They didn't treat her as a nobody but as an essential part of the clockwork that was Andrea and her artists.

People greeted her, kissed her cheeks, flirted with her, offered to get her drinks and congratulated her on the birth of TJ because for most people it was the first time they'd seen her since the baby bump.

She had eyes on Andrea, in case she was needed, but otherwise had a drink too many and was enjoying herself – not as a PA or a mommy but as Hannah, just Hannah. And it felt good. Her life had been going just fine. The boys were getting bigger, childcare cheaper. Then she'd fallen pregnant with TJ. She adored her baby but hadn't been ready for her life to be commandeered by children for a third time.

And as she thought that, she felt a pang of guilt. She shouldn't be happy to be free of her family but damn it, sometimes she needed a break from nagging and tears and her husband leaving the toilet seat the eff *up*.

Thankfully, she didn't have time to get bogged down in her personal dilemma because a bigger problem was about to unfold.

Rosalie stepped into the room, drawing the eyes of admirers, both men and women alike, as she managed to shine in a floor-length gold dress that not even Carrie Bradshaw would have been able to pull off. As soon as Andrea noticed her, she made a beeline for her. After all the help Rosalie had given Hannah lately, she wasn't about to let Andrea tear strips off her about her outfit selection.

Both women came in and out of view as Hannah worked through the crowd, arriving at Rosalie's side at the same time as Andrea.

Andrea had a face like thunder. Hannah watched Andrea open her mouth to speak but her jaw stayed loose and no words came out, her focus no longer on Rosalie. Hannah followed her gaze and realised that Andrea's eyes were trained on the man behind Rosalie, who was holding a woman's – his wife's – hand

and pressing his lips to her temple. That man and his wife were Rosalie's parents, Hunter and Loretta.

There was a beat of awkward silence that was not lost on Hannah. *Why?*

She hugged Rosalie, then Hunter and Loretta. Eventually, Andrea followed suit, hugging Rosalie, then kissing Loretta on each cheek whilst holding her at arm's length. Then Hannah observed as Andrea lengthened her spine and rolled her shoulders back, puffing out her chest like a lioness might to mark her territory in the wild.

Andrea held out her hand to Hunter, who had gone in for a hug, such that the pair ended up in a strained embrace, holding hands.

Hannah asked Loretta, 'Where is that dress from? I love it!' but she kept her eyes on her best friend and Hunter. She watched as he ran hungry eyes over every part of Andrea that was displayed to its best advantage in that dress. She watched as his eyes grew darker, heavier.

And in that moment, she knew.

As if the way they addressed each other and couldn't tear their eyes from each other wasn't confirmation enough, the uncommon flush of Andrea's skin and the way she fidgeted as she exchanged pleasantries with Loretta were also fairly damning evidence.

Andrea promptly excused herself from the group, grabbing a glass of champagne from a waiter on the way out of the room, downing it as she moved quickly into the corridor.

It was the nail in the coffin. Hannah was 100 per cent certain that her best friend was having an affair with her other best friend's dad.

'Holy mother of fuck,' she whispered under her breath, meeting Hunter's nervous gaze.

In This Together

On wobbly legs, Hannah excused herself, told Rosalie she would find her in a while, and went in search of Andrea, not sure whether she wanted to kill her first and reason with her later, or the other way around.

How could she do this? How could she lie about this? How could she cast aside Rosalie's feelings, as if years of friendship stood for nothing?

She pushed through the door into the ladies' restroom and saw Andrea, braced with her hands on a wash basin, looking at her own grey complexion reflected in the mirrors. The picture Hannah found told her the answer to all her questions, and it was worse than she had first thought.

She stared at her friend, not the powerhouse music exec but the vulnerable woman, who had lost her mother as an eight-year-old girl and brought up her younger sister whilst her dad found solace at the bottom of a whisky bottle. The woman who had grown up hiding her emotions and didn't know any other way, but who, deep down, was compassionate and complex and had spent her life caring for others – her friends, her sister, her dad, her musicians – without ever asking for the same in return. A woman who could be promiscuous but who was afraid to ever let her guard down because she had been terrified for thirty years of getting her heart broken. A woman who had just seen Hunter, her lover, with his daughter and wife, and endured the agonising reality that she was that *other* woman.

'Oh, God,' Hannah said. 'You have feelings for him, don't you?'

Andrea heaved in a breath.

'How could you do this, Andi? How could you do this to Ros?'

'I don't know, okay? Damn it! I didn't mean for this. I just... don't seem able to stop it.'

Hannah shook her head, refusing to feel sorry for Andrea.

'Of course you can't stop it. This is perfect for you. A man that you can't ever commit to. It's signature Andrea. Except this time, you've crossed the line, and you need to stop it. Or maybe that's your master plan? Push the few people you have let close to you away, one by one.'

8

ROSALIE

Rosalie was midway through telling Tommy Dawson how to feng-shui his new city apartment. Tommy had been on and off the scene in the past, having had numerous flings with Andrea. She had first met Tommy shortly before he and his band were plucked from Andrea at Sanfia Records by XM Music Group. Funny, because she always thought when Andrea and Tommy were working together they were perfect for each other, but it had never come to anything serious.

Tommy had bought a flashy penthouse apartment in a sought-after building in the city, and it was the kind of project even Rosalie would end her sabbatical for.

Their conversation was cut short when Sofia, looking uncommonly flushed and bothered, appeared nearby with Seth, Frankie, Billy and a young woman Rosalie didn't recognise but who looked to Rosalie distinctly like a music artist – call it intuition or call it long feather earrings, a hippie-style dress and purple streaks in her hair.

'Sofia, over here!' Rosalie called, pulling her into a hug. 'This jumpsuit looks incredible on you, and I love the slicked hair.'

Sofia looked down at herself. 'The what? Oh, thanks. You look as great as ever.'

Rosalie held up a hand in greeting to the others then quietly asked Sofia, 'Are you okay? You seem flustered.'

'I'm fine.' Then she shook her head. 'Just a bit of a delay getting out of the house, that's all.'

Rosalie felt her brows furrow as she looked around the space nearby. 'Isn't Jay with you?'

She noticed Sofia swallow deeply before she confessed. 'That was sort of the delay. He had a big night last night and...' Sofia clearly feigned a smile. 'Nothing he can't sleep off. Hey, I haven't introduced you to Dani.'

Sofia ushered the purple-haired musician forward and said, 'Dani, this is my friend, Rosalie.' Then she told Rosalie, 'Dani is recording her first EP at Sanfia. She's going to be a hit.'

Rosalie enquired about Dani's music but as she listened to the young woman's passion for country music, her attention was drawn to Seth, not shaggy and unkempt tonight but looking... well. Very well. His scuffed suede boots had been swapped out for polished leather. His dirty ripped jeans had been replaced by butt-hugging indigo dress jeans, and where he had worn a white T-shirt and a flannel shirt, he was wearing a black fitted T-shirt and a suave jacket. If it weren't for his seemingly signature dog tags and fiercely blue eyes, he would be barely recognisable.

Their eyes locked momentarily before Seth was yanked forward into a rough embrace with none other than man-of-the-hour, frontman of Armstrung, a Billboard-topping rock band, whose name was Randy Jonson – possibly the crudest stage name in the business.

Seth impressed her. Despite being in the presence of real fame and riches, Seth seemed to be taking everything in his stride, shaking hands with the other members of Armstrung, laughing and joking. Rosalie knew them all from a brief time she spent dating the lead guitarist.

But how did Seth know Randy Jonson? Seth hadn't even released his first single yet.

Since the music industry was all about *who* you know, Rosalie was going to find out. She neatly introduced Dani to Miley Delap, a young British pop artist who had recently left a well-known girl band to go solo. Rosalie knew Miley's family through a friend of a friend. With the girls happily chatting, Rosalie made a beeline for Randy and Seth.

She watched as Randy took a cigarette from the inside pocket of his leather jacket, hung it between his lips and went to light up.

'Outside, Randy!' someone called, making Randy laugh. Rosalie watched him pat Seth on the back and tell the people around him, 'Babysit my kid brother.'

Brother? Seth Young was Randy Jonson's brother? This was gold. She had to tell Sofia.

But as she turned on the spot, she was nearly rocked off her heels by Graham Shelton, organiser extraordinaire. He was speaking frantically to a producer Rosalie recognised from one of the big labels.

'What do you mean he's too sick to go on stage? Give him a pill or something. He's on in less than twenty minutes,' Graham said.

'I'm sorry, man, but he's in no fit state, believe me.'

'I hope he knows he's fucking up his career. What the hell am I supposed to do?'

'I'm sorry, man, I really am, but he's just a warm-up act. Can't one of the others play an extra track or somethin'?'

'At this stage in the game?' Graham yelled. 'Fuck!'

As Rosalie rubbed her battered arm, she listened to the

exchange, her mind whirring with an idea. A way of paying Sofia back for teaching her the ropes. A way of making a small dent into the professional side of the industry.

Before she had a chance to second-guess herself and whether Seth was ready for what she was about to propose, she said, 'Graham, maybe I could help you?'

* * *

'Are you crazy?' Seth snapped at Rosalie. Then he turned to Sofia. 'This is insane. I can't do this.'

Seth paced up and down in the gents' toilets, one hand in the pocket of his denim pants, the other rubbing the back of his neck.

'Please don't call me crazy,' Rosalie said. 'You should be thanking me. I'm using my contacts to get you a break here. Plus, I've seen it done before. Do you remember, Soph? Three years ago, Andrea took one of her musicians along to the CMAs. An act pulled out of a day slot and Andrea seized the opportunity, telling the organisers that her latest talent could fill the spot. It went a long way toward making his next single a hit in indie terms, hitting the indie charts at... what was it, Soph, like twenty? And just breaking into the Billboard top 100 Hot Country Songs. So, you see, you just need to take your opportunities.'

She chose not to highlight that the difference between what Andrea had done three years ago and what she had just committed Seth to in fifteen minutes' time was about ten thousand people (growing every minute), a significantly larger stage and, well, Madison Square Gardens.

Oops, maybe this was insane.

As Seth continued to pace, Rosalie motioned to Sofia to step in. He was Sofia's artist, after all. Surely she had some words of wisdom.

'Look, Seth, Rosalie is right,' Sofia said calmly. 'She's heard your single and wouldn't have suggested this – I wouldn't be in agreement with this – if we didn't think you were up to it. I want the world to see what you do. I want those people out there to hear your lyrics, the way you play, that voice.'

'You're the complete package, Seth,' Rosalie added. 'I mean, I had my doubts when I first saw you, believe me. Those ripped jeans and scruffy boots and... I digress. Tonight, though, you look... you know.'

He stopped pacing and looked at her as if he were contemplating her words. Then he smirked.

'So maybe look at it this way,' Sofia tried. 'You've been shot at and you've kept people alive in the middle of a war zone. All I'm asking you to do is go on stage, with Billy and Frankie, and sing like you would have to your platoon. Like no one else is there. Just you, sitting on some turned-up crates at your FOB.'

Shot at? He was a soldier?

Rosalie watched him rub the dog tags that hung down his chest, then he looked down to his feet and she truly had no idea whether he would do the show or not. God, maybe she was irresponsible after all.

Then she stood taller and asked firmly, 'Do you want this, Seth? Do you want to be an artist?'

He raised his eyes and Rosalie saw the answer in his determined look.

'Then you're going to have to get used to big stages and screaming fans because you've *got. It. All.* You're going all the way. I believe that. Sofia believes that. And you need to too. I'll give you two minutes to decide, and if you choose not to go on stage, I'll go and tell Graham that you weren't up to it. But my best advice, for what it's worth, is don't waste life's opportunities. Take them for those who can't.'

She left the bathroom, letting the door close behind her. In the corridor, Billy and Frankie were leaning up against the wall, wondering whether they would be going on stage in a matter of minutes.

She twisted one side of her mouth and raised her arms from her sides as if to say, *We'll see,* hoping that this wouldn't come crashing down around her and Sofia.

Why did she think she could meddle in a business she was fast realising she didn't know at all?

She came to stand between the guys, and the three of them waited for the bathroom door to open, counting long seconds until eventually, the door opened. Sofia appeared first, followed by Seth's imposing frame filling the doorway.

They waited for Seth's response. Rosalie held her breath.

Seth cleared his throat and asked, 'What about the piano?'

As Billy and Frankie quickly got excited, Rosalie exhaled slowly, relieved.

'You're going to have to play the piano, Soph,' Seth said.

'The stage isn't for me,' she said. 'You can go on without the piano. The guitars sound great anyway.'

'In the studio, you said the piano makes the track and I agree, so it's the single with the piano or no show.'

Reluctant though Rosalie was to admit it, from what she had heard in the studio, Seth was right; the piano did carry the melody, particularly in the opening of the track.

She thought quickly. 'Can't someone else just play the piano? Billy, you can play piano, right?'

'Yeah, I can, musical genius, but then we'll lose the bass guitar and—'

She held up a hand to quash his sarcasm and told him, 'Billy,

I'm nothing if not a lady with contacts. You guys get ready and I'll find you a bass guitarist to blow your socks off.'

* * *

The feeling she had was a feeling she rarely got and one that Rosalie knew only came when something truly great was about to happen. Rosalie rushed over to Hannah and Andrea, tottering at almost a light run as best she could in her heels, finding her friends deep in conversation with Calvin Richards. Calvin was a radio DJ capable of making or breaking artists, and Andrea would doubtless be tapping him up for airtime.

'Ladies, we need to get to the stage for the next act,' she announced, breathless. 'You too, Calvin. You're not going to want to miss this, let me tell you.'

'What? Who is it?' Hannah asked, already falling into step behind Rosalie as she led the way to the arena stage.

'Someone who is about to make history, magic and the front page of every glossy magazine in the country. Hurry!'

They hustled to the stage with Calvin Richards in tow, turning heads as they made their way, until they were part of a large group of others who tapped into their frenzy and filed into the arena, coming to stand in the press area immediately in front of the stage.

Sofia was already standing dead-centre in front of the set, her hands forming a steeple over her nose and mouth as she breathed into them.

'What's the big deal?' Hannah asked, seemingly giddy without knowing why, as they reached Sofia.

'Did you bring Calvin?' Sofia asked, less than her usual chilled self. Rosalie and Hannah separated to give Sofia sight of Calvin behind them.

'Hey, Calvin,' Sofia called to him. 'This is the track you're going to be playing to death next week.'

'We'll see about that,' Calvin said in return.

And Rosalie told him, 'You know we will.'

Rosalie would remind him of the helping hand she gave his younger sister when she started NYU and desperately wanted to make a complete U-turn on her gothic look to go preppy. His sister became head of the cheer squad and now had a sweet pad overlooking Central Park, where she lived with the starting quarterback for the Jets, all thanks to Rosalie's wardrobe overhaul, a few foils and some major laser hair removal.

When Calvin dropped his head back, laughing good-humouredly, Rosalie's wide, signature smile broke, showing her perfectly straight teeth beneath red-painted lips. She winked at Sofia, who finally seemed to relax.

Andrea and Sofia looked alike in many ways – they had similar features and the same green eyes. But Rosalie had always found Sofia's looks more beautiful. She had softer angles, her frame was daintier and less imposing, and she had the sweetest creases at the sides of her mouth to match the small dimple in her chin.

In fact, Sofia's personality was all-round sweeter and more relaxed, though she and Andrea could come to blows big style. It was rare but they had been at loggerheads a couple of times since Rosalie had known them.

The first time was when Sofia wanted to rush into marrying Jay – in honesty, Andrea was right about him. Jay had fooled everyone at first but soon his own insecurities were clear and it became obvious that he would put Sofia down to make himself feel better.

The second time was when Andrea ditched Sanfia Records to move to XM Music Group, though they disguised the truth of that argument behind something much less meaningful, so meaningless Rosalie couldn't even remember what it was.

'So, why did we run here?' Hannah asked.

Just then, the arena lights went down and they were standing in near blackness, looking at a dark stage. Rosalie could just about make out figures moving around. A guy with a guitar she assumed and hoped was Seth approached the central microphone.

They stood in a row – Andrea, Rosalie, Hannah and Sofia. Rosalie watched Sofia take a deep breath – had she pulled this off? – then her attention was drawn to the stage as the sound of a piano began to play. The melody was pretty – slow but not melancholy, just how the guys had rehearsed in the studio.

The stage lights came up. As two lights streamed the audience, Rosalie noticed the arena was already half-full and growing, ready for the headline acts. On the stage, the man she had seen moving as a silhouette with a guitar was now standing under a central spotlight, his guitar strapped across his shoulder. Seth had discarded his jacket and wore simply his jeans and plain black T-shirt that allowed her to see that he was toned – muscly, in fact. He had facial hair but didn't look as ragged as the others on the stage – Billy, playing piano, Frankie, playing lead guitar, and the secret weapon she persuaded to help out his younger brother was playing electric guitar. Her heart fluttered with excitement and satisfaction.

Hannah leaned toward Sofia and asked, 'Is that Randy Jonson?'

Sofia's gaze was fixed on the man at the front of the stage, who was staring back at her as he began to play his guitar. Sofia nodded and Rosalie wondered if the gesture was in response to Hannah's question or to reassure her artist on stage. It was a move that reminded Rosalie that, as ever, she was just the helper on the periphery of someone else's story.

As the melody picked up, an indication lyrics were imminent, Rosalie felt Sofia stiffen beside her and wondered whether Andrea might put an arm around her sister. True to form, she didn't. Andrea was great at a lot of things, but she was completely emotionally inept.

Then all other thoughts left Rosalie's mind as Seth started to sing.

> Maybe I was wrong.
> Maybe I fell for you when we were too young.
> But we both learned from a broken heart
> and now we can move on.
> I'll never forget that first kiss.
> You know I will always remember.
> Baby I was crazy about you.
> But you aren't here no more.

His voice was velvet – old, familiar and smooth. It wrapped around her like a warm bath and made her want to sink down under luxury brand bubbles. Rosalie wasn't as talented as Andrea and Sofia when it came to music, but she had been around it all her life, first with her dad, endlessly listening to vinyls at home. Then with the many musicians she had dated – a member of Randy Jonson's Armstrung included (if you could call it *dating*). And latterly because of Andrea, Sofia and Hannah. So she felt qualified enough to know that the man on stage – his voice, the way his fingers effortlessly commanded his guitar, the lyrics, which were no doubt his own if he was working with Sofia, the whole look – had it all.

If her own opinion wasn't enough, when she looked to her

left and saw Andrea's wide eyes and slightly open mouth, she had back-up. When she saw the glazed look in Sofia's eyes and the way she shivered when Seth dropped into his lower register, she knew Sofia thought he was the real deal.

Rosalie leaned into Sofia's ear and told her, 'You can stop holding your breath now.'

Sofia's lips broke into a smile, then a laugh. Then she shook her head and quickly swiped a rogue tear from under her eye.

If Andrea wouldn't show any emotion, Rosalie certainly could. Instinctively, she wrapped an arm around Sofia's waist and they pressed their heads together long enough for Sofia to regain some composure. Sometimes, people just needed to feel loved and lately, Rosalie felt like she had more love inside her than she was able to give.

As the track built to a crescendo, Randy Jonson announced through his microphone, 'Madison Square Gardens, meet Seth Young.'

The ever-growing crowd roared, and Seth did what most artists forgot to do – he paused for a moment and took it all in. As far as Rosalie could tell, he would have to get used to people screaming his name very quickly.

Her hips swayed and she tapped her foot in her fine high-heeled shoe as she stood among her friends.

'Sofia, Seth is fantastic, well done, you,' she shouted above the roaring crowd and her own applause as the track ended.

Sofia was beaming. 'Thanks, but it's mostly him, I assure you. He's incredible – voice, lyrics, guy.' Sofia shook her head as she looked at the stage Seth was leaving, seemingly in awe.

As the noise in the arena calmed, Rosalie saw Andrea place an almost rigid hand on Sofia's shoulder and tell her, 'He is good. With the right support, he could be really something.'

Well, that was about as close to an endorsement as Andrea

was likely to give – a tiny chink in her otherwise imperishable armour.

Sofia didn't have a chance to respond before Calvin Richards raised his closed fist for her to bump.

'I'll be more than happy to give him airtime, Soph. Send over the track. I want an exclusive.'

Rosalie watched as Sofia's mouth curved into yet another smile. 'It's yours,' she told Calvin.

Then, with a gentle but large hand pressed to her shoulder, Rosalie was politely asked to move aside by none other than Seth Young – who suddenly seemed taller, broader and even more ruggedly handsome than he had appeared to her before.

When Seth spoke to Sofia, the southern twang that decorated his voice when he sang was even stronger.

'I was once told that a man should never argue with a woman because women are always right,' he said.

Sofia blushed, uncommonly so, Rosalie silently mused. 'I don't know about that but a good producer always knows what's best for her clients.'

Seth laughed – a soft, rich laugh – as he rubbed the light covering of stubble around his jaw. 'Yeah, all right, I'll give you that. Thank you.'

Rosalie held her breath, grinning as she waited for Seth and Sofia's gratitude. It had, after all, been her initiative that got Seth a slot and her sharp thinking that got Randy Jonson up on the stage with him – something she knew would bring Seth countless hits on social media and pictures in the rags as showbiz columns wrote about the newest face in country rock.

'You were great up there, Seth,' she gushed.

Seth turned to her with a scowl as Sofia said, 'I'm not sure if that was brave or ridiculous, Ros, and I don't know whether to thank you or curse you.'

Oh. If Sofia hadn't shaken her head with a glint in her eye, Rosalie might have felt the exact opposite of praised.

But Seth didn't offer a smile as he folded his big arms across his chest and said, 'You know, Sofia may forgive you for putting us in that situation, but I won't thank you. It was a stupid thing to do, way before I was ready for it, and it could have ruined my career before it even got started. Not just that but Sofia knew, because *she* is my producer, *not* you, that I don't want to ride on the back of my big brother. *Hell,* I didn't want anyone to know he's my brother, not if that's going to be the thing that gets me on the stage over my own music. But I guess this is how your life of pretty things and parties works, right? Be seen with all the right people. Daddy gifting you record labels you have no clue how to run. Prancing around in high heels and sparkly dresses and acting like life isn't real.'

Before Rosalie had a chance to even process her shock, Seth had been pulled into another conversation, leaving Rosalie feeling winded.

The feel of Sofia's hand on her now cold skin reminded Rosalie to breathe. 'He's still wired from the show. Try not to take it to heart. But he does have a point, Ros. Next time, maybe you could ask first and act once we've all thought it through?'

As tears welled behind her eyes, Rosalie offered her brightest smile and nodded. 'Of course. I'm sorry. Silly me, always acting before thinking.'

9

ANDREA

It was nearly 1 a.m. when Andrea, Hannah, Sofia and Rosalie took up seats around the corner of a kitchen bar in East Village. It lacked lustre and finesse. The choice of wine and beer was limited to whatever they'd decided to stock that week. The walls were decorated in old music posters that had been stuck right onto the plaster, rather than put into frames, and were, consequently, worn and discoloured. Andrea had always suspected that the low lighting was more for disguise than mood-setting.

In fact, this was far from what Andrea wanted to be doing right now. She would have ranked bed, preparing for tomorrow's presentation to her board, or wallowing over the fact she'd been having an affair with a married man and had to endure his romance with his wife at the concert tonight as priorities far outweighing sitting at this bar.

But this was tradition. After a big concert, Andrea, Hannah, Rosalie and occasionally Sofia would come to this very bar for the best sliders in Manhattan. And tonight, of all nights, Andrea was considering where her true loyalties lay – to her family, to her friends, to her lover or to herself. She knew where they ought to lie and so, regardless of whether she wanted to be here or not, she had been unable to say no.

'There's something stuck on my knife,' Rosalie said, holding the knife from atop her white paper napkin in front of her face. 'Why do we always have to come here? Can't we, just one time, break with the norm and go somewhere *nice*?'

Despite herself, Andrea smiled. Rosalie was as sweet as she was dumb, as smart as she was uppity. Rosalie wasn't like an onion with lots of layers to be peeled; she was more like a banana, with just one layer. On the outside, she was all glamour and – for want of a better word – simple. She cared about clothes, shoes, fine dining. Spending on her father's credit card whenever he did something to annoy her. Finding Prince Charming. But on the inside, she was smart. She had investments across Wall Street and private funds, Andrea knew. What had once been a healthy but not remarkable inheritance and trust fund income, Rosalie had turned into a gold mine. True, she had advisors, but Rosalie was no fool. Very few people knew that. Beneath her superficial exterior, another thing people didn't see was the size of Rosalie's heart.

As Andrea looked at her friend now, laughing with Sofia and Hannah about the grubbiness of the bar they were sitting in, she felt a surge of guilt. What she and Hunter were doing was wrong. She had to stop it, she knew, but she didn't know if she was strong enough – and that was not something she had ever thought before.

Hannah was right. Andrea did have feelings for Hunter. What had begun as an accident, then turned into an exciting affair, had somehow become something deeper. It had to end. She had to go back to her life before Hunter. Her. An apartment. A job. The strength of will to take on anything.

'Andi… Andi?'

Andrea was pulled from her thoughts by Hannah, whose disappointment in her was clear in every look they exchanged.

'Marco is asking what you want to drink.'

She looked up into the expectant eyes of the slightly shaggy-looking bartender, then looked along the row to see what the others were drinking – red wine, Hannah; white wine, Rosalie; bottled beer, Sofia. 'I guess I'll take a glass of white.'

'What's up with you, Andi? You seem out of sorts,' Sofia said.

It always struck her as peculiar when Sofia asked how she was. It was as if their God-given roles were flipped on their heads. It had always been Andrea's job to keep her younger sister safe.

She twisted her lips into a smile. 'I'm fine. I was just thinking about work.'

It had been the wrong thing to say; better than *I was thinking about the affair I've been having with Rosalie's dad,* but not good. Andrea's leaving Sanfia Records for the giant of XM Music Group had been swept under the carpet. In the first weeks, months even, after her switch, Sofia had avoided Andrea, and Andrea had been too consumed by making a good impression to seek her out. Time passed and softened her sister's anger, but they had never truly resolved the conflict that Andrea's move had caused between them.

In Sofia's eyes, Andrea had abandoned her family.

Perhaps she had. Perhaps she had wanted to do something for herself for the first time in her life. Or perhaps she was doing what she thought had been in her sister's best interests at the time. Andrea didn't like Jay. He manipulated Sofia, undermined her, made her question herself and her confidence. But he was ultimately Sofia's choice and as a couple they wanted to have a family. That changed things. Andrea leaving Sanfia Records had been the only way she, Sofia and Jay could all exist harmoniously.

Sofia nodded. If there was any animosity left, she hid it. 'How's it going at Stellar?'

Andrea could have gone into her struggles, her need to prove herself to her executive board, but wouldn't that be weak? She was the big sister. She was supposed to be strong and successful, an example. 'Fine. But I want to know more about Sanfia and that guy you put on stage tonight.' There was no other option than to tell her sister, sincerely, 'He's a talent, Soph. He needs some fine-tuning but he's got something.'

Sofia sipped from her bottle of beer, not hiding her turned-up lips. 'I won't argue with that.'

'Does Sanfia have that kind of money?' She regretted the question as soon as it left her mouth, but she couldn't take it back, and it was a legitimate question. Sanfia Records didn't have the kind of budget an act like Seth Young deserved, or needed.

Sofia set her bottle down on the bar with a clunk. 'I have a strategy.' And with those four words, what she told Andrea was, *It's no longer any of your business.*

Andrea itched to discuss it more. To understand how Sofia intended to promote Seth Young. From where she believed she could find the funding. But she respected her sister's choices.

'Well, you know where I am if you would like any… if you'd like to chat through your ideas.'

'And you know where I am when you want to talk about what's really eating you tonight,' Sofia countered. Because, though she hated to admit it, there were very few people who had insights beneath her armour, but Andrea was sitting in the presence of three of them.

Andrea picked up her wine, raising the glass toward her lips, and said, 'Touché.'

'Where was Jay tonight, Soph?' Hannah asked, breaking up the terse exchange.

Jay. The wedding of he and Sofia being possibly the biggest argument she and Sofia had ever had, putting place of employment aside. He was a waste of good air and a leech. The truth was, even if Sofia ever stopped loving him, she would stay with him because that was who she was – loyal to the end, through thick and thin. It was a trait Andrea had to respect in her sister but that she often thought was naïve and misplaced. Sofia thought that their mom had paid the ultimate sacrifice for her family – giving up cancer treatment to have Sofia and dying just months after her birth. Sofia felt like she should give her all to family, too. But what she failed to see was that their mom had decided to leave her husband and eight-year-old daughter to fend for themselves. She had sacrificed for *Sofia* but she did *not* sacrifice for all her family.

Sofia scratched at the white, unbranded label on her bottle of beer that simply said 'light beer'. 'Well, Jay got overly acquainted with two of his old friends before the concert. I left him to sleep it off.'

Andrea bit down on her lip to stop herself from speaking in advance of processing her thoughts. Jay was an asshole regardless, but the concoction of Jay, alcohol and drugs made for a demon.

'Oh, don't all look at me like that,' Sofia said, swigging from her bottle again. 'It's not like last time. He's had a couple of benders – work-related, I should add. I'll talk to him tomorrow.'

Andrea's scoff left her before she could stop it. 'He's an addict, Sofia. To add to his long list of undesirable qualities.'

Of course, she knew it was ironic to give her sister couples advice when her own love life was less than ideal.

'For a bright woman, Sofia, you have let yourself get into a ridiculous situation.' Just like her, Andrea thought. 'You keep expecting Jay to change, to be an upstanding husband and start a glorious family with you, where he picks up the kids from daycare whilst you work your dream job. Leopards and spots, Soph. He won't change.'

Leopards and spots. God, she was an idiot. Hunter was never going to leave his wife. He was never going to fall in love with her. They would never have a normal relationship. Did she even want that?

And as she realised she had been venting as much about Hunter as Jay, she noticed three pairs of eyes fixed on her.

Okay, she had overstepped, but that didn't make her statements – whether about Hunter or Jay – any less true. 'He's taking you for a fool,' she said, before draining her wine and wagging a finger at Marco to top her up.

She waited for Sofia's retort and an argument to ensue. She would deserve the embarrassment of a showdown in the middle of a public place. Sofia rolled her jaw, glowering at Andrea. Then she inhaled deeply and said... nothing, which was somehow worse.

They'd fallen into uncomfortable silence until Rosalie said, 'Hannah, how is TJ doing? Is he over his bug fully now?'

'Was TJ sick?' Sofia asked, finally breaking her stare.

'Just a twenty-four-hour thing but nursery wouldn't take him for two days. Ros was an absolute godsend, in a million ways. Cleaning up sick, cleaning my *house*, bringing TJ into the city. I thought he wouldn't want to come back to me.' Hannah chuckled, resting a hand on Rosalie's knee.

Rosalie looked down to Hannah's hand, then suddenly said, 'Ladies... I think I'm going to have a baby.'

At that unfortunate moment, Andrea's mouthful of wine sprayed out across the counter – it was that or choking.

'You're pregnant?' Hannah asked, shock as evident in her voice as in Andrea's spit up.

'No, not yet, but I'm going to be.' Rosalie reached for her purse on the counter and took out her phone. Tapping in her passcode, she pulled up a website and displayed the screen for them all to see. 'I've found this agency called Swans. It matches you up to a baby daddy.'

'Like a sperm donor?' Hannah asked.

'Kind of but not exactly. So I'll fill in a checklist of what I consider essential and what I consider desirable in a man who would be the father of my child. Somewhere, a man will have done the same about his ideal mommy. The Swans agency matches our profiles and we, you know, make a baby.'

'Wait, wait, wait,' Sofia said, sitting up straighter in her seat. 'So you guys – man and woman – both want to make a baby? Then who gets the baby?'

Rosalie beamed. 'Well, that's why it's so much better than a donor. We both do.'

Andrea was aware of how comical she must have looked as she rubbed her temples and scratched her brow, trying to follow the idea. 'It's like a dating agency but for people who want to make babies?'

Rosalie sipped her drink and shook her head. 'No, we both want to have a baby but haven't found the right person, so we agree to make the perfect baby together, and we share custody. It's just like parents who got divorced. Except much nicer because we won't fight. See?'

'Ros, I hate to point out the obvious here but there are no perfect babies,' Hannah said. 'Besides that, I mean parenting isn't easy sharing it with the man you love, never mind a stranger.'

Rosalie drew her lips into a pout and nodded slowly. 'I see. Silly Rosalie, that's what you're all thinking, isn't it? She isn't responsible enough for a child. She isn't responsible enough to have a demanding job or husband. She only loves shoes, and purses, and... and clothes and...' She stood from her stool and stuffed her cell phone back in her purse. 'Shame on you, my so-called friends.'

God, she could be dramatic and ridiculous... in equal measure. Babysitting a tantrum-taking Rosalie was even lower on Andrea's list of priorities than sitting in this bar. Still, she stood and reached out to grab Rosalie's hand before she stomped away.

'Rosalie, sit down. We are your friends and we love you, which is why we want to make sure you've thought this through. I mean, you did spring this on us. How long have you been thinking about it? What brought this all on?'

Rosalie's bottom lip protruded before she replied. 'Hannah has kids. Three! Is it so strange that I would also want someone to love and take care of? Someone to hang out with all the time and who would love me back?'

Andrea sighed. 'No, Ros, it isn't. It's lovely. But why don't we all chat it through some more? You would usually have a baby daddy to discuss things with in these situations, wouldn't you? It's not an easy decision to make on your own.'

Rosalie resumed her position at the bar, as did Andrea. The whole thing wasn't worth an argument given, knowing Rosalie, it was a fad that would change direction with the next wind.

'Have you spoken to your mom and dad about it?' Hannah asked, wincing slightly in Andrea's direction.

Of course, because here she was, the woman fucking Rosalie's father, giving her advice about the birds and the bees.

'Marco!' Andrea called, raising a hand to the bartender. 'We're going to need another round.'

* * *

At 6.30 a.m., having had less than four hours' sleep, Andrea had decided not to rouse Hannah from her child-free slumber and had completed her presentation to the board of Stellar herself. At 9.30 a.m., armed with a double-shot, full-fat mocha latte, she had stood before the all-male board of directors and told them her ideas for growing and strengthening Stellar division of XM Music Group.

Now, armed with a large bottle of sparkling water, having demolished the Jarlsberg bagel Hannah had picked up for her on the way into the office, she could admit she was failing to work through her hangover and failing to impress her colleagues.

She was gently pacing the floor of her office, her high-heels tip-tapping, one hand on her hip, which was covered by a grey pencil skirt, the other fiddling with the double collar of her blouse. Clouds hovered in a low line over the backdrop view of Manhattan, the tips of One World Trade Center and 432 Park Avenue poking out above. Her office felt as grey as she did.

'Knock, knock.' She turned to see Hunter in her favourite of his suits – light grey with a dazzlingly white shirt beneath and his top three buttons undone.

'You know, you can't just say "knock knock" and enter. It's a call for a response, like the Beale Street blues.'

Hunter's lips curved. 'Smart as well as beautiful, that's my girl.'

Andrea felt her eyes widen as she shot a look at the office door, relieved to see Hunter had closed it behind him.

'I wasn't your girl last night.' She knew it was a bitter and childish response but that was something close to how she was feeling.

Hunter gave her a look that felt as patronising as his words

In This Together

and she thought, in this moment, it would be easier to end their affair than she had been fearing.

He crossed the room toward her and she took a step back toward the window. 'That's why I'm here,' he said. 'I know last night must have been... less than ideal.'

She scoffed. Less than ideal? Understatement of the millennium.

'I want to make it up to you.'

Shaking her head, she moved behind her desk. 'It's the middle of the day and, frankly Hunter, I'm not in the mood.'

With his hands resting casually in his pockets like he couldn't give a damn about how she was feeling, he made for her office door. 'I meant later. I'll come to your place tonight. We'll talk and I'll show you how much you mean to me.'

As he closed the door behind him, Andrea took a steadying deep breath. *How much I mean to him?* Hunter never spoke to her about feelings. Neither of them ever spoke about feelings. Was this a turning point? Maybe seeing her next to his wife had triggered something in him. Made him realise what he could have with Andrea. But did *she* want it?

She watched him walk along the corridor out of sight, then typed her password into her computer and got back to procrastinating. What she really needed to do was think of an idea she could present to the board to show her true value – whilst pretending she wasn't screwing the ultimate boss. Instead, she typed 'Seth Young singer/songwriter' into her search engine.

There wasn't an abundance of hits but enough to fill the first page of searches – she recommended to her artists (even the newer ones) that at least the first five pages of search results must be about them and they should do whatever it took to make that happen.

The first hit was a link to Seth's own website – well, at least he had one of those. Second, already, was a YouTube video from last night's performance at the Presley John concert. The third, a blog article titled 'Who is Seth Young?' The fourth, *Seth Young: Spotify*.

She clicked the YouTube hit and replayed what she could admit to herself was a very special stage debut – on a *real* stage – last night.

His voice was ruggedly remarkable – a quality she hoped he wouldn't lose. His lyrics were... Well, she was watching with a lump in her throat, which told its own story. And the way he held himself on stage – in front of the mic, the casual movement of his arm as he strummed his guitar, the confident way his fingers plucked the strings – it was all effortless and... sexy.

She found herself simultaneously charged by what he offered and immensely proud of her younger sister for recognising his talent. On her screen, the crowd roared as Randy Jonson shouted his brother's name into the arena. She cleared her tight throat when the video ended.

The next video that rolled on YouTube was titled 'The Singing Soldier'. On screen was a man dressed in the khaki-coloured casuals of a US serviceman. He was sitting on what looked like a crate in the middle of a group of similarly dressed men wearing Santa hats and holding bottles of beer. The cameraman stood behind the group and the poor quality of the video suggested he was using an old cell phone.

The ground around them was sand. Military vehicles were parked in the distance. A compound wall surrounded them.

Even in his uniform, despite the shades covering his eyes and the Santa hat covering his hair, the way the man held his guitar and rocked to the beat of his own strum, he was unmistakably Seth Young.

And he started to sing, a song she had never heard:

> We see kids playing in the streets
> No socks or shoes on their feet
> They live in hope of better days
> When the men they should look up to
> When they correct their ways
> And we're here
> And we're fighting
> To make a better place
>
> We're supposed to be tough
> But these things we see
> Goddamn they're rough
> We question everything
> Except our hope
> To make a better place
> Lord knows, I couldn't get by
> Without my brothers

Infallible as she tried to be, Andrea found herself pressing her thumbs to the corners of her eyes to stem her impending tears as she listened to his words and the sincerity in his voice.

Then she laughed as a soldier took off his Santa hat and threw it at Seth on the video. 'It's fucking Christmas, man!'

She watched Seth laugh and burst into a rendition of 'White Christmas'.

Then she took a breath and exhaled the words 'Dear God.' Seth Young had it all. He was the complete musician, who had faith and decency and love inside him. And, of course, his brother was none other than Randy Jonson. He was a ready-made star and *boy* was he exactly what she needed for Stellar right now. The board couldn't doubt her if she landed someone like Seth Young. They would nurture him, build him up whilst keeping the rawness and truth of his own sound. They would pump so much money into promoting him in all the right channels that he'd be printing money for the label in no time.

But he was signed to Sanfia Records. He was signed to her sister. Their family label, though not so much hers any longer since she had given up her directorship and stock holding as a requirement of her contract with Stellar.

'Urgh,' she groaned, suddenly feeling another wave of exhaustion and hangover.

She leaned back in her desk chair. She was being so unproductive, she might as well get through the 'must-do's for the day and go home, pour herself a hair-of-the-dog and wait for Hunter. And when he turned up for a screw and to leave, she would tell him he could leave without the screw and not bother coming around again. Ever.

* * *

Andrea had bathed and shaved since arriving home and was sitting on her sofa, wearing a silk dressing gown, with her legs folded beneath her, the Hudson and New York's skyline her backdrop. A smooth jazz channel played on her vintage radio. The wall-mounted fire flickered above its grey pebbles, not putting out real heat but providing ambience. Andrea held a glass of red wine in one hand and various contracts relating to Stellar that she had been asked to review and sign off on in her lap.

Hunter hadn't given a specific time that he would come over, but she was fed up with playing her words over and over in her mind. Whatever shape they took, they needed to have the same end result. She and Hunter were done. *Finito*. She would not be the *other* woman. She would not wait for her heart to be broken. And she would not continue lying to her friends and family.

The wine was both medicinal – hangover cure – and Dutch courage. She took another sip and as she did, she considered her image to someone who walked through the door. Her attire and demeanour did not suggest *I'm breaking up with you.* They suggested *Come get me.*

'Yoga pants. I need yoga pants.'

She set her contracts and wine glass down on the coffee table in front of her and stood, but before she had a chance to change, her door buzzer sounded.

With another mouthful of wine, she told Hunter to come up and set about pouring him a glass too. She could at least soften the blow with the light-headedness of alcohol and, who knew, maybe they could talk afterwards. Try to establish a platonic relationship again. Lord knew it would be awkward enough in the office for a while after this.

After one strong rap, she opened the door to her apartment to reveal Hunter – one hand resting on the frame, the other holding his suit jacket across his shoulder. He was still in his tailored grey slacks and white shirt from the office. She squeezed her thighs together and reminded herself of the plan.

Hunter took in her silk gown, which she knew she should have changed, and his eyes seemed to darken. 'Baby,' he said appreciatively.

Flattery was nice but it didn't change things.

'Come in,' Andrea said, walking to her kitchen counter to retrieve the two glasses of wine.

As she turned to hand a drink to Hunter, he cast his jacket aside and pressed his lips to her neck, groaning against her skin, his tongue gently licking her collarbone.

Oh God, she felt that everywhere he intended. He pulled her against him, digging his fingers into her buttocks and allowing her to feel him against her.

'Hunter,' she managed to say hoarsely. 'Stop. We need to talk.'

He rolled his pelvis against her and moaned his displeasure before he pulled away. 'I know.'

Andrea was still holding both glasses of wine as he retrieved his jacket from the countertop and reached into the inside pocket. At the sight of a small, rectangular, velvet box, she put the drinks down.

He stood in front of her and opened the lid of the box to reveal a dazzling bracelet that looked to be a continuous row of diamonds and sapphires.

She felt her eyes widen. No one had ever bought her anything like this. It was beautiful, sparkly and, without a shadow of doubt, expensive. 'Hunter, I...'

He set down the box and unleashed the bracelet. 'Hold out your wrist.'

She did, still focused solely on the way the gemstones glinted under the soft lights of her apartment.

He fastened the bracelet around her wrist then kissed the palm of her hand. 'I know last night must have been tough. I hated it, too. I hated that you were put in that situation.'

Last night. Yes. The concert. Rosalie. His wife. 'Hunter, listen, we can't keep—'

'This gift is to show you how much you mean to me, Andi.' *Oh.* 'I want you to know that I am committed to you. To us.' *Huh.* 'I know that things aren't... straightforward. But I want to be with you.' *You do?* 'What we have is something special, kiddo.' *It is.*

Just like that, what she had thought was going to happen tonight was obliterated.

She dipped her head to compose herself. Hunter raised her chin. 'I love you, kiddo.'

He loved her? He... *loved* her?

Every nerve ending in her body tingled as he held her and pressed his mouth to hers. She dug her fingers into his hair and pulled him harder against her. Their tongues entwined as they swallowed the sound of each other's moans and whimpers.

Love? He loved her? It was a line. Surely, it was a line. Did she love him?

'God, you're beautiful,' he told her, lifting her onto the kitchen counter.

She had spent the day preparing herself for their relationship to end and now, here he was, in her home, expressing his commitment and showing her that what they had physically was not just about his pleasure but hers too.

And he *loved* her?

He couldn't. She wouldn't.

She rewarded his efforts by leading him to her bedroom, letting sex take her out of her head.

* * *

For the first time, Andrea woke under the bright light of the sun shining through her linen curtains and under the weight of Hunter's arm.

The first thought that came to her was, *How is he going to explain this to Loretta?*

She was grateful that today brought the weekend. They had a lot to talk about. She was supposed to end things and Hunter had declared his love to her. Was that even real?

She needed to be rational for both of them. She would nip out for coffee and pastries. They could plan their next steps – like how and when to tell people about their relationship. No. *Relationship?* That was not something she had been looking for.

It would hurt people they cared about. Would he move in? Would they be girlfriend and boyfriend? That was ridiculous. She had never called herself anyone's girlfriend. By choice.

She lifted Hunter's arm and rolled onto her back, staring at the ceiling. Rosalie. His wife. What would Sofia think of her? Some kind of role model. Her father. What would he say?

Hunter murmured, snored and rolled over until his back was turned to her. She stared for a moment at the dark hairs that lightly covered his back and shoulders. She hadn't noticed them before, but now she thought it was peculiar that the dark colouring was a contrast to his silver hair. She wondered if his wife had ever had the same consideration.

Urgh, she was driving herself crazy.

She glanced at her bedside clock. 07.59. It was as good a time as any to break her cycle of thought.

After slipping out of the covers, she pulled on a pair of stonewash jeans and a Rolling Stones T-shirt from her closet. Having found her sneakers and located her purse, she gently closed the apartment door and headed to her favourite bakery, three blocks away.

This was the best time of the week for Andrea – early on a Saturday morning, before shoppers, tourists, dog walkers and families with strollers hit the streets. When Williamsburg was waking up. The sun had risen but wasn't yet too hot. Before cars were noisily filling the air and before the stalls were being set up for Smorasburg market. She didn't need to wear tailored clothes or make-up. She could just be herself, with herself, please herself.

She closed her eyes on the sidewalk when the first scent of fresh bread and pastries reached her nose from the bakery. The only thing that could possibly rival that smell as the best in the world was the scent of fresh coffee being brewed.

She smiled to an elderly man, whose name she didn't know but whose face she recognised as the one that always took up a seat at a small iron table outside the bakery. As usual, he dipped his head today without speaking.

Stepping inside the corner building, she was immediately thrust into sensory overload. Baskets filled with fresh baguettes, sourdough and bloomers lined the walls. The glass counter was filled with macarons, fresh fruit tarts, vanilla slices, every kind of Danish imaginable.

'Hey, Andi!' She smiled to Aliza, who was already reaching for a takeout coffee cup in anticipation. 'The usual?'

Aliza had been serving Andrea every Saturday morning for the last two years. Every week, without fail, she smiled and offered a bubbly welcome. She was only slightly plump, which Andrea thought was nothing short of miraculous, given she worked among such decadence. The plumpness suited her personality in the most stereotypical of ways and with her cupcake apron tied around her front, everything about Aliza made Andrea envious. To the naked eye, she had such a straightforward life.

'Hey, 'Liza. Actually, I'll take two filter coffees and two almond croissants today, please. Then I'll take the usual rosemary focaccia and a date and walnut loaf.'

Aliza paused somewhat comically, with the coffee cup in her hand and her jaw loose. Andrea couldn't help the short laugh that escaped her.

'Not alone then?' Aliza asked with obvious playfulness.

Andrea smiled. What would it be like to say, *Hunter and I are doing this or Hunter and I are doing that*? She hadn't much considered it before now. Then, Hunter had never so much as hinted that he might feel more for her than a bit of fun on the side.

It sounded odd and, honestly, not like something she could ever imagine herself saying.

Armed with breakfast, she strode toward home with her shoulders back and her chin high.

With coffees balanced on a tray and bread tucked under her arms, she fumbled for her keys in her pocket but before she got them in the lock, the door to her apartment was pulled open.

Hunter stood in front of her, dressed in last night's clothes. He replaced his shock very quickly with a smile but not quickly enough.

'I was wondering where you got to,' he said.

Was he leaving? Really? 'I went to get breakfast. Were you leaving?'

'N-no, I saw you coming, I was getting the door.'

He turned his back, not taking anything from her, and led the way to her kitchen.

'What did you get?' he asked.

Not quite sure what to make of the situation, she simply told him, 'Coffee and croissants,' and set about putting the other items in her bread bin.

He remained standing as he tore off a large chunk of croissant and put it in his mouth, washing it down with coffee, barely chewing and making a sipping sound.

Andrea watched him, a little repulsed. 'I thought maybe we could have breakfast and, you know, talk about last night.'

He regarded her for silent seconds before he said, 'You like the jewellery, don't you?'

'Of course, the bracelet is beautiful.'

He grinned. 'Good.'

She sighed. 'Hunter, last night you told me you love me. Was that just... I mean, did you... Do you mean it?'

He walked around the counter to her on the opposite side

and pulled her waist until they were inches apart. 'I have to go to Europe next week on business. Come with me.'

'*With* you?'

'*With* me, yes.' He laughed at her *again*. 'We could have gelato in St Mark's Square, bratwurst in Berlin.'

'That sounds...' Scary? Odd? Unlikely?

He turned back to the counter and put another chunk of croissant in his mouth, then slurped coffee. With his mouth full, he said, 'You can clear it at Stellar. Say you're legitimately scouting for talent in Europe who could make it in the US.'

Andrea scoffed when confronted with her own stupidity. 'More lies. More hiding. God, I'm such an idiot.'

She walked calmly to her bedroom. Then back to the kitchen, where she placed the black velvet box and its contents that he had given her last night on the counter in front of him. 'You have no intention of ever telling her about us. You've no intention of us ever being together. Telling me you love me was the oldest trick in the book and I slept with you anyway.'

'Now, hey, where has all this come from? We've got a good thing going here, kiddo. Why rock the boat?'

'Hunter, you're so full of shit. Take your jewellery and get out.'

'You're being irrational, Andrea. I have a life, a family. I can't just throw that away. They depend on me. You... You're independent. Fine on your own. This works for both of us.'

'Hunter, I don't want you to throw anyone away except me. Get out.'

'Andi.'

'Get out, Hunter.'

'Kiddo.'

'Get the fuck out!' she screamed.

What in God's name had she been thinking? To risk Rosalie over this? To risk Hannah and Sofia?

She threw the black box after him and as soon as her apartment door slammed shut, she broke. Her legs gave out and her tears fell. She knew, without doubt, that Hunter would forget about her long before she ever got over what she had done to the people she loved.

10

HANNAH

The thing about being a mom was, she constantly wanted a break from the crying, the feeding, the cleaning and the squabbles. But when she got a break, she felt guilty about it. The concert on Thursday had been fun. Hannah had been granted time to be an adult woman, dressed nicely, having drinks with her girlfriends. She had enjoyed herself but felt a low level of guilt in the back of her mind the entire evening. She had left all three children being 'babysat' by their father – she wouldn't even get started on the fact Rod considered looking after his own kids as 'helping her'.

She had endured Andrea at work on Friday – long in the face because, surprise surprise, the woman having an affair with her best friend's married father was getting hurt. By the time she had taken the train back to New Jersey on Friday evening, she was desperate to see her kids.

Until… she had arrived home, pushing the door against her eldest's school backpack that had been dumped in the porch. Four sets of shoes – including the baby's – had been kicked off in all directions. As she bent to straighten the shoes, she heard an almighty scream. Running into the house, she found the middle kid crying and shouting at the older kid for God knows what and chasing him with slime. TJ was lying in his bouncer chair watching what looked like *John Wick 2* in the lounge, where empty beer bottles and snack wrappers covered the coffee table.

'Babysitting clearly involved Daddy's friends last night,' she muttered to no one.

'All right, you two, calm it. Now! Jackson, put the slime away. If I have to wash that stuff off my walls again, there'll be big trouble, mister. Luke, you're supposed to be grown-up. Get over here and tell me what happened – no lies.'

'He will lie. He always lies,' Jackson shouted.

Hannah gave him stern eyes. 'Young man, you'll get your turn next. Go and put that slime away like I've told you.'

She headed into the lounge, unstrapping TJ from his bouncer and hooking his legs around her hip. 'Go ahead, Luke.'

'He was taking forever to eat his Shake Shack. I thought he'd finished, so I ate his last fries, then he started screaming like a little girl.'

'I'm not a girl!' Jackson said, coming into the lounge *sans* slime. 'He ate my fries 'cause he's a big fat ass.'

'Jackson! We don't call each other fat asses. Luke, apologise to your brother for eating his fries. Jackson, apologise for calling your brother a fat ass.'

'He is a fat—' She silenced him with a look.

'After three, you'll each say sorry.' She had learned not to ask one to go before the other and start a *new* fight. 'One. Two. Three.'

'Sorry,' they said in huffy unison.

'Now, why were you eating Shake Shack for dinner? Where's Dad?'

'In the garage doing weights,' Luke said.

Sure he is. What else would he be doing after picking up our three children from school and putting them on a trash-food high?

'Okay, I'm going to find him. You guys... Be nice.'

With TJ in tow, she made her way to the garage, where Rod had his headphones in his ears, doing shirtless pull ups on his multi-gym.

Sure, she was mad at him but that was pretty much the normal state of play, so why couldn't she take a moment to enjoy the way his abdominal muscles flexed, his quadriceps tensed, his biceps bulged? That his artwork was framed in sweat was somehow even more of a turn-on.

Wait, why had she come to see him again?

When he caught her looking, she raised a hand but she would not smile, *no siree*. She was cross with him, after all.

She glanced one last time from across her shoulder as she walked away and received a 'Hey baby', accompanied by a knowing grin, in return.

The next time she had seen Rod, he had been leaving the house smelling of cologne, heading for beers with the guys. Apparently, Hannah's one night off in seven months warranted Rod's one hundredth.

Naturally, his beers had led to him snoring all night and Hannah getting up every hour or two, thanks to TJ teething.

Now, she was standing on the sideline of one football field with TJ strapped to her front, cheering on Luke, whilst Rod was standing on an adjacent football field cheering on Jackson. They switched kids on a weekly basis to ensure they both got to see each child play without being accused of favouritism (this had happened in the past).

This was her life – football, arguments, sleepless nights. Thank heavens for mommy friends, who knew how much fellow mommies needed coffee.

'White, no sugar,' one of the school moms said, approaching Hannah with a tray of mugs from the clubhouse.

'You're my angel,' Hannah said, taking the cup and wrapping both hands around it.

After football, they went to see Granny – Rod's mom – in her care home. That was a long hour of mixed-up names, snarling at the kids, and repeatedly asking everyone to stay quiet.

Then they'd gone to a panini chain, where they spent a small fortune on sandwiches she could have made at home, apples and juice boxes. She and Rod broke up a fight between the eldest one and the middle one over the banana that Hannah tried to feed TJ but that he turned his nose up at.

Now, they were headed home in the car she called a bus, which they'd been forced to buy to fit in a teenager, a lanky middle kid and a child-seat kid, with trunk space big enough for groceries and a hand-me-down pushchair. TJ and Jackson were sleeping. Luke had his headphones stuck in his ears watching something she probably wouldn't approve of on his iPad.

These fleeting moments of calm and quiet were what she lived for. She leant back in her seat and turned her head to look at Rod. He glanced to her then placed his hand on her thigh. She took hold of it and closed her eyes.

'Han. Hannah. Light of my world.'

She opened her eyes to see Rod standing at the passenger side door on their driveway with TJ in his arms.

'Oh God, I fell asleep,' she said.

'Yeah, I got that when you were drooling and calling out my name. Rod, oh Rod, take me to bed, baby.'

Despite herself, she laughed. 'In your dreams.'

'No, baby, in yours.'

'Jackass,' she whispered, just loud enough for him to hear as she climbed out of the car.

He held a hand over one of TJ's ears. 'Not in front of the kid.'

* * *

'Homework time, please,' Hannah called up the stairs to Luke and Jackson. It was the usual routine – an hour's stint on spellings or math on either a Saturday or Sunday, depending on plans. In Luke's case, she wasn't sure she and Rod could even help any more.

As predicted, she received grumbles and lies for five minutes before they gave in and went quiet. She tiptoed up the staircase and checked on both boys – who were, in fact, doing their homework. A rare but beautiful moment.

Back downstairs, she prepared a dinner of pasta for four – with chili for grown-ups and without for kids – and blended sweet potato for one. TJ wasn't feeling solids greatly, still preferring milk to anything else, and in truth, he was a tad too young. But he was a hungry little monster and now that he was at nursery, they had to get him onto solids.

One by one, Rod, Luke and Jackson came into the kitchen, took a plate of food and headed into the lounge. Hannah put TJ into his high-chair, took her own seat at the kitchen table beside him and set down a plate of pasta in front of herself but far enough away from TJ's grabby hands.

'Let's see how you like sweet potato, buddy, shall we?' She filled a plastic dinosaur spoon with the orange-coloured mush and flew it like an airplane toward TJ's mouth. 'Neeoum.'

He seemed to swill it around his mouth, then swallow it down and stick out his tongue like a lizard over-and-over again.

'Yummy, right?'

Hannah filled the spoon again and repeated the process. 'Neeoum.'

As soon as the food touched TJ's tongue, it came flying back out of his mouth and all over Hannah. She wiped remnants from her face then picked a lump from her chest.

'I'll take that as a no then, shall I? Try one more for Mom, please.'

He shook his head and made disgusted noises but swallowed the next spoonful.

She took a congratulatory forkful of her pasta. And so they continued for the next fifteen minutes, until TJ's boredom emanated in a scream.

She had managed one third of her own meal before she began pacing the kitchen floor, bouncing TJ gently on her hip.

By the time TJ had settled, the other three were lying on the sofas in the lounge, laughing at something they were watching on TV. Three plates stood dirty and empty of food in various positions around the lounge floor.

She set TJ down in his playpen and picked up the plates, rinsing then depositing them in the dishwasher. She poured herself a glass of red wine and took it with her upstairs to the main bathroom. She contemplated running a bath and decided it would be pointless. Her kids had a sixth sense for when she was bathing and generally chose that moment to need a poo.

No. She would just sit on the toilet for five minutes with her glass of wine, then go back to life.

She turned to put the lid down on the toilet and was greeted by skid marks – probably Rod's – and a floating ball of poo – most likely Jackson's. She flushed the toilet, brushed away the skids, put down the lid and drank her wine.

It turned out that the others had been watching the recent *Jumanji* in the lounge. She enjoyed a second glass of wine and made Rod an El Dorado 15 with Coke. An argument ensued which they had heard a thousand times, about Luke taking his driving test and getting a car for his eighteenth birthday, which they simply could not afford. The argument resulted in Luke slamming the front door on his way to a friend's house nearby.

Eventually, the other two kids either walked or were carried to bed.

'Finally,' she said, sighing as she came to sit on the sofa next to Rod. It had been years since she had lost the ability to sit or stand without audible expressions.

'Come on, Han. Sit down next to your man.'

She slipped under Rod's arm and rested her head on his chest. 'Can we not watch sports and maybe listen to some music? Smooth jazz, like your dad used to play?'

'On this occasion, I'm going to bow to my woman.' Rod hit one remote to turn off the television and another to turn on the music player.

Hannah wanted to finish her wine and fall asleep, right there on his firm chest. But two minutes (maybe less) into the first Louis Armstrong track and Rod's hands were wandering. She knew every one of his strokes and touches, what they meant depending on their pace and location. The way he was using just the tips of his fingers to roll up and down her spine was asking for sexy time.

These were the moments where she had to muster. Not because she wasn't attracted to Rod. She absolutely was. But because TJ had been a result of their slack attitude to contraception when they were just starting to get their lives back on track – no nurseries, the childminder fees almost a memory, both able to start thinking about things they wanted to do for themselves. Unfortunately, their excitement at getting their nights back to themselves had led to a forgetful incident, which ultimately led to TJ. Now, she had to dig deep and wake up her sleepy libido.

Rod took her wine glass from her and set it down on the

coffee table, then rolled her onto his chest. He lifted her chin and nudged her with his nose as his hands roamed over her butt.

'Have I told you how amazing you did to get right back into these tight little jeans?'

She giggled. 'That's because you always wanted me to have a bigger ass.'

He gripped her rear harder. 'Too right. A fine ass it is.'

She laughed and kissed him, melting into his big lips. She loved his lips. They were always warm and soft. Even when they were having rough and ready sex, his lips were gentle.

Kissing him and feeling his desire grow beneath her, she found herself waking up and squirming against him with arousal. He was a dangerously sexual and beautiful man. She had three pregnancies to show for that.

He pulled her harder against him as she ground her pelvis against his and moaned into his mouth. Then... the unmistakable wailing of TJ over the intercom.

They stilled. 'Maybe he'll go back off,' Hannah said hopefully.

Rod kissed her again.

TJ screamed louder.

'I'll be back,' she said, slipping off her husband.

Twenty-five minutes later, she came back downstairs to find the television on and a second rum and Coke in Rod's glass.

'Sorry, where were we?' she said, not feeling like resuming where they were at all.

He glanced at her with a look of disappointment, as if *she* had made TJ cry. *He's half of you, too* she wanted to say but didn't bother.

She picked up her wine – the fuzz of the first two glasses now faded – and sat next to Rod.

Still looking at the television, he said, 'I accepted the coaching job in Queens.'

Hannah coughed through her next mouthful of wine. 'Come again?'

'The coaching job in Queens. I took it.'

'Yes, I heard that part. I think what I was missing was the part where we discussed you accepting an interview in Queens, going out there, then accepting a job, all without consulting with me.'

'Baby, come on, it's a good opportunity for me. I told you I was taking an interview. The school has a new principal and he wants to put a lot of money behind the varsity team. If I could...'

She did now have a vague recollection of his interview. 'Rod, it's in *Queens*. We make our life work because I drop the kids and commute into the city. You start and finish early and work in New Jersey to pick them up. If we both worked in New York, we'd have to... It's not possible. TJ isn't even six months old. Imagine the childcare fees. Luke can't be expected to look after Jackson and TJ, it isn't fair. Plus, he'd forget them whenever he got a whiff of a girl in cut-off daisies.'

'Baby, I've already said yes.'

Hannah scoffed, her eyes on fire, her hands trembling with rage. 'Sure you have, Rod, because it's something *you* want to do. What about anything *I* want, huh? Just... just for *once*... could you not be so fucking selfish?'

She left her husband, her wine and whatever shit was on the television and she went upstairs to the bathroom, where she put down the toilet lid, sat on top of it and cried.

There had to be more to life than this.

11

ROSALIE

Rosalie's apartment at Central Park West was her ultimate sanctuary. She had waited years for a suitable property to come up in the area. Fortunately for her, a nasty divorce left the place in a matrimonial settlement to the glamorous wife of a business tycoon, who wanted a quick sale to cut all ties. She had, in any event, received a newsworthy settlement and the apartment was merely a snip of that.

It hadn't been to Rosalie's taste when she had first moved in. The walls had been white and plain, with signs that large artwork had been hung on them which had probably been grotesque but acquired due to its obscene expense. The floor had been tiled black. The surfaces chrome, glass, black marble – probably perfect for snorting a line, not that she was one to stereotype.

The apartment was the project Rosalie was most proud of to date. She had put all her interior design skills to use and created a homage to true style. The theme was vintage luxe, with an emphatic nod to the 1920s. The vast open-plan living area was bright, thanks to the large windows that looked out toward Central Park.

She was sitting in a high-back chair by the window, with a cafetière of coffee on the brass-legged coffee table in front of her and her laptop resting atop a velvet, dusty-rose-coloured pillow on her lap. She had read about the possibility of laptops having negative effects on a woman's fertility and whether it was true or not, she couldn't risk it now.

Around her, the walls were painted with texture paint, various rich shades of blue and green. The furniture was structured and finished with fine fabrics – ochre and burnished gold were a recurring theme. Her dining table was permanently set with fine china – she mostly ate out in any event. And she had a bar table that she had acquired at auction, which had been used on the set of Leo's *Titanic*. That too was laid out with gold-rimmed champagne glasses and an ice bucket.

Though the music that filled her home was being streamed, the mix of soundtracks was being played through what appeared to be a vintage radio. Soundtracks were Rosalie's music of choice – and if they had jazz tracks, the world was smiling in on her. She could escape to a world where Gatsby pined for his first love, where Audrey Hepburn portrayed a glamorous, though a little eccentric, socialite.

She hummed along to Andy Williams's 'Moon River' as she performed her usual Monday morning routine. She was reviewing the weekly statement her investment manager sent to her.

Interior design was her somewhat part-time(ish) job, she supposed – she had a company and clients. Investments were something of a hobby that happened to be the source of wealth that kept her in the lifestyle she was accustomed to. And she was quite good at her hobby.

She had been investing by way of her trust fund and inheritance from her grandparents since she was eighteen. Fifteen years later, she'd learned a few tricks. Though most of her investments were managed on her behalf, she did take on a few projects of her own.

She had amassed quite a number of silent investments in new or struggling companies – mostly loose acquaintances – in recent years. The first time had been a favour to a friend, the second time a friend of a friend. She liked helping people. She would invest her money to help people get off the ground or out of trouble with their business, then she would take back her money with interest. She didn't take part in business decisions, she simply gave people the opportunity to do something with their lives, though she was confident her lawyer made sure she couldn't be screwed over. Her lawyer had described her as an angel of sorts, which she liked just fine as a title. And her hobby kept her in new shoes. What it didn't do was occupy her for lengthy periods of time and, if anything, it isolated her, rather than giving her a route to human interactions, which she so loved.

Confident she was making and not losing money and that everything was A-okay, she closed the investment report on her screen and turned back to her primary focus for today. She was calling it Project Swans, after the company that would match her to the perfect daddy for her soon-to-be baby.

Swans was like a dating agency that matched potential mommies and daddies. Or sometimes, daddies and daddies, or mommies and mommies. It sold itself as the company that could get you what you wanted no matter how busy you were, how long you had been putting your life on hold for other commitments, or how truly catastrophic you were when it came to finding love (paraphrased). The latter was most true of Rosalie.

She hadn't been too busy working on other commitments to make a baby, she'd only been too busy wasting time on all the wrong men.

What she wanted – no, *needed* – was a man like her father. Honourable, hard-working, successful whilst being devoted to his family. She had come to realise that such men didn't grow on trees – or certainly no tree she had come across.

What had changed? That was what the girls had asked her after the concert last week. Was it her latest break-up? Was she bored? Andrea had had the audacity to ask the last one.

It wasn't any of those things. Nothing had changed, as such, but her days babysitting TJ had shown her how much she wanted her own baby to take care of, to love and be loved by, to dress up and take for days out. Her heart had nearly burst every time that little guy had smiled at her. Imagine if it was her own child smiling at her, hugging her, gurgling and chuckling because she made a funny face. She would never have days waking up and wondering what she should do or who to do it with. She would have her little man or lady to fill her days. Plus, soon she would have the recording label and her life would be bustling with people, adventures, admiration and love.

And why should she wait to have it all? She could be a mother without a man. Despite what some people thought, she was responsible. She was capable of caring for a mini-Rosalie. And she had more than enough time to look after a child.

She poured herself a fresh mug of coffee and leaned back in her chair, staring across the lush green of the park.

She knew how ridiculous it would sound if she ever said it aloud, but she was… lonely. She had so many possessions, and she had friends and living parents. Yet she spent a lot of time alone or in department stores with shop assistants who would listen to her tales for so long as she was handing over her credit card.

The more she thought about it, the more she was sure that she was doing the right thing. She pulled up the Swans website on her laptop and trawled the pages of information about how the programme worked.

She had already signed a confidentiality agreement. Today was the start of the process. At 2 p.m. she was going to the agency's office on Broadway to be interviewed by a lady called Carmen, who would ask about her expectations, what she wanted from her baby's father, and generally how she felt a baby would fit into her life. If she liked the agency and the agency liked her, she would pay fifteen thousand dollars for them to find her the right baby daddy.

After her interview, she would take a DNA test. Her results would be compared to the potential fathers on the agency's programme to check for genetic compatibility, which she presumed to mean a 'peculiar diseases and anti-incest test'.

Finally, she would fill in a questionnaire about values and morals, which would also be matched to potential daddies who shared the same values. In her mind, both she and her baby daddy would have to concur with Elle Woods – orange would never be the new pink.

The agency would then provide her with a list of names that matched her, and she would select anyone who piqued her interest enough to meet.

The website was silent about the conception part of things and how childcare would be divided, which was something she would ask about later today.

She took a deep breath and exhaled slowly. 'I'm really doing this.' Then she imagined herself in a café with a little girl dressed in a tweed two-piece, drinking a babyccino, holding her hand

and telling her tales of the things she had learned at school, and she smiled so wide it ached her cheeks.

After finishing her coffee, she showered, slipped into a tailored dress and blazer, draping pearls around her neck. Then she headed out to the salon, where she would have a blow-dry and mani-pedi, because what kind of new mother would she present as in her interview if she wasn't well kempt herself?

* * *

Rosalie bounced her foot as she sat cross-legged in the waiting room of Swans agency. She was sitting on one of two leather sofas in the magnolia-painted room, which was brightened by Jack Vettriano prints and fresh flowers. The lady who had told her to take a seat and was intermittently tapping away on a computer behind the reception desk kept looking over. Whenever Rosalie caught her looking, she would look away too quickly to be subtle. It was making Rosalie nervous. Was she dressed inappropriately? Had she said something wrong? Was the woman tapping scrutinising notes to pass on about why Rosalie shouldn't be allowed to make a baby?

She picked up a copy of last month's *Vogue* from the table in front of her and tried to distract herself. She was the only person in the waiting area and she couldn't decide if that was a good thing – less competition for the best baby daddies – or a bad thing – the agency didn't work.

'Rosalie?'

A tall woman, perhaps in her forties, with Ellen DeGeneres-style hair, appeared from behind a door and leaned her head to one side as she smiled at Rosalie, offering her hand to shake.

'Yes,' Rosalie said, her voice betraying her nervousness as she stood and accepted the hand.

'I'm Melissa. Have you come far to get to us today?'

Rosalie followed Melissa along a short corridor, making polite small talk until they reached her office.

There was a desk with chairs either side, hosting nothing but a computer. Behind it were bookshelves which held more treasures – a snow globe, a fancy paperweight, a picture of Melissa and another woman smiling with their arms around each other.

'Let's sit on the sofas,' Melissa said, gesturing to the other half of the room, which was set up like a small lounge. 'Can I get you a tea or coffee? There are cookies and brownies on the tray there.'

Rosalie took a seat on one sofa whilst Melissa poured them both tea and added a brownie to the saucer before handing it to Rosalie. The informal setting relaxed her and she found herself liking Melissa as she took a seat on a sofa opposite Rosalie.

'Oh boy, that's a good brownie,' Rosalie said, covering her mouth with her fingertips as she chewed.

Melissa smiled. She was warm and friendly. Rosalie felt at ease around her. 'So, you obviously know about Swans and what we do. Before we start, do you have any general questions about the agency – our ethos, when we started, why we started? There are no right or wrong questions or answers today. I just want us to get to know each other. If you want to slip off your shoes and put your feet up, feel free.'

Melissa did exactly that and sipped her tea from one corner of the sofa with her legs curled beneath her. Rosalie realised there had been no need to get a blow-dry or new nails. She needed to be herself, just like Melissa.

Was herself enough? Was herself responsible enough?

'Rosalie, I can see you're nervous. Most people are when they first come here. I'd be more worried if you weren't. Having a baby is a huge deal and finding the right partner to do it with is so important.' Melissa took a bite of brownie and set the rest on her saucer. 'I co-founded the agency with my partner three years ago, almost to the day, in fact.'

Melissa pointed to the photograph of the two women that Rosalie had noticed on her bookshelves. 'That's my wife, Lauren. We married eighteen months ago but we've been together for four years.'

Rosalie looked at the picture again. 'She's beautiful. Congratulations.'

'Thank you. Lauren and I have two children – a girl and a boy. Three and one. Both terrors and adorable in equal measure.'

Rosalie chuckled.

'I needn't state the obvious, I'm sure, but Lauren and I didn't make babies together the conventional way.'

Rosalie blushed.

'A friend of ours set us up on a blind date of sorts. It was funny because at the time we'd both sworn off relationships, but we both felt like our biological clocks were ticking and we wanted to have children. Our mutual friend knew this and suggested we meet. That night we discussed both wanting children and by the time we went away in our separate cabs, we'd decided to co-parent.'

'Wow, just like that,' was all Rosalie offered.

Melissa smiled. 'Yep. We met up a few more times soon after that and really got fixed on the idea. We talked through our options – adopting, donors, surrogacy – and decided that for us, surrogacy would be best. That way neither of us could be jealous of the other having carried the baby. Anyway, as it happened, we fell for each other and we were a couple before our first child was born.'

'And that's why you started the agency?' Rosalie asked.

'Exactly. We were lucky to fall in love with each other but our main focus when we met was having children. It made us think about how many other people out there were in a similar position for whatever reason. Maybe they focused on a career and suddenly found themselves in their early forties with no partner. Maybe they hadn't found the right partner, or thought they had and the relationship had broken down. Maybe they just wanted to have a child and co-parent but not be in a relationship. So we started Swans. We match people who want to have children. If those people fall in love and live happily ever after, great. If they choose to be individuals and stick to a shared parenting schedule, good for them. The "how's", "when's" and "why's" are up to the couple. Our aim is simply to match you to someone you have parenting compatibility with.'

The way Melissa explained things made perfect sense. Rosalie understood what the girls had said – what if she met the right guy whilst she was pregnant or had a young child? Wouldn't it be easier to start a relationship without that burden? But who was to say Swans wouldn't lead to romance too? And if she later found a man who couldn't handle her having a child, he wasn't the kind of family man she wanted in any event.

'So, tell me about you, Rosalie. Where are you from? What made you contact Swans?'

'Where to start... Well, my mom used to be a supermodel. My dad...'

Rosalie went through her life history from her birth, to schooling, to work, investments, and every failed relationship she'd endured.

At the end of it all, she asked, 'Do you think I'm doing the right thing? People have said I'm not responsible enough. I think they see me as superficial, you know? That can't be a good place to start as a parent, can it?'

Melissa offered her warm smile again and reached forward to

take Rosalie's hand. 'I think you have a lot of love to give, Rosalie. In my experience, the main thing a child needs is love. We all get things wrong. There's no rule book. But if you love a child, they'll forgive you for needing to work it out.'

Rosalie nodded. She did have love to give. And she had time. Time she wanted to be filled with unconditional love. Maybe Melissa was right. She could do this. She would be a good mom.

Melissa sat back on the sofa. 'Practically speaking, you have the means to give a child a good life too. I'd say the only thing you need to do is find the right daddy.'

'This all feels very surreal.'

'But exciting, too. Now, would you like more tea? Do you have any more questions? If not, we can get your DNA testing started.'

'Mmm, I do have one question. About the, erm, the...' Rosalie felt her cheeks blaze.

'Conception?' Melissa asked, taking the words out of Rosalie's mouth.

Rosalie nodded, pleased not to have to enquire about the birds and the bees aloud.

'Well, that's really up to you and the father. You should discuss what each of you would be comfortable with when the time comes. One option is for the man to effectively act as a donor. I have had couples use IVF so that they could choose the sex of the baby – some people feel precious about continuing family traditions. Or you could use a surrogate.'

'Oh, no, I think I want to, you know, have the full experience.'

'Most women do. The other option for heterosexual couples, of course, is to do things the conventional way.'

'You mean... have sex?'

'That's what I would call conventional. What I would suggest is that you include your preference in the values test I send you home with. There's a section dealing with conception and gestational preferences. Of course, I'd encourage you to remain open to Daddy's views, too. The one thing we can't change for you is the gestational period, unfortunately.'

Rosalie laughed. Oh heck, did they just share a baby-making-agency joke?

* * *

Later that night, Rosalie poured herself a cup of rose tea and sat on her sofa with a hard copy of the Swans morals and values test.

Q: What environment would you like your child to be raised in?

A: In the city, perhaps with weekend trips out to the Hamptons. I would like to expose my child to Europe. Trips to Italy, France, Germany.

Q: How would you like your child to be educated?

A: Reputable schools. Ultimately college.

Q: How much screen time would you allow your child?

Rosalie paused with her pen between her lips. Screen time? How on earth was she to know the right answer to that?

She picked up the receiver of her vintage-style landline and dialled Hannah. After explaining the background, Rosalie asked, 'So, what should I say? I don't want to give a high number of screen hours so they think I'm not fit to be a parent and I never find a baby daddy. Equally, I figure they have to have some time for, like, development and stuff, right?'

Hannah laughed. 'Hell if I know, Ros. I have a seventeen-year-old who only leaves his computer games for food and girls. My eleven-year-old stays quiet if I give him an iPad. Sometimes dinosaurs on television make TJ sleep.'

'So what do you suggest I answer? As much screen time as they want so long as they're quiet?'

'If it's meant to be an honest questionnaire, yeah.'

Rosalie laughed. 'Thanks for the help, Hannah.'

'Any time. And Ros, for all our sakes, don't choose a baby daddy who answers "none" to screen time. In a similar vein, have you thought about how you would make a baby and a recording label work alongside each other? Oh, crap, I've got to go, TJ just face-planted trying to crawl.'

12

ANDREA

Andrea was sitting in on a marketing meeting being led by her head of marketing, with Tommy Dawson's management team. Tommy Dawson, whilst publicly stating he would *not* be leaving his band, was taking some time to focus on a solo album. Andrea had heard some of the sample tracks, and what was lacking due to the loss of the band Tommy made up for with raw and emotional lyrics. In her opinion, it was a stripped-bare example of him and his music. She was more than happy to have him making the solo album under the Stellar label.

They were playing one of his new tracks in the meeting room. She took her coffee from the large oval table where his management team and several of her colleagues were sitting to stand in the window. She watched the clouds slowly glide through the horizon as Tommy sang about making changes to his life.

There had been a time she could have fallen for Tommy. They had always gotten along well, right from the early days. She'd enjoyed working with him. More than once they'd spent a few weeks 'together' and each time had been bliss between the sheets. He lived up to his reputation and then some in that department. When it was just them, lying naked in a hotel bed, their bodies entwined, his fingers gently stroking her skin as he spoke to her, there were moments of real soul to Tommy that did not present in the rock star version of him.

The problem was, Tommy's rock star persona and Tommy's real life were a blur, and Andrea hadn't needed a man in her life any of the times they had been together, so she'd had no patience in waiting around for those fleeting moments of tenderness. Their random hook-ups since the last of those few intense weeks had been just that, hook-ups. Great sex until they were exhausted, then a test of will over who could politely leave quickest and get back to the important things in their lives.

But as she listened to his music now, the mellow beauty of the guitar, the slower pace of the tune, the soft husk of his voice, she wondered if he really did want to make changes. More than that, she considered whether it was time for her to make changes too. Starting with getting rid of Hunter.

As Tommy sang about being an innocent child before that innocence died, she asked herself how she had gone from being a happy young girl to a sometimes ruthless woman. A woman who was capable of having an affair with a married man, the father of one of her best friends?

Could people really change? God, she hoped so. Could she be that smiling little girl again? That, she doubted. Those happy days, before her mom left her, were nothing more than faint memories. Since then, she'd seen her father be a drunk, brought up her sister as best she could, taken control of the family business and now brought more responsibility upon herself as the CEO of Stellar.

There was a knock on the meeting room door, which interrupted her self-analysis. Hannah held it open.

'Hi, everyone, this one couldn't stand you all talking behind his back.'

Tommy Dawson chuckled as he stepped into the room in all black – jeans, leather jacket and shades – with two large suited security men in tow.

He glanced around the room, then his eyes fell on Andrea. He took off his shades and his cheekiness creased his bright eyes – noticeably brighter and cleaner than Andrea had seen them for a long time.

'Bringing out the big guns for me, huh?' he asked.

Andrea glared at him. 'Too much of a star to be on time, huh?'

They both laughed and Tommy pulled out a seat at the table. His guard dogs stood like statues at the back of the room. Tommy greeted everyone as he poured himself a glass of water.

In times gone by, Tommy – if he came to a meeting at all – would have slouched in his seat, tapping out a beat with his foot and drumming his fingers on the tabletop as he wrote a melody in his mind. Then he would have asked for a whiskey on the rocks – a poison he and Andrea could agree on and which they'd shared too much of in the past. He would not have taken off his shades, politely conversed with his management team and poured H-2-O. *No siree.*

Who was this man?

'Guys, I gotta tell ya,' Tommy said, 'this album is my baby. I want to be heavily involved in every aspect of what we're trying to achieve here.'

A general chorus of assurance followed.

'I've had a few ideas,' Tommy continued. He took a small black notebook from the inside pocket of his leather jacket and Andrea almost choked, for one of two reasons.

Either he was about to share his little black book of women –

which didn't seem big enough to reflect the reality of his one-night stands, unless it contained only the ones he'd been sober enough to remember. Or he was a man who made business notes now. The second option was by far the most shocking.

'Don't worry, it's not as full as my little black book,' he joked, winking at Andrea as if she'd spoken her thoughts aloud. Despite herself, she smirked.

He was still a rogue but perhaps a redeemable one in this moment.

* * *

Though she hadn't intended to sit in on the entire meeting, two hours, two coffee runs and a plate of baked goods later, the meeting about Tommy's solo album drew to close.

Hannah reappeared to show everyone out of the room and to the elevators. Andrea stood at the door, shaking hands as each person passed, as if she were part of a wedding line-up.

Tommy was last to leave. He waved his team off and asked Andrea, 'You got a sec?'

'Sure. Do you want to come along to my office? I think this room is booked out.'

They made their way along the corridor, with Tommy's personal security following closely behind and with Tommy turning the heads of every PA as they walked by. Andrea smiled to herself, remembering the early days, when Thomas Dawson was nothing more than a freeloader, sofa-surfing his friends, including, once or twice, Andrea. Turning up to Sanfia Records in the same pair of track pants day after day alongside his band members. He had been talented then but he hadn't known how good he was as a frontman.

Boy, how times had changed.

It was the remarkable thing about the music industry. Sure, there were mediocre artists who could sing and play but couldn't blow anyone away, whose lives never changed much from release to release. They earned a living doing what they loved. They had a steady fan base. Then there were the people like Tommy, who gave up everything to commit to their dream. Who had a spark, something magical in their music, and whose lives were projected by the industry from rock *bottom* to rock *stars*.

'Nice digs,' Tommy said when Andrea showed him into her office, his security standing watch like mastiffs in the corridor.

Through the glass panes, the PAs continued to ogle Tommy, until Andrea threw them a scowl that was intended to have the effect of an ice-cold power hose on their horny libidos.

'Make yourself at home,' she told him, gesturing to the suede sofas that occupied one half of her office space.

Tommy walked beyond the sofas to the wall of shelves stacked with LPs that Andrea had collected over more than two decades and didn't have space for in her apartment.

'Would you like a real drink?' she asked, moving to the bar table in the corner.

Tommy kept his eyes on the records, pulling out a Jimi Hendrix album, *Band of Gypsys*, and looking over the track list.

'No, thanks, I'm trying to cut down,' he said. He turned quickly and added, 'Not stopping. Just keeping it for dark.'

Andrea removed her hand from the bottle of Macallan whisky she'd chosen and moved to Tommy's side.

'That was his best album,' she said, nodding to Jimi Hendrix in bright colours on the record cover. '"Machine Gun" arguably did more for the industry than the King himself.'

'Agreed,' Tommy said, setting the album back on the shelf. 'These days people take distortion and feedback for granted. Though I probably wouldn't go around busting Elvis's ass.'

Andrea smiled with amusement. 'So, what did you want to see me about?'

'I wasn't expecting you to be in the meeting today.' He moved to sit in one corner of the sofa as he spoke.

'I hadn't intended to stay, to be honest.'

Tommy looked around the room they were in, then took in Andrea, in her pencil skirt and tailored blouse, the high heels she'd finally gotten used to wearing at work all day. Just as she felt he was scrutinising everything he saw, he shifted his attention to look out of the window, rubbing the gruff of his chin contemplatively.

'Do you miss being in the studio?' he asked.

She'd been too busy recently to think about being in the studio, but whenever she did, she definitely missed working with artists, being creative. More than that, she missed the early days, before she'd become so heavily involved in the business management of Sanfia Records, when the big decisions at Sanfia were made by her dad and she was able to focus on the music. When she could turn up to work in jeans, a sweater and sneakers.

She nodded as she came to sit in the opposite corner of the sofa to Tommy. 'I'm mostly too busy to think about it.'

'Do you remember those first EPs we made together?'

She nodded again, smiling at the memory of being blown away by Tommy and his band. Back then he'd had a great sound, but it was rough around the edges and he was shaggy looking, unintentionally, not like the polished, intentionally unkempt rock god he was now.

They'd spent weeks in the studio, often working into the early hours, collaborating to make the kind of music that Andrea felt in her core.

'It was fun, wasn't it?' Tommy continued.

'Yeah. Yeah, it was. But, you know, you went on to bigger and better. And I did more and more of the business side of things at Sanfia and, now here, that's pretty much all I do at Stellar. I guess we can't have it both ways.'

He nodded, watching her a beat too long, until she squirmed in her seat. 'So... you wanted to see me about...?'

Shifting his body to face her, he pulled a knee up to the cushions. 'First, I want your view of the music. Honestly, what do you think of the sample track?'

Even Tommy Dawson has doubts, she thought.

'Honestly? I'm blown away by it, Tommy. It's stripped bare, it's raw. It's heartfelt and you've kept that... edge, or... electricity you have these days. It's like early-days Tommy Dawson, pouring his heart into his lyrics with not two dimes to rub together, meets a seasoned artist, accomplished and fine-tuned. I... I love it.'

He didn't smile or even seem to react; he simply kept staring at her.

When eventually he spoke, he said, 'Have dinner with me tonight.'

It took Andrea a second to get over the flattery of Tommy asking her to dinner. Not because of who he was but because he had never asked her to dinner before. In the past, they'd ended up in bed after a long day in the studio, and later, they'd met at shows, shared impromptu drinks and screwed. Then, he or she always left and it would be months before they next saw each other.

She scoffed and brushed invisible dust from her skirt as she stood, walking toward her desk and coming to stand behind it, physically shielded from the man on her sofa. 'No.'

He followed her, standing across the desk from her, his arms folded across his chest, his bottom lip almost protruding like a petulant child. 'Why not?'

She matched his stance. 'For one thing, you don't mean dinner, you mean sex.'

'Huh. Someone has a big opinion of herself, doesn't she?'

Andrea raised an eyebrow incredulously.

'Okay, I take that back. But I asked you to dinner and I meant dinner. At my new place, not a hotel, and I'll cook.'

Now she laughed. 'You cook? Since when?'

'All right, I'll order in. But I'll order in nice. I've told you, this is a new me. New home, new music, maybe even a few morals. It would just be nice to... hang out... talk music, catch up.'

She smiled. That did sound nice. But... 'No.'

'Why?'

'Let's suppose you really mean dinner. So we'll eat this great food you order in. We'll drink some single malt on the rocks. We'll sit by your open fire.'

'I live in a penthouse apartment.'

'Fine. We'll sit by your electric fire. We'll get talking. We'll laugh. We'll flirt. We'll dance. Then we'll sleep together.'

'I mean, that kinda sounds... No, no, I'm just playing with ya. I promise no sleeping together.'

She smiled in response to his hands held out in surrender. 'No, Tommy.'

'You're a hard woman to crack. Look, I'd really like it if you were involved in the new album, whatever way they'll let you be, but I get if you can't make that happen. I just miss the old days, you know? Anyways, you've got my number. The offer stands.'

He started to walk away and Andrea said, 'For how many seconds?'

She heard him laugh as he walked out of her office. She watched him lean on Hannah's desk and say something to her, then tap his hand down and walk away.

'Probably giving *her* his number,' she mumbled, but found herself laughing.

If nothing else, Tommy's visit had taken her mind off Hunter.

Who happened to be walking past Tommy in the opposite direction… toward her office.

What did he want? She'd already said everything she had to say to him. Now, what she really needed was space to get past him. Oh, but he was wearing her favourite light grey suit.

'Psst, Hannah. Hannah. Hannah!'

Hannah jumped on the final shout, turning in her desk chair positioned outside Andrea's office. Andrea ushered her in subtly with her hand.

Hannah glanced in the direction of Hunter then looked around her desk, grabbed a bunch of papers and hurried into Andrea's office.

The women stood on either side of Andrea's desk, staring and pointing at the paper stack between them. Andrea dared a discreet glance and saw Hunter was almost upon them.

'You need to call, erm… ah… Sean Deacon, over at ah… the… ah…'

Hannah's nerves were making Andrea more nervous. 'At Platinum Management?'

'Yes,' Hannah said. 'And don't forget about the thing… the, ah, erm, urgent thing.'

'The urgent thing?' Hunter's voice was as smooth and assured as ever. Clearly breaking off their affair hadn't made him flounder at all. 'Now that sounds very important.'

Andrea stifled a nervous laugh when Hannah said under her breath, 'Dick.'

'Ladies, how are you both?' he said, swaggering into the room. Andrea had never noticed the familiarity of his swagger before. But it came to her now. It wasn't sexy, at all. It was *Liberace*.

'Very busy, Hunter, I'm afraid. Did you need something?' Andrea spoke with her shoulders back and her chin high because, yes, finally, she was doing the right thing and taking the moral high ground.

He slipped a hand in the pocket of his tailored slacks, drawing Andrea's gaze to his crotch. *Damn it!*

'Right. With very *urgent* things. I do need to speak with you and this is *urgent* too.'

He eyed Hannah in a way that said, *I don't care if you're my daughter's friend or not, get the hell out.*

Ultimately, he was the big boss so Andrea knew that Hannah could do nothing more than offer an apologetic look and pick up the math homework pages she had printed using the work printer, probably for her middle kid, from the desk between her and Andrea.

Hannah kept the office door open, which Andrea silently thanked her for.

'What can I do for you, Hunter?'

'I saw Tommy Dawson leaving your office.'

She folded her arms across her chest. *Jealous, are we?* 'He had a meeting about his new album.'

'In your office?'

She smiled at him in a way that told him she was on to him. 'Was that all, because I really do have work to do.'

He exhaled heavily, the way a flame-breathing dragon might. Then he extracted a familiar velvet box from his inside pocket and set it down on the desk. Andrea glanced to the corridor outside her office, thankfully finding no one was watching them.

She nudged the box back to Hunter. 'We've discussed this and I have nothing more to say on the matter.'

His lips curled up like a cunning fox. 'You're still taking a tantrum then?'

Her hands trembled with fury she couldn't unleash. 'I'm not a child, Hunter.'

'Then stop behaving like one. Take the gift.'

'Have your circumstances changed since the last time we spoke?' Damn it, why was she even asking this? But she waited for the answer, holding her breath, her stomach tied up. What if he said yes?

His silence was the only response she needed, and she found herself relieved.

'If there's nothing else...' She looked toward the exit.

'I'll come to your place tonight and we can discuss this like adults.'

'No.'

'No?'

'No. Even if I wanted to, which I don't, I'm busy tonight.'

He snorted. A grotesque sound. 'What, like, washing your hair?'

She scowled. Didn't she have anything else in her life besides work and her illicit affair with her boss? Was she that predictable? 'Yes, I will be washing my hair, right before I go out. See, I have a date.'

'A date? With who?'

'It's with *whom*.'

'Touché. With *whom* do you have a date?'

Oh God, she was such a shitty liar, except, apparently, when it came to banging Hunter. 'A man.'

He laughed in a way that made her want to bring her trembling hand across his cheek. 'Which man?'

'You don't know him.'

'Okay, Andi. Well, if your date doesn't transpire, I'll be at your place around eight.'

She watched him leave. *Fuck him. Fuck him so. Damned. Hard.*

Urgh, she was so angry her eyes were stinging and her body was shaking. He was so... arrogant. What had she ever seen in him? Maybe Hannah had called it spot on. Andrea went with Hunter because he was off limits and now, she realised, not a man she could have ever fallen for seriously enough to get her heart broken.

She stomped to her window, hoping if she watched the Hudson for long enough she would calm down. And all she could think about was how, all her life, men had been telling her what to do. That it didn't matter whether she was now a CEO of a label, because her ultimate boss and *ex*-lover still held the power. That it hadn't mattered when she was running her own indie recording label because *she* was the one who was told to look after the business – by her father, even by her sister's new husband. That it hadn't mattered when she was just a girl who deserved to have her own independence; that she had been told to look after her kid sister and take her *everywhere.*

'So, you have a date tonight, huh?'

Hannah's voice was tentative. She could read Andrea as easily as she could read a highway sign.

Andrea kept watching the Hudson and the ripples that followed a power boat. 'You heard that?'

'Yes. But I was intentionally eavesdropping and the other girls have their headphones in, so they didn't hear anything.'

Andrea nodded once, sternly.

'You did good, Andi. I'm proud of you.'

Her porcupine prickles softened slightly. 'I don't think proud is a word you could use in the same sentence with my name and Hunter's.'

Hannah came to her side. 'You're doing the right thing, now. Here.'

Andrea looked at the small piece of paper Hannah held out with a phone number on it. 'What's that, the number of a good therapist?'

Hannah smiled. 'Tommy left it on his way out. In case you changed your mind and don't have his new number. I figure, since you need a date tonight...'

* * *

Tommy's penthouse apartment was amongst the quieter streets of downtown, in the Tribeca district, nestled, Andrea knew, alongside other A-listers, like Beyoncé and Jay-Z, Justin Timberlake and Jessica Biel, Taylor Swift. Celebrities in New York tended to congregate in clusters, where their security could almost be shared.

She paid the cab driver and headed inside the building after being buzzed in and presumably checked off a list at the front desk. *Tommy Dawson Girl Number 6,000, tick!*

The concierge at the front desk told her to wait in the vestibule, where she was met by one of Tommy's security who had been at the office earlier today. 'Ms Williams, I'll take you up.'

She rolled her eyes. These guys must be versed in picking up women at the front desk for Tommy. 'It's Andrea, or Andi. And you are?'

'Mike,' he said, turning his back on her and pressing the button to call the elevator.

'Well, it's nice to see you for the second time in a day, Mike.' Her heels clicked on the marble floor tiles as she followed him into the elevator. 'Nice to learn your name, too.'

They rode five floors in silence. Andrea slipped off her leather jacket, fussed with her first-time-on blouse, and checked her skinny jeans were sitting right against her strappy shoes. 'Just so you know, Mike, I'm not like the other girls. I've known Tommy for years. We used to work together.'

Mike was unresponsive, his hands held together in front of him, his suit from earlier today having been replaced by a black, long-sleeved top and black slacks that showed his impeccably muscled frame.

Well, whether he responded or not, she knew herself that she wasn't like the other girls. She wasn't just coming here for a lay. No, she was coming here to chat. To catch up with an old friend. And, above all else, to give her a genuine excuse to avoid a certain person whose name would not cross her lips tonight.

There were only two doors on the top floor of the building. Mike led the way to one, knocked and opened it. Before she even stepped inside, Andrea heard the unmistakable sound of U2 and B.B. King's 'When Love Comes to Town'. Ironic, given magazines had, on more than one occasion, likened Tommy to the greatness of Bono.

'Damn, I love this song.' Mike took her leather jacket, in silence, and hung it on a coat stand by the door. 'You know, they recorded this track in Sun Studios, Memphis. The old-fashioned way.'

'And you were just a little girl with pigtails in your hair when this was recorded.' She turned to see Tommy, barefoot, which was something of an irrational turn-on. He came toward her wiping his hands on a towel, wearing stonewash jeans and a black fitted T-shirt with a chain hanging down the front and his usual leather bracelets around his wrist.

'You're giving away my age,' she said coyly.

'Hey, it's nothing to be ashamed of. Don't I know it. You ought to be twice your age for everything you've accomplished.'

She laughed. 'Starting with compliments. I thought I told you this wasn't a date. What's with the towel?'

'I was breaking ice and it was fucking freezing.'

'You don't say,' she said, chuckling.

'Come on, smart ass, I'll show you around *my* office.'

He headed down the rosewood floor of the corridor, the white walls of which were covered in framed prints. She glanced behind her to see where Mike was but he had vanished. 'Where'd the guard dog go?' she called out, slowly making her way past each of the prints.

'The team lives in the apartment next door,' Tommy called back.

'Sure they do,' she muttered to herself.

Her shoulders moved of their own volition in time to the music as she took in the framed images – Jimi Hendrix playing at Woodstock, the Rolling Stones live at Earls Court, Led Zeppelin at the Los Angeles Forum. She followed the prints to the end of the corridor, where she inhaled the scent of something spiced and exotic, her stomach rumbling in response.

She tried not to look in awe as she stepped into the vast open space of the apartment, with views as far as New Jersey. The theme of whitewash walls and music memorabilia continued. The space was big and had little furniture, but something about it felt comfortable, homey even. Perhaps it was the smell of food. Or the fact Tommy really did have an electric fire on one wall in front of two large L-shape sofas that formed a broken U around a cow-skin rug.

She had been in celebrity homes, frequented more charlie parties in celebrity homes than she could count, such was the industry. But Tommy's pad was impressive.

'Ouch, fuck!'

She spun quickly from where she had been looking over a picture of Tommy on stage at the Super Bowl two years ago and saw Tommy wafting his burnt hand in the air.

'You never did cook?' she said, rushing over to him.

She took hold of his hand and saw a small red mark. 'That's fine, you big baby, just run it under cold water for a minute.'

He did as she instructed and Andrea closed the cooker door.

'No, I ordered in, the best,' he said. 'I was just stirring it. I thought you'd want a drink first?'

She found herself laughing, again. 'Only you could burn yourself on takeout.'

'It's not just any takeout. That's a biryani and a tikka masala from the best Indian restaurant in the city.' He dried off his wound and handed her a crystal glass of liquor on ice from the marble-top kitchen counter. 'Macallan single malt,' he said.

They carried their drinks as Tommy showed her around the impressive penthouse. She noted the super-king-size bed set with satin sheets in the master bedroom. The hot tub in the main bathroom. And the awards for platinum albums, million-copy sales, best rock artist, and best single decorating the 'office'.

Once the tour was done, Tommy poured them both a second drink and they came to sit on the sofas by the fire. 'I had this installed today, after your comment,' Tommy said, pulling his legs up onto the sofa so they were lazily spread in front of him as he reclined against the sofa cushions.

'You're lying,' Andrea said, mirroring his pose after unbuckling and slipping off her heels. Boy, it was nice to take a load off. No work. No randy boss. Great music playing in the background – now Tracy Chapman's 'Give Me One Reason'.

Tommy smiled in response. 'This track always makes me want to pick up the guitar.'

'It makes me want to go sit in a bar on Beale Street and drink Tennessee bourbon.'

'You get down there much these days?'

She shook her head. Her mother was buried in Nashville and she had spent her early years there when her mom still performed in the bars on Broadway, before her dad moved them back to his home town in New Jersey and set up Sanfia Records. At Sanfia she had ventured south fairly regularly for concerts, recordings and the CMAs. But in recent years, she'd had no reason to go.

'And leave the office?' she said. 'How could I?'

He fell silent and she wondered if he was also remembering their backstage romp after he played at the Grand Ole Opry for the first time, back when the band's sound was more country rock than mainstream.

'So, tell me, Tommy Dawson, rock god, notorious bad boy, are the new lyrics honest? Are you really changing?'

'Slowly, yes.'

At that moment, four paws came running from the hallway, not breaking stride as they leaped onto Tommy's sofa and started furiously licking his face. Tommy laughed like a child, making Andrea laugh, too.

'All right, boy. It's good to see you too, buddy.'

'I take it he's yours?'

Andrea wasn't up on her dog breeds but she could admit Tommy's four-legged friend was a good-looking hound. It was dark brown, with a shiny coat and white fur that looked like socks on its feet. It was chiselled and looked well walked, the structure of its face almost good enough for *Vogue*.

Tommy set his drink on the floor and wrestled the mutt, taking hold of it and carrying it over to Andrea. She leaned back as it tried to lick her face. Tommy held the dog's paw and offered it to Andrea who, after a pause for thought, took hold of it and shook it. 'Hello, dog.'

'This is Rocky.'

'As in Balboa?'

'As in rock star,' Tommy said with a cheeky glint in his eye.

Andrea laughed again, something she hadn't anticipated from their evening based on her recent mood. Tommy set Rocky the rock star down and sent him on a hunt for his food bowl.

'Where did he appear from?' Andrea asked, perplexed.

Tommy resumed his position on the sofa – reclined, drink in hand. 'One of the guys next door will've walked him and brought him back.'

'Right, the staff.'

Tommy smiled through her insolence. 'I usually walk him myself but tonight we made an exception for you.'

'I'm flattered,' she said in good humour. 'So, I hate to ask this but, I mean, was he, like, an accident?'

Tommy chuckled. 'I got him about six months ago. Adopted, not self-made, though noted that you likened me to a hound.'

'Or the mother.'

'Ouch! No, he was recommended to me, or at least the idea of getting a pet was recommended to me, by my therapist.'

Andrea almost spat out her next mouthful of whisky. 'Tommy Dawson has a therapist?'

'Is it so strange?'

'Can I ask why?'

'Well...' He scratched his head, as if pondering his next words. 'I just couldn't find myself, or remember who I really was, I guess. I'd been on the road for two years straight. I didn't have any roots anywhere. I'd lost touch with most people I knew before' – he gestured to the expansive space around them – 'before all this. I was drinking too much. Not that I couldn't stop, just that it was the accepted protocol, you know? Drink before stage, during stage, after stage. Drink through the night, sleep through the day. Rinse and repeat.

'I'd been having these... I don't know... moments of uncertainty, I guess. Like, I wasn't sure any more what the point of it all was.'

'The music?'

'Anything. I'd just lost any sense of perspective.'

'So you decided to see someone?'

'Not straight away. Around the same time, we found out that my old man had dementia.'

'I'm really sorry to hear that, Tommy.' She had met his dad once at a concert and thought he was a true gent.

'Yeah, it pretty much sucks. He's already in a care home. Too much for my sister and my mom, and I'm never around much.'

'Is that why you moved back to New York?'

'I think so. Mostly. It's easier to see him from here but I probably could have visited from anywhere. I think the combination of everything just took its toll. My writing started to change and it wasn't a match for the band's sound, but it felt right to me. Natural. Anyway, through it all, I decided I needed to talk to someone who wasn't invested in me. It felt like no one would just talk to me on a level because they all wanted something from me. The band wanted the rock star and the carefree lyrics. My sister wanted help with Mom and Dad. The road team wanted me to stay on the road.'

'I wish... I mean, I know we're not that close any more but I hope you know you can talk to me. I used to like you keeping me in the studio until the early hours talking my right ear off.' The sincere turn up of her lips was reflected by Tommy.

'I actually think having someone who didn't know me at all and who really couldn't give a fuck about my career was helpful. It definitely was. It made me realise that there's more to life. I love music, but the trimmings – the parties, the booze, even the women – they mean nothing. I don't want to be lying on my death bed wondering why I went for one more lay or one more drink, and why I don't have people I love around me.'

She processed what he said. It was right, of course, and made her think, what would her last thought be? Would it be that she wished she'd spent more time in the office or more time sleeping with married men? She didn't want to get into those thoughts now. She brushed them aside and asked, brightly, 'And the dog?'

Right on cue, the dog came back to them, wagging its tail at Andrea then jumping onto the sofa and curling up by her feet. Meh, he was kind of cute, even if she wasn't an animal lover. If nothing else, her feet were warmer with him snuggled on top of them.

'The idea is, he gives me responsibility, for myself. Now it's strange being in this place without hearing his feet pitter-pattering on the floor. He makes me feel like I have a home. And when I'm travelling, he comes with me. I know he needs to be walked, fed, played with and so I have a reason to say no to another drink or another party.'

'He's like a guide dog for the drunk.'

Tommy laughed. 'Hey now, I'm not a drunk. And, on that note, do you want another?'

She looked at her glass, surprised it was empty. 'Sure, but I'm not ready to move now that my toes are warm.'

'How about dinner on the sofa?'

No Hunter. No work. Laughing. Lounging on the sofa with Tommy's dog on her feet. Oddly, she was in.

Tommy insisted she stay where she was whilst he brought another round of drinks and – *sans* more skin burns – laid out the Indian meal: poppadums, naan breads, dips, curries, and all on a coffee table he manoeuvred to the rug in front of them.

'Oh my God, this biryani is to *die* for,' Andrea said, lost in a world of slow-cooked-lamb-bliss.

'I told you, it's the best Indian food in the city,' Tommy said, not bothering to pause between bites.

They worked their way down 70 per cent of the meal before they called it quits and gave the dog the scraps he was allowed to eat.

They lay back on their sofas, groaning about their gluttony and consequent bloating, and bickering about which song they should listen to next.

Andrea couldn't remember the last time she'd spent a night like this. Fully relaxed, in company she truly enjoyed. It was a shame it would be six-to-twelve months – based on historic experience – before she saw Tommy again. She liked the new him, who was very much like the old him except a little more mature and worldly.

They were playing a game of one person naming an artist or band and the other choosing their best song. Currently, Bon Jovi's 'Bed of Roses' was playing, which Andrea considered to be the band's best track. Tommy wholly disagreed.

'It's hands down "Always",' he said.

'No way. "Bed of Roses" is incredible. The melody, Jon's voice. That build right before the chorus. Would you just listen to that, please?'

'I'm listening, baby, and I'm saying you called it wrong.'

There was something about the way he called her 'baby' that made her think about Hunter for the first time in hours. In hindsight, she couldn't stand the way he had called her 'kiddo' all the time, especially in a post-coital moment. What was that? Some kind of reference to her being his daughter's friend? A power play?

The way Tommy called her 'baby' right then was nothing like the same. It was affectionate, familiar, not intended to be demeaning at all, despite the fact they were bickering.

'Hey, you still here?' Tommy asked.

She realised she had been lost in her own thoughts. 'Sorry, yeah, I'm here. Ah, who next…? Chris Stapleton.'

'That's easy. "Millionaire".'

'I disagree. His best is "Broken Halo" but I'll let you have it since I happen to have a soft spot for most Chris Stapleton music.' She drained her drink as the song began to play into the apartment.

'"Broken Halo", huh? And I thought I had problems.' He gave her a mocking look. 'So, in the theme of being honest, are you going to tell me why you changed your mind to come here tonight?'

She pulled up her legs, needing the comfort of wrapping her arms around her knees in the absence of the dog on her feet. She shouldn't say anything about Hunter. No one could find out. Wasn't that the main reason she'd ended it? But if anyone would listen to her promiscuous indiscretions without judgement, it was the man sitting opposite her.

'Honestly? Please don't take this the wrong way because I'm having a nice time tonight.'

'But?'

'I got out of a relationship of sorts this week and I thought maybe spending time with someone else would take my mind off it.'

He seemed to nod as he looked at her, not giving much away. Had she offended him? From memory, Tommy didn't offend easily.

'I get that,' he said eventually. 'I didn't realise you were with anyone.'

She took a breath for courage. 'That was part of the problem. No one could know.'

'Ah. Got ya. Who ended it?'

'Me.'

'How long?'

'Six months-ish.'

'Messy?'

'Very. Like, work-colleague-meets-father-of-a-friend-bad.'

He whistled. 'That's covering a lot of bases.'

'Yup.' She held up her empty glass. 'My turn.'

She helped herself around his kitchen, making them drinks as Tommy talked to her from the sofa. 'Would I know him?'

'Would it matter if you did?' she asked.

He shrugged. 'I'm just curious to know if the scowl Hunter gave me as I walked past him in your office today is anything to do with this.'

She froze, mid putting the top back on the bottle of Macallan. 'Was it that obvious?'

'He's pissed. He's missed out on a great woman.'

She scoffed. 'Yeah, for his wife. I should never, *ever* have gone there. It just sort of happened.'

She handed Tommy a fresh drink and he patted the sofa next to him. She sat with her back pressed to his shoulder, their legs stretched along different sides of the L-shaped sofa.

'Do you think I'm a terrible person?'

He pressed his cheek to her head and she made no move away. She couldn't remember the last time anyone had comforted her. Not that she deserved to be comforted, she knew.

'I think you made a mistake,' he said. 'That isn't an automatic pathway to hell. God knows I've made plenty. We all do.'

'Some are worse than others, Tommy.'

'Yes.' He draped his arm across her shoulder and she leaned deeper into him. 'You're no saint, Andi. You're a human being. That means we fuck up, we recognise the errors of our ways, we make amends as best we can.'

'That sounds like it came directly from your therapist.'

She felt his humour as his chest chugged against her. 'Food, whisky and therapy. Baby, you can't afford me tonight.'

She closed her eyes and hummed as Chris Stapleton's 'Tennessee Whiskey' started to play.

She felt Tommy suck in a breath before he started to sing, 'You're as smooth as a Tennessee whiskey.'

Chris Stapleton and Tommy Dawson; she couldn't have screwed up *that* badly because she'd been allowed into heaven. Stapleton's words and Tommy's voice traversed her veins just like the Macallan had been doing for hours.

'Dance with me?' he asked.

She shouldn't. She had turned up at the *new* Tommy Dawson's house. They had drunk liquor, too much liquor. Now, he was singing to her, and if they danced…

He stood and took her drink from her, setting both glasses down on the coffee table. Then he offered her his hand.

She looked up to him. An incredibly handsome man. 'Will you keep singing if I do?'

One side of his lips curved up and she already knew how they would end the night before she slipped her hand into his and before he pulled her in close to him. Before he wrapped his arms around her and sang, as she laid her head against his chest.

She nudged into his neck, smelling his musk that was *all* man. When she pressed her lips to his skin, he lifted his head. As he sang, she kissed his throat, his jaw.

He swayed them in time to the music. 'You should know, if I kiss you, tonight is only ending one way.'

She looked into his eyes and let him know she heard his intentions. She wanted him, too.

He pressed his mouth to hers and stretched his fingers into her hair. He parted her lips and she tasted the way he wore his whisky.

He swayed them again, singing to her as her hands roamed his back, his chest, beneath his T-shirt. She slid the fabric up, kissing his skin as she went. He raised his arms and took the T-shirt over his head, kissing her as soon as it was off, pressing his warm torso against her. God, she wanted to feel his skin on hers.

He took off her blouse and expertly released her bra. When her naked breasts pressed against him, she moaned, the touch teasing her already hard nipples.

She felt his pleasure coursing through her own alcohol-rich blood. This felt like more of a sin than anything she had done with Hunter. It was the ultimate guilty pleasure and she couldn't get enough.

Her times with Tommy had always been good, but this was... different. Slower, deeper, a smooth ride to heaven.

Afterwards, Tommy collapsed against her chest until their breathing calmed. 'Stay?'

She nodded in response, knowing he couldn't hear her answer but that he somehow knew it was yes.

Sometime later, they took the bottle of Macallan to the satin sheets of his bedroom and made love again, and again.

* * *

She had fallen into a sated sleep and woken under the weight of Tommy's arm, with a head that felt like it was made of concrete and a throat so dry it felt like someone had taken a razor blade to it.

What had she been thinking? Nothing beyond needing to be taken out of her head, out of her thoughts of Hunter, for one night. Tommy had been a gentleman last night, but the saying went 'a leopard can't change its spots', didn't it?

Tommy had been the perfect hook-up. Now what she needed was a cab, an aspirin and a long black coffee.

She slipped out of his bed and found her clothes in the lounge. She hushed the dog with a finger across her lips as she tiptoed past it, carrying her shoes. Unhooking her coat, she snuck out of the door and back out of Tommy's life. This time, it would be for good. He'd talked about change; well, it was about time she made some changes too. No more promiscuous Andi. No more sex until she meant it. No more of the stuff that had her head in turmoil. Just no more.

At least not until she got her shit together.

13

ROSALIE

Ordinarily, Rosalie would have grumbled about the trek to Williamsburg for brunch – which was admittedly more like a short drive – but it was a working day, which meant the other ladies were stationed there and, more importantly, she had made a brunch reservation at Meadow Sweet. She would take a cab any distance for their Venetian Spritz and ricotta toast. Plus, the girls hadn't been together since the night of Presley John's memorial concert, which was almost four weeks ago.

She arrived first, was greeted by the staff, who knew of her love of the Venetian Spritz and brought one to the table within minutes. Meadow Sweet was like the seventies meets modern NYC. The flooring had the sort of distorted geometric pattern her grandmother's rug had in photos she'd seen of her mother as a teenager. The yellow and green hues were reminiscent of the period. The wood tables and bar, the tan leather upholstery and the exposed beams all vibed *That '70s Show*. But the stools at the bar, where guests could sit to drink or dine, said modern Manhattan. The food was quirky and had the finest flavours – who didn't love truffle? Modern art decorated the walls and there was a cute mezzanine level with live plants – a nod to the anti-chemicals, pro-vegan trend. Or perhaps it was a nod to flower power and the revolution.

Regardless, the restaurant played to her bent for interior design, love of delicious cocktails and scrumptious food. Plus, she would have to stop with such treats if she got pregnant – there were more foods on the list of things expectant mothers shouldn't eat than those they should, and all her favourites: shellfish, nuts, carpaccio, ceviche, soft cheese (occasionally). And if she had her way, her pregnancy would happen soon… just as soon as the Swans agency matched her to the right male counterpart, whose sperm would greet her egg with the respect it deserved and produce the idyllic offspring – long dark ringlets, brown eyes and a fine set of teeth (optional but preferred).

She sipped her drink as she waited for Hannah and Andrea to join her. In general, it was good to be fashionably late, but these were her working friends who couldn't spare an extra fifteen minutes if she made them wait and, in any event, with these ladies, Rosalie didn't need the pretence.

Rosalie stood when they arrived and pulled out the shopping bags she had tucked under the table. 'You're here. Hey! These are for you, Hannah,' she said, handing over two bags that were bursting at the seams with faux fur, metallic pink, pink suede, very tightly curled shaggy wool and sequined cushions. 'I thought they would look incredible on that old grey love seat in your lounge. They'll totally brighten the space and the grey-pink combo is very *in* this season.

'Andi, this is for you… You can open it later but it's a little silk something for you to enjoy with your secret.' She finished with a wink that made Andrea frown with confusion, but Rosalie had heard many things, the latest of which was that her friend was currently enjoying a fling with an old flame.

Once all three of them were seated – Hannah on the black leather cushioned seat with Rosalie; Andrea in a chair opposite – Rosalie waved over the staff, who brought her pre-ordered bottle of champagne (from the Champagne region of France, *naturellement*).

'Fizz?' Hannah asked with one raised eyebrow.

Rosalie slipped a hand onto Hannah's leg and said, 'My treat. It's been four weeks since we were all together at Madison Square Gardens already and we have so much to celebrate.'

'We do?' Hannah and Andrea asked in unison.

Rosalie would tease out the reason for their *misère* soon enough but for now, she said, 'Yes, we do! Seth Young is taking the world by storm, thanks to my little moment of ingenuity at the Presley John concert. I've heard that song he played at least three times on the radio. Calvin Richards really did me a good turn. All of this means that when I go to Sanfia Records today, Sofia is bound to agree to continuing to teach me the ropes.'

'He certainly has the right connections and backstory for a winning formula,' Andrea said. 'I mean, an ex-serviceman always tugs on the heartstrings – especially some of those YouTube videos I've seen of him in barracks with his troop. But the fact he's also Randy Jonson's brother. Sheesh, he's just a goldmine waiting to be extracted.'

'You're not thinking of poaching him for XM now, Andi, are you?' Rosalie teased.

Straight-faced, Andrea told her, 'I know you think I have an iron heart but I wouldn't do that to my sister. You and I both know that his success is great, but the big labels will be swooping in if he continues to hit the billboard charts. They're likely already looking into the guy who made his debut appearance on stage with Randy Jonson at Presley John's remembrance concert.

Sanfia Records doesn't have the clout or money to keep someone like that.'

'Okay, well, nice attempt to kill the merriment there. Back to celebrations. Andi, a little dickie-bird tells me Tommy Dawson is rocking your world again? That gift I gave you might make a little more sense now.' She finished with a mischievous giggle.

'Hey! How did—'

Rosalie waved off the objections. Sometimes Andrea could be such a prude. They could talk about her bed being a-rockin' once the champagne had limbered her up. 'Hannah's turn now,' she continued, cutting Andrea off. 'Hasn't Rod started a new job?'

'Huh, well, yes, but—'

'Uh-uh. I'm not finished just yet. And *I* have started my baby-daddy dates.' She clapped her hands quickly three times. 'So, raise your glasses, ladies. To three thirty-odd-year-old women winning at life.'

With less enthusiasm than her own, Hannah raised her glass first and said, 'Meh, take your wins where you can get 'em, I suppose.'

Rosalie held her glass against Hannah's, and they waited for Andrea to join them. Andrea bore holes in Hannah with her eyes but eventually raised her glass too.

They quickly ordered food, to make sure the others could eat and get back to work. Andrea also ordered a ginger-based mocktail.

'Don't you like the champagne, Andi?' Rosalie asked. 'I could choose another?'

Andrea shook her head. 'It's great, Ros, and a nice thought. I've just been struggling with terrible indigestion these last few days. It's like fire in my chest. It wasn't helped by Hannah buying me chipotle for lunch yesterday, though.'

'Hey!' Hannah said. 'I got you lunch, didn't I? Nothing like being grateful, huh?'

Rosalie was used to seeing Andrea and Hannah bicker. They were the oldest friends of them all – closer even than Andrea and Sofia's sisterly bond – but there was a snappy tone about them both today.

'It is part of your job to get me lunch. That is, when you're in the office,' Andrea jibed.

Ouch.

'My kid has been sick.'

'There's always one of your kids sick.'

Wow, okay, that was vicious.

Hannah's head snapped back as if Andrea had slapped her. 'That's a low blow, Andi. Don't have a go at me when you're actually just pissed that... Forget it.'

Thinking quickly of something to say to break the arctic air, Rosalie said, 'Andi, actually, I have a little favour to ask of you. You know how Sofia has been helping me to get some experience in the music industry, like, more production-y type stuff? Well, I was thinking I could come to XM and see how you do things some time, too. I mean, I know you won't have the time to show me all the digeridoos and what not but if I got that from the indie side, like you trained, then you showed me the more exec side, then I'd be...'

'What? You come to XM?' Andrea snapped. 'Ros, I don't have time to have you playing around in my office. I have a job to do.'

Rosalie gasped, unintentionally theatrically. '*An*-drea. I need all the experience I can get to prove to Daddy that I can run my new label. And he always talks about you, so I figured if I—'

'What label?'

'The recording label. That Daddy is giving to me at XM.

We're going to be music label sisters.' She beamed as she clapped in her seat.

'Is this a joke? Hunter is going to gift you a label? He can't do that. There's an exec. A board. And besides the obvious governance issues... you don't have the first clue about running a music label.'

Stunned, Rosalie could only stare at her so-called friend.

'Andi,' Hannah admonished quietly.

'No, Hannah. It is ridiculous. You can see that. It's... farcical.'

Rosalie pressed her hand to her pounding heart in her chest. 'I *knew* it. You *do* think I'm ridiculous. All the... All the things I do for you and I ask you for one small thing, just one time.' With her napkin, she dabbed at the wetness that had formed in the corners of her eyes. Andrea could be so cruel.

Then she felt Andrea's cold palm on top of hers on the table. 'I'm sorry. When you have your label, of course we can swap tips. Okay? I didn't mean to upset you.'

'You're just saying that because you think I'm causing a scene.'

'No. No, I'm not, Ros. I mean it. It's just this damned heartburn has got me in a foul mood. Promise.'

'Come on then, Ros,' Hannah said. 'Tell us about your baby-daddies.'

'Oh, yes.' She bounced on her seat. 'Well, I had my first daddy date last week.'

'I thought the idea was that you were looking for fancy sperm, not romance,' Hannah said.

'Oh, it's not really dating in the romantic sense but describing it as a meet-up to interrogate a potential sperm giver doesn't quite have the same ring to it now, does it?'

Hannah chuckled, her bicker-fest with Andrea seemingly forgotten. 'It's like Tinder for sperm. It's Spinder.'

'Which is scarily close to spinster.' Andrea laughed good-naturedly.

Rosalie protested but she could admit it was quite funny, and at least her friends were back in good spirits. 'Well, it's quite possible I'll die a spinster because my first date was with a gay daddy.'

Silence descended on the table just in time for their food to be set down. Rosalie inhaled the smells – truffle, garlic, lemongrass – from around the table. Whilst she drifted to a culinary heaven, she noticed Andrea's face screw at either the sight or scent of her lunch portion of pappardelle.

'Is it okay, Andi?' Rosalie asked.

'Mmm hmm.' She nodded. 'Just this indigestion knocking me sick.'

Whilst Andrea played with her food, Hannah continued to quiz Rosalie on her gay daddy date.

'But, like, when it came to the baby-making part?' Hannah asked.

'Yes, well, in his case, there wouldn't be conventional vaginal conception,' Rosalie said. 'I mean, unless he... Well, no, I guess it wouldn't work.'

'Oh my goodness, I'm dying over here. Ros, you are the perfect medicine for me,' Hannah said, dabbing tears from her eyes as she laughed.

'What? It's okay to say vaginal,' Rosalie countered. 'My mentor at Swans says it's important to use the correct terms and get comfortable with the process and my body. My vagina, womb, cervix, all of that.'

'On a serious note,' Hannah began, 'would having a gay father for your child bother you?'

Rosalie shrugged. 'You mean in terms of values and lifestyle?'

'I guess,' Hannah said. 'I'm not saying I have an issue with gay people here, or gay couples having children, don't misunderstand me.'

Rosalie put a hand to her friend's arm. 'Of course you're not.'

Hannah was the least discriminatory person Rosalie knew, if there was such a thing. Hannah had been through struggles with perceptions and awkward conversations about her being white, Rod being black and their kids being of mixed heritage, at least a thousand times, that Rosalie knew of.

'I guess you mean because the baby would have a heterosexual experience with Mom and a homosexual experience with Dad, right?'

'Well, yeah,' Hannah said.

Rosalie chewed a mouthful of food. 'I've definitely thought about it, but I think where I get to is that it wouldn't be the most conventional start to life in any event and later, I guess it would become just the same as if Mom, me and Dad were divorced, except they'd never put the kid through all the fighting and hate to get there.'

'In some ways,' Hannah said, 'it would be great that the child got to see different options, too. It doesn't have to be straight, or gay, or feel guilty about being whoever it wants to be because Mom and Dad are clearly open to anything.'

Rosalie smiled. 'Exactly. As it happens, I don't think last week's guy is going to be the sperm to my egg…'

Hannah choked on her next mouthful of fizz. Rosalie patted her back as she continued.

'But I wouldn't say "no" to daddy-dating another gay man. I suppose it might be a shame to completely rule out the idea of romance, but that's not the main driver here. I checked the "open to options" box on my agency form. Plus, I totally love the gays. Wouldn't my kid be more fashionable in the city that never sleeps with a Mommy and a Gaddy? It would have, like, supreme emotional intelligence, taste and class. And, I'm not going to lie, if I never have to compete with the baby daddy's younger wife with pert boobs and a perfectly formed butt, I won't be sorry.'

'Hell, I'm convinced. I think I'm going to trade in Rod for a gay daddy,' Hannah said.

'So, Ros, how has Sofia been recently, at the studio, I mean? Has my dad been at the studio a lot?' Andrea asked.

'Actually, I'm pleased you asked. I wanted to mention something but I didn't want it to seem like I was telling tales.'

'Go on.'

'Well, Jimmy is helping out and I think it's because Jay is using again. I overheard some of Sofia's artists complaining that Jay hadn't shown up for their recording sessions.'

With pursed lips, Andrea nodded. 'Thanks, Ros. It's good to know you're there to keep an eye on her. Sofia hardly tells me anything these days. And asking about Jay is like lighting her fuse.' She shook her head. 'I wish she would see Jay for what he is before he ruins both their lives.'

'Is anyone having dessert?' a waiter asked as he cleared their plates.

'Oh, let's take a peek,' Hannah said, glancing to Andrea, who seemed to subtly give the green light to Hannah in her PA capacity.

'So, Andi,' Rosalie began, taking the dessert menu that was handed to her. 'Tell me about you seeing Tommy Dawson again.'

'Hannah should learn to hold her water. And I'm not *seeing* Tommy. I have never been *seeing* Tommy. He's hardly the kind of man someone has a relationship with.'

'Permission to rephrase?' Rosalie asked, setting down her menu and deciding against dessert for the sake of her waistline, no matter how much she wanted one. 'So, Andi, Hannah tells me you had a night of romping Tommy Dawson.'

With clear reluctance, Andrea laughed with them. 'If you must know, it was one extremely long, hot, spine-tinglingly great night. And then it was done.'

'Oh, tease. Tell me more,' Rosalie said.

Andrea smiled and, if Rosalie hadn't known her better, she might have even thought she blushed. 'There's nothing more to tell. Tommy and I get each other. But we understand each other for a few hours at a time. He's not the kind of guy who settles down. Despite what he says about turning over new leaves.'

'But would you want to... if he did?' Rosalie probed.

'God, no. The timing would be awful.'

'Really? How so?' Rosalie suspected the timing would be just fine, which meant Andrea would never risk going for it, in case it actually worked out.

'Ah... well, I... erm... with the promotion. Work is so busy,' Andrea fumbled.

'But work will always be busy, won't it?' Rosalie asked. 'I mean, look at Daddy. He's so hardworking but he manages to be a great husband and father too. You can find a balance, like Daddy has.'

Andrea fiddled with her water glass, seemingly unconvinced, though Rosalie could understand that. Her father was an incredible man, and probably most men in his position – CEO of XM Music Group – wouldn't have the best of every world. They'd probably be divorced or cheating or doing neither of those things but underperforming at work.

'But, Andi, Tommy was so sweet at the Presley John concert,' Rosalie pressed. 'He kept asking about you.'

'He did?' Andrea asked.

'He did,' Rosalie and Hannah said in unison.

'Plus,' Rosalie said, 'correct me if I'm wrong here but hasn't it been, like, a reeeeally long time since you've been with a man?'

Andrea's eyes shot wide. Oh, she could be a prude. 'And, on that note, we need to settle the check and get back to the office.'

Once lunch had been called to an abrupt end, Rosalie decided to walk to Sanfia Records. Her job was now twofold. One, she had to learn everything she could about the indie music scene. Two, she was going to make it her mission to find out just how bad things were between Sofia and Jay and report back to her big sister. Rosalie wouldn't sit back and let Sofia suffer.

***

By the time she had reached Sanfia Records, Rosalie's feet were red and swollen, her skin was flushed and her hair had lost its bounce. Why on earth had she decided to walk?

Stepping inside the studio, she took a moment to compose herself, slipping her feet from her heels one at a time and wiggling her toes before replacing her feet in her shoes.

As she tangle-teased her long locks, she overheard who she thought was Jimmy, speaking with Sofia in the studio office along the corridor.

'What happened to your eye?' Jimmy snapped.

'We had an accident. Spilled milk,' Sofia told him. 'Really, Dad. The milk carton spilled. Jay and I both bent to clean it up at the same time and we... I don't know, clashed somehow. It looks worse because it's on the bone.'

Rosalie tiptoed closer to the office door. After a pause, Jimmy spoke softly.

'I want you to promise me one thing, Sofia. If there's ever something you feel like you can't get out of, you tell me. All right?'

'Dad, it's a milk injury, that's all,' she snapped.

'Life doesn't give us points for being a martyr, Sofia. Some things, some people, they can't be fixed.'

As Rosalie snuck a glance around the frame of the door, Sofia, who had her back to Rosalie, slammed her hand on her desk and turned to face Jimmy. 'I know what you're implying. I know what you think of Jay. Hell, I know what *everyone* thinks of Jay. But I married him, Dad. He's my husband. In sickness and in health. My family. What would I do…? What would it make me if I walk away when he needs me the most?'

'He's our family too, Sofia. Yours, mine and your sister's. Now, maybe we haven't been the strongest advocates of him in the past, but we don't want to see him out of his head. For your sake *and* his.'

Sofia nodded and appeared to swallow deeply.

'But, kiddo, this isn't a one-off. When people get sick, they get help. If he won't get help, he's not sick, he's a drain on my daughter.'

'He. Is. My. Husband.'

Jimmy scoffed. 'Sometimes, I blame myself for this sense of… pride or foolishness you have. Loyalty should be rewarded, not abused. You have a choice.'

'Like Mom did? Did she have a choice?'

'That was different. Your mom was stuck in a situation with two unfair options. You're not trapped, Sofia. You don't have to be.'

She sucked in a breath. 'Dad, could you please just *not*? The last thing I need right now is a lecture. I'm worn out from it all. I came here to get away and I've had some great news about Seth. Can we not focus on that?'

His stern face softened and his shoulders dropped from their rigid position. 'Let's talk about Seth. Are you calling him?'

'He's coming in shortly. I think I'd like to tell him in person. We're finishing the EP today.'

'Another chart hit, for sure,' Jimmy said, tugging Sofia into his side and dropping a kiss to her temple.

'Let's hope so.'

'You know, I hate to state the obvious here, but chart positions mean Nashville will come knocking.'

It was exactly as Andrea had said over lunch. Someone like Seth would be highly sought after; with chart hits, a famous brother, a military background to pull on the heart strings. The thought of him being snatched away from Sofia and Sanfia Records made Rosalie feel sad. Sofia didn't deserve that.

As Rosalie adjusted her weight on her sore feet, the floor creaked beneath her. She quickly knocked on the open door and smiled as Sofia, just as quickly, put on a pair of white trimmed sunglasses. Her hair was still part wet, as if she had let it dry naturally after washing. Her skin looked pale and her jeans, lumberjack shirt and boots looked less casual style and more downtrodden today.

'Knock, knock,' Rosalie almost sang.

'Ros, hi,' Sofia said, surprised.

'I know I'm here unannounced but—'

Before she could offer Sofia the gift she had brought, Billy, Frankie and Seth burst into the studio, all joking and chatting loudly, until they reached the office and Seth paused, his eyes narrowing as he took in Rosalie's presence.

'Hey,' he said to Sofia. 'Hey, Jimmy,' he said, shaking Jimmy's hand. He ignored Rosalie completely.

'Let's head into the sound booth, there's more space,' Sofia said, and the others led the way, leaving Rosalie limping along behind them, with her gifts in her shopping bag.

If there was one thing Rosalie hated more than fashion faux pas, it was being ignored.

Clearing her throat, loudly, she said, 'I brought some gifts. For you, Sofia, and one for you, Seth. To say, you know, well done for hitting the billboard charts and, I guess, as an apology for acting rashly at the Presley John concert.'

Setting her shopping bag down on the sofa where Frankie had flopped down, she took two wrapped photo frames and handed one each to Sofia and Seth.

As they unwrapped their gifts, she explained, 'A friend of mine was the official stage photographer at the concert and I just loved these. Sofia, you have Seth and the guys. And, Seth, the photographer got a great shot of you and Randy, hugging at the end of the performance. And don't worry, I told him that shouldn't go anywhere. That you don't want to, you know, play on the whole brother thing.'

She watched Seth as he considered the photograph, leaning back against the wall, unmoved and quiet. 'Well...? Do you like it?' She wasn't at all used to this level of delayed gratification.

Seth looked up to her as he set the picture aside and simply said, 'Thank you.'

Thank you? Not, *You didn't have to buy me a gift*. Or, actually, *Rosalie, I realise I was a complete asshole to you at the concert and I'm sorry*. Just, thank you.

Scowling, she told him, 'It's a shame you hadn't kept that style from the concert. You looked much more palatable with a facial hair trim, polished shoes and a jacket.'

It was childish but he made her say it.

Sofia chuckled, then said, 'I love it, Ros. I'll put it on the wall in the sound booth. Thanks, so much.'

'Yay! So, it's okay that I'm here?'

'Of course it's okay, Ros,' Sofia said, already replacing a

framed picture of The Beatles on the wall with the picture Rosalie had gifted to her.

Despite her pouting and planting her hands on her hips in waiting, Seth didn't confirm her presence was okay. What was his problem?

'Seth, perhaps you could hang yours in your apartment,' she quipped. 'I have no idea where you live. In fact, I dread to think. But I can tell that you need to seriously feng-shui, my friend. Your aura is needlessly prickly.'

At that, Jimmy, Frankie and Billy laughed, dragging a half-smile, which Rosalie could admit was quite a treat, from Seth.

14

HANNAH

Andrea had been stomping ahead of Hannah into the office after their lunch with Rosalie at Meadow Sweet. Her temperament was always volatile but it had been especially so in recent days. Was it that she missed Hunter? Was it that she walked out on Tommy after their night together and now Hannah was having to field his calls, wondering why the heck Andrea had left him? She didn't know. She would never know because when Andrea decided to shut down, she couldn't be prised open.

What she *did* know was that Andrea's hips were swinging with prime-time swagger as her stilettos pounded the sidewalk as best as their skinny heels could.

Hannah had learned that silence was best in these situations. Until the volcano finally erupted, Hannah had no way of telling whether that hot lava was coming after her in a friend capacity or in her capacity as an executive PA.

They reached the revolving entrance doors to XM Music Group's office block. Andrea paused, then sighed, then spun those doors so fast that Hannah decided it would be safer to let her complete the revolution alone.

And she did complete the revolution. After a full three-sixty walk through the revolving doors, Andrea was back on the sidewalk, facing Hannah, on the verge of eruption.

'Isn't it enough that everyone in this place thinks I slept my way to the top?' she ground out through her teeth. 'Now, everyone will be saying, *There goes Andrea, CEO of Stellar label, who slept with the boss and screwed her clients to keep them.*'

The way her arms flailed as she spoke and her cheeks flushed red made the situation almost comical.

'Is that why you encouraged me to go to Tommy's? Huh? So you could tell everyone? Gossip to whoever will listen?'

Hannah felt like shaking Andrea's shoulders hard, both in anger and to stop the hysteria. She raised her arm and forced her fingers to point instead.

'*You* decided to go to Tommy because you were mourning the loss of dirty grandpa from your panties. *You* decided to fuck Tommy. Yes, I thought seeing Tommy was a better idea than pining after that douchebag, Hunter. He's a significant improvement from screwing your friend's dad.

'You like Tommy, whether you can admit it to yourself or not. And he likes you. Hence him calling my desk every second to find out why you're not taking his calls and why you walked out on him, *again*. Which, by the way, is a question only *you* can answer because, despite the fact you *do* like Tommy and you've gone back there a thousand times in the past, *you* left *him*, again.'

'That's none of your business, Hannah, and it's certainly not your story to go gossiping to Rosalie about.'

Hannah raised her hand to say *stop*. 'I'm not finished.'

Andrea straightened, dropping her hands on her hips and pulling her lips into a pout. But she didn't move from her spot on the sidewalk.

'You sleep with someone like Hunter for six months and walk

out on someone like Tommy, who you get along with. You're terrified of being with anyone who might stick. You're afraid to be committed to anyone.'

'I have been committed to people all my life,' Andrea snapped back.

'You lost your mom. You took care of your dad when he needed help. You brought up Sofia as if she was your responsibility. You have never committed by choice and you're terrified of doing so.'

Andrea lowered her voice, glancing at passers-by on the street, whose attention had been drawn by the showdown. 'You're the prime example of how that statement is bullshit, *Professor* Hannah. I've never walked away from you. Or maybe that's because I feel a sense of responsibility to you too, huh? With a million mouths to feed and a lazy, selfish husband to take care of. Well, let me tell you something, Hannah, I've had enough. I've had enough of playing friend instead of boss when you take endless days off for sick kids. When you leave early because Rod got a new job and didn't have the decency to discuss it with you first.'

Hannah saw the proverbial red mist. 'Do. Not. Talk. About. My. Family.'

'Yeah, it's shitty when someone spreads crap you don't want to hear, isn't it?'

Hannah squared up to Andrea. 'I told our friend – one of your best friends – that you slept with Tommy. I wasn't gossiping, I was putting her as far off the scent of you fucking her dad that she could get. That's the joke, Andi, I was protecting you. And why? So that you could badmouth me and my family? I've stood by you for years and you're currently throwing it back in my face because I've called you on your shit. You're terrified of getting hurt. Well, aren't we all, Andi?'

Andrea's shoulders heaved and Hannah almost felt bad. She knew Andrea's insecurities and had just exposed them in the street. But not unprompted.

'You need to decide whether you're my friend or my assistant and realise that there's a line you can't blur.'

Hannah scoffed. 'We've blurred the line for years. I'm *always* looking out for you, Andi, no matter how bad your mood or what stupid things you decide to do.'

'No, Hannah, I'm always looking out for you. Any other boss would have kicked you out on your ass already, not brought you over from Sanfia Records and kept giving you pay rises to help with the ever-growing family.'

What stung Hannah, what made her feel like someone was driving a stake through her heart, wasn't the words being thrown at her but the person saying them. She looked through the revolving door to the office. She did need her job. She needed the salary and the stability, now more than ever. But she could find these things closer to home, where her commute would be negligible.

She stayed with Andrea because she was her best friend. Because Andrea needed Hannah more than she would ever admit. Because working with Andrea had always made her feel like she was just a city gal, free as a bird. Her own person, not a mom or a wife.

Today, though, Hannah wanted to tell her so-called friend where to shove her job and her apparent pity vote. She had always defended Andrea. She knew Andrea behaved the way she had because she'd had a tough life in many respects. But times change. And since coming over to Stellar and getting her promotion to CEO, working with Andrea had changed.

She moved her focus to Andrea, who was looking back at her. *Say sorry,* she willed. *Apologise to me for being a dick.*

But Andrea stood defiantly, her hands in her pockets. *Of course she won't apologise.*

'I'm going home,' Hannah said.

'We've got work to do,' Andrea told her, not an ounce of compassion or remorse in her tone. Just cold, bitter Andrea. Shut down and in protection mode.

Hannah shook her head as she walked past her friend.

'Are you coming back?' Andrea asked, a hint of feeling breaking her steely demeanour.

Hannah let the words reach her back and decided not to respond. She had had enough. Enough of Andrea's shitty attitude. Enough of her digs about Hannah's family, as if Andrea's life, with her spacious, empty apartment and nothing but work and men she fucked, was better than Hannah's children and husband.

She walked without purpose, not knowing if she would go back, until she reached the river. Then she walked alongside the Hudson, dipping away and coming back as the sidewalk wound around buildings and through parks. She walked until the low heels of her ankle boots made the balls of her feet ache.

Coming to sit on a bench, she looked out in the direction of Manhattan. There had been a time – a long time ago – when Hannah thought she could be anything she dreamed of. She had been one of the most attractive girls in school, when she was a teen. Back then, the thought of being a model or a movie star, or that the mess-around sessions in Andrea's dad's studio recording herself, Andrea and Sofia singing along to Destiny's Child tracks would lead to fame and fortune, had seemed possible.

Then responsibility after responsibility started to pile up and dreams were replaced by a need to keep a job, to make money and to try to keep a semblance of independence.

She was tired. So incredibly tired. From nappies to gym class uniform, to back-chatting. From a husband who felt like he didn't need to run life decisions by her and whose sleep deprivation seemed to trump hers. From the fact that no other person in her house would leave the toilet seat the *eff* down.

Work was as much her escape as it was a necessity. Work meant she commuted into New York each day in smart clothes – though admittedly occasionally covered in puke – with her hair done and a little make-up to make her look human. It meant she sat on a train with people around her who didn't know how many kids she had or that her dreams of college graduation and whatever else had been dashed by a youthful pregnancy. That she earned halfway decent money and had adult conversations with people, where her opinion mattered.

But recently, her opinion hadn't mattered. The level playing field that had always existed between her and Andrea, despite any hierarchy in employment, had tipped against her.

Was it that Andrea was unhappy and taking it out on Hannah? Or had things changed between them? Was Hannah actually below par at work? Was Andrea doing her a favour by keeping her on?

Andrea had always needed Hannah. They both knew that, despite the fact it had never been said. Andrea had demons that most people couldn't see. Hannah recognised them and kept her friend's head above water when they started to creep in. But she had failed recently.

The Andrea Hannah knew could be promiscuous, but she would not have had a six-month long affair with a married man, let alone the father of one of her best friends. She wouldn't have yelled at Hannah in the street and badmouthed her family.

Sure, they had had fights before, but lately it felt like their crossed words were chipping away at years of friendship. They were losing touch with each other. Keeping secrets.

Hannah missed their days at Sanfia Records, when Andrea was producing and happy. When she asked Hannah for her opinion on music and the management of artists. When Sofia was carefree and didn't have Jay anchoring her. When Rosalie would pop into the studio to show them her latest pair of shoes and flirt with the artists.

Times changed. What mattered now was that she had four mouths to feed at home. That Rod was excited about his new coaching job in Queens and she wanted him to be happy and to feel satisfied. He too had had dreams, bigger dreams than hers, and they had been shattered, not by children but a broken back. He could never change that, no matter how old and independent the kids got. Those boys and Rod were her life and they were what mattered, not an argument with Andrea over her sex life.

Hannah stood from the bench with renewed purpose and headed back to the office.

* * *

Hannah and Andrea had passed the remainder of the week in the office with stoic silence, neither one of them speaking to the other, communicating through blunt email exchanges. Hannah was now standing in packed Penn Station staring at indeterminate train delays, thanks to a jumper.

'People are so selfish,' one commuter said.

'Couldn't they have jumped from a bridge or a building or something?' another said.

'All I want is to get home on a Friday night with my bottle of wine,' said another.

Whoever said humanity was dead?

Though, despite having a little more compassion, Hannah

couldn't disagree with the inconvenience they had all been caused.

It was the first week of Rod's new job in Queens. She was frantically trying to get hold of him, wondering where he was and when he would make it home for the kids, since the sitter got off at 5.30 p.m. She wasn't worried about Luke, or even so much about Jackson – they were old enough to fend for themselves for a few hours – but TJ was not.

Rod finished work earlier than Hannah, but he also had to pass through Penn Station and she had no idea if he had already made it through.

She tried calling his cell again. No answer. She called home. No answer. She called the sitter. No answer.

'Doesn't anyone answer their goddamn phones?' she shouted into the station, her voice lost in a mass of noise.

As if the big man upstairs had heard her taking his name in vain and wondered what the heck was up, her cell phone rang.

'Rod! Where *are* you?'

'Babe? You there? Han?'

'Rod? Can you hear me?'

'Hold up, one sec.'

'Rod?'

'Yeah, yeah. I can hear you, babe. Whatssup?'

'I'm stuck at Penn Station. Are you with the kids?'

'No, babe. My first week, the guys wanted to take me out for a drink, you know, welcome me to the team.'

'That's great, Rod, but the sitter finishes in...' She checked the digital clock on the train departure board. 'The sitter finished twenty minutes ago.'

'No, babe, I got her to stay until six.'

'I hate to state the obvious here, Rod, but neither of us will be home by six.' At that moment, God was definitely looking in on her because the departure board refreshed and gave her four minutes to get to the platform for her train home. 'Rod, I've got to go, the train is coming.'

She ran toward the designated platform, pushing and shoving other commuters, feeling like Kevin McCallister's mom in *Home Alone,* eventually making it onto her train in time.

Squished like a sardine in a can, she managed to dial the sitter and bring her phone to her ear. After a broken conversation, the sitter, Hannah thought, agreed to stay until 6.40 p.m., at which time she absolutely *had* to leave.

Hannah watched the minutes tick by on her cell phone, working out with each passing second how long her kids might be left unattended between the sitter leaving and her arriving. *How much harm can come to them in five or ten minutes?* A teenager, an eleven-year-old and a baby... *Oh, hell.*

She had visions of TJ choking to death as his brothers played computer games. Or worse, lying in a heap at the bottom of the staircase, where they had fought on the landing and tumbled to their deaths.

When the train pulled in, Hannah ran from the station, hardly breaking stride – despite her heels, despite the fact she had not run the distance since track in high school – until she arrived home.

She burst through the front door to the house. 'Kids?' she managed, panting.

Music was blaring upstairs – some godawful rap; the teenager's latest fad. That she couldn't hear any child was disconcerting enough to make her energy-drained legs carry her up the staircase.

She followed the rhythmic expletives to Luke's bedroom, where he was lying on his bed, playing computer games.

She picked up his headset and plugged it into his stereo,

stopping the racket. 'Is everything okay? Where's TJ? Where's Jackson?'

'They're fine. They're making potions or something in the bathroom.' He snatched the headphones from her, pulled them over his ears and continued playing the game he hadn't paused.

Without the sound of rap music blazing in her ears, Hannah could hear TJ's childish giggle coming from the bathroom. *He's alive, at least,* she thought.

'Splash!' she heard Jackson say. 'Splash!' This time louder.

She opened the bathroom door to find Jackson holding her only bottle of perfume in his hand, about to drop it into the loo.

'What are you doing?' she yelled, grabbing the bottle from him. She next saw TJ lying on his back on the bathroom rug, giggling as he held his foot to his mouth.

Scooping up the baby and doing a quick check for any major injuries, she turned back to Jackson. 'What are you doing?'

'Playing splash. TJ likes it. He thinks it's funny.'

His pants were soaked through and he was shirtless. *What the...?*

Then, she peered into the loo and all became clear as she saw her toothbrush, a tube of toothpaste, a razor and a bar of soap in the bottom of the pot.

'I bet your smelly bottle would have made the biggest splash,' Jackson said.

Closing her eyes, she inhaled deeply. 'You're eleven years old, Jackson, not five. Go change your pants,' she said. Because what was the point in labouring the point to her child who already knew better that he was a little shit for putting all those things down the loo, which she would have to fish out before she could take a pee? Surely his retort would be something like, *You abandoned your kids, what did you expect?*

She closed the bathroom door, then put down the toilet seat and held TJ to her chest as she slumped down on top of it.

She was failing as a mom. She did nothing but snap at her husband. Her best friend currently wasn't speaking to her. And she was so exhausted, she couldn't tell her own ass from her elbow.

Either she needed to quit working in the city, which she didn't want to do, or they needed to move home, which they couldn't afford to do.

'Or I need to sell you kids to the highest bidder,' she said, stroking TJ's wiry black hair and kissing his temple, knowing there was no way on earth she would ever sell her boys... Unless... No, she couldn't give up the babies.

She sighed. 'But something does need to change, little man. Mommy can't continue like this.'

15

ANDREA

Reading contracts on the train was knocking her sick. Or had she been feeling sick before getting on the train, when the smell of coffee in the station had made her stomach turn? For sure, the motion of the train speeding along the tracks now was making her feel worse.

Andrea tucked the documents into her bag and opted instead to look out of the window at the sun bouncing off the multitude of buildings as she crossed from New York City into New Jersey.

It had been a good while since she'd ventured to New Jersey, her dad's hometown. Hannah still lived a few blocks away. Still as close as when Andrea and Hannah had walked Sofia to school. That was how it was when they were kids. Hannah was always with Andrea, even on days when they'd fallen out over something and nothing, and Andrea was always watching out for Sofia.

Some things don't change, she thought. The sun was beating down on her skin through the train windows, too powerful for the air-conditioning onboard. Though she was wearing thin jeans and a loose-fitting T-shirt, she was feeling the heat. She slipped the wide neck of her top off one shoulder and sipped the cool ginger ale she had picked up in the station.

The relative quiet of New Jersey struck her as soon as she waved off the train. Putting her sunglasses in position, she headed for the place she used to call home. For a moment, it occurred to her that she could drop in on Hannah whilst she was here, but given they hadn't been getting along well of late, adding a sixth day of seeing each other in a week was probably a bad idea.

In fact, Andrea and Hannah hadn't been getting along particularly well since Hannah came back to Stellar from maternity leave. Some of that, she suspected, was due to Hannah's tiredness and being strapped for cash. And the problem with having your best friend working for you was that you still needed them to do their job, regardless of whether TJ had colic, Jackson had a sickness bug, Luke was taking teenager hormone-related tantrums and Rod was sporting his usual selfish persona.

But that wasn't all of it. Though blaming Hannah for their fallouts would be easy – and her big mouth was certainly to blame for the most recent argument – Andrea knew that some of it was down to her own guilt. Her affair with Hunter had started when Hannah was heavily pregnant and preoccupied. Maybe if Hannah had been around and not on maternity leave, it would never have happened or gone on for as long as it had. Once she was caught up in it, Hunter became like a drug to Andrea. A symbol of her defiance for once.

Hannah's return to the office and finding out about the affair made the shame of what she was doing real. She knew that Hannah hadn't forced her into having an affair but she couldn't help feeling like her friend could have stopped it in the first place.

Maybe Hannah was right. Maybe Andrea had slept with

Hunter because there was no chance of it ever going anywhere. Or perhaps... Andrea had been lonely without Hannah around, with Sofia more concerned with Jay and Sanfia these days.

But she didn't need people. People needed her. Andrea wasn't dependent on anyone. She never would be – she remembered how much it hurt as an eight-year-old girl to lose the one person she'd truly depended on. It hurt too much.

Before she knew it, Andrea had battled with her thoughts all the way to the porch of her father's home. She knocked but entered without waiting for a response.

'Dad?' she called, moving inside the dated terrace. 'Jimmy?'

By habit, she flicked through the mail she'd picked up from the floor to make sure there was nothing he wasn't on top of. She ran her finger along the stair rail, checking for dust as she kicked off her sandshoes and headed along the hallway toward the kitchen, dipping her head into the lounge – no sign of Jimmy – and the dining room – no sign of Jimmy.

The kitchen was in worse shape. The countertops were cluttered with things that hadn't been put away – a loaf of bread, a chopping board and knife, a block of cheese. Dishes were scattered around the sink, unwashed.

Instinctively, she started to run the hot tap and fill the sink with soapy water. Admittedly, she'd seen the place in a shoddier state than this. The superficial mess aside, the place seemed clean enough and the walls looked like they had enjoyed a refresh of pale yellow paint.

The toilet chain flushed upstairs, then Jimmy appeared in his usual attire – stonewash jeans and a lumberjack-style shirt.

'You don't have to clean those,' he said, putting away the food items from the side. 'I thought we could have coffee in the yard, since the weather's good for it.'

Coffee. Just the mention of it made that sickly feeling come back. 'I'm off coffee but I'll take tea.'

Jimmy set about making tea as Andrea finished up the dishes and they settled into the small yard, sitting around an old rickety table and chairs.

'New parasol?' Andrea asked, noting the replacement for the rusty green and white striped version that had adorned the table for the last decade.

'The old one wouldn't open so it left me no choice.'

Andrea smiled behind her cup of tea. Jimmy hated parting with things. He was a stickler for habits, just like Sofia. Which, incidentally, was the reason she had made the trip out to her dad.

'So, you're working back at the studio,' Andrea said, moving directly to the point of her visit.

'I'm helping out, yeah. It's not like I had much of a choice,' Jimmy said.

Andrea scoffed. 'Great, let's start with a dig about me moving to XM Music Group, huh?' Would he ever let it drop?

Jimmy scratched his head and visibly lowered his shoulders from around his ears, making Andrea realise that she, too, had been uptight. 'Let's not fight, Andi.'

'Then let's not make smart remarks at each other, Dad.'

'Deal. It was a shot and I apologise for it.'

Andrea nodded her acceptance. 'So Jay is what, drinking, taking drugs, both?'

'I think both. You know what Sofia's like, she won't badmouth him. I take what she says, add a multiplier and think I'll come close to the truth. What I do know is that they're in a bad way. Jay is definitely back to drinking and god knows what else.'

'And the bruise on her eye?'

Jimmy shrugged. 'She said it was an accident, cleaning up milk or suchlike.'

'Do you believe her?'

Jimmy sipped his coffee and squinted as he raised his face to the direction of the sun. 'Whether I do or don't, I could believe that he'd hurt her. He's a piece of work, whether he's drinking or not. The way he speaks to my girl...'

And it came to her, tumbling like black thunder clouds rolling down a hill, her being a little girl stuck at the bottom, waiting to be hit. *Guilt.*

Sofia was her little sister. The one person she was supposed to protect, and she'd walked out on her and Sanfia Records to go to XM Music Group. It had been as much about giving Jay and Sofia a shot at making things work between them as an advancement of Andrea's career, but had she done the right thing? Was a chance to work what Sofia had really needed, or had she needed to see that Jay was a manipulative leech, whether he was on a bender or not?

'I tried to tell her a thousand times, Dad. He was bad news when she first met him and I told her that. I told her before she got married but she thought I was... jealous.' She scoffed. 'Sofia wants the fairy tale – the career, the husband, kids. If Jay is her fairy tale, it's her choice. She's stubborn as an ox.'

No, she couldn't keep feeling guilty about her move. If she had her way, Andrea would still be producing, even if that meant for less money. The reality was, Sofia wanted to fend for herself. She wanted to build a life with Jay, start a family. And Andrea and Jay just couldn't get along. She'd left Sanfia Records to give them a chance at being happy and to salvage her relationship with her sister. Not that anyone else, Jimmy included, saw the move in that way.

'Yeah, well, she married him and *she's* loyal to the bone,' Jimmy said.

She's loyal. 'God, you're incredible. You see nothing but her, do you? She did marry him, Dad, and she *is* loyal.' Andrea stood, anger making her legs lively. 'But, you know, maybe she's loyal to a drunk because she never had to see what living with one is like. How... how soul-destroying it is to see your own father stumbling home, fumbling with his keys in the lock, bouncing off walls, bringing women home to screw them in the lounge. Maybe she doesn't know because she was kept locked in her bedroom, in a crib or wrapped in a duvet, with the sound of her mom's music playing her to sleep through the stereo.

'I've done everything my whole life for her and for you, yet you throw the one thing in my face that you don't like. Yes, I left Sanfia. Yes, I've left my sister with a drunk. But *he* was an asshole with or without the drink and *she* wants to be there. She chose that life.'

Feeling her eyes sting, Andrea walked to the bottom of the yard, where she instantly felt shitty about calling out her dad on those years after their mom died. He'd got sober, for them, that was what she had to remember. In his shoes, if she'd lost the love of her life, how would she have reacted? She didn't know and she would never let herself be in that position to find out.

She sensed Jimmy come up behind her.

'I'm sorry,' he said.

She took a breath. 'Me too.'

Both facing each other, they said more in the look they shared than either of them could say in words. He was her father. He had done his best in a shitty situation.

'I don't know how to help her if she won't leave him, Dad.'

'Nor do I. Thing is, the sicker he gets, the more Sofia will feel an obligation to stay with him.'

Andrea thought about that statement and the truth of it. Their mom had died slowly, with Jimmy by her side, caring for her. Those were the things Sofia committed to her memory, not the long months that followed the funeral, or the turbulent years that followed their move north.

'We have to help him,' Jimmy said. 'We'll help get him clean.'

Reluctantly, Andrea agreed. 'But if he's clean again, she'll stay. He'll continue battering down her confidence, changing her and trying to make her change the business. It'll be like rinse and repeat.' What Sofia needed was a real out. A real split. A clean break.

'I got clean and stayed clean,' Jimmy said.

'You had two girls at home and you were never a shitty person to begin with, Dad. You just... had it tough for a while.'

'I really am sorry for everything I put onto you, Andi.'

She wanted to say that it was fine, but the words wouldn't come. 'Why don't you talk to Jay? Man-to-man, from someone who...'

'Has walked a mile in those shoes? It's okay, it's true. You're right and I'll try it. I don't think he's in a frame of mind to listen, but I'll try it.'

'Sofia could do with a break from him. Maybe she could see what life would be like otherwise. Maybe that's a good thing, maybe not, but it would give her some perspective either way. I know of some clinics that aren't crazy expensive. If you can get him to agree, and I doubt whether you can, I'll look into it. If insurance doesn't cover it...'

Jimmy held up a hand to stop her. 'If insurance doesn't cover it, I'll find a way.'

Though she had every intention of revisiting that conversation if, or when, the time came, for now, she understood that Jimmy needed to wear the situation himself.

* * *

By the time she sat back down on the train to return to the city, Andrea felt drained. They had a plan now. Stage one was up to Jimmy. If anyone could reason with an alcoholic, it was a recovering alcoholic. Stage two was on her and if she had a chance of making it work, it was when Jay was in recovery. For now, she would keep it to herself. Ultimately, she could free Sofia once and for all. With near certainty, she would cause a rift between her and her sister that might never be resolved.

She leaned her head back against the seat and closed her eyes, just for a moment, and she saw her mom. Her long brown waves of hair. Her fiercely green eyes. The hippie dresses and cowboy boots she used to wear. The way she would sing Andrea to sleep, stroking her temple. The memory was like a blanket wrapping around her, warming her, comforting her, making her feel as if she wasn't alone.

'The next stop will be Penn Station,' the driver announced over the tannoy, interrupting her thoughts.

She was back on a dirty train, alone. On the fringe of making a rift between her and her sister even bigger, having dredged up the past with her father, she and her best friend in the world barely tolerating each other, having slept with her other friend's dad for six months. For so long, she had tried to be all the things to all the people who needed her, and now that she'd managed to shatter every relationship that mattered, she found herself wondering...

* * *

'What's the point? If I'm not the mother-cum-big-sister. If I'm not the best friend who pays over the odds for a PA to help her out. If I'm not the friend who *isn't* romping with your father and tries to rationalise your crazy thoughts. If I'm not the daughter who just sucks it up and I'm no longer the award-winning producer because I'm sitting behind a desk looking over financial statements. Then who the hell am I?'

Tommy's lips turned up as he popped the ring on a club soda and set the can down on the countertop in front of Andrea, where she was sitting perched on a stool, with Rocky 'the rock star' at her feet.

'What are you smiling at?' she asked.

'The fact you're a hot mess,' he said, his voice decorated in good humour and somehow enough to make Andrea smile too.

'Gee, thanks. Aren't I glad I turned up at your door? The sympathetic ear.'

Tommy took up a stool on the opposite side of his kitchen island. His hair was dishevelled, he was dressed in a plain black T-shirt and ripped jeans, and he had nothing on his feet. He looked perfectly normal and perfectly edible.

'I am,' he said. 'It's nice to know that other people get lost sometimes, selfishly. How d'you think I got here, taking some time off the road, going back to grass roots and pouring it all out into lyrics? Sometimes, being all things to all people is exhausting. It's too easy to forget who we really are.'

Andrea turned her can on the worktop. 'You know what terrifies me more than any of it?'

'That without being all those things, you don't actually know who you really are?'

She shifted her attention from the can to Tommy, wondering whether he'd spoken those words or if she had. She watched his pupils slowly dilate and her gaze dropped to his lips, the lips that kissed her so well.

'So, you really don't drink in daylight hours,' she said, distracting herself from the urge to cross the island between them and fall into his arms, get lost in him, lose herself and her mind, the way he could make her do.

'No. Not any more.' He stood up and busied himself opening cupboards and the refrigerator. Suddenly, Andrea wondered what on earth she'd been thinking coming here. Why had she called him from the train station after three weeks of avoiding his calls?

She stood. 'I'm sorry, Tommy, I shouldn't have come here like this. You don't want to listen to me whine about my life. I'm not even one to moan, usually. I don't know why I—'

'Would you just sit your ass down and stop fretting about everything?' He stared at her until she took her seat back on the stool. 'I think I've got everything to make a club sandwich. Are you in?'

'Yeah, I'm in,' she said, her mouth shaping into amusement as he turned his back to her and started pressing random buttons on the oven. 'Need any help there, sparky?'

'It's an oven. How hard can it be?' He continued to press buttons, turning lights on and off.

Andrea moved to his side and turned on the grill. 'I assume it's for chicken?'

His eyes narrowed and he rolled his chiselled jaw. 'Smart ass.'

They made two impeccable club sandwiches, side-by-side, then ate them at the kitchen worktop, talking about where in the world had the craziest fans – Japan – and which was Tommy's best-ever gig – the Super Bowl. They talked about NFL and Tom Brady versus Patrick Mahomes. About the Yankees and the last ball game they'd been to. They talked about everything and nothing of consequence and it was the best time Andrea had had in a while. No burdens. No arguments. No pressures.

After lunch, they went to Tommy's music room – a spare

bedroom he had sound-proofed – that played host to no less than seven guitars on stands and a baby grand piano.

She noticed sheets of paper strewn across a side table, scribbled with words and a pen sitting on top of them. 'Are you in the middle of something?' she asked.

'I was when you booty-called me earlier.' He picked up a six-string acoustic and sat on a music stool. 'It's called, The Only Woman Who Ever Walks Out On Me. Repeatedly.'

Andrea covered her mouth to stifle her chuckle but when he winked, she couldn't hide her laugh. 'I did not booty-call you.'

'But you do leave me after you use my body for sex. Every time.'

She straddled the piano seat, facing him. 'A girl's gotta keep a guy on his toes.'

'You certainly do that when I'm running after you.'

'Why are you doing that?'

He started to strum. Andrea watched his fingers move over a D7 chord, a G, then A minor. A classic combination.

'Why am I running after you?' He shrugged and chuckled then sobered quickly. 'Because having women fall at your feet, waiting for you to invite them to speak and when they do speak, having nothing to say except nonsense about how they can't believe they're screwing Tommy Dawson, gets old.' He started to finger-pick a tune. 'I say that knowing how arrogant it sounds.'

'At least you know. That makes it semi-redeemable. I think referring to yourself in the third person was a real low point.'

'Well...' He slipped back to a four-beat strum. 'I also, backhandedly, called you interesting and smart.'

He started to sing...

> 'Let 'em talk 'bout what they think they see
> Let 'em talk 'bout how they see us be

> 'Cause baby, we got nothin' to prove
> The world is yours and mine, you and me
> We earned our scars and put in our time
> Let 'em show, for everyone to see
> Babe, I'm gonna love you anyway'

Then, as he continued to play, Andrea picked up a guitar and, following his sequence, picking up his rhythm, she played in harmony as he continued to sing.

'You should key change there,' she said, 'right after the second verse. Play it out and let the story sink in. Try this.' She strummed a key-changing chord progression.

'Yeah, yeah,' Tommy said, picking up again, improvising with a hum in place of lyrics. 'I like it.'

They played and sang and wrote, lost in a bubble, where no one could reach them. All the while, Rocky the dog lay on the floor, listening. Andrea fell in love, with the idea of a home, with a dog, and a husband who didn't want to take from her, who wanted to be a team. With the idea of making music for the rest of her life with a man she respected and admired.

And when she realised that, she hung her guitar back in its stand. Because things didn't last. People didn't stay. Love didn't last. When it died, it hurt. It hurt so fucking much.

'I should go.' She pushed her hands into her pockets, suddenly not sure what to do with them. 'I'll see myself out. Thanks, ah, for today. I, ah, bye. Bye, Rocky.'

She broke free of the music room and almost ran for the door of the apartment, stopping to pull on her shoes.

'What are you so afraid of?' Tommy's voice was calm and controlled and too close behind her.

She turned to him. 'Who said I was afraid?'

'You did. Every time you leave. Every time you catch yourself smiling and force yourself to stop.'

'Yeah, well, I'm not afraid. The fact is, Tommy, we... we have great sex but that's... that's all it is.' She looked to her toes, feeling vulnerable, fragile. She hated it. 'Look, you're... you. And I'm... me.'

He stepped towards her, bringing a hand to her cheek. She felt the nubs of his fingers, warm from guitar strings. She felt the heat of his palm against her cheek.

Why had she come here? What had she been thinking when she made that call? Why was it that he was the one person she seemed to be able to be herself with, or at least have a shot at working out who herself really was?

She felt his lips press against her closed eyelids and her body melting into his hold. 'Stay,' he whispered. 'Stay now and wake up here tomorrow.'

His lips met hers – slowly, tentatively. 'Stay,' he said again.

'I can't.'

He kissed her again, kissing away her conviction. 'Stay.'

'I can't.'

But his next kiss took away her fears.

She opened her eyes to find his bright blue irises full of strength, hope, heat. She took his lip between her teeth and tugged, then his hands were in her hair, gripping as he devoured her mouth with his, holding on as if he'd never let go.

Every reason she had not to be there, in that moment, in his arms, disappeared. All she wanted was to feel his skin against hers, for him to fill her, consume her.

She wanted more of this. She wanted more of him. Her heart swelled in her chest as the rest of her felt simultaneously satisfied and longing. He kissed her briskly, then took a breath and kissed her again. And again. Until her arms were wrapped around his neck and he was carrying her to his bedroom.

* * *

She woke in the middle of the night. Tommy's bedroom was tinged blue by the low floor lighting outside the room, seeping through the gap under the door. From under Tommy's hold, she reached out and found his cell phone on the side table. It was 03.18. She should go.

Then a long, strong arm snaked around her, took the cell phone from her and set it back on the side table.

'Don't you dare,' he said, burying his head in her neck and pressing her tightly to him, where she felt his equipment, semi-hard against her rear.

She turned to face him and ran her fingers through the hair at his temple. What if she stayed? What then?

She didn't have time to answer her own questions before he rolled her onto her back, taking his weight on his forearms as he kissed her.

One way or another, he was making her stay.

16

ROSALIE

'Here she is, finally,' said Clarissa as she stood from her seat at a table in Astor Court.

Rosalie didn't miss the way Clarissa smiled in her direction, then rolled her eyes in the direction of the other two women now standing at the round table.

Clarissa, Madeleine, Kaitlin and Rosalie had been frequenting the St Regis dining room for years, always enjoying brunch in the luxury of high painted ceilings, fine tapestry and impeccable service.

The hotel had become something of a staple institution in their years of friendship. Kaitlin had stayed in the presidential suite the night before her first – no, second – wedding. Madeleine had been conceived on the balcony of one of the suites – something her mother was happy to discuss publicly, given Madeleine's father was merely the first of a string of husbands. Clarissa had spent months at the hotel playing mistress to a Russian oligarch who introduced her to bondage – a passing fad that secured her own adult wealth when she threatened to disclose his many indiscretions to the world and landed herself a seven-figure confidentiality arrangement.

And Rosalie? Yes, it was true, she knew the interiors of the finest rooms at the hotel. She had been introduced to flings and boyfriends in the King Cole bar over a glass or two of champagne. She had even woken up to find one of everything from the breakfast menu had been ordered for her after a night of lovemaking, though her date had already left the building.

But the truth was, those days were behind Rosalie now. She was in her thirties and wanted to move on to the next phase of her life. No more one-night stands with insanely wealthy men, when their wealth was her sole motivation. No more status flings with musicians that were sure to make the gossip rags. No more meaningless relationships. No more being dumped because she wasn't responsible enough, apparently.

She wanted and needed more in her life. The way Andrea had an amazing, all-consuming career, Hannah had a beautiful family.

Rosalie was going to become a mommy, with responsibility for something bigger than shopping and casual relationships. She was going to have a little human to love and be loved by, whom she could mould into a fine young lady or a handsome young man. She would impart her wisdom on them. People would say things like, 'Ros is such a good mom' and, 'That child is a credit to Rosalie.' Her friends and parents would be proud of her because she'd achieved something incredible. She would have someone to share all the love inside her that could be spared. Someone to fill her lonely days, be there to talk to always, to fill her empty apartment with noise and unconditional love. She was going to run a record label and demand respect.

The eye-rolling and gossiping were beneath her now.

The maître d'hôtel took Rosalie's short crepe jacket and showed her to the table, where she was air-kissed European style by Clarissa, whose voluminous yet sleek blonde locks engulfed Rosalie.

'What is that scent, Clarissa? You smell divine,' Rosalie said.

Clarissa flicked her hair back across her shoulder, displaying this season's Chanel pearls around her neck as she retook her seat and said, 'The latest treat from my beau.'

Madeleine stepped forward to Rosalie, performing the perfunctory greeting ritual and whispered, 'Another Russian. Probably staying in Trump Tower for free.'

Rosalie couldn't help but smirk. 'It's lovely to see you, Maddie,' she said, taking a step back to admire her friend's tailored pink dress with cream neckline and matching cream gloves à la Audrey Hepburn. 'This dress...' was all Rosalie could manage because Madeleine did not look like Audrey Hepburn in a garden of blossom trees; she looked like a giant marshmallow that was wearing gloves when it was expected to reach eighty-four degrees out.

It didn't matter because Madeleine finished the rest of the sentence in her own mind, gushing with pride. 'Oh, Rosalie, thank you. You always do know the right things to say.'

For a woman whose education must have cost her parents a small fortune, Madeleine really was just a little bit dumb.

Kaitlin's greeting came next – the red widow. Kaitlin had lost two husbands before she'd reached her thirtieth birthday. One went to a stroke and the other to a freak helicopter incident – both of whom left her a healthy proportion of their estates, pissing off their children who, in both instances, were older than Kaitlin. As far as Rosalie was aware, the third husband was still alive and kicking – for now.

Rosalie was the only one of the four women taking a seat and being tucked under the table by waitstaff in unison who had never been married. This was something the others liked to gloat about. Occasionally – like, every time she left these girls and felt strangely deflated, down on herself even, without truly knowing why – Rosalie would wonder if there was something wrong with her. She knew she wasn't ugly and she kept herself in decent shape. She enjoyed the finer things in life and dressed the part. So why had no man ever stuck around long enough to propose to her? Amongst these women, she felt like a failure in the romance department. In fact, *all* of her friends, with the exception of Andrea, had been married, and the lucky ones, like Hannah, were still happily married.

Without needing to be asked, a waiter brought a round of the hotel's famous Bloody Marys from the King Cole bar and set them down around the table. No brunch at the Regis was complete without a Bloody Mary.

Rosalie sipped her drink, resigned to having just the one because she wanted to have a clear head for her meeting later with Lance.

'Your problem is,' Clarissa had once told Rosalie, 'you expect too much from them. The kind of men we need don't want a friend or an equal, Rosalie, they want control. That's what we have to give them. In return, we get to live the lives we want and when they leave, they give us a big fat cheque for letting them indulge in their egocentric ways.'

Rosalie remembered this as she looked around the tables of wealthy people and thought that her friends were the elite of high-class hookers.

'Ladies, raise your Bloody Marys because we are celebrating,' Kaitlin said.

Rosalie raised her glass, thinking about her last lunch with Hannah and Andrea in Brooklyn and how they had celebrated new relationships, new jobs and Billboard successes.

Then Kaitlin said, 'Maddie has *finally* gotten rid of those ashy tones.' She turned to Madeleine, gently touching her refreshed blonde waves. 'I'm so happy for you, sweetie. It's been such a torrid three months for you.'

Rosalie watched as Maddie pursed her lips and leaned her head to one side. 'Aww, Katy-bear, you're the sweetest. It has been awful and I'm so happy to finally feel like myself again.'

Sipping her drink, Rosalie wondered what on earth she was doing here. Her life was shoes and clothes and men with these women. It wasn't real. It wasn't what she wanted any more. And it wasn't how she'd been brought up.

Her parents had been married for more than thirty years. They'd loved and respected each other. She wanted that. She wanted more than hair and shoes. Than being able to choose the best-looking men, who turned out to be idiots. She wanted to sit at a table and feel proud to talk about her business investments and a husband she loved, a child she adored.

She was jealous of Andrea, heading up a record label. Of Sofia running Sanfia Records. Of Hannah and her gorgeous family.

'So, Rosalie,' Clarissa began, 'what's new with you? Any replacement yet for – what was his name?'

What *was* new with Rosalie? This morning, she had made an investment into a bio-genetics company that she'd been monitoring for some time, in anticipation of its inevitable IPO. Later today, she was going to Sanfia Records to continue her learning. Tonight, she had a daddy-date with Lance, who ticked every box she could think of. A CEO, like Daddy. Living in Greenwich Village. Never been married. No pets. Wanted his kids to be empathetic and accepting. Likes theatre and fine-dining. Oh, and straight. Hopefully, a year from now, she would be sitting in the St Regis with a baby who relied on her for everything. She would be too busy juggling things that mattered to waste time celebrating the death of ashy tones.

She smiled and said, 'Not much to report. Though I did pick up Louboutin's limited edition stud bootie yesterday.'

Squeals preceded questions that preceded statements.

'There's no pleasure without pain,' Clarissa said.

'Are we talking about the Russian or shoes here?' Kaitlin asked, making them all laugh – all except Rosalie, who was ready to enjoy her egg-white omelette then swiftly return to the real world.

* * *

Rosalie's cell rang just as she got out of her Porsche at Sanfia Records. Struggling to balance the box of New York's finest cupcakes in one hand and her purse and cell phone in the other, she managed to hold the phone to her ear.

'Hello?'

'Hi, is that Rosalie?'

'Yes, speaking.'

'Rosalie, hi, great to speak to you. This is Jenna de Sanchez from *Rolling Stone* magazine. I wanted to speak to you about Seth Young.'

She walked and talked with Jenna de Sanchez all the way to the studio. 'All right, Jenna, let me speak with Seth and we'll fix a date. It's been great speaking with you. Tell Leonardo I owe him for this,' Rosalie said, entering the sound booth where Seth, Billy, Frankie and Sofia were listening back to a track.

'I have some great news and some less good news,' she said. 'I just got off the phone from *Rolling Stone* magazine and they want to interview Seth in advance of the CMAs. Now, it's going to have to be asap, preferably today by phone. I know the editor over there and he's willing to make this a feature. The next edition is already planned and it's out next week but they are really keen to get a piece on you and it's pretty much the best publicity you could get.'

All other eyes in the room had gone wide and were focused on her... in a good way. But... 'Thing is, I know you won't like this part,' she continued, her voice breaking as she met Seth's gaze. 'They want to mention Randy.'

Seth stood and moved close to her. 'Rosalie...' he said, with a tone that said whatever would leave his mouth wouldn't be good.

Nervous and suddenly afraid of the bizarre way her heart was pounding in her chest with him this close to her, Rosalie looked past Seth to the break between the tiles on the floor.

She took a deep, steadying breath. 'Look, you're this tough, hot soldier guy, who happens to have a killer voice, knock-out lyrics and can play a mean guitar. You've also burst onto the music scene, getting your first airplay hit right out of the box and you're lined up to play at the CMA Awards. *Rolling Stone* wants the scoop on you. But you also happen to be Randy Jonson's brother and that elevates you from interesting to mega scoop for the magazine.'

'You know I don't want to ride on Randy's rep. I want us...' He turned to Sofia and the guys. 'Sofia, Billy, Frankie and me, to do this.'

She tried not to show how sad it made her that he, like everyone else did, had dismissed her, failed to even acknowledge the part she was trying to play in making him a star.

'We are doing, Seth,' Sofia said, coming to his side, where they were both facing Rosalie. 'We're the A Team. The interview won't be just about Randy, and we can make that clear, but you've got to appreciate that people are curious about you guys. Like, where has this insanely talented brother been hiding, huh?'

He folded his arms across his chest and sighed. 'Yeah, thanks to her,' he said, gesturing to Rosalie. 'All right, Soph. I'll do the interview, but I'm doing it for us.'

'So I'll call the magazine and say we're on?' Rosalie asked, no longer excited at all about helping her friend.

Seth looked at her in a way that almost knocked her from her heels, which would have had devastating consequences for the box of cupcakes in her hand. 'I'll do it.'

'And maybe you could say a small thank you, just this one time? I mean, if only for the fact I called you a hot soldier guy.'

When Rosalie smiled, Seth Young blew her away with a laugh that threw his head back and came from somewhere deep inside him. 'Thank you for calling me a hot soldier guy, Rosalie.'

She pouted and scowled playfully. For the first time since she had met him, Rosalie didn't find Seth to be a poorly dressed ignoramus.

'And I brought cupcakes,' she said cheerfully, giggling when Billy, who it seemed only ever thought about his stomach, took the box of cakes from her.

'Let me lighten your load, sweet lady.'

'Ah, it's true, a man's belly really is the way to uncover his good manners.'

As she glanced, uncommonly shyly, up to Seth, who towered above her even when she was in heels, he was displaying that curiously sexy half-smile again.

'Say, Ros,' Sofia said through a bite of red velvet cake, 'why don't you tag along to Nashville with us for the CMAs? Seth got a last-minute slot. We'll go south for a few days.'

Rosalie gasped. 'Oh, oh, oh! I could totally dress Seth. Get him out of those godawful lumberjack shirts and make him look like a real rock star.'

'Now then, what's wrong with a lumberjack shirt?'

The voice belonged to Jimmy, who had appeared at the studio door wearing his usual stonewash jeans and checked shirt. His appearance prompted Rosalie to consider the attire of every other person in the room and found them all wearing some variation of the same thing.

She shrugged, offering an angelic smile, and said, 'You know what I mean.'

As everyone laughed, Jimmy's expression changed. 'Soph, I don't want to break up the mood but I need to speak with you. It's about Jay.'

* * *

Seth's session was over for the day but he was hanging around waiting for Jenna from *Rolling Stone* magazine to call for a telephone interview. They had a photographer in the city who was going to come out to take pictures of Seth in the studio the next day. They wanted the story badly and it pleased Rosalie immensely.

Sofia had gone home after dropping a bombshell that Jimmy had agreed to drive her husband, Jay, to a rehabilitation clinic, so Rosalie offered to stick around at the studio, as much to calm Seth's nerves and reluctance to do the *Rolling Stone* interview as anything else. Frankie and Billy had gone for pizza and beers.

Rosalie wondered whether Jay could get clean and stay clean. He'd never managed before but he had never had professional rehab before either. She wondered whether it would be a good thing if he got clean and Sofia stayed with him, and because of that she knew that somewhere deep inside, Sofia's loyalty would be battling with her sensibility. Rosalie hated to admit it to herself because in her eyes, Sofia had the job, the husband, the impending family, but Jay wasn't a nice person. He had started off great – fun, making Sofia wildly happy. But as soon as they married and he became involved with Sanfia, he started to change Sofia. First her style, then her spontaneity; like, her random calls to hit an open mic night after work stopped. Then he started trying to change Sanfia Records and the way Sofia ran things. Slowly, her confidence started to go. That was all before they kept having to battle the drink and drugs. Still, if Sofia loved him and if he was what Sofia wanted, then Rosalie wanted him to get clean and for them to work, for Sofia's sake.

The sound of the piano being played in the studio reached her ears as she sat in the sound booth, picking at the last of the cupcakes she had brought. It was an unexpected sound, since Seth tended to improvise on a guitar.

She stood from her stool, looking through the glass pane into the studio, watching him move his fingers over the ivory keys. Then he started to sing, not his own lyrics but a song she recognised by Brett Young, called 'Mercy'. In this instance, the surname was a genuine coincidence.

Listening to the words he sang made her heart stop beating and stole the air from her lungs. Could he love as fiercely as the man he was singing about? For a moment, she found herself indulging in the fantasy that someone, *he*, could sing those words about her.

Would she ever know that kind of love in her life?

Had Seth ever felt that way about a woman?

And, despite his crabby attitude towards her, Rosalie wanted him to be singing to her. She willed him to look up and meet her eye. Why? She didn't know.

Before she could second-guess how much her very presence would irritate Seth, Rosalie had slipped her sore feet back into her heels and found herself walking down the steps into the music studio, coming to sit on a stool behind Frankie's drum kit.

And she closed her eyes, letting Seth's voice soothe her. She thought of nothing else. Not the pain in her feet. Not her posture. Not the way everyone saw her as a joke and how her loneliness broke her heart every single day. Not about the person people expected her to be and the image of herself she always played up to.

She thought only about the voice in the room and the sweet melody of the piano. How could such a beautiful voice come from such an incredibly ill-mannered, poorly dressed man?

17

ANDREA

Andrea pulled a brush through her dark hair and leaned across the wash basin toward the wall mirror to put on a moisturising lip gloss. She didn't need to look fancy for her long drive and she certainly didn't need to look good for what she had planned today.

The combination of the heartburn she had been suffering for weeks now – which she really needed to get checked out, when she had a spare moment – and the anticipation of what she was about to do, had her feeling nauseous.

She crouched by the toilet and pressed a hand to her chest, swallowing until the sickness subsided.

She was playing God today, meddling in people's lives and, though she knew her motives were justified, if her plan backfired, Andrea could lose her sister forever. There was no way of knowing for sure which way the cookie would crumble.

Pushing up to stand too quickly, spots of purple and yellow flashed in her vision. She closed her eyes briefly, until the spots subsided, then made her way from Tommy's en suite, through his bedroom, where they had spent another blissful night of rolling around in his sheets, and into the living area.

Seeing Tommy's naked back as he made coffee in the kitchen, wearing only lounge pants, made her pause to enjoy the view.

Without turning, still focusing on making himself coffee, Tommy said, 'Didn't you get a good enough look last night?'

She grinned, thinking she would never get enough. Somehow, over the last few weeks, she had started to crave Tommy – his counsel on matters of the music world, his support of her work, the way he held her in his strong arms, the way he didn't judge her, the way her opinion on his new songs mattered to him and the way he made her laugh, like no one had made her laugh for years.

It scared her and she was having to fight her instinct to run but somehow, the instinct to stay was winning out for the first time in her life. Her plan, currently, was to try not to think about what would happen if things went pear-shaped.

'Good morning,' she said, approaching him and slipping her arms around his waist, pressing her lips to his shoulder blades. 'Domestication looks good on you.'

He turned, tugging her tighter against him as he leaned back on the kitchen counter. He stroked her hair with a touch so tender she closed her eyes and leaned into his hand.

'How are you feeling?' he asked.

'The same. Like this could be a terrible idea and it could backfire massively... but like it's the right thing to do. I just want to get this over with and come back here to see you.'

His lips curved slightly at one side, then he kissed her brow. 'How about I take you out tonight?'

'Like, out in public?'

'Like, out to dinner in a place where the policy is discretion and no Press.'

Rumours about Andrea's personal life had been rife ever since she got the position of CEO at Stellar. Was it worse to have people say that she slept her way to the top by screwing the exec or that she was keeping the post by banging one of XM Music Group's biggest stars?

As she asked herself this question, she also knew that there was a part of her – though small – that knew the outcome of today could swing some of those rumours around. Getting ahead at work was *not* her motivation today, but she could admit that the right outcome could be the move she needed to make on the chess board of the Stellar label exec.

Was today just about freeing her sister? Or was it also self-serving?

'Hey, did you hear me?' Tommy asked, still holding her.

She nodded. 'Okay.'

'Just *okay*?'

She kissed his brow. 'Okay.' Then she took the takeout tea she assumed he had poured for her, knowing she was still enduring a fallout with her beloved coffee, from the counter and made to leave.

'Would you look at that woman's ass?' Tommy called out.

She put extra swagger into her hips as she and her form-fitting cream pants left the apartment.

As she drove the I-495 out of the city, Andrea's head spun with a thousand questions. How had she and Tommy seemed to slip into something extremely close to resembling the early stages of a relationship? Where were things going between them and where would they end up? Was she ready for this? Was she over the whole mess with Hunter? What if they did decide to be together? What happened when he inevitably got bored of domesticity and went on tour? The groupies. The wild nights.

Andrea stuck in Williamsburg wondering what in the hell he was getting up to.

She drained the last of her tea and physically shook the thoughts from her mind, then pushed the button on the dash to turn on the radio.

'Here it is, this week's most requested track, "Moving On" by hot new country artist, Seth Young.'

Andrea turned up the radio, rolled down the windows of Tommy's Range Rover, and hummed along to Seth's hit.

Damn he was good. So good, she expected he would become the most successful act to come out of Sanfia Records since Tommy and his band had been picked up by XM Music Group with a contract that kept Sanfia afloat for years after. Now was a good time for Sanfia Records – or the good times were on the horizon, at least.

And that thought brought her full circle to the reason she was driving out to the Hamptons to pay an unexpected visit to her brother-in-law (and *only* in-law as far as she was concerned), in rehab.

As the roadside turned from concrete jungle to long stretches of sand dunes and beach shores, Andrea inhaled the fresh air deeply. Then was struck with the overwhelming need to throw up.

Checking her mirrors, she swung off to the side of the road, slammed on her brakes and barely managed to open the door before she vomited on the ground.

Wiping her mouth, she leaned back in the driver's seat and closed her eyes. Heartburn. Sore breasts. Off coffee. Now, nausea.

Holy fuck. Was she pregnant?

No, surely not.

Maybe.

It was possible.

She and Hunter never used anything, but they had a combined age of nearly a hundred; surely not.

She and Tommy had gotten carried away on more than one occasion, but how likely was once or twice?

'Let's be rational here, Andi. You don't know anything. Get on with your day and take a test later. You'll see,' she told herself.

She pulled back onto the road and continued her drive to Jay's rehab facility. She thought about what her father had said to her when they last discussed Sofia.

I've told her I'll come back to the studio full time. She's tied to Jay morally and in business. It's a nasty combination. The hardest thing as a father is to accept that your baby girls need to do things on their own sometimes, work things out for themselves. She knows that when she's ready, I'm here. There's not much more I can do without pushing her away. You should know that as well as anyone.

Sofia had always been Andrea's responsibility and whether Sofia ever understood how much Andrea loved her or not, Andrea would always look out for the best interests of her sister.

That was the important thing today. *That* was her sole focus.

* * *

It was half an hour later, after she had gotten through the security check-in – a thousand interrogating questions about who she was and why she was visiting the client – that Andrea stood on the edge of the lawn to Jay's clinic. With the whitewash building – that looked more like a cosy retreat than a substance abuse rehabilitation centre – behind her, she looked out to sea. A light breeze whipped up her hair and chilled her skin where she had gotten hot in the car from the sun beaming through the windows, despite the air conditioning.

She was pleased she'd decided to wear flat shoes as the lawn mixed with sand made for a soft surface. Beyond the lawn, the grass gave way to dunes that tumbled down the short bank to the water, which gently lolled back and forth, making short white waves.

She had known friends with homes in the Hamptons over her years working in the music industry. She'd had a fling or two that wound up in dirty weekends locked in the summer homes of artists and executives, who rarely had time to enjoy them.

One such executive she had been sleeping with for more than half of the past year. As she had that thought, she realised her hand had come to rest on her lower abdomen, as if confirming what she wasn't ready to have confirmed.

'I'm not sure you're the *very* last person I expected to see but you're certainly down there on the list.'

Remembering that she was here on… business, of sorts, Andrea turned to face Jay. She analysed him like a doctor looking for disease. Clean sneakers. Jogging bottoms. A pressed *Coldplay* merchandise T-shirt. The way his hair had grown shaggy and too long but looked, at least, clean. She clocked his bare fingers and noted that the gold band that usually decorated the fourth finger of his left hand was not in place. Then she assessed his eyes, finding them to be white – as clear as she'd ever seen them.

'Have you come to gloat?' he asked sourly.

'No,' she replied honestly.

He walked toward one of numerous white Parisien-esque tables on the lawn. Andrea followed and a member of staff automatically brought them each a glass, filling them with cucumber-infused water as they sat silently.

How should she start this?

'You look better,' she said. 'Good.'

His bemused look showed from behind his glass as he drank.

'I know we don't see eye-to-eye, Jay.'

He scoffed and said, 'Understatement,' just loud enough for her to hear his petulant tone.

'Like I said. But I am glad that you're finally getting the help you need.'

He scratched his head, his knuckles white with strain as he clearly battled his annoyance or frustration, perhaps both.

'There's clearly nothing wrong with Sofia, otherwise you would have opened with that or maybe not even come at all. Fuck knows. Whatever you need to say couldn't wait another fifteen days until I get out of here. So how about you say what you came to say and be on your way?'

She nodded. There weren't many things she could respect about Jay. There were many things she could hate, like the way he'd manipulated his way into Sanfia Records, which, she suspected, had been a major factor behind him seeking out Sofia in the first place. Like the way he tried to change Sanfia Records, wanting to introduce dance music and drum and bass, basically using an established label for his own preferences, rather than having the balls to set something up for himself. Or the way he spoke down to Sofia and demeaned her without her even realising it. The way he had changed and continued to change her bright, quirky and happy younger sister into someone plain and unhappy. But if there was anything about Jay she could respect, he, like her, also liked to cut to the chase.

She slowly sipped her water, knowing that she could be the bigger person but unable to let Jay have control of the situation.

'You're not wearing your wedding ring,' she said, looking out to the ocean.

She saw from the corner of her eye as he wrapped his right hand over his left. 'That make you happy? You'd love it, wouldn't you? If this was it for Sofia and me?'

'I want what I've always wanted for my sister – what's best for her.'

'Regardless of what makes her happy?'

God, he was poison. He'd been poison since the day they met. Always talking into Sofia's ear, making her think she needed him, that she wouldn't find someone else. Sofia wanted the complete picture – career, husband, family – and Jay preyed on that.

'What you'll figure out one day, maybe sooner rather than later now that you're sober – for however long that lasts – is that what's best for Sofia will also make her happy. You're scum, Jay. You're a leech. You wanted Sanfia Records as much as you wanted Sofia, and don't you dare tell me that isn't true. You came from nothing and you thought your dreams of being a music producer would be made by Sofia. So you're right, nothing would make me happier than to see her rid of you. Not because I don't like you, which I don't, but because *she* deserves a hell of a lot better than you.'

She paused as her voice rose, glancing around to make sure they had no prying ears. It wouldn't be good to be seen cursing the patient, would it?

When she looked back to Jay, she was surprised to find his eyes on the brink of tears and his skin red as he stifled a sob.

Now, she looked around wondering what the heck she was supposed to do with a crying Jay. She had said things in the heat of the moment that she had wanted to say to him for a long time. Yet it didn't make her feel good at all.

'I know she does,' he said, before quickly swiping at his cheeks and sniffing back his upset, straightening his back as if his blip in composure was over and never to be seen again.

What surprised Andrea more was, though she didn't feel good about releasing her venom, faced with a broken man, in tears, she still felt nothing but loathing for him.

'It's why I'm here,' he said, stronger and clearer than just seconds before.

'Some things are too little, too late, Jay. Sofia will stand by you, of course she will. It's what she does. But why should she? What did you ever do for her?'

He gazed out to sea, as if contemplating, then told her, 'You're a bitch.' It wasn't said viciously or in distress, it was matter of fact, which was somehow worse. Like the first time your parents tell you they're disappointed in you, rather than being angry, like the first time your sister keeps something from you as big as the fact she's engaged because she knows you wouldn't approve, and the worst part is, you know it's true; you understand their reasoning.

Was she a bitch? She had been screwing Rosalie's dad, a married man, for six months; of course she was a bitch.

She was here now, meddling in business that most people would consider wasn't hers, even though she thought she was doing it for love. She loved Sofia liked she was her daughter, not her sister.

And that was perhaps the scariest realisation of all – she could be a bitch in the name of someone she loved like a child.

She thought of the thing that was maybe growing in her stomach.

She couldn't be a mother. She wasn't fit to be a mother.

She needed to get out of here and back to some place where she could take a test and find out what was going on with her.

Reaching into her purse, she retrieved a white envelope and slid it across the table to Jay, drawing his attention from their surroundings.

'What's this?' he asked, holding up but not opening the envelope.

'It's an offer. A business proposal.'

His eyes narrowed.

'Open it,' Andrea demanded.

He read the short letter and took in the figure printed on the cheque attached to it.

'You want to buy Sanfia Records?' he asked.

'Not entirely. I want, on behalf of my label, to acquire your shares in Sanfia Records and I think you'll find that sum more than fair value.'

He looked at the cheque, then at her, then back to the cheque. For God's sake, he was slow.

She waited for his brain to catch up with the opportunity that had been presented to him.

'Let me get this straight. Stellar, of XM Music Group, wants to acquire Sanfia Records?'

She tried but failed to stop her eyes rolling.

'Soph will never go for this. Has she agreed to this?'

Finally. The crux.

'She doesn't need to agree because I'm not offering to buy Sanfia Records, I'm offering to buy your shares in Sanfia Records.'

And the proverbial light bulb...

'You want to buy me out.'

'Yes,' she said, crossing one leg over the other, relaxing minutely now that the proposition was out in the open. 'I want to buy you out and I want you out of my sister's life.' She stood, knowing her answer would not come today. 'It's a great offer. And when you take it, you'll take it subject to one condition.'

'What?'

'You'll file for divorce. You'll let Sofia move on without you.'

He stared at her, not displaying shock or anger, or hatred even. Nothing she might have expected. He considered the cheque again.

'Wouldn't it be nice to have money for a change?' Andrea

asked. 'Rather than taking loans and remortgaging the apartment when a potential star comes along? Wouldn't it be nice to take the money and start up as a producer, working on the kind of stuff you want to do? I'd be paying over the odds for your shares, in the circumstances.'

He scoffed. 'Enlighten me.'

'Sanfia is mortgaged up to the hilt. I know Sofia has put everything on the line for Seth Young.'

Jay's eyes shot wide. As she suspected, he'd been out of the decision-making loop of Sanfia Records for some weeks.

'One of the producers is an addict,' Andrea continued, sealing the coffin. 'If you love her. If you *ever* loved her. Do the right thing by Sofia.'

'She would hate you more than she already does if she knew about this.'

Andrea's stomach sank. *Hate?* But there was every chance his words were true. Regardless, she loved Sofia and this was for her.

'Lucky for me, a good person like Sofia can only have so much room in her heart for hatred, and she's used a whole load up on you and your habits.'

She started walking away, weaving through the tables on the lawn, and she heard Jay call out... 'Sofia is right, you never do anything if there's not something in it for you.'

His words made her freeze. *Sofia said that?*

'I suppose it hasn't occurred to you that you'd get one of the biggest indie labels on your books, huh? You'd get the so-called star-in-the-making on your books.'

She spun quickly, aware that the centre's staff were closing in on her. 'If I wanted to bring Seth Young over to Stellar, I would.'

They glared at each other as a woman in a black uniform – tunic and pants – took hold of Andrea's arm. 'I'm afraid I'm going to have to ask you to leave,' she said.

'Don't worry,' Andrea said, her eyes still locked on Jay's. 'I know the way out.'

* * *

She clenched her jaw as she wound her way out to the car park, swallowing down emotion that threatened to break from her throat. Inside the car, she pulled down the visor, looked at herself in the small square mirror and said, 'No! He doesn't get to upset you.'

Except, it wasn't *Jay* who had upset her; it was his declarations. Did Sofia hate her? Was she a bitch? Those were the questions she played over and over in her mind as she drove back in the direction of the city.

Was her motivation for trying to buy out Jay solely Sofia? She couldn't deny that getting Sanfia Records on the label's books and, in particular, Seth Young, if things kept showing as much promise as they currently were, would be good for her reputation. It would, undoubtedly, stop her peers thinking she'd slept her way to the top. It would silence their wagging tongues when, or if, her *thing* with Tommy, whatever it was, came out.

Tommy.

She swung off the road at the next opportunity and wound up parked outside a pharmacy. She took three pregnancy test kits from the shelves and smiled awkwardly at the cashier as she paid. Next door to the pharmacy was a coffee shop. After purchasing a bottle of water, she went to the bathroom and did the deed on all three little white sticks. She jammed them back in their holsters, dropped them into her purse and washed her hands.

Back in the car, she counted down the seconds as she continued the drive back to the city, waiting the allocated time before looking at those little sticks again as they taunted her from her purse on the passenger seat.

A mother, Andrea?

She hadn't thought about having kids, not seriously. She had never got that burning desire women seemed to get, like Sofia had, like Rosalie had developed. There was no hidden maternal instinct inside her, like Hannah had in abundance.

In any event, she had spent most of her life mothering Sofia. She didn't need any more practice, nor any more proof that she would be a terrible mother.

For another thing, she didn't have time in her life for a child. She was career focused.

Moreover, she was... a bitch. A hated woman.

God, if she was pregnant, her spawn was either the result of an illicit affair – most likely – or another fling with a rock star she bedded for a few weeks every year or so.

Taking the tests from her purse, she leaned her head back against the headrest and closed her eyes, because she knew without looking that everything that was going wrong in her life just got trillions of cells worse.

She tried to refocus on the road ahead of her, but her mind was spinning.

When? How? Was it Hunter's? Was it Tommy's? When was her last period? Had she missed a period?

How would she tell them? Would she even keep the baby?

What would people say? Hannah. Sofia. Her dad. Rosalie.

Oh, fuck, Rosalie. This could be Rosalie's brother or sister growing inside of her.

She let out a sob right before throwing up into her lap.

As she looked down to the vomit, she felt... THUD!

'Fuck!'

Her car swerved right and left until she pulled off to the side of the road and the car she had just driven into the back of pulled up in front of her.

She watched the driver as he leapt from his car and came charging toward her.

'Pull yourself together, Andi.'

She stepped out of Tommy's Range Rover to receive a barrage of yelled abuse and finger pointing from the other driver. Ignoring him, she went to the front of Tommy's car and saw the damage. It wasn't horrendous, most likely thanks to both cars moving in the same direction, but it was bad enough to cost Tommy an insurance job.

As she ran a hand over the dinted surface, the incessant whining of the man behind her kept going. And suddenly, she flipped.

'Look, it's a fucking car. Accidents happen. I've had a really fucking shitty day. I'm covered in vomit...' Then tears sprung from her eyes. 'And I'm goddamn pregnant. So would you *please* just take my insurance details and back the hell off?'

'I... ah... erm... Are you, like, okay?'

'No, I'm not okay!' she screamed. She was a raging, pregnant, emotional, terrified, fully-fledged lunatic. And now she was going to have to return this car to Tommy, battered and bruised, whilst she was covered in sick and had pregnancy test kits scattered around the passenger seat.

After swapping insurance details with the other driver, Andrea pulled herself together. The reality was, she was in a situation that would not resolve itself and would not be resolved with tears. She wasn't entirely sure how best to resolve it right now, but she needed to think it through, strategically, piece-by-piece.

There was one glaringly obvious way to resolve the problem and go back to the life she had just hours ago.

What she needed to do first, though, was return the beat-up Range Rover to its owner and clean herself up.

The thought of driving through the city to Brooklyn and getting back to Tommy even later than she already would, with his expectation of taking her out to dinner, was too much. She made a pit-stop at a shopping centre outside the city and picked up a pair of jeans and a T-shirt. She hated the look of sympathy the store assistant gave her and the way she offered to discard Andrea's own clothes out of pity. Yes, she was a wreck – a pregnant woman, covered in her own vomit, with mascara under her eyes from crying over some little bump in a car. This was not her. She was a CEO of a world-renowned recording label.

Outside Tommy's building, she typed the code for the underground garage into the keypad at the entrance to a downward slope and waited for the roller door to rise.

The code was unique to Tommy's penthouses – his own and the one that was home to his team – and they would have been alerted to her return.

Parked in the designated spot, between two of Tommy's other cars, she threw the positive pregnancy tests into her purse, just in time before Mike from Tommy's security team arrived at the side of the car.

Mike, in his usual black uniform, opened the driver's side door. He considered Andrea's outfit and she figured his usual astuteness would have clocked her change of attire, perhaps even the lingering smell of sick in the car. She had attempted a quick wipe around of the upholstery, given most of the vomit had landed on her person, and she had clipped a new air freshener to the dash, but she could still smell the sick.

She tried to smile but couldn't manage it. Seeing Mike was a reality check. A reminder that she really did have something growing inside her. That she didn't know who the father was.

That Tommy was upstairs, expecting her to go to dinner and continue their fling until he next went on the road, and she was down here, in the basement, thinking…

She dragged in a sharp breath… Thinking she wished the baby were his.

Clearing her throat, she stepped down from the Range Rover. 'Hi, Mike.'

'Andrea.'

She rolled her eyes at his usual stoicism – an impressive rival for her own.

Before she had a chance to make one of a number of confessions, Mike asked, 'Are you okay?'

She felt her eyes widen. Did he know? Was it written all over her face? Could he sense that she was pregnant?

He inclined his head in the direction of the scratched hood of the car. 'The damage.'

The car. Shit.

Relief flooded her. 'I'm sorry… I… A car just… I went into the back of someone. I gave the driver the insurance details from the glove box. I don't think there's much damage. A few dints and scratches. She's driving fine.'

He took the keys from Andrea and walked around the car to get a better look at the damage, bending to rub each mark, making her feel even worse in the process.

How on earth was she going to explain this to Tommy? She couldn't exactly say she was in a fluster, mulling over whether she should get rid of the child inside her or not. *Oh, that's right, I'm pregnant, funny thing. You're not cross? No, it may not be yours. It could in fact be the child of my best friend's dad.*

She backed away from the car, gripping the strap of her purse on her shoulder for support.

Mike looked up to her. 'Where are you going?'

Where was she going? Anywhere. Nowhere. There was nowhere she wanted to be, except with Tommy, where she couldn't be. She had nowhere to go.

'Please, tell him I'm sorry,' she said, before making a run for it.

18

ROSALIE

As she stood outside arrivals with Seth, Billy, Frankie and all their gear, waiting for a minivan to pick them up, Rosalie inhaled the southern air. There was something so homey and provincial about the south.

'You all right there, Rosalie?' Frankie asked. 'Kinda look like you're smellin' a burger truck.'

She pursed her lips, brought her Dior shades to the tip of her nose and, looking over the rim, told Frankie, 'Do you really think I would relish the thought of a fatty burger?'

'Now that you mention it...'

Replacing her glasses, she smiled. 'You boys only ever think about your stomachs, don't you?'

'No, sometimes I think of my mouth, and how it would like to taste a burger and a beer before they hit my stomach,' Billy said. 'Is anyone else starving?'

'Don't worry,' Seth said. 'If there's one thing we know how to do in the south, it's feed people. My old man will have had the grill stoked all afternoon, smoking meat for us. Wait 'til you taste his ribs.'

'Oh, are we going to visit your dad before we go to the hotel? Or are we dropping our things to the hotel first?'

Seth seemed to scowl from behind his thick black shades. 'We're staying with my old man. He offered, Sofia was grateful, and down here, somebody offers you hospitality and you turn it down, we have a word for that. It's *rude*.'

Before Rosalie could retort or protest, a black minivan pulled up in front of them and the guys loaded their gear inside. The van smelled of cheap air-freshener and the leather on the seats was coming away at the edges. Rosalie considered her pink wrap dress and the damage those seats would do to the crepe material. She looked at the dirty step up to the van and feared for the cream leather of her Aquazzura bow-embellished sandals, bought new for the trip. Oh, she couldn't do it to them. Her beautiful shoes.

'Are you going to get in the van?' Seth asked, appearing at her side in his staple stonewash jeans and scruffy boots. How could he possibly understand the dilemma she faced?

Was it too late to arrange herself a luxury transfer? Why hadn't she checked the schedule Sofia had given her in more detail?

'All right, let's go,' Seth said.

Rosalie squealed as she was hoisted into the strong arms of Seth's tall, extremely masculine frame. 'Put me down,' she yelled, kicking her legs as Seth held her as if he was about to cross the marital threshold.

Ignoring her entirely, Seth stepped into the back of the van with Rosalie in his arms and set her down on the front seat.

With his body leaning over hers, Rosalie breathed him in, surprisingly affected by his scent – soap and natural musk, that was manly and disturbingly delicious. She found herself wetting her lower lip as she released her grip on his neck and the tips of her fingers traced the line of his ever-present dog tags, taking advantage of the closeness to his firm chest and enjoying the brief investigation into what was under his T-shirt.

To her surprise, when she glanced up to him, Seth's eyes were firmly fixed on hers.

'You can't just manhandle me like that,' she said.

Shaking his head, he moved to the back of the van, muttering something about time, his death and Rosalie getting in the van.

It was going to be a long three days. Made even longer by the fact she was likely to be spending it in a sleeping bag on some worn sofa in a tiny little wood hut with four men who all wore ripped stonewash jeans and smelly, styleless shirts without exception.

But as the van moved into motion, Rosalie had a thought. 'Ooo, I almost forgot...' Digging into her purse, she took out a small paper bag and clumsily got up from her seat, moving to each of Billy, Frankie and Seth, handing out the gifts she had bought them for the trip – mostly in an attempt to win them over.

'They're solid gold plecs. Not really for use but as a little memento of the occasion. See, on one side, they say Seth Young, CMA and the number one. You know, because its Seth's first CMA. And on the other side you have your own name. So either Billy, Frankie or Seth. Do you like them?'

Billy bit down on the plec between his teeth. 'Yep, solid gold.'

'They're pretty neat,' said Frankie.

And Rosalie raised an eyebrow, eyeing Seth until eventually, his straight lips broke into a chuckle and he said, 'It's sweet. Thank you.'

Rosalie smiled. Mission accomplished. 'I have one for Sofia too,' she said, retaking her seat. 'It's such a shame she didn't feel able to make it. She would have been so proud of you guys. But I totally get it. I mean, she just felt like she shouldn't have fun and leave New York with her husband in rehab.'

'Jay's a jackass,' Frankie said. 'You have to want to get clean to get clean. He's no more likely to get off the drink and drugs this time than any other.'

'Yeah, I'm with you, man,' Billy said. 'It kills me watching Soph run herself into the ground, scrimping and scraping to keep Sanfia afloat, when he spends every spare dollar they have on his habit.'

'God, I want this… us… to work out more for her sake than my own,' Seth said. 'I know she's breaking the bank to help me out and I can't give her anything back right now.'

'I overheard her telling Jimmy that the bank won't lend her any more cash on her apartment. It's mortgaged to the hilt,' Frankie added.

'Oh my goodness,' Rosalie said, turning in her seat to face the guys. 'I had no idea things were so bad. Why wouldn't she ask me for help?'

'Because, Ros, Sofia is a great producer, with or without her big-shot sister. She wants to make her own way,' Seth snapped. 'Not everyone wants to live on handouts.'

She wanted to retort. She wanted to argue that she made her own money. But something told her to save her breath.

Turning her back on the guys, Rosalie considered her designer outfit, her perfectly manicured nails and the large platinum diamond flower decorating her finger. She wouldn't be able to convince Seth to take her seriously any more than she could convince anyone else. But her dad had faith in her. He was signing over a recording label to her. And when she made the label a continued success, maybe even more successful than Andrea's Stellar label, everyone would take her seriously.

But right now, in a van full of people, she felt sad and lonely.

'Crank the tunes, driver!' Billy called out. Country music filled the vehicle as the highways and city lights of Nashville turned into fields and open country roads.

After forty minutes, they took a left onto a bumpy track that was lined with trees and horses in fields beyond. Rosalie's jaw dropped as they approached the huge ranch that Seth's dad called home.

'Are you shitting me?' Billy asked. 'Man, you didn't say you were loaded.'

Seth laughed. 'I'm not. Randy bought the ranch for the old man a few years back. Before that, we had a much smaller place.'

Seth's attire, coupled with the whole struggling musician, ex-military thing, had led Rosalie to assume he would have come from not much at all. But, of course, when you had a rock star brother, things changed. And Rosalie found herself smiling. Not because she wouldn't have to stay on a grotty sofa for three nights but because she found herself thinking that one day, Seth would be a star, too. Something told her he would also be quick to spend his money on his loved ones.

'Randy Jonson is a decent fucking guy,' Frankie said of Seth's brother. 'Who knew?'

They pulled up by the porch that ran the length of the large house. White decking was surrounded by white railings that broke in the middle to allow for wood steps leading up to the front entrance. Two large swing chairs and two bench seats were positioned on the porch to look out across the ranch's land. The driver came around to the side of the van and opened the door. Putting her shades in place over her eyes, Rosalie moved to the open door, looking left and right, taking in the beauty of the place. The silence of the fields. The vibrant green of the grass. The fresh air.

Well, almost fresh, she thought as she made to step out of the van.

'Watch out for the—'

But whoever shouted was too late. Rosalie screamed when her foot squelched into a freshly laid pile of horse poop.

'It's still warm. It's on my skin!' she yelled. 'I'm going to vomit. Someone help me!'

But the only help she got was an old man coming running from the porch, a driver holding out a hand and three musicians doubled over with laughter behind her.

'I am not a bad person!' she snapped at them whilst holding her nose with one hand to cover the stench and reaching out to the driver of the van with her other, letting him lead her to cleaner ground.

'Don't worry, I've got you covered, darlin',' the older man said, before throwing a bucket of cold water over Rosalie's soiled foot.

'Is it any wonder I don't come to the south?' she cried, mostly for her own ears, as the older man, with a slightly smaller frame but strikingly similar features to Seth, was stepping out of an embrace with his son and greeting Billy and Frankie.

'Good thing I brought ten pairs of shoes. I'm going to need them,' she muttered.

'And this must be the boss,' Seth's dad said, holding out a hand to Rosalie.

'Ah, no,' Seth said. 'Sofia couldn't make it. This is Rosalie.'

'She's a groupie,' Frankie said, draping an arm around Rosalie's shoulder, laughing as he did so.

'I am *not* a groupie. I'm actually helping out whilst I'm training to take over my own recording label. It's nice to meet you, Mr—'

'Tim. Just Tim.'

She nodded. 'Well, it's very nice to meet you, Tim.'

Tim looked from Rosalie to his son, whose hand was in his hair, his arm shielding his face and his reaction to the unspoken conversation the two men seemed to be having.

They watched the minivan drive away and eventually, Tim said, 'How's about we get this lot inside and I'll give y'all the southern welcome?'

'Grilled croc?' Frankie asked.

Tim laughed. 'Let's start with wings, Tim's famous hot sauce and a fine Tennessee whisky. It'll put hairs on your chest.'

He patted Seth's shoulder affectionately and the group lugged their gear indoors. Rosalie took off her soggy sandals at the door and put on the pair of spa slippers she'd brought with her, in case hotels in the south didn't provide them.

The house was big and bright, which surprised Rosalie. Where she would have expected old, dark furniture, maybe even a musty smell of a home lived in by only a man, she found high ceilings, beams in place of walls, slate tiled floors, a large modern log fire, cosy yet bright and clean cream sofas, a brand-spanking-new farmhouse-style kitchen. It was like a home from a magazine and one Rosalie would have been proud to have decorated.

One corner of the living space had floor-to-ceiling shelving, packed full of vinyl records, and in front of them was an upright piano and two six-string guitars set in stands.

As she looked around the space, for reasons she couldn't fathom, tears came to her eyes. Perhaps it was the beauty of the home. That it felt warm and welcoming. She had never lived in a place that felt this way and, oddly, she felt soothed by it. As if the home were wrapping its arms around her and saying, *Within these four walls, you'll never walk alone.* Or perhaps that was the words of Elvis singing in the background.

Rosalie cleared her throat and fiddled with the rose-gold

chain around her neck until she had composed herself. 'You have a lovely home, Tim,' she said.

'Not much to do with me, darlin', but thank you. Now, there're two bedrooms down here going spare and two upstairs.'

Frankie and Billy volunteered for the downstairs rooms and made their way through the kitchen with their gear. Tim took Rosalie's luggage from her, ignoring her protests, and led Seth and her upstairs.

She held on to the stair rail to steady herself as she walked through Seth's jet wash – that scent that had thrown her in the van. For some reason, Seth seemed to abhor Rosalie and, frankly, she wasn't fond of his crabby attitude. Nevertheless, as she walked behind him, his triceps were taut, and his muscles contracted as he lugged his guitar in its case in one hand and his holdall in the other. He had discarded his lumberjack shirt now and wore only his white T-shirt and stonewash denim pants. He had kicked off his boots and socks on coming into the house and now he walked barefoot up the stairs. She loved how he slipped into the home as if he'd never been away, how his southern drawl had ramped up a notch in his dad's presence and, most of all, how that *fine* ass of his flexed as they mounted the stairs. She gripped the stair rail just a little bit harder. Window shopping never hurt anyone's credit card.

Tim nudged open the door to the first bedroom they came to at the top of the staircase and Rosalie followed him inside. The smell of outdoors blew in from the open window that looked out across the paddock. A large oak bedframe commandeered most of the space in the room and was covered by white cotton sheets.

'There's a wardrobe there and a chest of drawers,' Tim said. 'The sheets are fresh on; I pressed them myself.'

Rosalie turned from the view across the thriving green fields and smiled. 'By all accounts you make a mean grill. If that vinyl collection downstairs is anything to go by, you have great taste in music. *And* you're domesticated? Tim, where do I find one of you and how on earth are you single?'

Tim chuckled. 'Well, now, I do have certain lady friends from time to time.'

Rosalie laughed, more at Seth shaking his head and saying, 'All right, Casanova, let's leave her to it.'

Tim nodded. 'Bathroom's down the hall, and the vinyl collection is much bigger in the music library.'

'You have a music library?' Rosalie asked.

Tim shrugged. 'For want of a better name for it. Help yourself to a look around, it's the next room from yours.'

'Thank you, Tim. For the room, the food, for having us.' And thank the lord this home was so much better than she had expected.

'Nonsense. Thank you for bringing my boy home. I thought he was going to re-enlist for a time there.'

Re-enlist? In the military? Rosalie looked at Seth leaning against the door frame, his guitar case still in hand, his hair rugged from where he had pulled his fingers through it out on the porch. The thought of him ever risking his life seemed as brave as it was terrifying.

'I'm pleased he didn't do that,' she found herself saying, all the while looking at Seth.

'Do you have everything you need?' he asked.

Everything. She had air in her lungs, warmth in her heart, a beautiful home full of love and music.

She nodded and watched Seth walk away with Tim, listening to the father and son banter as they walked down the hall.

As Rosalie took in the enticing view from her bedroom window again, the breeze cooling her skin, she realised she had never been in a home quite like this before. Not her childhood home. Not her own home.

Here, she could imagine homecooked meals, children riding the two brown horses outside, helping her little girls with their homework, family nights eating s'mores by a fire in the yard. What a different life that would be to her own.

After unpacking a few bits and pieces to cover her for the three nights she would be staying at the ranch, Rosalie put on an untarnished pair of Louboutin sandals and took her toiletries in search of the bathroom to freshen up.

Walking to the end of the hall, as Tim had directed her to do, she reached out for what she suspected was the knob of the bathroom door, then jumped back in shock as it was pulled open from the inside.

As the bellow of steam cleared, she was faced with a sight that dried her lips and made her mouth open as she ogled shamelessly. Seth was naked but for the white towel tied around his waist and the dog tags that always hung around his neck.

Her gaze went first to the spot where the towel was tied, then to the cut of his muscles just above his hips. She followed the light trail of hair up his navel and his chiselled abdomen, to where the hair spread across his toned chest. His jaw flexed as he swallowed, then her hungry eyes met his and the yearning she felt was unmistakable.

'Oh my goodness. I was... Me, I... You're wet.'

'I showered,' he said, stating the obvious, his eyes still fixed to hers.

'Right. Me too. I mean, not yet. I'm going to. Freshen up, I mean.'

He nodded. 'Bathroom's all yours. Don't take hours, grub's up.'

And just like that, his attractiveness was gone. As if she would take hours, she thought, rolling her eyes as his *very* nice back walked away from her.

***

Rosalie could smell Tim's smoking grill as it wafted in through the bedroom window. She could hear the guys outside – Frankie, Billy, Tim and Seth. Whilst she would have preferred a colourful salad ordinarily, she had to admit to herself that she was positively salivating.

Tottering in her heels to prevent any indentations in the hardwood floor of the hallway, Rosalie was making her way outside when she remembered the music room Tim had invited her to look around.

It was the size of the bedroom she was staying in. Tim hadn't been exaggerating. Two walls were full of vinyl records. The kind of collection it would take years to amass, even for a true lover of music.

The flooring, like in her guest room, was wood but a large square rug lay in the middle and on it sat two high-back leather chairs. Between the chairs was an old record player in the style of the fifties, with its lid open, ready to accept music. Five guitars – acoustic, electric and bass – hung on a third wall and around them were black and white prints of Randy and his band Armstrung playing live. She moved closer, inspecting them, so intricately she could see the beads of sweat on Randy's brow. Tim was clearly a very proud father, as he should be.

Then she noticed on the wall behind her more family photographs of Tim, Randy, presumably their mother, and a young Seth. He was cute as heck – all full cheeks, not like the streamline structured face he had now, a mop of dark hair and striking brown eyes, even then. He had most resemblance to

Tim, where Randy had more of a look of their mom; softer eyes and a more pronounced nose.

Next to the family pictures was a large portrait of Seth in his full military uniform – formal breasted jacket and standard issue hat. He was clean-shaven and looked strapping and proud. In truth, she was in awe of Seth and men like him, who would knowingly go into danger to serve their country.

Beside his portrait was a picture of Seth with a group of other soldiers, sitting around on crates and folded out chairs, at what looked like an operating base. He had one knee bent up as he perched on a tower of crates with a guitar in his hands.

Moving to the shelves, she realised the music had been arranged in alphabetical order by artist. Someone had lovingly worked through the collection and sorted it this way. It must have taken hours and hours of time.

She slipped out a few records – Bob Dylan, Dean Martin, Dolly Parton, Frank Sinatra, Guns N' Roses. It was quite a collection. Whilst she was hovering in the 'G's area of the shelves, she came across a record that stole her breath. *Grace*, a self-named title.

Taking the record from the shelf, she admired the close-up of the woman on the cover. Her roman nose and high cheekbones, her painfully exquisite smile that lit up her eyes, which were a reflection of Andrea's and her long dark hair, the same colour as Sofia's.

Settling into a high-back chair, she admired the image of Andrea's mother until she was looking at it through wet eyes. How sad it must have been to lose her mother at such a young age. A space in her life that could never be filled. Rosalie had never lost any close relatives in her life, yet she could understand feeling like something, or someone, was missing.

'Rosalie?' Frankie called from somewhere in the distance.

'You ready for beer and wings? I feel like my throat's been cut here and the others are telling me I've got to be all chivalrous and shit.'

Rosalie chuckled. 'On my way.'

She breezed onto the lawn towards the guys and the long table that was laid with food from the grill. 'Looks yu—'

Catching herself right at the last, Rosalie yelped when the heel of her shoe dug into the mud, making her stagger-stumble forwards.

'Nice choice of footwear for the lawn there, pretty lady,' Billy called out.

Tim appeared at her side. 'Darlin', I think I've got some spare boots from summer harvest that might fit you, if you like?'

'Oh.' Rosalie laughed off her tumble. 'Not to worry. Us city girls can handle our shoes, Tim.'

Nevertheless, she was grateful for the arm he offered, linking him as he helped her to the picnic bench-style table.

Staring at the spare spot next to Seth, she contemplated how she was going to get her legs over the seat gracefully in her dress.

'Need a hand?' Seth said with irritation in his voice.

Rosalie wanted to stick out her tongue in response but refrained. 'I'm fine, thank you,' she said, bending to sit on the seat and pressing her knees together as she swivelled over the bench seat. 'There. I'm in.'

'Now that the lady's here, let's dive in,' Tim said, lifting a plate of sweet-smoky wings from the centre of the table, holding them up for Rosalie in his red apron that read *My son is a rock star*.

Rosalie stared at the plate, wondering how she was supposed to get the sticky meat to her plate, feeling all eyes on her.

Well, she could always wash her hands afterwards, she supposed, as she took two wings between her fingers and popped them onto her own plate. As she did, she told Tim, 'You might need an apron that says my *sons* are rock stars soon.'

He beamed like the proud father he was. 'That I will, darlin'.'

Rosalie glanced to Seth, offering a smile, but got nothing in return, except the usual stone-faced Seth, as he seemed to be only with her.

Rolling her eyes, she picked up a wing and gently nibbled the food between her teeth, being careful not to mess her lipstick. Then the taste hit her tongue and, moaning, she wrapped her mouth around the chicken. Forgetting herself completely, she spoke through a mouthful of food. 'Oh my goodness, Tim, these are soooooo good.'

As she bit hungrily into the wing again, all the men laughed. 'Seriously, Billy, you're going to love these. Dig in.'

'Yes, ma'am,' Billy said, as eager as Rosalie with his food. 'Oh yeah, that's good grill, sir.'

'Tim, where did you learn to – Oh, pants!' The wing she was holding slipped between Rosalie's fingers, and as she fumbled to catch it, her elbow caught the edge of her plate and in a split second, two chicken wings covered in sauce had rolled down the front of her pink dress and landed in her lap.

Not knowing what to do, she stared down at her dress, open-mouthed. The stain would never *ever* come out of the fabric.

'Oh good Lord,' Tim said, rushing to her and rubbing her dress with a cloth that spread the sauce further.

'Oh hell,' Tim said, pulling back in a fluster.

Right then, Billy laughed. Frankie laughed. Seth stifled a laugh, and Rosalie... well, what else was there to do than laugh with them.

Once their giggles had subsided, Seth stood and offered her a hand up. 'Come on, I'll get you some clothes of mine that might be more appropriate. You can throw as much food down them as you like, promise.'

Accepting his moment of no doubt fleeting kindness towards her, Rosalie took Seth's hand and let him lead her into the house, upstairs to his bedroom.

'Here, try these,' he said, handing her a pair of jogging bottoms and a hooded sweater. 'Not quite your usual glamour but better for stains, I think.'

Rosalie took the clothes. 'Thank you.'

He nodded, staring at her but not speaking.

Inhaling deeply, she took the opportunity to ask him, 'Seth, why do you hate me?'

He folded his arms across his chest, biceps and pecs bulging. 'I don't hate you, Ros. I've just known girls like you and that hasn't worked out well for me.'

She stepped back and sat down onto the edge of his bed. 'Tell me?'

He shrugged. 'I was engaged once. To a girl called Connie. And she was a heck of a lot like you. Shoes, clothes, spending all the time. Trying to buy her way out of problems.' He stepped back, leaning against the bedroom wall, a sign Rosalie took to mean he was going to open up to her.

'When I was younger. Before I enlisted, and then when I was on leave, I used to go to a lot of Armstrung's gigs, with my brother and the guys. They always had groupies around, you know? Anyway, then there was Connie and she took an interest in me. I fell for it.

'It's kind of hard to believe now but I thought she was... the one. Right before I went away on my first tour of Afghanistan, I proposed and she said yes. That was it for me, you know; the house, the family, the rest of our lives.'

'What happened?'

'Whilst I was away, I got a letter telling me she'd found someone else. Turned out to be another musician. She sent it to me with an extortionately priced jacket, as some kind of conciliation prize.' He shook his head again. 'I think she only ever wanted to get closer to my brother and the band, looking back.'

'And that's why you don't want to be associated with Randy?'

Seth shook his head, moving off the wall and letting her know he was about done talking. 'Randy and I chose different paths, and I want to make my own way. It's not to do with Connie.'

'But not liking me is?'

He didn't reply.

'I'm not like that, you know, Seth. I do have substance. I'm sorry that someone did that to you but you shouldn't let it colour your view of people before you take the chance to get to know them.'

He stared at her, then nodded but didn't seem convinced. 'See you outside.'

'Thanks again for the clothes.'

* * *

Rosalie stood to the side of the stage and watched Seth jog into position, picking up his acoustic guitar and pulling the strap over his head as he went. There was an incredible crowd, given the time of day – late afternoon – and that Seth was still relatively unknown, despite his first single having been an airplay chart hit.

Her heart swelled with inexplicable pride as she watched the crowd cheer, eagerly anticipating this hot new artist's set at the CMAs. Like he had done at the Presley John concert, Seth took a moment to absorb the venue and the crowd. It was a wonder he could see with the combination of the late afternoon sun shining directly onto the stage and the overhead lights on full beam.

He took a seat on the stool positioned before his microphone, exactly where he had sat the day before for his sound check, and Rosalie watched as he took a deep breath. But he didn't look nervous; he looked every bit a star. Black shades shielded his eyes. He wore the pair of jeans that he had worn the night of the Presley John concert – much fancier than his usual stonewashed pair and slightly fitted, just enough to hug his butt and thighs – and a plain khaki-coloured fitted T-shirt, with his signature dog tags hanging down his chest. What she had once thought were a teenage boy accessory, she now respected as his nod to his brothers in arms.

'How're y'all doin' tonight?' he asked the audience, his southern twang as thick as ever.

Rosalie smiled at the wolf-whistles and screams Seth received from the field in front of the stage.

Then Billy counted them in and Seth kicked off with a medium tempo track from his album, one Rosalie had loved the first time she'd heard it in the studio. It took a line, maybe two, but Seth settled quickly into the performance, singing and playing as well as he ever did, teasing the crowd as he built the track and found his stride.

When he kicked on after the second chorus, Rosalie closed her eyes and let the rhythm of the music rock her body. When the song ended and the screams and cheers had died down, Seth thanked the audience, then started talking to them. Rosalie missed what he said because a kerfuffle of noise started up behind her. Turning to look across her shoulder, she saw a tall, broad guy in black jeans, black shades and a black leather jacket. With his messed-up rock-star hair, she could have sworn it was...

'Randy?'

Seth's rock-god brother finished signing the breasts of a woman and came to Rosalie's side. 'If it ain't the designer lady.'

'Hi, Randy. I didn't realise you and the band were playing?'

Randy folded his arms across his chest and leaned casually against a large amplifier that wasn't in use but was on standby at the side of the stage.

'We're not.' He gestured with his head toward Seth, who was starting up his most upbeat track, strumming his guitar and smiling like fun knew no limits. 'I came to see him.'

Rosalie knew that Randy was amidst a tour with his band, Armstrung. She had no idea how he'd managed to make it to Nashville and she doubted he could be staying any longer than a night. She felt an overwhelming affection toward him on Seth's behalf.

'Randy Jonson, aren't you just full of surprises? One minute you're signing a girl's breasts and the next you're a doting brother.'

Randy shrugged. 'He's my brother. I'll always have his back.'

'It's really nice that you came.'

'Just nice to see he's finally doing what he was born to do. Ain't no one in this life deserves it more than my kid.'

Rosalie smiled. 'He looks like he's been doing this all his life.'

She watched Seth tease the crowd, singing to them, winking at them, playing tricks on his guitar.

'How did you know he was playing? Your dad? He's out in the crowd, by the way. He wanted to get the whole experience.'

'He's always preferred being in the crowd,' Randy said. 'No, Seth told me he was playing and I couldn't pass up his first show without me.'

They turned back to the stage and watched Seth command the set. Rosalie dialled Sofia on video call and held up her phone to let her friend see the incredible product of all her hard work. When she got back to New York, Rosalie was convinced she was going to offer Sofia an investment in Sanfia to help promote Seth.

After a second upbeat number, Seth said, 'How's about we bring it down a notch or two? Would that be all right?'

A girl right in front of the stage called out, 'You can do anything to me and it'll be all right.'

Seth laughed into his microphone. 'I'm gonna take that as a yes, then.'

Six minutes later, a sweaty Seth came jogging off the stage. Rosalie handed him a towel and a bottle of water, then Randy pulled him into a rough embrace and said something into his ear.

Before even Frankie and Billy had made their way off stage, a group of young girls wearing lanyards that said they were VIPs swarmed Seth, asking for his autograph and selfies.

Seth glanced to Rosalie, somewhere between humbled and embarrassed. Rosalie rolled her eyes and laughed. 'Get used to it,' she said, though she wasn't sure he heard her over the sound of the young girls.

She gave towels and water to Frankie and Billy, then went in search of Tim in the crowd and ushered him inside.

After Tim had congratulated his son on a great performance, Randy announced he'd had enough – by which he meant enough of every person backstage: groupies, stagehands, managers, artists, everyone accosting him for pictures and autographs. Randy had a car waiting for him and offered to take Tim and Rosalie home. Seth and the guys wanted to soak up some atmosphere first and have a beer. He told Randy and Tim they would meet them back at the ranch.

* * *

Randy and Tim had been sitting on the porch, eating burgers that Tim had thrown on the grill and drinking beers. Wearing Seth's joggers and sweater from the night before, freshly showered and with still-wet hair, Rosalie made her way outside.

'Do you mind if I join you?' she asked.

'Hell, no, darlin'. Grab a seat on the swing seat there and I'll get you a burger,' Tim said.

'Why are you staring at me like that, Randy Jonson?' Rosalie asked. But she knew why…

'I've just never seen you in anything other than fancy dresses, with your hair all done up and your make-up on.'

'It's shocking what sits behind the mask, isn't it?' She laughed as Tim handed her a plate with a burger on it and offered her a bottle of beer.

She pondered the beer. It wasn't really her thing, but then none of this scene was, really. So she took the beer with a shrug and sipped the cold drink straight out of the bottle, coughing as it went down the wrong hole.

'Nope, the uptown girl is still in there,' Randy said, making all three of them laugh.

'I like it here,' Rosalie said after clearing her first bite of Tim's delicious grilled meat from her mouth. 'The air. The ranch. The music. Do you know, I haven't heard a car horn or a siren since I've been here? And it's like, you can walk outside and not worry about who might see you, what they might say about you, whether you'll be snapped by a magazine and have awful comments made about you like, *Socialite not eating after break-up* or *Following her break-up from business tycoon, daughter of supermodel looks like hell.*' She laughed sadly. 'Who would have thought I'd feel happy in a pair of oversized jogging bottoms and a borrowed sweater, drinking beer from a bottle with no make-up on?'

'Hell, not me,' Randy said, making her laugh again.

'It's nice,' she said thoughtfully, chewing her food as she watched the silhouettes of Tim's horses grazing in the nearby paddock.

It wasn't long before Seth, Billy and Frankie turned up to join in the food. The guys brought out their guitars and Rosalie was, remarkably, having one of the best nights of her life, listening to Randy and Seth play ridiculous songs they'd made up as kids. Watching Billy and Frankie having a 'play-off' to decide who was best on the electric guitar, which didn't work, since they were declared to both be incredible.

'Not quite Jimi Hendrix, but good,' Tim had said, offering a reigning endorsement that made Billy and Frankie huff and the others highly amused.

There were no bright lights, no shops. There was no fine dining or champagne. Yet her life felt as full as it ever had.

After a while, Tim and Billy declared their night (or rather morning) was over and took themselves to bed. Frankie and Randy, who had developed a fondness of each other, or perhaps it was a mutual appreciation of bottled beer, were standing inside, choosing LPs to play on the record player, the dulcet tones of Florida Georgia Line and Tim McGraw drifting out to the porch.

Seth sat up from where he had been lying back on the porch swing opposite the one on which Rosalie was sitting. He spread his long legs out in front of him and offered Rosalie that half-smile she was becoming quite fond of.

'You look genuinely happy, Ros.'

'I must look like a crazy lady, having let my hair dry naturally in this humidity.'

Seth smirked. 'Admittedly, your hair appears to have a life of its own, but you look pretty. Don't quote me on this, but you're kind of beautiful, Rosalie.'

Usually, Rosalie was great at taking compliments. She lived for compliments. But *Seth,* commenting on her au-naturel appearance; that made her blush.

'Thank you.' Clearing her throat, she said, 'Since we're complimenting each other, which is no doubt more beer talking than anything, you were great today, Seth. Beer or no beer. Listening to you is… I don't have a word to describe it but you give me goosebumps.'

'I scare you?'

She laughed and enjoyed the sound of Seth laughing with her.

'Another beer?' he asked, leaning from his seat into a coolbox.

'No, thank you. A crate's my limit.'

She enjoyed the way his eyes seemed to sparkle when he was amused.

When he came back to rest, Rosalie pulled her legs up to the swing seat and asked a question she was very curious about.

'How come your dad is on his own?'

Seth picked at the label on his bottle as he told her, 'Mom walked out when I was five. Never seen her since. He's had relationships here and there but I don't think he ever got over her breaking his heart.'

'So he's never really tried again?'

Seth exhaled slowly. 'Have you ever had your heart broken, Ros? Truly?'

She thought about her answer, then confessed, 'Probably not, in honesty.'

Seth nodded. 'Well, it's hard to let your guard down after you have.'

'Is that why you haven't?'

He smirked as he drank from his bottle. 'Maybe. Or maybe I just haven't found the right kind of girl.'

'Do you believe that people can have a type? Like, no one could, you know, break the mould?'

'I'd be open to being proved wrong but, yeah, I think there's a type.'

'But you could overlook someone who's perfect for you because you've typecast them. Isn't that a huge shame?' As she thought that, Rosalie considered her baby daddies and the checklist she'd prepared. Wasn't that exactly what she had done? Hadn't she requested a type – suits and shiny shoes, well-paid, likes theatre and over-priced schools?

'Come on then,' Seth said. 'Prove me wrong. Tell me what makes you different to the *it girl* stereotype.'

'Well, I'm not just material and dumb. I do want things from my life. I manage investments. That's actually where my money is from, not from Daddy, like people assume. And when I have my own label, I'm going to prove to people that I am someone to be taken seriously. I'll prove people wrong. I'm also looking for a baby daddy right now.'

'A baby daddy?'

'Yes. I've signed up to a programme to be matched with a suitable baby daddy. I figure, why keep putting my life on hold waiting for the right man to come along when I can make the life I want myself?'

'Wow, so, you're going to start a new business and be pregnant at the same time?'

'Yes. What's wrong with that? I'm capable of it. See, you're just like everyone else, you don't think I can do it but I can.'

'Hey, I never said you couldn't do it. My point is, creating a new life or starting to run a new business are both all-consuming things in their own right. Why do you need to do both now?'

It was Rosalie's turn to pick at the label of her bottle and sigh. 'Promise you won't think I'm pathetic?'

'Pinky swear.'

She shrugged. 'I want to prove I can be responsible. Both things do that. But I want a baby because... I want to come home to someone. I want someone to spend my time with. I want to love something, wholly, and for them to love me back, unconditionally. Like, no questions asked. If I'm having a bad day, they'll love me anyway. They won't judge me or think I'm ridiculous. I won't have to buy things to keep up with them or to make them want to be around me.' Without realising, tears had trickled from Rosalie's eyes, wetting her cheeks.

Seth stood from his seat and moved to sit next to her, taking an arm around her shoulder. It was a move Rosalie was unfamiliar with. It was completely unexpected. Yet it was so welcome that she leaned into it, dropping her head to Seth's shoulder.

'You think I'm pathetic, don't you? I have so many things in my life. Anything I want, but I'm lonely and unhappy. It *is* pathetic.'

Seth held her chin between his forefinger and thumb and gently teased her head up until Rosalie was looking at him. 'I do not think you're pathetic, Ros. And actually, I think I've been unfair on you. I'm sorry for that. For comparing you to people I've known. Like you say, I don't know you well enough to do that. But I do think that maybe you're not sure what you want. Can I say that?'

She sniffed, looking down to her lap. 'I'm not sure you can, actually,' she protested weakly, without moving from Seth's embrace.

'Look, I think you're kind. Your heart is always in the right place. But do you actually want to run a record label, or is it about your dad proving that he trusts you enough to give you a label? Do you really want to be a single mom, or do you want real loving relationships in your life? I think when you can answer those questions, you'll know what to work at. But in my experience, *things* don't make people happy, Ros. Knowing who you are and what you want is the only way to make yourself truly happy.'

'That's rich coming from someone who is striving for superstardom,' she argued, sitting up and moving out of Seth's hold.

Seth shook his head. 'Honestly, I'd be happy having enough money to get by, my family around me, a guitar on my lap, a pencil and notebook in my hand, and the air in my lungs. You laugh at my jeans and checked shirts. I like wearing jeans and checked shirts. I don't need expensive leather jackets and designer sunglasses. I've been approached by a giant music label already and I turned them down because Sofia was the first person to believe in me one night in a dive bar. She was the first person to take a chance on me and I want to be a success for her.'

Rosalie considered his words and surprised herself when she said, 'I wish I could be more like you, Seth.'

He met her gaze then and told her, 'Stop trying to be like anyone, Rosalie. Be who you want to be.'

Did she? Did she try to be like other people? Was being like Andrea the reason she wanted a recording label? Was being like Hannah the reason she wanted to have a baby? Was being like Clarissa, Kaitlin, Madeleine, even her own mother, the reason she surrounded herself with material things?

What did she want? Who did she want to be?

'I think I'm going to go to bed,' she said, suddenly overwhelmed and exhausted.

'Are you okay?' Seth asked.

She tried to smile but it didn't come. 'I will be.'

Seth nodded. 'Let me walk you up.'

As she followed Seth upstairs again, she felt a strange mix of annoyance and affection for him. He had no right to tell her that she didn't know who she was. Yet he cared enough to say it.

He pushed open her bedroom door and flicked on the light, then turned to her on the threshold and stroked her wild hair back behind her ear. 'I think you're a good person, Rosalie. Maybe I should have stopped at that downstairs.'

'Maybe,' she said, smiling at him before reaching up on her tiptoes and pressing her lips gently to his cheek. 'Or maybe you told me what I needed to hear.'

She watched his chest inflate as he inhaled deeply, his palm pressed to her cheek. Right now, she was grateful for his warm tender touch.

'Thank you for letting me tag along this weekend,' she said.

'Sweet dreams, Ros.'

''Night, Seth.'

19

HANNAH

'You're late. Again,' Andrea snapped before Hannah even made it to her desk outside Andrea's office.

She was hot, flustered and irritable from a combination of New York's smouldering early summer and power-walking from the subway station, thanks to TJ's reflux causing him to need another day off nursery.

'I'm sorry but TJ was sick and...'

'TJ is always sick!' Andrea retorted, storming into her office and slamming a bunch of papers down on her desk.

Hannah would usually back down because, ultimately, Andrea was her boss. But lately, her boss, her friend, whichever personality was turning up to work, was being a dick. And today... today Hannah was in the mood for a fight.

She marched into Andrea's office, closing the door behind her. 'What's your problem today, Andi? Huh? Seems like there's always something happening in Andrea's world lately that means she has to treat everyone else like shit.'

Andrea stood behind her desk and crossed her arms. 'Excuse me?'

'You heard me. I'm seven minutes late to the office, after having to get an emergency sitter, waiting for her to arrive, then running for my train and missing it by one minute. Then taking the next train and having to run for the subway, then running from the subway to the office. I'm seven minutes late!'

'Don't you have a husband? Isn't the dad supposed to help? What the hell else are they there for? I bet Rod was on time for his new dream job, huh?'

'No. You do not get to badmouth my husband and my family. I don't care how long you've known me.'

'I'm not badmouthing him more than any other man. That's the truth, isn't it? Women have kids and that's the end of their life as they know it, while the man, oh he just keeps going to work, or on tour, and doing the things he loves, not giving a damn about you.'

Of course, she did take more weight than Rod. He did swan off to work and leave her in the shit, too often. And, yeah, she needed help. She really needed support with three kids, a hell of a commute, and a full-time job with a freaking cantankerous ass of a boss of late. But she wasn't going to cry on Rod's shoulder and beg for help. This was life. This was her life. This was a working mom's life. She could do it. Damn it, she could manage.

'Rod gives a damn about me,' she said. 'Don't you ever say he doesn't.'

Andrea threw her hands in the air, uncharacteristically dramatic, and walked to the window, where the argument seemed to fade into nothing.

'I know he does,' Andrea mumbled. 'I'm sorry, it's just, if he did more, then maybe you'd have more time, for...' Then she sighed, her usual straight back and broad shoulders seeming to deflate and taking with them Hannah's fight.

'For what?' But Hannah didn't need Andrea to answer that

question. She never would and Hannah already knew the answer. *Me.* 'Are we still talking about me being seven minutes late to work here, or is something else going on?' Hannah asked.

The question seemed to fall on deaf ears, as Andrea continued to stare out of the office window. As she waited, Hannah's attention was drawn to the bundle of documents Andrea had thrown down on her desk just moments before and in particular, the name blazoned across the front of them. *SANFIA RECORDS.*

She picked up the papers, feeling Andrea turn and shift her attention to Hannah as she read the sub-heading *Acquisition of Stock*.

She turned then to face her boss, who stared at her silently. And she knew, this was Andrea's way of telling her something, *without* telling her.

'You're trying to buy Sanfia Records?' Hannah asked.

Andrea didn't move or speak.

'Silly question, maybe, but does your sister know?'

Andrea drew in a breath but didn't speak.

'I'll take that as a no.'

'I'm not trying to buy Sanfia Records outright, I'm trying to buy Jay out.'

'Andi, I know you've been looking for something to make your mark at Stellar but—'

'It's not about that,' Andrea said calmly.

Immediately, Hannah understood. Andrea was trying to get rid of Jay from Sofia's life, once and for all.

Hannah set the papers back down on Andrea's desk and walked to the window, where they stood next to each other, looking out across the river. For long minutes, Hannah thought about the most appropriate response.

'Andi, for as long as I've known you, you've tried to look out for Sofia and do the best by her. I know that there was a part of you that made the move to Stellar to try to give Sofia and Jay space to make a go of things.'

'I told him Stellar would buy his stock on the condition that he files for a divorce,' Andrea said.

'You did what?' Hannah was unable to hide her shock. 'Andi, that is *not* your call to make.'

'And yet, I made it,' she said, shrugging, with her hard-faced bitch persona firmly in place.

'Andi, what the hell is wrong with you? You live in your own world sometimes. You aren't God. You can't meddle with people's lives like this.'

'She isn't people,' Andrea said calmly. 'She's my sister and I know what's best for her.'

'What if what's best for her is Jay? He's getting help now.'

Andrea turned to look at Hannah. 'Hannah, you know everything I know. He's bad news. He always has been and, thankfully, I don't believe Sofia loves him any more. How could she? My sister is afraid of being alone, afraid of letting people down and, most of all, afraid of admitting that sometimes, being family just isn't enough to stop bad things from happening.'

Hannah scoffed. Andrea was unbelievable. 'You know, for years, I have defended the way you behave. For years, I've thought that the way you are with Sofia is maternal instinct. But this... This is too far, Andi. I mean, God, is this really just about Sofia?'

'What is that supposed to mean?'

'You know exactly what it means. Is this about you not wanting to let go of Sanfia Records and wanting to prove something to the exec board at Stellar? Seems funny that Sofia finds a chart hit with Seth Young and you're all of a sudden interested in buying the label.'

'How dare you? You of all people should know that this isn't about me! I want to give Sofia a way out. She's tied to Jay financially, in business, in misplaced loyalty.'

'And that's her decision. Not yours.'

'If I don't help her, who will?'

'You're bang out of line, Andi, and when this thing backfires, I won't help you pick up the pieces.'

Andrea glared at Hannah, her nostrils flared. 'You have work to do.'

Hannah laughed sardonically. 'That's right. The truth isn't easy, so let's run. Typical Andrea.'

They stared at each other, each of them breathing hard with anger, until Andrea said, 'There's a memo on your desk to be typed up.'

Hannah finally took up her post at her desk and felt drained. Her morning had been frantic, made worse by Andrea's revelation. She had been put in the middle of Andrea and Sofia again.

She was tired of it. Tired of everything. She *did* need help.

How was it that Rod could wake up, get dressed, and swan off to work without a care in the world, whilst she panicked and fretted about everything in their lives?

What on earth was she supposed to do about Andrea's latest move? Did she tell Sofia?

Why did she constantly have to think about everyone else and no one ever thought about what she might want or how she might be feeling?

Her cell phone chimed with a WhatsApp message...

ROS

Lunch, ladies? I have so much to tell you. Rx

And the next thing, Andrea shot out of her office running in the direction of the bathrooms. Hannah replied to the message.

> Count me in.

She could use a lunch catching up on Rosalie's latest shenanigans. Nothing took Hannah out of her real life quite as easily as a catch up with Rosalie and her distinctly *un*-average life.

She set her phone on her desk and picked up the memo that Andrea had scribbled all over. As she read, she noticed Andrea come back out of the bathroom, pale and wiping her mouth with a tissue. A number of things occurred to Hannah...

First, the arguments she had endured with Andrea over the last few weeks about heartburn and inappropriate lunch choices.

Second, Andrea had replaced her three mugs of coffee each day with tea.

Third, Andrea had been way more irritable and emotional than usual lately.

Fourth, it seemed she was throwing her guts up in the morning.

Fifth... She scrutinised Andrea's breasts as she passed by, the way they now tugged at the buttons of her blouse, which usually fit perfectly.

Oh, shit.

She turned to find Andrea's eyes already on her and in a look, Andrea confirmed Hannah's thoughts. She was pregnant.

Oh God, was it Hunter's? Was there a chance it could be Tommy Dawson's? The rock god whose snake was generally in a new cave every week, or the asshole, cheating scumbag CEO.

Suddenly, nothing else mattered. The arguments, the bickering, the slanging matches; they were forgotten because Andrea needed her.

But before she made it to Andrea's door, the asshole, cheating scumbag of the hour was making his way along the corridor toward Andrea's office.

Did he know?

'You wanted to speak with me?' he said, entering Andrea's office.

Andrea glanced from Hannah to Hunter, with a look that said *Help!*

'Yes, but not here.'

Hunter knocked the office door, which began to slowly shut. 'Well, I haven't got time for anywhere else. What is it?' he said, clearly still sour about the break-up.

The door shut and Hannah felt helpless. She didn't want to stare but she couldn't look away either. She wanted to go inside and put her arms around Andrea. This would rock her world. She never spoke about kids, except negatively. Her only maternal instincts were in respect of Sofia and were otherwise non-existent. Andrea was terrified of commitment, and a child was the antithesis of non-committal.

Hannah watched as Andrea came to perch on the edge of her desk, facing Hunter, who looked arrogant as ever, with his hands in his pockets and pushing the tails of his flashy suit jacket open.

Andrea spoke.

Hunter's composure broke.

He rubbed his chin and paced the floor of the office.

Andrea looked down to the ground. *Disheartened? Apologetic?*

Oh no, she was not accepting this as her fault.

That bastard.

It takes two, fuck-weed! Hannah wanted to scream.

Then Hunter was in front of Andrea, flinging what looked like a credit card in her face. Andrea recoiled, startled. Hunter flung open the office door.

'Get it done,' he said.

As he marched down the corridor, Hannah ran to Andrea, who was unmoving, still perched on the edge of her desk, Hunter's credit card on the floor in front of her.

'Leave me,' she mumbled, her eyes fixed on a spot on the floor.

Hannah stepped forward. 'Andi...'

'Please, Hannah, just leave.' She looked up to Hannah, her eyes full, and whispered, 'Please.'

Hannah hated him. She hated that bastard. She wanted to drive a stake through Hunter's stone-cold heart and tear it to shreds.

* * *

It wasn't her fault, Hannah knew that, but as she walked into the French boulangerie and saw Rosalie waiting for her, Hannah's lips curled, almost snarling. There had been a time in all of this that Hannah had felt terribly sorry for Rosalie, unsuspecting as Andrea screwed her dad. Now, all she saw when she looked at Rosalie was Hunter's child and the fact Hannah had just bore witness to that vile man throwing a credit card at her best friend and telling her to go kill her unborn baby.

She had to separate the two things. Lunch had been a bad idea, in hindsight, but she had fretted about Andrea too long before realising it was too late to cancel on Rosalie, especially since Andrea, for obvious reasons, had done a no-show.

But there was a sickness in Hannah's stomach that wouldn't go away. It was hatred for Hunter, combined with disgust over Andrea and Hunter's affair, mixed with sympathy for her best friend, who would be feeling truly lost. She knew exactly how lost Andrea would be feeling because she remembered being a young woman, barely more than a child, in the middle of college, finding out that she was pregnant and not having a clue what to do, or how to tell people, or what Rod would say. With everyone who should have supported her being disappointed in her.

The difference was, Hannah had never thought, not for a second, that she wouldn't have the baby. Rod had never thrown money at her and told her to sort it. She couldn't imagine what she would have said to someone who told her to abort her child. Her parents had alluded to it and that was part of the reason, seventeen years on, that she didn't have a good relationship with them.

Yet here she was, kissing Rosalie on her cheeks and trying to pretend like her dad wasn't a murderous dick.

'Are you all right?' Rosalie said as they took seats opposite each other. 'You look... bothered.'

Hannah was staring at her friend, in a moment when she could air it all – the affair, the baby, the abortion – but knowing that it wasn't her story to tell. There would come a time, who knew when it would be, that everything came out in the wash. Would she lose Rosalie's friendship then? Wasn't Rosalie as much a victim in all of this as that unborn child?

But Andrea meant everything to Hannah. They had always been by each other's side. Andrea had been the only person there for Hannah and Luke in her darkest days. Hell, Hannah suffered an agonising commute every day to work for Andrea and she knew that, without Hannah, Andrea had no one to truly rely on, or at least that was what she believed.

And so, Hannah told Rosalie, 'TJ is out of nursery again.'

'Oh, that poor mite. You know you can call me when you're stuck, right? I'll be there in a flash.'

Hannah gave a soft smile, hating that she was lying to Rosalie. 'Thank you. Should we have a look at the counter? This place does the best focaccia.'

She knew what she would pick for lunch, though she had no appetite, but feigning looking at the options in the glass counter bought her a few minutes to centre herself. It was Rosalie. The same Rosalie as yesterday. Her friend.

They paid the cashier for their orders and resumed their spots at the table.

'I'm hoping you're going to tell me all about this perfect baby daddy you've found,' Hannah said, as brightly as she could manage.

'Perfect baby daddy? Ohhh, Lance?' Rosalie asked. 'Oh, you know, I'm not sure that's going to work out, after all.'

'But I thought he was perfect. Good job on Wall Street, matching values, all that jazz?'

'Good looking, too. Like, Idris Elba good-looking.' Rosalie smiled from behind her coffee cup.

'Let me get this straight, he ticks all of your boxes and he'd make gorgeous babies with you but you don't think it will work out? Didn't you get along when you met?'

'Oh yeah, we really did. He's funny and sweet. Obviously smart. I like him a lot, but I got thinking about, you know, what kind of baby I want...'

Hannah bit down on her lips to stop herself from saying something unkind. Rosalie. Andrea. What was it with the women in her life that they thought they could pick and choose which babies they had or didn't have or what kind of baby they had? No one ever asked Hannah and she adored all three of her kids, regardless of whether they had been planned, what shape or size they were, whether they were smart or just a little bit dumb, whether they were athletic like Rod or anti-athleticism, like her.

'...and the thing is, I want a baby that looks like me.'

Hannah felt her features twist in confusion. 'I thought the idea was it was your baby? Your egg, womb, all of that.'

'No, it would be, I don't mean, like, have my nose or whatever.'

Then Hannah understood. 'What do you mean?' she asked fake breezily.

'You know... Like, when I was looking after TJ, people asked if I was babysitting or whatever. They didn't look at TJ and think he was mine.'

Hannah felt her temper rise. 'You mean because he's black?'

'I... Well, yeah, I think, mostly. I don't mean that I have a problem with black kids, or anything...'

Oh. My. God.

'Just that I want my kids to look like they're mine.'

Hannah stood, her chair screeching against the tiled floor. 'So my kids don't look like they're mine because they're mixed-race? Is that what you're saying?'

'No! No. I... I'm sorry, this isn't coming out right. It doesn't even matter any more because I don't think I'm going to go through with the whole process.' She sighed. 'Look, I just think if I had a white baby, people would know... I mean, it's different for you because you have Rod. If I went down the Swans agency route, then my baby wouldn't necessarily have a dad around when I was out with it, so it would need to look—'

'Enough!' Hannah yelled, drawing the attention of other diners. 'How dare you? I'm so sick of you, and Andrea, and your first-world problems. Babies aren't toys, Rosalie. They aren't trash you can throw away when you're done with it or because you never wanted them in the first place. You think that a baby will cure the fact that you're bored with your shoes and your handbags and the fact you have nothing meaningful in your life.'

Rosalie stood. 'How dare *I*? How dare *you*! I don't want a baby to cure boredom, Hannah. I have meaningful things in my life.'

Hannah grabbed her purse. 'No, Rosalie, you don't. You want a designer baby that you can pick up when it suits you and dress in fancy clothes and take for babyccinos then drop him off to Daddy, who is straight and white and rich, just like your daddy because isn't Hunter just goddamn perfect?'

'Don't bring my dad into this!'

'I will because the reason you can't find a decent man and a father for your child is that you think the sun shines out of Hunter's ass. You would overlook a decent man because he isn't the CEO of a music label or because, god forbid, he isn't a rich white man. Well, news flash, Rosalie, your dad is a lying, cheating scum of the earth. If that's what you want from life. If that's someone you want to father your child, I don't think I want to know you.'

Hannah stormed from the bakery with Rosalie hot on her heels. 'What are you talking about? Why are you saying those things about my dad?'

Hannah spun and found herself inches from Rosalie's face. 'Because he's a heartless, cheating bastard.'

'He is not! How would you even know that? Why would you say that?'

'No? He isn't, huh? Ask Andrea if she agrees with that.'

Fuck. Fuck-fuck-fuck.

Hannah startled herself, straightening her back as she sucked in a breath. What had she done?

'Andrea? Andi? What are you saying?'

There was no going back. She released her breath, resigned. 'I think you know what I'm saying.'

* * *

Hannah felt faint as she made her way along the corridor to her desk. What had she done? She had outed Andrea and Hunter to Rosalie in a moment of rage. She had destroyed Andrea's trust. Ruined a friendship. Made everything a thousand times worse for Andrea than it had been this morning.

As she neared her desk, Andrea stepped out of her office and stood calmly, with her hands by her sides. Hannah was going to have to tell her the truth. Today of all days. Despite what Hunter had done to her this morning.

There was no going back.

She swallowed the bile that rose in her throat as she reached her best friend.

'Andi, I have to tell you something.'

Andrea spoke calmly. 'You're fired.'

'Andi.'

'Pack up your things.'

'Andi, the kids.'

'You had kids before you had lunch with Rosalie, perhaps you should have thought about them then.'

Then she turned her back on Hannah, walked into her office and closed the door on their decades of friendship.

20

ANDREA

Rosalie hadn't said anything that wasn't true when she had called Andrea, yelling at her down the phone after Hannah had broken her silence about Andrea's affair with Hunter.

Andrea was a liar, a terrible friend, a horrible person, a homewrecker. She was all those things and worse.

She could add to that a shitty boss and an awful example of a leader. Since firing Hannah, on the spot and in front of the entire secretary pool, no one in the office had spoken to her unless they absolutely had to, which she understood was entirely deserved. She'd let emails slip, lost documents and failed to show up to a meeting.

Not only was she alone and realising how hard work life was without Hannah, she also had zero motivation. Work was, for the first time since she could remember, pointless. Admin and accounts, meaningless crap that nobody gave a damn about.

She had fired her best friend, with three children. The fact Hannah outed her to Rosalie at all meant Andrea had lost her trust even before she'd fired her.

Worse, she had fired Hannah for exposing her relationship with her *other* friend's father.

How had she gotten here? How had she put sex before friendships and people she'd cared about for years?

This wasn't her. She was supposed to be the one who held other people together when *they* were broken.

She had promised herself as an eight-year-old girl that she would never fall to pieces again. She would never be hurt the way her mother had hurt her by abandoning her.

There weren't many people in a position to break Andrea's heart and that was how she liked things. But of those who could, she had left her sister with Jay, forced Rosalie out of her life, and pushed Hannah away.

Now, there was a little person growing in her stomach and she had no idea who the father was.

Was it Hunter's? Who was probably having affairs with multiple other women and still lying to his wife. A self-obsessed A-hole.

Was it Tommy's? A rock star turning over a new leaf, who could head out on tour with his band at any time and get back to sleeping with another groupie every night.

Did it matter whose child it was? Because Andrea was no better than either Hunter or Tommy. She had lied to those closest to her, just like Hunter. She had run out on Tommy countless times because... because...

She squeezed her eyes shut as she sat in the waiting area for her obstetrician, trying not to scream or stomp her feet in frustration or cry a thousand tears.

She had run out on Tommy countless times because deep down, she cared for him. They had so much in common. They loved music and, more, they loved making music, together. He *had* changed, she knew that. But what would happen when he left her? Because that was what people did when you loved them; they left or they died or they turned to drink and shut you out.

'Andrea Williams?' the doctor called as she stepped out of her consultation room and into the waiting area.

Andrea held her breath, staring at the doctor with what felt like steel legs, unable to stand. She managed to nod her head, to which the doctor responded by saying, 'Come on in. Take a seat, Andrea. I'm Doctor Stead but please call me Maria.' She smiled from her seat behind the desk as she gestured to the blue chair opposite for Andrea to take. 'I can see you're nervous. There's no need to be.'

Andrea said nothing. What was the correct response? *Doctor, I am nervous but I'm fairly certain I'm pregnant.* When what the doctor would surely be expecting was, *Doctor, I'm nervous in case my home test kits showed a false positive.*

'I assume you've taken a test?' Maria asked.

Andrea nodded. 'Yes. Three.'

Maria smiled. 'They were all positive?'

Andrea nodded again.

'Well then, I think it's safe to say you're pregnant, Andrea. Congratulations.'

'W-wait. Don't you need to do something... a test? To verify.'

Andrea's panic was replaced with shame as the smile Maria had been wearing changed to something that looked very much like disappointment. 'Sure, we can, yes.'

As Maria moved around the room, Andrea's nerves built. This was it. After today, if the doctor confirmed she was pregnant, she could no longer think about that slither of doubt before trying to sleep at night.

'There's a restroom at the end of the corridor,' Maria said, handing Andrea a sample pot.

Even as she went about the necessary to complete the test, Andrea knew, in her heart, that there was no doubt.

So when she was faced with Maria telling her a matter of minutes later, 'You're officially pregnant,' Andrea could only stare at her, expressionless.

'This is the point when a lot of people jump for joy or recoil in shock,' Maria said, scrutinising Andrea's face, as if looking for dysfunction – emotional ineptness, inhumanity.

'When?' she eventually managed.

Maria nodded, as if accepting that Andrea was not one of those people who could sit in a chair and bare her feelings until she was cured of heartlessness.

'You said the first day of your last monthly was April tenth.'

'About that.' Andrea shook her head. 'I don't know. I can't... I can't think. I can't remember. Sometimes it's three and a half weeks, sometimes five. When I'm especially stressed I miss.' She gave a sombre short laugh. 'I'm stressed a lot of the time.'

Maria reached out and pressed a hand to Andrea's knee. 'Look at me. We're going to work this out. Take a deep breath for me.'

Was she losing it? Oh, God, she was losing it. She took a deep breath and nodded quickly. 'I'm good now.'

Maria smiled. 'Try to think of something around the time of your period. Maybe an event, a meeting, a dinner, where you were irritated you had your period or it was awkward having to slip off to the ladies' room. That often helps.'

Of course, there was something that came to mind. *Hunter.* She had been nearing the end of her monthly the night she got promoted. She'd worried when he took her in her office that she might leave a mark. Her vision tunnelled and came back to light, then she darted for the biological waste bin and threw up. It wasn't morning sickness. She threw up again and again at the thought that the spawn growing inside her was Hunter's child.

When she stopped, Maria handed her a tissue and they started to work through dates. The doctor estimated that Andrea was due in January. The precise date hardly registered because what really concerned Andrea was the date of conception.

'Well, generally, we would say fourteen days from the first day of your last period is the most fertile point of a woman's cycle. In your case, because your periods aren't regular, it is more difficult to pinpoint the date. Sperm can live inside a woman for five days and there would be scope for a couple of days either side for ovulation. It's safe to guess at the end of April, though.'

End of April. She thought about the last time she had slept with Hunter, right after the Presley John commemoration concert. And the first time she slept with Tommy a matter of days later and they got... carried away.

'Is there a date that's more... likely?'

Maria sat straight in her chair, the proverbial lightbulb above her head turning on. 'I see.'

'I'm not – I don't just sleep around.' Didn't she? 'There just happened to be one person who I was... in a relationship with.' As far as an affair could be called a relationship. 'Then the guy that I'm... who I *was* seeing.'

'Are you single now?'

For the first time, she truly missed Tommy as she said, 'Yes.'

'Would it have an impact on your pregnancy if you knew who the father is?'

Andrea knew the question was a polite way of asking if she would terminate the baby. Would she?

If the baby was Hunter's, would she want it? She felt her eyes begin to fill and her throat tighten. No. She didn't want Hunter's child. How could she want his child? He had thrown his credit card at her and told her to terminate the pregnancy. He was married. He was *Rosalie's* father.

Christ, the child would be Rosalie's brother or sister. Hell, she felt sick again.

What if the baby were Tommy's? A mini rock star. An empathetic, talented child. It would love music and he or she would play guitar and sing like Daddy. They would play records like *Grace,* her mother's first charted album, and sing the baby to sleep.

But then Tommy would go on tour. What was she supposed to do? Give up work and travel the world with Tommy, a baby and Tommy's groupies and band? Or stay home, a single mother struggling to hold down a job and bring up a child? Never seeing it because she worked long hours, or abandoning her career to be a good mother.

What kind of mother would she really be? She wasn't a good person.

She looked down to her non-existent bump. *You could be my little boy or girl,* she thought. *Mine and Tommy's.* Her heart swelled and she brought her hand to her tummy. Did it know she was its mother yet?

God, what if it did? What if it could hear her thoughts?

'Andrea, can I make a suggestion?' Maria asked. 'I suggest you go away and decide whether you want to have a baby. For you. Only you. Forget the father for now. Believe me when I say, lots of women not as strong or as stable as you manage this without Daddy being around.'

'They do?'

'Yes. You're stronger than you think, believe me. If the father chooses not to be around, or isn't around, for whatever reason, you can do this. The real question is, do you want to be a mom?'

A mom. She thought of her own mother. Her sweet face, how

she would play the guitar and sing, sitting on Andrea's bed until she fell asleep.

But she had left. She'd left Andrea and Sofia and Jimmy. And it had hurt every day since.

'I'm not sure. How am I supposed to know that?'

'Take some time out. Maybe get away for a few days and clear your head, if you can. There's no right or wrong decision here, remember that.'

'What if I decide that I don't want to keep it?' Andrea asked, already wondering whether she could go through with a termination.

'It's still early days so the procedure is quite straightforward.'

'What if I only want to keep it if... When could I find out who the father is?'

'The earliest time we can check is around eight to nine weeks.'

Andrea took a slow, steadying breath and nodded. 'Okay.' She had no idea what she meant by that – *okay, I'll keep it; okay, I don't want to go through with it; okay, I'll keep it if Tommy is the father and not if it's Hunter's.*

What in hell was she supposed to do?

'The last thing I would say is, if you ever *do* want Daddy to play a part in Baby's life, you should think about telling him sooner rather than later.'

Andrea shook Maria's hand and for the first time in as long as she could remember, she didn't run from one appointment to another. She hung her purse over her arm, covered her clouded eyes with her sunglasses, and slowly walked along the riverbank, turning every question she had asked herself in Doctor Maria's office through her mind.

The stark reality was, Andrea was not fit to be a mother, and she couldn't do it alone. Alone was exactly what she was. No

Hannah. No Rosalie. And once Sofia found out about all of this, she would be so ashamed.

For years, she had been so angry with her mom for leaving her. For choosing Sofia over her. Now, she had never wanted to be able to speak to her mom so much in her life.

She squeezed her eyes shut but this time, she couldn't stop her tears from falling, wetting her cheeks as they dripped to the ground.

'What should I do, Mom?' she asked, desperately needing an answer.

Andrea had rarely spoken to her mother in the years since her death. She had spent a night crying herself to sleep after they'd said goodbye to Grace. Then her sorrow had turned quickly to anger – anger because her mother left; anger because her father turned to the bottom of a bottle, rather than looking after her; and anger because she was just a young girl, left without a mother, with a baby sister to look after and shield from the endless hours that Jimmy had spent inebriated.

'Please speak to me, Mom. I know you can hear me. What would you do?'

But even as she asked the question, she knew what Grace would have done. Grace would have sacrificed everything. She had given her own life to deliver Sofia.

As she pressed a hand to her stomach, for the first time, Andrea saw things as they had been in Grace's mind. She hadn't chosen to leave Andrea; she'd fought to save her unborn child. Grace had been faced with an impossible situation and Andrea realised now, in her mom's mind, she had no choice but to try to save both her daughters.

A sound stole Andrea's attention, drawing her eyes to a park bench, where a woman bounced a young girl – maybe eight months, at best guess – on her lap. The girl wore dungarees with a pink long-sleeved top underneath. She had crazy hair – blonde and messily curled, as if it had never been cut. And the sound of her laughter brought Andrea to a stop. She smiled when the girl's mother caught her looking, but she couldn't take her eyes away from the joy on the girl's face or close her ears to the sound of the childish giggle.

She watched a man approach the woman and child from behind the bench, pressing his lips to the woman's hair before handing her an ice-cream in a cone.

He came to sit next to her, taking the baby so that Mom could eat her ice-cream.

Andrea's heart ached. Her stomach ached.

She knew what she wanted and who she would want to sit on a bench with one day as she bounced her child and ate ice-cream.

Her knowledge came with a million reservations and doubts, but the only thing she knew, for certain, was that she couldn't give up on her baby, no matter who the father was.

21

ROSALIE

'I don't even want to buy these shoes,' Rosalie sobbed as she sat on a beige leather seat in Gucci on Fifth Avenue, turning her feet right and left, considering the classic pump in Gucci's signature shamrock colour.

A store assistant handed her a cotton handkerchief, no doubt adding a pack of them to her account.

'I don't want to run to shoes and clothes because I have troubles. It isn't healthy,' Rosalie said, pausing to blow her nose in as ladylike a manner as possible.

The assistant propped his hands up on his hips. 'Oh sweetie, I know. But sometimes we need a little something to help us feel better than talking it out can.'

Rosalie shook her head. 'It isn't going to work. Not this time.'

The thing was, she couldn't talk about the fact that her dad had been having an affair with one of her best friends. She couldn't tell anyone. Kaitlin, Clarissa and Madeleine would love it – imagine the gossip and the speed at which it would fly around those socialite circles. Everyone who was *anyone* in New

York would know about the affair within *hours*. And Rosalie hadn't even worked out what to do about her mom yet.

Was she supposed to tell her mom the truth? How should she break it to her own mother that the man she called husband and father to her child, the man she had thought she had been in a trusting and honest relationship with for more than thirty years, had cheated on her?

Rosalie needed advice but the people she would turn to – Hannah and Andrea – had betrayed her. Andrea was dirt as far as Rosalie was concerned. The lowest of the low.

True, Hannah had told her the truth but only after they'd got in a fight about Lance and Hannah effectively calling Rosalie *racist*!

As crazy as it was, she thought about Seth, about their conversations in Nashville. How he'd listened. But the only place she knew to find him was Sanfia Records. And Sofia must have known about the affair. Andrea was her sister. Did she know? Had Sofia known the whole time Rosalie had been in the studio lately? That thought took her sadness to a new level, where it weighed heavily on her heart and in her limbs.

'So you don't want the shoes?' the store assistant asked.

Rosalie looked down to the pretty shape of the pumps and her feet wearing them and whimpered. 'No. I have to find a new way of coping with tragedy.'

The assistant slipped the shoes off her feet and placed them back in their Gucci protective bags, before placing them in their box. Then he stood, collecting the Rajah shoulder bag Rosalie had picked out to try with the shoes.

'Oh, I'll take the purse,' Rosalie said, snatching it back from him. She wasn't that strong yet. One step at a time.

She left the store with her new purse and the other bags of shopping she had picked up on Fifth Avenue – not because she was buying her way out of her troubled state of mind but because she'd needed certain staple items, such as new perfume and beauty products, lingerie and a blouse to match a tapered pant that she already owned prior to her entire existence falling apart.

It had been days since Hannah had blurted out the affair. Days since she had immediately called Andrea and screamed at her down the phone. Rosalie had shifted between denial, rage and hurt, all by herself. She hadn't been able to tell anyone. There had been no one to put an arm around her and tell her that things would be okay eventually. She wasn't sure they ever would be.

As she made her way back to her apartment on the Upper West Side and dropped her bags inside the door, Rosalie looked around at all her *things*. She had all this *stuff* and yet nothing and no one.

Was she more like Kaitlin, Clarissa and Madeleine than she thought? She truly hoped not.

Was Hannah right to storm out of their lunch together? Rosalie was *not* racist. That she refuted wholeheartedly. But Hannah had challenged Rosalie's suggestion that a baby with Lance wouldn't 'look like hers' and Rosalie *had* meant in saying that, that the baby would be mixed race.

She brought her hands to her mouth and shook her head. What a horrific thing to have said, and to have said to Hannah of all people. She hadn't even meant it, had she?

Seth was right, things couldn't make you happy and Rosalie needed to seriously consider who she was and what kind of person she wanted to be.

A diary reminder chimed from inside her purse that was still dumped on the side table at the entrance. Tonight, she had dinner with her parents.

Her life had become a clusterfuck.

* * *

Rosalie parked parallel to the sidewalk outside her parents' home and turned off the headlights, but she rested back in the driver's seat and listened to Lady Gaga's 'Million Reasons' until the track ended and Calvin Richards' voice came over the airwaves. As the song ended, she braced herself to face the real music.

Zapping her car to lock, she spoke to Luisa through the intercom, who buzzed her through the front gate. Luisa had worked for her parents since they had lived in the four-storey city townhouse – almost six years, Rosalie worked out. Six years of lies.

Luisa opened the front door in her usual button-up style of dress, with an apron tied around her middle. Rosalie forced herself to give a bright greeting as she stepped inside.

'Such a lovely evening,' she said. Sniffing, she got the distinct smells of garlic and rosemary. 'Oh, Luisa, it smells like you've been hard at work, as ever. I can't wait to see what culinary delight you've prepared for us tonight.'

Luisa's shoulders rose toward her proud smile as she tapped the side of her nose and said, 'It's a surprise.'

'I can't wait. Are Mom and... Daddy in the lounge?' Her voice weakened at the thought of coming face to face with her dad, in the presence of her mom.

On Luisa's instruction, Rosalie's pumps tip-tapped against the solid wood floor of the vestibule as she made her way through the bohemian luxe décor, under the crystal chandelier and up the staircase to the second-floor lounge.

She paused on the landing to consider her mother's portrait – one of her younger modelling pictures – blown up to six by four feet in a brass frame. In the picture, her mother looked fresh and young. Her now lifeless features had not been 'enhanced' and her natural beauty and flawless skin, decorated with strong dark features, were striking and mesmerising. The iconic portrait was one that displayed the very reasons her mother's services had been in such high demand back then.

Rosalie scoffed. Perhaps her mother would have been better accepting that lifelong invitation to Hefner's Playboy Mansion after all. At least then she would have expected that she'd be cheated on.

'Rosalie? Darling? Is that you?'

'Yes, Mom. I'm just admiring your picture. Have you had it reframed?' she asked, buying time to compose herself.

'No, darling.' Her mother appeared from the lounge, stepping onto the landing and coming to stand next to Rosalie to admire her own picture. 'Though we had the wall paint touched up this week. Can you smell it? Perhaps it has made the brass look brighter.'

Rosalie nodded. 'That must be it.'

Steeling herself, she turned to her mom, who said, 'Hello, my darling, you look wonderful. A little dull perhaps but very pretty.'

Rosalie had teamed her new Gucci bag with a simple silk wrap dress, which was the same colour as her mood – grey.

'Thank you.' She took in her mother's Bardot claret dress and statement bauble necklace. 'You, too.'

Then Rosalie threw her arms around her mother and hugged her tightly, all the while feeling a huge wave of sympathy for her poor, unsuspecting mom, who hadn't done anything to deserve her husband cheating. And thinking, simultaneously, what a farce her life was. The dress-up, the play of happy families and righteousness.

'Now, now, be careful with my hair, darling,' Loretta said, gently touching her French roll. 'Giovanni spent two hours pinning me this afternoon. Come now, Luisa has made us a round of dirty martinis.'

Rosalie followed her mother into the even more opulent lounge, where burgundy leather sofas formed a square around a marble coffee table and above them hung another crystal chandelier. The walls were covered in Versace's neo-classical style paper, and Greek-style sculptures stood in the corners of the room. A replica of William-Adolphe Bouguereau's *The Birth of Venus* hung prominently above a mahogany side-mantel.

On a gold-rimmed bar table stood a decanter filled with what she knew would be her father's preferred port and two cocktail glasses that harboured cocktail sticks, each holding three olives.

She'd chosen to drive to her parents' house on the basis she might want to make a sharp exit, but one dirty martini might prove more of a help than a hindrance, she thought, accepting a cocktail from her mother and coming to sit on a sofa.

'Where's Daddy?' she asked, crossing one leg over her other.

Loretta swallowed a sip of martini before saying, 'Do I ever know? Likely still at the office. He's always so hardworking.'

Rosalie scoffed. 'Yes, good old Daddy. Ever the upstanding man.'

In her parents' home now, she understood it was this that had shattered her heart more than the affair with Andrea itself. It was the thought that Rosalie's father had fallen from the pedestal he was on and the realisation that the only person who had put him there was Rosalie herself.

She had always thought that her parents were better than those of Clarissa, Kaitlin, Madeleine and the people she knew in those circles. She had thought, every time they enquired about why *she* was single and why *she* hadn't married, that she was holding out for the real thing, like her parents had. That every time someone broke up with her, it would be fine in the end because she may be alone for a time but then she would find her true Prince Charming. Smart, attractive, hardworking, challenging in the best of ways. Someone to fill her empty days with love, purpose, conversation.

That was what made her better than those women.

But it had all been premised on falsity.

An hour and two dirty martinis passed, with Loretta gossiping about 'friends' and affairs and the drug-related death of a man she was once 'familiar' with. The entire time, Loretta's facial expressions did not, or could not, change, Rosalie observed.

'Loretta,' Luisa said tentatively, entering the lounge. 'Dinner is ready. Would you like me to keep it warm or serve?'

Loretta set down her empty glass and rose to stand in her strappy sandals. 'Oh, let's eat. Who knows what time Hunter will make it home.'

Had it always been this way? Rosalie thought back to the number of family meals they had scheduled when Hunter had turned up late. She had always put her father's absence down to being busy with work. Had every time been a lie? Had there been other women before Andrea?

No. She couldn't believe it.

Rosalie took a seat in the dining room, at the large, intricately carved walnut dining table. She sat opposite her mother and they left a space at the head of the table for Hunter. It had never bothered her before that her father was the head of the house and the head of the table, even the head of hers and Loretta's lives. But tonight, her skin prickled with irritation.

A real role model, she thought.

As Luisa set down light cheese soufflés in front of the women, Hunter appeared.

'I'm here,' he announced, floating in, kissing Rosalie on the head and Loretta on the cheek, then taking a seat, setting his two cell phones upside-down on the table next to him.

Was one a work phone and one an adultery phone?

'Where've you been, Daddy?' Rosalie asked, her tone clipped, unable to be her usual chirpy persona.

She adored her father and loved seeing him but tonight, she felt nothing toward him except anger, distrust and shame.

Hunter was clearly taken aback by her tone. 'At work, darling. You don't seem happy. What's happened now?'

The way he asked her, as if she was some kind of drama queen, irked her. She scowled, trying to decide whether to call him out for romping with her best friend behind her mother's back. Then she looked at Loretta and knew this wasn't the right way to go about things.

Luisa reappeared with a third soufflé and poured Hunter, then Loretta, each a glass of Hunter's preferred red wine. When she came to fill Rosalie's glass, Rosalie held her hand over the top.

'No, thank you, Luisa. I'm driving tonight.'

'Driving?' Hunter asked. 'Why would you drive? You don't usually drive.'

'Why would anyone do anything that wasn't expected of them?' Rosalie quipped.

Hunter dabbed the corner of his mouth with his napkin and set it down on the table, holding Rosalie's glare.

'I need to speak with you,' Rosalie said.

'Oh, Rosalie, if it's about me gifting you a recording label again, I've already told you, no.'

Rosalie gasped. 'You didn't. You said if I got experience I

could have a label.' She scoffed. 'You never had any intention of following through, did you? Gosh, you really *are* a liar. You think I'm stupid. Silly Rosalie and her silly ideas.'

'I do not think you're stupid, Rosalie, though you are being extremely dramatic.'

'Rosalie, what has gotten into you?' Loretta asked.

'Maybe I'm just finally seeing the sky through the clouds, Mom. *Daddy,* I *want* to speak with you and it *isn't* about a recording label, though it is related to your lies and deceit.'

The response she received – which was Hunter staring knowingly at Rosalie – confirmed what she already knew. But there were more questions and answers she wanted.

'After dinner,' Hunter said, reaching for his wine.

The remainder of the three-course meal Luisa had prepared was endured mostly in excruciating silence and partly in painstakingly pointless snippets of conversation led by Loretta.

When Luisa offered Rosalie after-dinner coffee, Rosalie declined, staring at her father.

Hunter nodded in understanding, rising from the table. 'Luisa, I'd like a glass of port in the library.'

'Yes, sir,' Luisa said.

'I think he meant to say "please", Luisa,' Rosalie said, realising that everything about her father was arrogant and wondering if he had always been this way.

Rosalie followed Hunter to the third-floor library, which was lit only by lamplight from the desk that sat on a rug in the middle of the dark wood floor, the walls around them full of books.

Hunter perched on the edge of the desk, facing her. 'You wanted to talk.' It was not a question but a statement. It was cold and direct and Rosalie had an insight into his work manner.

'How long?' she said.

He unfolded his arms and rested his hands against the edge of the desk either side of him. Confident. Bold. Unafraid.

'How long what?' he asked.

His conceit was the final straw. 'How long have you been *fucking* Andrea?'

He wasn't startled, or affronted, or ashamed. In fact, his demeanour didn't change at all as he told his daughter, 'It's over. It was a mistake and I can understand why you're upset but I ended it weeks ago. She begged me not to but I did because I knew it was wrong. I knew it would hurt you.'

Rosalie had known that it was true. Hannah wouldn't have lied. Yet her stomach sank. Her dinner was in danger of making a reappearance. The way he spoke told her it had been more than a one-off. And *he* had ended it. She wasn't sure what would have been best – that he had ended it, that Andrea had ended it, or that they had mutually decided a onetime mistake should never be repeated.

What she did know was that her heart broke again when she thought it was already broken entirely. She shook her head, willing herself to stay strong.

Hunter stood and walked to his daughter, reaching out to her shoulders.

Rosalie shrugged him off. 'Don't touch me.'

He dropped his hands. 'I know you thought she was your friend, Rosalie, but look how she treated you. You just don't have the best judgement when it comes to people and I'm sorry you had to find out this way.'

'Sorry I had to find out in a certain way or sorry I caught you out at all?' she snapped. 'How dare you blame this on my judgement of character? *You* did this to me, to Mom, to our family.'

'And I ended it, Rosalie. What more do you want?'

He shook his head as he walked back to the desk. 'You know,

I blame myself for your ignorance. You've been too sheltered from real life.'

'Excuse me? Are you really trying to say this is okay? That you lying to us is acceptable?' She paced the floor with anger that made her hands tremble. 'You're not even remorseful, are you?'

Hunter sighed, as if Rosalie was taking up precious time he couldn't be bothered to give.

'I'm sorry it was Andrea and I'm sorry I've hurt you, Rosalie. But you're a grown woman and it's about time you stopped being so naïve. Life isn't all love songs, flowers and chocolates.'

She stopped pacing and confronted him. 'What exactly is that supposed to mean?' she yelled, unable to contain her temper.

'It's supposed to mean' – Rosalie turned to see her mother, moving from the doorway into the library to join them – 'that your father and I have a very nice life. It works for both of us and it has always worked for you.'

'You knew?' Rosalie asked, her shock making her words barely more than a whisper.

'I realised it was Andrea the night of the Presley John commemoration concert. I told your father I didn't approve and that it would hurt you if you found out. He assured me he would end it.'

Rosalie tried to process what she was being told. 'I just don't... I can't understand this.'

Loretta moved to Hunter's side and placed a hand on his forearm. 'Rosalie, your father and I understand that we both have needs that we can't meet for each other.'

'Have there... been more women?' Rosalie asked, terrified of the answer.

'Yes,' Hunter said. 'And men,' he added, inclining his head toward his wife.

Rosalie stared at her parents, seeing them for the first time in more than thirty years in a completely new light. Naïve indeed. What a fool she had been, always searching for a man like her daddy. Aspiring to have a life like theirs – wealthy, stylish, indulgent, proudly deserved, full of love. The perfect life that ticked every box on her own checklist.

She looked at them now, the picture of a happily married couple, and she had no idea who they were, or who she was.

With nothing left to say, she turned her back on them and their illusion of a perfect home.

22

HANNAH

'Have a good day! Be good. Be safe,' Hannah called down the stairs in response to Luke and Jackson heading out for the school bus.

She was finishing off the small amount of make-up she ordinarily wore to work and hoping that Rod would leave the house on time, before Hannah was expected to leave the house to drop TJ to nursery on her way to work.

On the day Andrea fired her, the first thing Hannah should have done was tell Rod. Confess that Andrea had been having an affair with Hunter, that Andrea was pregnant and Hannah was terrified she might get rid of the baby because Hunter had told her to. That she had lost her temper with Rosalie over her stupidity, accused her friend of being racist, which she knew wasn't true, and taken her anger with Hunter and Andrea out on Rosalie. That she had told Rosalie about the affair and deserved to be fired by Andrea for what she'd done.

But she hadn't told Rod on the day she was fired and now, days later, she still hadn't confessed to Rod. Instead, she had been pretending to drop TJ at nursery and go to work. She had been keeping him home from nursery and cancelled the sitter, lying to her children about getting home from work early in the evenings, because she was afraid.

She was afraid that she had let down Rod and her whole family. They needed her salary to make ends meet. Even keeping TJ out of childcare wouldn't save them enough money for Hannah to stop working.

All her adult life, she had strived to be better than her own mother. To put her family and her kids, especially, ahead of everything else. To prove her father, who had wanted to abandon her for having Luke, that he was wrong, that she could take care of her kids on her own.

Hannah's family was her primary responsibility and she'd failed them.

Rod came into their bedroom, picking up TJ from where he was lying on his jungle mat on the floor, ready for nursery. He threw the baby three inches into the air and was rewarded with TJ's high-pitched giggles and limb-flapping as he repeated the move once, twice, three times.

'Okay, okay. Enough, otherwise he'll throw up,' Hannah said, unable to help herself laughing at the sound of TJ's happiness.

For that brief moment, she forgot that she was deceiving her husband.

'Rod...'

He set TJ back on his mat.

'Yeah, babe?' he said, before pressing a chaste kiss to her lips.

How should she begin...? 'Nothing. Have a good day.'

He kissed her again and was gone.

'Well, TJ, it's just you and me again, baby boy. Where should we clean today?'

***

After two hours of emptying, cleaning and refilling each cupboard and drawer in the kitchen, Hannah's arms were aching. She was hot and flustered and in need of a coffee.

She turned to where TJ was in his bouncer chair on the tabletop, giggling as George the Giraffe swung back and forth from the rail above his head.

'I would have normally had three coffees by now with the girls at work,' she told her son as she stepped down from the chair she had been using to reach the top cupboards. 'Today I haven't even had one.'

She tugged off her rubber gloves and considered them, then her son. 'What would you be doing at nursery, bubble? More than watching Mom clean the kitchen, huh?'

Dropping her gloves into the sink, she said, 'I've got an idea. Let's go out for that coffee, shall we?'

The summer was upon them when Hannah stepped outside with TJ strapped to her front, legs dangling in his carrier, his soft cap in place atop his increasingly unruly black curls of hair. Hannah had swapped cleaning clothes for a pair of yoga pants and a thin workout top. She walked briskly, happily building her heart rate as she and TJ headed toward the local park, where she knew she would find an exceptional oat milk latte and a fine Italian biscotti.

She passed other moms with their babies in strollers. Teenagers skated by her on roller blades and skateboards. A woman riding a bike chimed her bell to ask Hannah to step aside as she cycled the narrow pathway that was overhung by full trees.

All the people Hannah passed looked carefree. There was a part of Hannah that was loving her days off with TJ – she adored spending time with her kids. But the overwhelming feelings she had were guilt – guilt because she was lying to Rod; guilt because she had spent six bucks on a coffee and a biscotti when she was no longer contributing to the family finances – and a general sense of being out of sorts. She had no routine, no goals, no purpose.

She'd thought that trying to work alongside having a family was exhausting. In fact, sleepless nights due to *not* working were worse.

Taking a seat on a park bench, she unstrapped TJ from her chest and bounced him on her knee, tickling him until he giggled.

'You know I love you, buddy, don't you? But this just isn't me.'

TJ gurgled.

'Why? Well, I'm used to... being needed, I suppose. In a different way to how you and your brothers need me.'

She pressed her nose to his. 'And you, mister, have been the neediest kid so far. All that yucky sicky. That's right, you laugh at Mommy.'

She kissed his brow and bounced him on her lap again.

'Aunty Andrea will come around. She'll give me my job back, I know she will. She needs me.' Her stomach twisted with the thought of Andrea facing her pregnancy alone. It terrified her that Andrea might consider aborting her baby. She felt immeasurably horrible that she had been the one to bring Andrea's affair with Hunter out into the open. And now she had ditched her best friend. True, Andrea had fired her, but Hannah hadn't put up much of a fight. Andrea had been the one person Hannah had been able to depend on when her own parents turned their backs on her when Luke was a baby and Rod was still at college. When it came to Andrea and her first pregnancy, Hannah had walked away.

TJ screeched as she bounced him more vigorously, making her laugh, too.

'The thing is, I don't know if I want my job back, Teej. I don't know. I mean, we need the money, and I like the structure. I miss the girls, so much. And, you can't understand this, but I'm the most *me* I can be when I'm in the city. I'm not Mommy or a wife. I'm Hannah.

'But it's exhausting. And when I'm at work, I miss you guys. I hate not being home when your brothers get in from school. I hate that there's a chance I'll miss your first steps because I'm working.

'Your dad... he tries, I know he does, but he's equivalent to having another child in the house; a very large, hairy child.'

At that choice moment, TJ belly laughed. 'Is that funny? That Daddy is a big hairy monster, does that make you laugh?'

She turned TJ, bringing his back against her stomach, and she leaned her head back, lifting her face to the sun's rays. And she was struck by a stark reality – Hannah really had no idea what she wanted because she had never truly put herself first. Since she fell pregnant in college and dropped out, since she took a job with Andrea and followed her to XM Music Group to make sure that she was okay, because everything she did was led by thoughts of Rod and her children and the money their family needed.

She was in her late thirties, with three kids, one of whom would be looking to go to college very soon. If she didn't do something for herself now, would she ever?

She thought about Andrea and how alone she must be feeling. Assuming Hunter was the father of the baby and he didn't want anything to do with it, Andrea wouldn't be alone generally but when it came to home life, she would.

Her heart panged for her friend, despite everything.

And she realised something that she had been overlooking for a very long time. *She* wasn't alone. She had a husband and maybe it was time for her to stop being a martyr.

What do I want, for me? she thought.

Working out the answer to that question was her number one priority. Right after she had faced the music and confessed to Rod that she was unemployed.

23

ANDREA

The sight of a Range Rover with blacked-out windows escaped Andrea's attention as she walked past it, heading home from the office. It had been a long day of figures and administration, all of which, she realised, took a heck of a lot longer without Hannah, which meant she had spent her Sunday in the office, alone, working through a backlog of tasks.

The sky was dark, despite it being June, which told her without needing to check a device that she had been in the office late into the evening. Her stomach growled with hunger, since she hadn't eaten since breakfast. All she really wanted to do was crawl into bed, but there was something the size of a small vegetable growing inside her that needed to be fed.

As she crossed the street towards her apartment building, the door to the Range Rover opened and the person who stepped out of it made her pause in the middle of the road.

Tommy.

She was rooted to one spot, watching him close the door and fold his arms across his chest as he leaned back against the vehicle.

'It's been repaired,' he said, gesturing to the front of the Range Rover.

She suddenly felt extremely weak, her legs drained of energy. In the middle of the road there was nothing to hold on to, and she swayed.

'I'm sorry about that,' she managed, still unable to take her eyes off Tommy and get a handle on the tightness in her chest and stomach at the sight of him.

It had been just over a week since her trip to The Hamptons, since her car accident, since three pregnancy test kits gave her a positive result, since she ditched the damaged car with Tommy's security guy and left without explanation.

It felt like it had been much longer. Her body yearned to go to Tommy, to throw itself into his arms. Her mind reminded her of every fear she had – that he had no idea she was carrying a child, that she didn't know who the father was, that there was a chance she had been stupid enough to get pregnant with Tommy when things had maybe, possibly, had a chance of working out between them.

'I'm not bothered about the car, Andi. I'm here because I've given you more than enough time to get in touch and explain why you ran out on me, again.'

He stood straight, taking his back off the car. 'Could you please get out of the road?'

At that moment, a cab came hurtling towards her. Her eyes widened but she didn't move as the cab passed so close by her, the force blew her hair back from her shoulders.

Instinctively, her hands covered her tummy. *Sorry, Bean. I'm sorry.*

Tommy's concerned gaze moved from Andrea's face to the hands covering her unborn child, and back to her face. His eyes narrowed and his brows furrowed, but he said nothing as Andrea crossed the road towards him, thinking she had to face up to him at some point. Now was as bad as any time.

'Come up?' she asked, moving beyond Tommy and opening the entrance gate to the apartment block. 'Can I get you a drink of something?' She stepped into her apartment ahead of Tommy and flicked on the lights.

'You tell me,' he said, folding his arms across his chest, again, and coming to lean against the lounge wall as Andrea set down her bag and work papers then removed her jacket. 'Will I be here long?'

She sighed. 'Could you at least try not to be a dick? I've had a long day and an even longer week.'

She flicked on her record player, and the last vinyl she had been listening to started to play. It was an EP from a relatively up-and-coming indie artist whom she had an eye on to bring over to Stellar. Her lyrics were so beautiful they were almost poetic. Her voice was soft but she could rock out in a chorus and spice up a key change.

Hazarding a glance at Tommy as she headed past him and into her kitchen, she found him stone-faced. How in the hell was she supposed to start this conversation? How should she reveal the truth of everything?

As those questions made her mind spin, her body's lack of energy made her sway. Gripping the kitchen countertop, she closed her eyes, willing the room to still around her.

'Andi? Andi, are you okay?'

Tommy's arms came around her waist and she felt a stool press against her legs. Taking a seat, she came back to herself and felt like a damsel in distress – pathetic.

'I just need to eat something,' she said. 'I'll be fine in a minute.'

She tried to stand but Tommy pressed down gently on her shoulders. 'Stay. I'll fix you something.'

'There's bread by the refrigerator,' she said, in no position to argue.

Tommy set a glass of water in front of her, hung up his leather jacket, and set about making noise and mess behind her.

Andrea turned on her stool to watch him move around her kitchen, overwhelmed by a sense of homeliness that she had never felt in her apartment before. Those pregnancy hormones were no joke.

Tommy didn't speak as he set about cracking eggs into a pan and toasting bread. She wondered if he was also struggling for the right thing to say.

'I'm sorry for leaving the way I did,' Andrea said. Tommy stilled momentarily, his back to her, then continued going about his business in silence. 'I'm also sorry about the car.'

Then he glared at her, and she got the point that he really didn't give a crap about the damage to the car. He started to chop a pepper Andrea hadn't even realised was in her refrigerator. *Boy, he's a tough audience.*

'It had been a really rough day,' she continued, turning her water glass between her fingers in her lap.

Finally, Tommy spoke. 'I'd like to think we were maybe getting to a point where we would share a rough day with each other.' His tone was curt.

Oil spattered as he dropped the cold peppers into a hot pan. For as long as it took Tommy to turn out an omelette and two slices of toast and set them down on the countertop in front of Andrea, the pair remained silent.

As Andrea tucked into what was a surprisingly tasty plate of food, Tommy pulled up a stool on the opposite side of the counter.

'Who is this singing?' he asked.

She covered her mouth of half-chewed food with her fingertips and said, 'Her name is Hayley Pearce. Do you like her sound? She's indie and I'd like to work with her.' She scoffed once her mouth was empty. 'Not that I get to do much with artists these days but I'd like to bring her to Stellar.'

'She's good,' Tommy said. Then he clasped his hands and leaned his forearms on the countertop and asked, 'Do you want to be with me, Andi? Like, forget anything else, just answer me, right now, just you and me, nothing and no one else. Do you want to be with me?'

She swallowed the mouthful of food she had, almost choking.

'Look, I know I'm not the world's finest prospect,' he continued. 'I know that we'd have to work through schedules and touring. I have a past and I'm sure me telling you I've changed isn't enough to scratch that. But I'm asking you, in this moment, if you want to try?'

'Tommy, I—'

'Do you want to try?'

His eyes bored into hers and she knew, honestly, if there was nothing and no one else, then, 'Yes.'

He hung his head and sighed. His unexpected relief was enough to bring tears to Andrea's eyes.

She set her empty plate aside and reached out for his hands, wrapping hers around them. 'But, Tommy, it isn't that simple. I need to tell you something.'

He slipped a hand out of hers and took something from the back pocket of his indigo jeans, then set it down on the counter between them.

'Is it anything to do with this?' he asked.

She peered down to what was a receipt for three pregnancy

test kits, her mouth opening and closing but not forming coherent words.

'It was in the car when you returned it last week. Andi, are you pregnant?'

With his words came the stark reality that she'd been paying lip-service to him as far as she could. Warm tears fell from her eyes and rolled down her cheeks. 'Yes.'

Tommy exhaled and ran a hand through his hair. 'Mike found this when he was cleaning up the car. I've had it for a week. And I've played out every scenario in my mind. You found out you weren't pregnant. You found out you were. It's my baby. It's not my baby. I'm going crazy, here, Andi.

'But today, I asked myself what I just asked you – do I want to be with you, regardless of anyone and anything else? The answer is yes. So I need you to level with me. Tell me what I need to know, Andi.'

She wasn't sobbing, yet her tears kept rolling down her cheeks. 'I don't know whose baby it is, Tommy. I'm so sorry. I'm so ashamed, for me, for you, for the baby. It could be Hunter's. It could be yours. I can't find out for another couple of weeks. And I'm sorry that I ran but I was afraid. I've never thought about having children. I'm pretty sure I'd be a disaster as a mom. Then I thought it must be Hunter's and I told him...'

Then she was sobbing. 'He threw his credit card at me and told me to fix it.'

Tommy moved his stool so he was sitting next to her and tugged her into his chest. It was uncomfortable and... terrifying. She'd never sobbed on anyone's shoulder since she was a girl being comforted by her mom. But she was broken, and in Tommy's arms she fell apart. She wasn't the CEO who had her shit together, she wasn't the quasi sister-mom-wife she had been forced to be for years, she wasn't the friend who kept things together for others. She was just a woman, scared and in need of someone else to prop her up.

When she calmed in his arms, she realised Tommy was pressing his lips to her head, over and over, as he sang to her barely above a whisper.

Sitting up, she wiped her eyes. 'I'm sorry, I think you just got thirty years of repressed tears.' A short sombre laugh escaped her.

'I'll take all of your tears, Andi, as your partner or your friend. Do you hear me?'

She exhaled an unsteady breath. 'Quit being so nice to me, Tommy. I've made a mess of everything.'

'Do I need to give you a biology lesson, here? Academia isn't my strong point but I do know about the birds and the bees.' She laughed. 'It takes two people to make a baby, Andi. Talk to me.'

'Well, it turns out the dates mean that the baby could be Hunter's or yours.' She shook her head and looked down to her lap. 'At first, I was adamant I didn't want it but the obstetrician told me I needed to decide for myself whether I want a baby, no matter who the father is and, Tommy, I do want him or her. I'm frightened but I can't get rid of my baby.'

He held her chin and encouraged her to look at him. 'And I want you. So how about you stop being your usual self and let me take care of you?'

'I…' Her tears fell again, as if she had an endless supply. 'What if it isn't yours?'

'Then I'll love it because I love you and I want you to be my family. We'll all be a family.'

Her stool screeched against the floor as she stood and took his face in her hands, pressing her lips to his. 'I so want it to be yours.'

He kissed her again, more fiercely. 'It will be.'

* * *

Andrea woke on Monday morning wrapped in Tommy's arms. She had no idea what the future held, how she would deal with it or how to prepare for it. But she also knew that Tommy was going to be by her side. For the first time in her life, she wasn't alone. She was going to have a family of her own, to love and be loved by. She would have a partner she admired and respected and who would test her and push every one of her buttons – she would expect no less of a man like Tommy.

There was every chance she could end up hurt one day but the risk would be worth it.

As she lay peacefully, trailing her fingers up and down the strong arm across her chest, she wondered what Sofia was doing. For the first time, she understood that she didn't have all the answers, nor did Sofia, and she couldn't plan Sofia's life for her.

Not everything had to be perfect. That was a revelation to Andrea. And she knew, in that moment, how wrong she was to have meddled in her sister's life. She had to tell her, before Jay got out of rehab and told Sofia himself, that she had offered to buy out Jay's share of Sanfia Records if he agreed to file for a divorce.

In doing so, she would find out whether news of her affair with Hunter had made its way to her sister yet.

Then she needed to speak to Rosalie. Who would probably refuse to ever speak to her again.

'Stop. Over. Thinking,' Tommy mumbled, pulling Andrea tighter against him and nuzzling her neck.

She desperately hoped her baby was Tommy's.

* * *

Andrea's heart was pounding and her legs felt unsteady as she neared Sanfia Records. She played over and over in her head how she was going to tell Sofia what she had done. The deal she had offered Jay to walk away from Sofia and Sanfia Records.

She came to an abrupt stop as she rounded a corner and turned on the sidewalk outside of the terrace house that her own father had once transformed into a recording studio. Outside, Billy, Frankie and Seth looked deep in conversation, pausing to look up when they saw her.

'Andi, it's been a while,' Frankie said.

'Hi, guys,' she said, loosely holding up a hand in greeting as she neared them. 'Is Sofia around?'

'Probably best to hold off for now, Andi,' Billy said.

'Jay's here,' Seth added.

'Jay? I thought he was in rehab for another week?' she asked. But the evidence spoke for itself as Jay broke from the building, storming past Andi and deliberately crashing his shoulder into hers, almost knocking her from her feet.

Then there was an almighty bang from inside the building.

'What happened?' Andrea asked Seth, who was the closest person to her, and the first to reach out a hand to her elbow to steady her on her feet.

Before he could answer, the door of the studio was flung open again and in the open doorway stood Sofia – red-faced, mascara-stained eyes and undeniably livid.

'Isn't it enough that you tried to steal my label?' Sofia yelled, dragging all eyes to her as she strode towards her sister. 'That plan failed and so you go after my best artist. You are *fucking* unbelievable, Andrea!'

'Wow, Soph, we were—'

Sofia cut Seth off with a scowl. 'This isn't your business. It's between her and me.'

'Sofia, calm down,' Andrea said. 'I came here to talk to you. I wanted to tell you about Jay.'

'So it's true?' Sofia yelled, face-to-face with her sister. 'How could you? How could you try to take over the label? Wasn't it enough that you left us? Why, Andi? Why try to take this from me?'

Andrea held up her hands. 'Please, let's just go inside and you can hear me out. I don't know what Jay told you but let me explain, please.'

'Jay told me the truth!' Sofia dragged her hands roughly across her face. 'God, you've always resented me, haven't you? Mom died and you had to take care of me and you *hate* me for it.'

Now it was Andrea's turn to get mad. 'I could *never* hate you, Sofia,' she said through gritted teeth. 'Everything I have *ever* done has always been with your best interests at heart. That I swear to you.'

'Bullshit! Did you leave Sanfia for XM for my benefit?'

Andrea felt her nostrils flare as she inhaled, straightening her back, becoming taller on instinct. Her voice rose as she spoke. 'Yes, I goddamn did. I *knew* you were never over that. I left Sanfia because I couldn't stand that ass of a husband you chose for yourself and if I had stayed, you would have chosen him over me when it came down to it. I gave you a chance to keep both of us.'

'That is such *crap*! You left because you thought you were better than Sanfia. And now you realise that I could manage just fine without you and you want to steal the label from under my nose.'

'Grow up, Sofia. I told Jay I would buy him out on the condition he filed for a divorce.'

'You did *what*?'

Andrea scoffed. 'Right, so he left out that part, huh? I tried to let you sort things out for yourself but he was dragging you down and you were the only person who couldn't see it! You would never have told him to go, so I did it for you.'

Sofia lunged for Andrea but she was grabbed around the waist by Billy, and she struggled against him as she shouted, 'You need to leave, right now!'

Andrea shook her head. Like every time Sofia took a tantrum, she needed a day to take the edge off her stubbornness. It had been a near constant battle for Andrea when they were younger and some things never changed. 'When you've come to your senses, let me know, Soph. We can have an adult conversation.'

Sofia visibly fumed, inhaling and exhaling fast and deep as Billy held her by the waist. 'I never want to speak to you again, Andi. *Ever*.'

The words tore through Andrea's chest and pierced her heart, but she would *not* let that show. As the two women stared at one another, as if they were strangers at war, the space around them fell silent. Until the click of heels against the sidewalk came quicker and louder.

24

ROSALIE

Rosalie reached them, hands on her hips and scoffed, staring at Sofia. 'So I guess you did know all along.'

Sofia, who was clearly fizzing with anger, now also played at looking confused. 'You guess I did know what?'

Rosalie pointed to Andrea. 'That *she* has been screwing my dad.'

Sofia recoiled. 'What are you talking about?' She looked from Rosalie to her sister. 'Andi?'

Andrea was motionless but for the movement in her neck as she swallowed deeply. 'Ros, can we go somewhere and talk, please? Let me explain.'

'Explain?' Rosalie yelled. 'Are you going to tell me you weren't having an affair with my dad?'

'No,' Andrea said.

Just like that. Just that simple. Wasn't everything just so simple to precious Andrea. As Rosalie's chest began to heave, Sofia appeared to process what was being said.

'Yes,' Rosalie told her, her hands firmly planted on her hips. 'Your sister has been sleeping with her so-called friend's dad.'

'What the fuck, Andi?' Sofia shot out. 'Is this some kind of joke? Hunter? You've been... How could you do that?'

Then something came over Rosalie. Something she had never truly felt. It gripped her with the force of a superhuman and wouldn't let go. As Rosalie launched herself at Andrea, Seth grabbed hold of her, but not before her hand connected with Andrea's cheek.

Andrea raised a hand to her cheek but didn't retaliate. What Rosalie saw in her expression was shame and remorse. But it couldn't change the facts and it couldn't stop the uncontrollable rage that had swept Rosalie up.

'Rosalie, I'm more sorry than you could ever imagine,' Andrea said. 'It was wrong. Terrible. Believe me, I hate myself for it.'

'You should hate yourself!' Rosalie yelled the words that were so desperately unlike her and ended in sobs. The force that gripped her had been replaced by the arms of Seth and as she watched Andrea's eyes fill with tears, a small part of her wanted to go to her friend and wrap her arms around her.

But the biggest part of her felt disgust.

'You've betrayed me,' Sofia snarled, 'and you've lied to everyone. When did you become so hateful, Andi?'

'Sofia, please,' Andrea pleaded.

'No!' Sofia snapped. 'Look at her!'

Rosalie felt, rather than saw, all eyes fall on her as she turned into Seth's chest, letting him hold her as she cried. Because there was no one else whose arms she wanted to fall into. And she had no other options even if she did. She had lost her best friends. Her only true friends. And the image of her parents she had always believed in had been shattered. She gripped Seth's T-shirt as he stroked her back, whispering soothing words into her hair.

'You need to go,' Sofia said. 'And, Andrea, I never want to see you again.'

Andrea's usual stone-faced expression was replaced by a sob. Covering her face, she turned and walked away.

'Do you have your car here?' Seth asked.

Rosalie pulled back from his chest and looked up to him. She must look horrendous, she realised, but she remembered Nashville, how Seth thought she was beautiful with no make-up on, crazy hair and ill-fitting clothes. But perhaps her mascara-stained cheeks were a bridge too far.

Yet Seth wasn't looking at her like he was judging her, he was looking at her like someone who understood the heartbreak of cheating. And in that moment, as he held her face in his palms and wiped away her tears with his thumbs, she had more in common with Seth than ever before.

'Why don't you let me drive you home?' he asked.

Rosalie could only nod.

'Ros,' Sofia said, approaching her side. 'I know you must feel like everyone was in on something except you, but it isn't true. I swear on my li—'

'Don't do that,' Rosalie said, cutting her off. 'Don't ever swear on your life.'

Sofia nodded. 'I didn't know. None of us guys knew, okay?'

Sniffing, Rosalie turned to face Sofia. 'I believe you but if you weren't arguing with Andi about the affair, what were you fighting about when I turned up here?'

Sofia inhaled, looking as sad as Rosalie had ever seen her. 'Maybe that's a story for another time. Suffice to say, I just lost my husband and my sister in one day.'

'Oh, Soph, I'm sorry,' Rosalie said.

Sofia tried to smile but the corners of her mouth barely

moved. 'Let Seth take you home and if you need a friend you can call me or come to see me anytime. In fact, I'd like that, okay?'

'Okay.'

* * *

'Come in,' Rosalie said, holding open the door to the brightness of her park view apartment.

Placing her purse on the sideboard and swapping her heels for the spa slippers she kept by the entrance, Rosalie glanced up to Seth, watching him scrutinise her home. For some reason, she cared what he thought of her favourite interior project to date.

'You can leave your boots on if you like, or I have guest slippers in the velour seat there.'

As if he had just remembered Rosalie was in the room, Seth looked to her, then to the small blue seat that was hidden storage by the door. He slipped off his loosely tied scruffy boots and popped his feet into a pair of spa slippers that were a match for Rosalie's.

Phew, she thought, not wanting her recently revarnished hardwood floor to be at risk of damage.

'Would you like a drink? Tea? Coffee? Something cold? I have fresh juices or champagne. I'm afraid I don't stock beer.'

Seth offered her the half-smile she now considered deadly, making her knees wobbly. It reminded her of Mr Darcy in *Pride and Prejudice*, when he finally sees Elizabeth and her 'fine eyes'. Mr Seth Young's smile was also *quite* fine on further acquaintance.

'Coffee would be good, thanks. Would you like me to make it? You've had a pretty rough day already.'

For the first time in days, Rosalie smiled. 'You have no idea how particular I am about my coffee.'

And when Seth told her, 'Oh, I can imagine, Ros, believe me,' Rosalie chuckled for the first time in days too.

'I'll make coffee. Feel free to look around. Make yourself at home. I usually take coffee in the window, overlooking the park. Oh, and put some music on if you like. I'm not sure we'll have the same taste; I mostly have soundtracks and jazz, but there's some country in the collection too.'

Seth nodded and she watched him move about her home before she remembered she was supposed to be making drinks.

'Ah, a compromise,' Rosalie said, coming into her lounge with a bronze tray set with coffee and its components. 'I love the *Walk the Line* soundtrack. I generally prefer instrumentals but who doesn't love Reese Witherspoon and Joaquin Phoenix as June Carter and Johnny Cash?'

She set down the tray in her window table where Seth had obligingly taken a seat, overlooking Central Park. 'You know, Joaquin gets some bad press but he's actually a very nice man.'

Seth gave a short laugh. 'Why am I not surprised that you know Joaquin Phoenix, Ros?'

She wasn't entirely sure of his point but as she took a seat, she told him, 'I know a lot of people from the music industry. As it happens, when he and Reese were recording the soundtrack to *Walk the Line,* that's when I met him. He's just a person, Seth, just like you and me. Just like Randy is your brother first and a rock star second. And in a few months' time, when young girls are screaming your name and throwing their panties at you on stage, you'll tell me you still just feel like Seth. The guy who lost a bet one night and ended up on the stage of an open mic night, where Sofia found you. You'll tell me you're just a soldier, a son, a brother' – she handed him a full cup of coffee on a saucer – 'and a friend, first.'

As he met her gaze, his fingers resting gently against hers as he took the saucer from her, Rosalie said, 'Thank you. For today. And for things you said to me in Nashville. You probably didn't realise at the time but you've given me a few things to think about, maybe just at the right time, too, as things have worked out.'

In typical Seth fashion, he silently sipped his coffee and they sat in what felt like companiable silence for minutes. It was odd to Rosalie, and she found herself wondering when she ever simply shared silence with anyone. Suddenly, birds were singing outside. The trees of the park seemed greener. She could hear car horns tooting as far away as 59th and Fifth. And she could feel Seth's presence next to her. How nice it was to have someone sharing her home.

'I'm sorry about your dad and Andrea, Rosalie,' Seth said, taking it upon himself to top up his own coffee and Rosalie's. 'I know what it's like to have the image of a parent shattered, no matter whether you're young or older.'

Rosalie tried to smile but she knew it was sheathed in weariness. 'Thank you for saying that. I think people probably think it's just typical Rosalie, over the top and as dramatic as ever, but it's not just my dad, it's Andi.' Her eyes began to feel heavy and clouded over.

She thought about Hannah and Andrea and how much she already missed them, no matter how mad she was with them. 'I have other friends, women I grew up with. Kaitlin, Clarissa, Madeleine. But they aren't like Hannah and Andrea. Recently, I've realised the sad truth that they aren't my real friends at all. They're part of a fake life that I couldn't let go.

'I challenged Daddy about his affair with Andrea and found out some other things about my parents in the process. Things I've just... overlooked, somehow. And it made me see that I've been striving for something false for a very long time. My ideals and values have been based on a lie.'

She turned the cup on her saucer with her fingertips.

'Would you like to talk about it?' Seth asked.

Rosalie smiled because it was such a small offer but one that she hadn't received since everything with Andrea blew up. She realised that that was what she had really been missing – someone to talk to. Someone to spend her days and lonely nights with. The concern in Seth's expression told her without doubt that his question was genuine.

'I would really like that, thank you. But not today. Today, I only want to say that you were also right when you said I need to figure out what I really want from life, for me. Whether I really do want a baby or just something or some*one* meaningful in my life to... love. Whether a music label is truly the right thing for me. Or, you know, words to that effect.'

He chuckled. It was a warm and lovely sound. 'You make me sound like the Dalai Lama. I'm not sure I said those things exactly.'

'Meh, maybe my interpretation was a little philosophical.' They laughed together, something Rosalie had been missing recently.

'Anyway, my point is, you made me ask myself some very important questions. When I looked behind the superficial reasons for having a baby, I understood that what I wanted was the kind of unconditional love that a child can give. I want someone to give all my excess time and love to. Something more than I have in my life now. But I wondered... I'm wondering, if I couldn't be loved that way by... a man, first. Not a man who ticks everything on the checklist of what is supposed to be Prince Charming but a man whose company I enjoy and whom I respect.

'When I think about running a record label, I know I don't have the instinct for it, like Sofia and Andrea, and even Daddy has. I guess I just wanted to be taken seriously. I wanted Daddy to take me seriously. Now, I can't take him seriously.'

She sighed. 'I think it's going to take me a while to work out what I'm really passionate about. What makes me happy, in here.' She held her fingers to her chest. 'Not fleeting happiness that I get from purses and shoes. Not the smugness I feel when Daddy won't give me what I want so I run up a nasty credit card bill for him.'

'Your dad pays your credit cards for you?'

Rosalie smiled. 'I thought you weren't the judging type?'

Seth smiled behind his coffee cup.

'Well, actually, I have my own money but I hold on to one of Daddy's cards for when I'm cross.' Then she laughed. 'Perhaps I should go max it out now.'

'But seriously, all of this...' Seth gestured around the apartment. 'This is all yours?'

Rosalie nodded. 'I have investments that I manage. My hobby, really. And I decorated the place myself. I love interior design. I'm actually trained. I've done some wonderful projects.' She stood from her seat and went in search of her portfolio, handing it to Seth as she retook her seat. 'I keep pictures of the homes I've decorated. I only do it for friends, just a bit of fun, but I love it. I love how happy it makes people, you know? Like buying gifts for people. I know you think, and maybe others think, that I try to buy, I don't know, loyalty or something, but honestly, I just love to see reactions, how people smile from a little act of kindness.'

Seth flicked through the pictures in Rosalie's leatherbound book, then looked up to her. 'Rosalie, these pictures, this place, this is what you should do. If you love it and you want a business, this is it. These places are like something out of a magazine.'

'Oh, well, two of the homes have actually been featured on *Cribs*.' She beamed with pride. 'Do you really think they're pretty?'

'Pretty? Rosalie, they're incredible. You have an amazing talent.'

'I do?'

He shook his head, smiling. 'Yes, Ros, you do. You should be really proud of these places.'

Feeling her cheeks flush, swallowing irrational emotion that rose in her throat, Rosalie fiddled with the cafetière on the coffee table in front of her.

'Seth?' She couldn't bring herself to look up to him. 'I hope you don't think that I'm like your ex-fiancée. I would never—'

'Ros, if I did, I don't any more.'

'Then... do you think... once I've worked out a few things about myself... maybe... would you consider dating me? Because I'd really like to find out everything there is to know about you.'

She dared to look him in the eye and found his face completely expressionless. She felt uncomfortable and wanted to fill their silence with words. But she had done enough talking. It was time to stop forcing people to be who she wanted them to be. So she waited, until eventually, Seth's lips broke into his signature smile and he said, 'I'd like to get to know you too, Rosalie.'

Her lips curved at one side, then the other, then her smile became so big it turned to a giggle. 'Well, that's good then.'

Standing, she took their empty cups on her tray to the kitchen and in the privacy of the space, she held her fingertips to her lips as she smiled, feeling a jolt of promise charging through her body. She wouldn't get her hopes up and she wouldn't try to make Seth fit a mould. She would simply see where things went from there, on their natural course. Scruffy boots, lumberjack shirts, cheating parents, absent parents and all.

Later that night, Rosalie lit her favourite orange-peel-scented candles, set the soundtrack to *Pretty Woman* playing on her record player, and she cleansed her home and her life. Every pair of shoes she had in duplicate, every item of clothing she wore for other people because, frankly, no one would ever feel comfortable in it, every purse she bought purely because it was the best of the then current season, she bagged up for charity. And when she had four sacks, filled and ready to be deposited for a good cause waiting by her front door, she turned to her plastics. The first card to fall victim to the scissors was the one her dad still paid for.

From now on, whatever Rosalie did would be because it enriched her life truly, not superficially, or because it was kind to others. No more illusions of who she thought people were. No more trying to be something she wasn't. No more leading a life to be more like others.

25

HANNAH

Sofia handed a glass of wine to Hannah and took a seat in the opposite corner of her sofa, both of them tucking their feet up to the cushions. Smooth jazz played into the room from Sofia's record collection – Hannah's choice.

'So, do you want to get it all off your chest?' Hannah braved to ask.

'How long have you got?' Sofia asked, laughing shortly.

'I'm here and I'm all yours for as long as you want me, Sofia.' Hannah was always Andrea's best friend first and a friend-cum-big sister to Sofia second. But part of Hannah felt like helping Sofia was, in a way, making up for not being able to help Andrea right now. If nothing else, she knew they were both hurting, and a little woman-to-woman solidarity never hurt anyone.

Sofia sighed. 'When Jay first turned up at the studio, I was just pleased he looked well. I'd wanted to see him in the clinic and though he had refused to speak to me or see me, I understood he needed time and space to get better. Yet being close to him then, all I could think of was how he'd slept with at least one other woman behind my back.'

'So, had he discharged himself?'

Sofia sipped her wine and nodded. 'A week early.' She shook her head. 'I told him he should have finished the programme. What was the point in taking 80 per cent of the steps he needed to take? But, of course, he told me he was *fine*. Clean.' She shrugged. 'He'll never change, I see that now.

'It was all so... off, you know? It felt, for the first time, like I was in a room with a total stranger and I could see it from someone else's perspective. As if I weren't me. Like I was you or Andrea, or Dad. I could see Jay for what he was and what he would never be.

'So, maybe I shouldn't have been surprised when he said he wanted a divorce and he wanted me to buy him out of Sanfia. Cheeky fuck. He only ever had a share in the label because of me. He was so flippant. He just said, "I want a divorce, Soph. And I want out of the label, too."'

Sofia rubbed her face with her hands. 'I was shocked. I mean, I thought if anyone was having doubts, it was, rightly, me. When Jay left for rehab he said he wanted to get clean and make a go of things, so it didn't fit.'

She took a large drink from her wine glass then stared into the chilled liquid, nursing the glass between her hands.

'Then he said, "There's something else I need to tell you."'

Sofia looked up to Hannah, who felt like she was being scrutinised, and she asked herself silently whether she already knew what was coming. And as Hannah took a sip of her own wine, she had a feeling she did have a good idea.

'Andi went to see Jay at the clinic,' Sofia said.

And Hannah didn't want any more lies between her and the people she cared about, so she confessed. 'I knew that much.'

Sofia nodded, more, it seemed, in acknowledgement than anger. 'Well, Jay said she wanted to buy his share of Sanfia. Or rather she wanted XM Music Group and the Stellar label to buy his share of Sanfia.'

Hannah watched as Sofia's eyes filled with unshed tears. 'He said she tried to poach the label from me, Han. Since Seth is doing so well, she wants to take Sanfia back.' A tear broke free of Sofia's eye and she quickly wiped it away with the back of her hand. 'How could she do that to me? Isn't it enough that she left, that I've had to mortgage my home to keep Sanfia afloat? That I work round the clock just... *trying*?

'So, Jay said he was telling me so that I could stop it from happening. He said if I buy him out quickly, he won't give up his share to Andrea.' Sofia scoffed, then sobbed briefly, shaking her head to stop the onslaught of emotion. 'I told him I don't have the money and, do you know what he said? He said I would have to sell the apartment.'

'Oh, Soph, come here,' Hannah said, moving to Sofia's side and draping an arm around her shoulders.

When Sofia composed herself, Hannah moved back to her own sofa, her heart breaking for her friend.

'I just can't believe it,' Sofia said. She took another large mouthful of wine. 'The two people in the world who are supposed to love me the most and they've betrayed me. Then again, I really wasn't anticipating what came next either. *God, what a day it was.*'

'So Rosalie flipped out big style, huh? It's hardly surprising.' Hannah shook her head. 'I don't know if Rosalie and Andi will come through this. I hope so but I'm just not sure.'

'And if they don't, it's all on Andi,' Sofia added.

Though Hannah was loath to ever not defend Andrea, she couldn't deny that the fault was not with Rosalie. 'Why was Ros at the studio anyway?'

'Well, I'm not sure if she came to the studio to work – she's been coming along to get experience for when her dad—'

'Oh, yeah, I know about that.' Hannah rolled her eyes. Another of Rosalie's fads.

'So maybe she was coming along for that reason and saw Andi there then flipped. But she was so angry, I think maybe she came to confront me.'

'That wouldn't be like Rosalie,' Hannah mused.

'I guess people do strange things when they find out their best friend has been screwing their dad.'

'Good point,' Hannah conceded.

'I'd been arguing with Jay and I told him to get out. Then when I was alone, all I could think about was how much I hated Andrea for what she did. I don't know, I guess I just saw red. I was storming out of the studio to go to confront Andi. As I walked out, Andi was there talking to Seth and I figured she was trying to poach him from me. It all just hit me like a freight train. I lost it. Started screaming at Andi. Seth, or Billy maybe, held me back because, honestly, Han, I think I could have murdered her in that moment. Then we hear these heels come tapping on the pavement and Rosalie is there.'

'Oh God.'

'Yup. She starts screaming at me, saying that I must have known about the affair and didn't tell her. Then she's screaming at Andi.' Sofia drained the wine in her glass. 'What a mess, huh?'

'What a mess,' Hannah repeated. The women fell into silence, contemplating just how huge a mess everything really was.

'Thank you for helping me pack up Jay's things, Hannah,' Sofia said, eventually breaking the silence. 'Clearing out Jay's stuff at least feels like the first step towards the new normal – no husband, no sister, clinging on to Rosalie's friendship by a strained thread.' She looked around the apartment, retro bold colours, shelves of vinyls decorating the walls, a vintage record player a feature on a seventies-style sideboard. 'It looks bare in here. Like those first days after you take the Christmas decorations down.'

'Men have a lot of shit but they like to call us the hoarders.'

Sofia smiled. 'It just feels so strange. I guess I'd thought that despite our problems, I'd be married to Jay forever. For some bizarre reason, I thought that was in my control. Like, if we were broken, it was my job to fix us.'

'It's funny,' Hannah said, 'I've been doing a lot of thinking about just that, lately. I've always thought it was my job to keep our family together and happy. To look after the boys, and Rod, the house and work. To try and save Andrea from herself.' She rolled her eyes. 'But look how that worked out.'

'I'm sorry about your job,' Sofia said.

Hannah shrugged. 'It's actually been good in some ways to have some breathing space, though the longer I pretend to Rod, the worse it's going to be to tell him.'

'Hannah, it isn't my place, but Rod should know.'

'I know. I just... I feel like I've failed, you know? I feel like I need to resolve things and go to him with a solution, rather than a problem. In truth, I thought that the whole thing would have managed to resolve itself by now and Andrea would have just given me my job back. Naïve, I know. I guess there's also part of me that doesn't want to give Rod a reason to fall out with Andi, too. I know, I know, you're hating on her right now.'

Sofia's mouth twisted. She was still hating on her sister and maybe she always would but... 'I wouldn't want you to leave her alone. She needs you.'

'I used to think so. Now, I'm less sure. I think it's time I gave you an apology for my part in all of this too, Soph.'

Sofia's brows furrowed.

'I knew about the affair with Hunter from the night of the Presley John concert. I guessed; she didn't tell me. Then I thought maybe if she just ended it, things would be fine. So that's what I tried to encourage her to do. And she did, for the record. Andrea broke things off with Hunter. She started seeing Tommy and I thought things would be okay, that maybe it was best if no one ever knew. Then, when she found out she was pregnant, I just couldn't—'

Sofia spat her next mouthful of wine. 'Come again?'

Hannah's expression turned to one of horror.

'My sister is pregnant?'

'Oh, fuck. I assumed you knew.'

* * *

Hannah opened her front door with TJ on her hip, surprised to see Andrea on her doorstep.

'Relax,' Andrea said. 'I'm not here to scream or yell, I'm here to apologise. You have every right to slam the door in my face and I would deserve it but I'm hoping you won't.'

Hannah stared at her friend, who frankly looked like death. Her face was gaunt. Grey circles coloured underneath her eyes and there was a light shadow on her cheek, which Hannah figured was from Rosalie having slapped her outside the studio, though Sofia hadn't explained it had been quite as good a contact as it clearly had been.

'Can I come in?'

Hannah stood aside to let Andrea step into the house, then led her through to the kitchen. Handing off TJ to Andrea, she asked, 'Would you like tea?'

Andrea looked up from where she was rowing a boat with TJ on her lap on a chair at the dining table. 'Please.'

When Hannah took a seat at the table, she placed down a plate of cookies and confirmed that Andrea could share hers with TJ.

Contented in Andrea's lap, TJ began to close his eyes and his head became floppy as he fell into his afternoon nap.

'How are you?' Hannah asked Andrea.

Andrea scoffed. 'It's me who should be asking you that.'

'Sofia? Rosalie?'

Andrea shook her head, confirming that neither her sister nor her friend were speaking to her. 'I can't say I blame them either. But that's not why I'm here,' she said. 'I guess there's no better place to start than to tell you I'm sorry, Hannah. I'm sorry for the affair and putting you in a shitty situation with Rosalie and Sofia, even at work. I'm sorry for taking everything out on you when all you tried to do was help. And I'm sorrier than you can imagine that I fired you and for the way I did it, in front of people.'

It was Hannah's instinct to accept the apology and go on to make excuses for Andrea's behaviour but, for once, she wasn't going to do that. She missed Andrea and she wanted her to know that she would always be there for her, especially knowing how much it would be killing Andrea that Sofia wasn't speaking to her. Hannah knew that she shouldn't have blurted out the affair to Rosalie in the manner she had either, but none of that excused Andrea's actions. Not this time.

'The thing is, Hannah, I miss you. It's like I've lost a piece of me without you around. You've always been there for me when I needed it, and even when I didn't realise how much I needed you. Sometimes the truths you've told me have been brutal and sometimes so nice I couldn't believe them. Well, now it's my turn to tell you the truth – you've done too much to help me, Hannah, even sacrificed at home, and don't say you haven't. I've never told you that because I'm selfish and I've been scared to lose you as my assistant but I'm more scared not to have you in my life every day. The thought of going through everything without you...' She glanced to her lower abdomen. 'And without Sofia and Rosalie, too. I can't bear it.

'I've been horrible. Selfish and hateful, I know. But I need you, Hannah.

'So, if you'll have it, I've also come here to offer you your job back, if you would ever even consider working for me again, anyway.'

Hannah smiled because, for once, Andrea had shared with Hannah what Hannah always knew she felt. 'You will never lose me from your life, Andi. No matter how big our fuck-ups. Just try it. I'd hunt you down and make you be my best friend.'

They shared a knowing smile.

'But...' This was harder than she thought it would be. 'I don't want my job back. I've done a lot of thinking recently about what I want from my life. It's twofold. I want to have more flexibility to spend time with my family, to be home when my kids finish school, to have the chance to hear TJ's first sentence and see his first real steps. But I also want, *need*, more. I need to be stretched and I need to push myself, to see how much I've got in me. I'm not exactly sure what that looks like at the moment but I'm working on it.'

Hannah braced herself for Andrea's reaction, and the one she received she should have expected. Andrea smiled and reached out to take Hannah's hand.

'You know something else I've never told you, Hannah? You could be anything you want to be. You're smart and organised, funny and great with people. Your taste in music is almost as good as mine.'

Hannah chuckled.

'I'm going to hate not working with you every day, Han. Not because I need you to run around after me, which, let's face it, I do, because I'm a hot mess without you.'

They both laughed.

'I'll hate not working with you because you're my family and I love you.' Andrea's eyes glazed over, which Hannah briefly noticed before her own vision clouded. 'I'm also glad that you're not going to take your job back. You deserve to have more. *Everything*. So when you decide what it is you want to do, and if that happens to be using your talents to manage in the music industry – I think you'd be great at it, FYI – I'm going to write you the best resumé and references anyone in the world has ever written.'

Hannah sipped her tea, trying to hide behind her cup how nice it felt to have Andrea's endorsement. 'Do you really think management would be a good idea for me?'

Andrea squeezed Hannah's hand. 'I think you'd kick ass at it.'

Hannah felt as if her chest physically filled with pride. 'Thank you. It means a lot coming from you, Andi. But before I deal with any of that, I really need to tell Rod that I'm currently unemployed.'

'You haven't told him yet?' Andrea asked, her surprise evident.

'Oh, please, like you're one to judge,' Hannah said with good humour, making them laugh again.

'Good point well made. Seriously, you do need to tell him, though,' Andrea said.

'I know. I will.'

Andrea bent to reach into her purse, being careful not to

wake TJ, who was now snoring. She took out an envelope and handed it to Hannah. 'This is your final pay slip. I anticipated you throwing my job offer back in my face, just not quite as politely as you have done.' She smiled, uncommonly bashful. 'You've been paid in lieu of notice, straight into your account.'

Hannah opened the envelope. 'Andi, this is six months' pay.'

'Yeah, well, I'm hoping you don't sue my ass.'

Hannah held her fingertips to her lips. 'Thank you.'

'It's only what you deserve.'

They spent an hour catching up on the fallout with Sofia, Rosalie's breakdown in the middle of the sidewalk outside of Sanfia Records when she bumped into Andrea, how Andrea was feeling in pregnancy and that she and Tommy were trying to make a go of things. Hannah relayed her weight loss from walking with TJ every day and how being at home had taught her, with certainty, that she could not be a full-time, stay-at-home mom.

'As they say, the grass isn't always greener on the other side,' she confessed.

Then, a very tired-looking Andrea headed back to her office.

Things were far from perfect in Hannah's life. Neither she nor Andrea would easily forget what had happened in recent weeks. But things felt more right after Andrea's visit than they had before and for that she was grateful.

* * *

Later that day, Hannah had decided to stop pretending that she was still working. Instead, she spent the afternoon preparing a three-course meal for Rod. When Luke and Jackson came home from school, she told them they would be on babysitting duties for the night and that she and Rod were having a date night downstairs.

By the time Rod came home from post-school training, she'd slipped into a little black dress that she hadn't worn for a very long time. She had even taken the trouble to shave her legs. Oh yes, she knew how to handle her husband. Feed him, give him beer, drop the bombshell, then seduce him.

Sitting at the kitchen table, their favourite smooth jazz playing in the background, two bottles of beer (Rod) and two glasses of wine (Hannah) under their skin, Hannah was about to break her news to Rod when he asked, 'So, is all this a pre-empt to you telling me why you've been staying home for the last week?'

'You knew?'

'Mrs Schinken said she'd seen you and TJ out walking a couple of days and Luke asked why you were really home in the evenings. I figured you'd fallen out with Andi. Am I right?'

'Huh.'

He leaned back in his chair and hung an elbow loosely over the back, tugging at the smart shirt he had put on for her after coming home to find her in a dress. His dark, firm skin blended with her wine to make her feel intoxicated by desire. It was the first time in months that she had felt like she wanted to tear at his clothes – the first time she hadn't been feeling truly exhausted.

'Babe, I may just be the jock from high school but I'm not an idiot.'

'I've never thought of you as an idiot. Please don't say things like that.'

'Well, are you going to let me in on the secret?'

Hannah steadied herself. 'Okay, here goes. Andi was sleeping with Rosalie's dad. I told Rosalie and Andi fired me. Wait, let me finish. Andi and I have made up and she paid me six months' salary but when she offered me my job back, I turned it down.'

'You're unemployed?'

'Temporarily,' she said quickly. 'Andi said she'll write me a reference to do whatever I want. In reality, if I can't find anything before the money runs out, she'll take me back. But I don't want to go back.'

Rod leaned back into his chair, waiting for more of an explanation.

'It's time to hear me out, Rod, about some things I should have said years ago. Now, I shouldn't have hidden things from you, I know that, but I also shouldn't have felt like I had to hide things from you. That's partly my fault for putting so much pressure on myself but it's partly your fault, too.

'I made a mistake, I hurt my friends and I got fired, deservedly so. I made an even bigger mistake when I didn't tell you right away.

'But here's the thing, I'm not infallible and that's okay. I've realised that I've been trying to look after this family almost entirely on my own for as long as I can remember. I've been trying to prove to myself and everyone else that I'm better than my own mother, that my kids will always come first, that the young girl who fell pregnant in college could raise a child without any help.'

'Hannah, you're not alone. You never have been alone.'

'I think I'm only just appreciating that. And I recognise my fault in that, I do. But you also need to start realising that we're in this together. I never got pregnant on my own. It wasn't my fault that your football career didn't work out. And, Rod, you're really just a little bit lazy.'

He opened his mouth to protest, then twisted his lips shut without retort.

'We're a team, Rod, and I need you to start playing for the team, instead of coming off the bench in the final quarter. Understand?

'I want to work and do something more than I have been doing but I need your support in that. I love the music industry and it might take me a little time to work out what I'm going to do but I'm on it, I promise.

'When I do find something, I need you to start pulling your weight. No more staying behind for work drinks without consulting me. No more leaving your shit around the house expecting the magic fairies to swoop in and clean up after you. And no more leaving the effing toilet seat up.

'I need your help. There, I said it. I need your help. And I shouldn't have to ask for it because you should want to be here for me, and the kids.'

Rod stared at his wife, seeming to process her words. 'Is this how you've been feeling? For what, years?'

Hannah nodded sadly.

'Babe, I thought you liked running around after us all.'

She raised one eyebrow in question.

'Yeah, okay,' Rod conceded. 'Who would like picking up after my shit, right?' He scratched his head almost comically. 'Look, Han, you're my world. I'm sorry if I take you for granted. I guess if I'm honest, I know I do. But I'd be nothing without you and the last thing I want is for you to be unhappy, okay? So I can do those things. I can do more. Or I can certainly try. But you've gotta keep talkin' to me, babe. Yeah? That's how we work. We might not be perfect but I've loved you, girl, since you were nineteen years old. That's never going to change. I've got your back, no matter what. You hear me?'

She nodded.

'Well, all right then. Tell me this, how long until that main course is ready?'

Hannah's lips curved up mischievously. She stood, moving to the cooker and turning down the heat. 'Long enough,' she said.

Then Rod was upon her, kissing her roughly, growling into her neck and pulling down the straps of her dress. When she laughed, he placed a hand over her mouth. 'Do you really want the zoo to come down here?'

With humour dancing in her eyes, she shook her head. He picked her up and carried her to the table, stepping between her legs.

'Oh, and Rod, one more thing... I want you to have a vasectomy.'

26

ANDREA

Andrea had suffered a restless night's sleep, tossing and turning. It was no wonder, since most things in her life were falling apart. She had slept alone in her own apartment because Tommy was in Los Angeles for a pre-recorded chat show interview about his solo work and wasn't coming back until later that day. All that had been going through her mind for the last four days was that Sofia *hated* her. And she had no idea if she could ever repair her relationship with Rosalie.

But on top of that, she'd experienced stabbing pains in her lower abdomen. At 3 a.m. she had made herself a hot water bottle, which had eased the pain enough that she'd managed to settle into a short sleep before her alarm sounded its wake-up call.

She had just ended a terse meeting with her executive board and was now pacing the floor of her office, trying to walk off the pain that was now a constant ache in her stomach. Was it wind? Had she eaten something?

She was trying not to be melodramatic but had decided to give things until lunchtime and if the pain hadn't subsided by then, she would put in a call to her obstetrician and confirm what kind of painkillers she was allowed to take whilst pregnant.

She was startled by the entrance of Bryant Matthews – the man who had been gunning for the position of CEO and who thought he was a shoo-in for the role ahead of Andrea – as her office door was opened so hard it clattered off the adjacent wall.

'Were you born in a barn, Bryant?' Andrea chided.

'What the hell kind of presentation to the Board was that?' he quipped, ignoring her remark.

Before she could retort, a stabbing pain struck Andrea's stomach and her mind went blank as she breathed through it, trying not to let her weakness show.

'I'm afraid you'll have to expand on that,' she told Bryant, forcing herself to stand upright and not fold forward.

He pushed his hands into the pockets of his suit pants defiantly. 'You presented a load of nothing, Andrea. Since you took the position of CEO, Stellar's books are down. That's a pretty impressive rate of profit destruction, wouldn't you say? Then you have the audacity to sit in that meeting and give us nothing – no way forward, no plans. What happened to your promise of luring in new stars, big-hitters? What happened to acquiring high-performing indie labels?'

Another strike of pain hit Andrea and she moved to her desk, leaning on it for support.

'Bryant, we need to do this another time, I have a meeting.'

With another wave of pain, she bent forward, gripping the edges of her desk, unable to hide any more as she sucked air through her teeth.

Bryant came to her side. 'Andrea? Are you okay? What's wrong?'

She shook her head, still gripping the desk with one hand and holding her stomach with the other. 'I'm fine.'

'The hell you are,' Bryant said.

What happened next was a blur. There was a flurry of shouting and activity around her, but Andrea heard nothing distinctive because her eyes were fixed to the tears of blood that came from underneath her skirt and rolled down her legs.

No. No, please, no.

* * *

'Shhh, let yourself go to sleep,' Hannah said as she stroked Andrea's temple and held her hand at the side of her hospital bed. 'Close your eyes.'

'Hannah, I'm so sorry. I'm sorry for everything,' Andrea said, grateful for her best friend.

'I know you are, sweetie. I am too. Just rest.' Andrea watched as a tear fell from Hannah's eye. 'I'm here.'

Andrea's breath hitched as she tried to breathe in. She'd been given painkillers, antibiotics and fluids but the intravenous plug in the back of her hand was currently empty as she lay in the small grey room.

She barely remembered the trip in the ambulance, what the doctors and nurses had been saying to each other and to her; she couldn't remember who had called Hannah from the office and at what point she arrived at the hospital. All she could see when she closed her eyes was the blood. All she could hear when the room fell silent was the absurdity of the doctor who told her she had 'lost' her baby, as if she might find it again some place.

'This is my fault,' she said, her throat hoarse. 'I deserve this for everything I've done.'

'Hey! You stop that, right now,' Hannah chided. 'This is awful, Andi. So, so sad. But it is *not* your fault.'

Andrea's chin quivered. She didn't bother to argue but she

knew it was her fault. It was her penance for sleeping with a married man, for causing her sister to hate her, for firing her best friend, who, despite everything, had rushed straight to her bedside.

'What kind of baby would have chosen me?'

Hannah ran her thumbs under Andrea's eyes for what felt like the millionth time in the last hour. 'Andi, one day, you are going to be an incredible mommy. I promise you that.'

Andrea turned her head on her pillow and looked at her friend, whose honest, good eyes told her she meant those words. But Andrea had nothing to say in return.

Behind Hannah, the pastel-pink-coloured door to the room was gently pushed open. Tommy saw her and was instantly at her side, lifting her to him and cradling her head against his stomach, where Andrea was happy to be held.

'I'm going to get a coffee,' Hannah said.

When Andrea heard the door close, her heart broke a little bit more and she wept in Tommy's hold. He shuffled her over on the bed and climbed on top of the white cotton sheets next to her. With her head cradled against his chest, she heard his heartbeat rise and him sniffing back his own tears.

They had decided to be a family, no matter what. And they'd only had four days to enjoy that together.

'I'm sorry,' she told him over and over again. 'I'm so sorry.'

He pressed his lips to her head. 'You're killing me, Andi. What can I do? I need you to tell me how to make this better, baby. We'll try again. We'll try again. I love you so much.'

'I've messed up everything, Tommy. Sofia hates me. She *hates* me. I don't want to be at Stellar any more. I've screwed up so badly with Rosalie. It's a miracle Hannah will even speak to me.'

He held her tighter against him. 'Nobody hates you, Andi. We all love you. You've made some mistakes. That's life. Losing the baby...' His voice broke. Once he had gathered himself, he continued. 'It's nothing to do with anything else except really shitty luck. It just wasn't your time. But it will be. It'll be our time.'

She wasn't sure how long they lay like that but in Tommy's arms, she finally felt like she could drift to sleep. 'I just want it to be like it used to be,' she murmured, before everything went dark.

27

HANNAH

Sofia had been at the studio when Hannah called her on the way to the hospital. As Hannah knew she would, despite everything going on between them, Sofia had dropped whatever she was doing and rushed straight away to be at Andrea's side.

So now she, Sofia and Seth, who had driven Sofia to the hospital, were sitting in the waiting room, for Hannah and Sofia's parts waiting for Tommy to come out of Andrea's room so that they could visit their best friend and sister.

Hannah was sitting in a leather chair next to Sofia, nursing what was now a cold coffee, staring out of the window at the stillness of the blue sky beyond. It seemed strange that it would be such a nice day outside. Even with her first pregnancy, as surprised as she was, Hannah had loved her baby before it was even a foetus. She just couldn't imagine the pain Andrea would be going through.

'I can't believe I never even got around to congratulating her on being pregnant, and now this,' Sofia said. 'I told her I hated her. I was evil.'

Hannah broke from her own thoughts, reaching out a hand to take Sofia's.

'She knows you don't hate her, Sofia. You love her. She knows that. I'm sure it hasn't always felt like it and I know she's gone the wrong way about some of the things she's done but Andi has always, *always* had your best interests at heart, Soph.

'She screwed up with Hunter and she knows that. Believe me, she's punishing herself more than anyone else could about it. But the stuff with XM Music Group and Jay, those things she truly thought she was doing in your best interests. Now, I'm not saying there weren't some perks for her along the way but just hear me out.'

Sofia looked to Hannah and nodded.

'Andi despised Jay, you know that. She never thought he was right for you. But when you decided to marry him, she realised you'd made your decision and, whether she liked it or not, it was not her choice to make. She didn't want to become embroiled in admin and finance tasks when she went to Stellar, Soph, but it was a good opportunity and she thought that the only way she could let you live your life with Jay and not fall out with her would be if she left Sanfia Records.'

Sofia's brows furrowed as she seemed to process Hannah's words. 'She left Sanfia so that Jay and I could run it together?'

Hannah nodded. 'Don't get me wrong, the lure of Stellar was big for her, but she only considered taking a meeting with them about the move in the first place because she knew something had to change at Sanfia.'

'She never told me that,' Sofia admitted.

Hannah gave her a sad smile. 'That's not Andrea's style. She's always tried to play the silent angel.'

'It doesn't excuse what she did with Jay. She tried to poach Sanfia.'

Hannah shook her head. 'I was hoping that you and Andi might have talked through this at some point and, again, Andi knows that she shouldn't have stepped in when she did. That was why she was coming to speak to you the other day at the studio. She's sorry for the way she went about things and she wanted to explain that. Of course, no one expected that Jay would sign himself out of rehab before his thirty days were up.'

'But Jay said—'

'I don't know exactly what Jay told you but here's the truth. Andrea and your dad were worried about you. You were exhausted, Soph, and when you got that black eye... Andi went out to New Jersey to see your dad.'

'She did?'

Sofia was right to be surprised, since Andrea never made the trip out to visit their dad. Hannah nodded. 'They talked and they both knew, in their hearts, that even if you were unhappy, you would never leave Jay.' Hannah smiled and gripped Sofia's hand tighter. 'You're too loyal for your own good sometimes. You always have been.'

'Funnily enough, I'm not feeling loyal at all today.'

'Andi asked Jimmy to try to convince Jay to go to rehab. She offered to pay anything that insurance wouldn't cover.'

'I didn't realise that.'

Hannah shrugged, as if to say, *Well, that's Andi for you.* 'Jimmy stuck to his end of the deal and, though he didn't know exactly what she had planned, Andi figured her role was to give you the chance to break free of Jay and have a chance at something, some*one*, better.'

At that moment, Tommy Dawson stepped into the waiting area, dragging a hand roughly through his hair. His eyes were red and Hannah knew in that moment that she had never misunderstood how much Andrea and Tommy had felt for each other in the times they'd briefly been dating in the past.

Hannah stood. 'How is she?'

Tommy tried to speak but his face contorted with pain and he shrugged. Hannah wrapped her arms around him and kissed his cheek, trying to convey her thanks that he was there for her best friend and that she was sorry for their loss.

Tommy brought his hands around her waist and as he held on to her, he said, 'She loves you, Hannah.' Then he pulled back and looked to Sofia. 'Sofia, she loves you so much. Please go to speak to her.'

Sofia stood and inhaled deeply, nodding. 'I will.'

'She's sleeping now but they'll let her out tonight. Maybe you could speak to her before then.'

'I will,' Sofia repeated.

Tommy seemed to notice Seth in the room then. He dragged in a breath, composing himself, and moved to him, holding out his hand. 'Hey, I'm Tommy.'

Seth stood and smiled sombrely. 'I know. Seth. I'm sorry, Tommy. I don't know what else to say.'

Tommy patted Seth on the arm. 'Listen, I was hoping you and I could talk?'

The look of confusion on Seth's face was a match for Hannah's and Sofia's but in that moment, it seemed neither of them had the energy to ask questions or worry about anything other than Andrea.

'Ah, sure,' Seth said.

The men left Sofia and Hannah, who went back to their seats next to each other. 'You were going to tell me about Andi visiting Jay,' Sofia said.

'Right. Well, Andi wanted to buy Jay out of Sanfia. What she actually wanted was to buy him out herself but she couldn't because she's contracted to Stellar and has restrictive covenants. So the only way she figured she could make it happen would be to have Stellar buy out Jay's share of the business.'

'So it was never about her taking Sanfia over to XM Music Group?'

Hannah shook her head. 'No. Obviously, it wouldn't have hurt Andi's reputation at Stellar and that's partly why she wanted to explain everything to you before you found out from someone else. But I saw the deal she had drawn up, Soph. If Stellar had bought out Jay's share, she was going to make sure that you were still able to run Sanfia as you wanted to do. But the part Jay didn't tell you was that Andi made the deal conditional on Jay filing for divorce.'

Sofia stood from her seat. 'She told me. I was... *am* furious.'

Hannah stood too. 'I know. She shouldn't have meddled and Andi knows that too. She was going to call it all off after she'd confessed to you.'

'She was trying to play Creator with my life,' Sofia scolded.

'She made a mistake. But she also thought it would be a test. See, in Andi's mind, if Jay didn't take the deal and he got sober, she would have left you to it and accepted that you had to be left alone to work things out between you. If he took the deal, it meant...'

'He didn't love me,' Sofia said sadly. 'As it happens, he didn't take the deal, so maybe he loved me enough not to sell me out to Stellar. Or maybe he just despised Andi enough not to want her to win but for him to still get cash. Either way, he still left.'

Sofia moved to the window and stared outside. 'Andrea was wrong to mess with my life with Jay. Yet I have Sanfia. And Jay has done what I probably could never have asked him to do –

he's left. In a warped and messed-up way, maybe things have worked out for the best.

'But I still have the problem of having to buy Jay out of the label,' Sofia said. 'I can't afford to do that.'

'Have you considered asking Rosalie?' Hannah suggested.

Sofia gave her a look of incredulity. 'In Rosalie's mind, I must be tied to Andi in this whole thing. She'll probably never speak to either Andi or me again, let alone offer to lend me money or buy into the label.' She looked back to the outside. 'I wouldn't want to abuse her friendship like that, in any case.'

'All I'll say is, Rosalie truly doesn't have a malicious cell in her beautiful, immaculate body. She wouldn't hold something that Andrea's done against you, Soph.'

Hannah retook her seat. 'Well, now you know the truth, how do you feel?'

Sofia shrugged. 'I don't know. I'm mad at Andi but I'm pleased I understand now what she'd been thinking. Ultimately, it doesn't matter now. She's my sister and she's hurting.'

An hour later, Hannah and Sofia crept quietly into Andrea's room, where she was asleep, fragile and pale. As Hannah took a seat at one side of the bed, Sofia leaned her head next to Andrea's on her pillow as she sat in the chair by the other side of her sister's hospital bed, both of them watching Andrea sleep.

Andrea had made a huge mistake getting involved with Hunter, but maybe it would have never happened if she hadn't felt like she had to leave Sanfia Records and let Sofia run the business with Jay. Her goodness had been misplaced when it came to her actions with Sofia and Jay, meddling in their lives. But her good intentions were there. Hannah was sure that, deep down, Sofia knew those good intentions had always been there.

'I don't hate you, Andi,' Sofia whispered. 'I could never hate you. I love you with all my heart and it's breaking for you right now.'

Andrea's hand rose and she brought it to rest on Sofia's cheek, her eyes still closed. 'I love you,' she whispered, turning to kiss Sofia's brow.

28

ROSALIE

Rosalie was reviewing her investment report over coffee when her intercom buzzed. She wasn't expecting anyone and was surprised to look in the viewfinder and see Andrea downstairs. She buzzed her in and went to find a clean mug from the kitchen to pour coffee for her.

Yesterday, she had been visited by Hannah and Sofia. They had each come under the guise of apologising to Rosalie. Hannah apologised for the way she broke the news of Andrea's affair with Hunter. Sofia apologised for, essentially, being Andrea's sister and thereby determining that implicitly, she had wronged Rosalie.

In truth, Rosalie hadn't needed their apologies; she was simply grateful that they obviously missed her too. She told them as much and over two pots of English tea, the women resolved to always be open and honest with each other and not to let things come between their friendship.

Rosalie had told them about her wardrobe and life cleanse, how she was looking into turning her passion for interiors into a business and how she and Seth were intending to date. Sofia filled her in on Jay leaving and how, even though she was hurting, she knew it was going to be the right thing for them both in the long run. Hannah told her how she was looking for a new job, one that might be more flexible, and how she'd opened up to Rod after all their years together, about how she needed his support.

In all, Rosalie couldn't have been happier for her friends and to have them back in her life. But, she explained, things couldn't go back to how they were because they would never be three best friends and a little sister again.

After that, Hannah and Sofia had explained a few things to Rosalie. Now, as she filled a mug full of coffee for Andrea, she wondered if Andrea had come of her own accord, or whether she had been sent by Hannah and Sofia.

She'd left the door ajar but Andrea tapped gently and called her name before coming inside.

'I'm in the lounge,' Rosalie called from her seat in the window. She had opted to sit, unsure how she should greet her old friend.

Despite it being a work day, Andrea wasn't dressed in her usual corporate attire. She wore jeans and a T-shirt, with flat-soled sandals. Her hair was roughly tied up and she looked pale, tired and... sad.

She hovered on the threshold between the lounge and the hallway, holding her handbag in front of her with both hands as she looked at Rosalie.

'Hi,' she said, not bold and confident like Andrea usually was but uncertain.

Rosalie had wanted to be stern and guarded but seeing Andrea this way was not what she wanted at all.

She thought about the baby Andrea had been carrying just days before and the tragedy of having lost it. She'd cried when

Hannah and Sofia had told her about it, even though she was still furious with Andrea. Because she loved her. Though she wished she didn't because she would be able to move on much easier if she didn't, the fact was, Andrea was one of Rosalie's best friends. Not of the Clarissa, Kaitlin or Madeleine ilk but of the real kind.

'I poured you coffee,' Rosalie said.

Andrea took the invitation and came to sit in the high-back chair opposite Rosalie, each of them looking out of the window at the view across Central Park.

'Rosalie, I know there's nothing I can say or do to ever make up for what I did. It was shameful and disgusting and I will forever be sorry for all the hurt I caused, to everyone, but mostly to you.'

Rosalie looked at her now and saw a stream of water running down Andrea's cheek. Andrea who never cried or got emotional about anything. Stoic Andrea.

It broke Rosalie's resolve.

'I'm sorry about the baby.'

Andrea's jaw tensed and she turned back to the window for a moment before glancing back to Rosalie. 'Thank you.'

'Was it...?'

'I don't know,' Andrea said, her voice catching. 'It's possible. I hoped it was Tommy's.'

Rosalie thought about that. About the fact that the baby could have been her family, too. Then she remembered what Hannah told her, that her father had thrown his credit card at Andrea and told her to get rid of it.

'He should never have told you to abort the pregnancy,' Rosalie said. 'I'm sorry he did that.'

Andrea let out a short, sad laugh. 'You have nothing to apologise for, Rosalie. This is all on my shoulders. I knew what I was doing. I knew how much it would hurt you… your mom, too. Yet I did it.'

Andrea's voice broke and her shoulders shook as she started to cry. 'I miss you. I know I have no right to say that but I do and I hope that, one day, we could be friends again. You'll never know how truly sorry I am, Ros. For everything.'

Seeing Andrea broken as she was, Rosalie's own tears spilled from her eyes. She clenched her fists to stop herself from reaching out and comforting Andrea.

'I don't know if I can ever forgive you, Andi. And I will never *ever* forget.'

She wiped the tears from her face.

'But I miss you, too. All of you. So… I'm willing to try.'

Her words turned Andrea's cries to sobs and this time, Rosalie could not stop herself from putting her arms around her friend's shoulders.

It would be a long, long time before Rosalie could ever trust Andrea again. But she knew she wanted to, one day.

EPILOGUE
ABOUT ONE YEAR LATER...

TOMMY DAWSON
World Tour

Supported by
Seth Young

The arena crowd roared when Seth played the first chord of his latest single that was still sitting at number one on the country Billboard chart.

The track had a killer opening sequence and Seth loved to play it. Rosalie loved to hear it. As she stood in the wings of the stage, her heart rate soared when Billy brought in the bassline then Frankie kicked up the beat on the electric guitar.

As Seth's newest session player pummelled the drums and Seth began to sing, Rosalie could see that he was in his element. He had never needed or expected the fame he'd received and when they were lying next to each other in bed, or sharing breakfast over the view of Central Park from Rosalie's – their – apartment, Seth was still just the guy who wore scruffy boots and lumberjack shirts. And though Rosalie had managed to get him in a suit once or twice in their six months together, actually, he had been a bigger influence on Rosalie's style. She loved that she could tap her feet in the sneakers she wore with her jeans and T-shirt without feeling any pain at all. And now that she was busy with her interior design business, she was on her feet a lot. These days, heels were reserved for awards events and fancy dinners with Seth or her best friends only.

Tonight was the last show of Tommy's world tour. Since he'd decided to buy Jay's share of Sanfia Records and bring Andrea back to the label to produce again – the way things used to be, the way she loved – Tommy, Andrea and Sofia had worked hard as a team to make Seth a star. Though Seth may have been the supporting act, the combination of Tommy and Seth had led to sell-out concerts on every night of the tour. And they were all planning to go out on a high, playing with more energy than ever for their home crowd in New York.

Seth sang about the woman he loved, how her hips could wreak havoc on a man, how her mind was as genius as it was a pain in the ass, how only a superhero could handle her. And he sang with a smile. A smile that filled Rosalie's heart because just nights ago, he had told her, 'If someone had asked me if I would have ever smiled again when I'd left the services and lost my fiancée, I would have said no. Yet here I am, one year after meeting a girl I'd misunderstood entirely, feeling like I hold the world in my hands. And damn it, you make me smile every day, Ros.'

The guys kicked into the chorus and Seth jogged to Billy, singing through his headset as he went, then they rocked out like they'd never rocked out before, as if no one was watching, like they were young kids with the whole world to live for.

Rosalie swung an arm around Sofia's shoulders where she

stood beside her and they sang out the song together – not at all pitchy – swinging their hips and their hair.

Because that was how Seth had made Rosalie feel, like she was just a girl, loved and in love, with the whole world to live for.

Seth ended the set as he always did, taking a beat to soak up the crowd and the atmosphere. Forever humble. His most admirable trait.

Then he glanced to the side of the stage and his eyes met Rosalie's. He winked and told her through his microphone, 'I love you.'

* * *

Andrea clapped and watched as Tommy congratulated Seth and the guys when they came backstage, sweating and on a high.

Then Tommy walked back to the dressing room sofa where he'd been sitting with Andrea. He leant down and kissed her temple, then kissed her rounded stomach.

'There's nothing quite like that feeling of coming off stage, the audience screaming your name and chanting for more,' Tommy had told her recently as they shopped for a car seat and a pushchair. 'But there are other incredible feelings too. Like your baby kicking for the first time in the tummy of the woman you love.'

'Knock 'em dead,' Andi said now, as she always did before he went on stage.

'Since you told me to,' he replied with a cheeky grin, making her smile. 'Daddy will be back soon, kid,' he directed to her bump.

Some things hadn't changed about Tommy – he was cheeky, a great musician and an incredible lover. Other things had changed in the best way – he was a wonderful husband, already a loving father, a fantastic producer alongside Andrea and Sofia, and, it turned out, quite happy to give up on 4 a.m. parties every night.

Making Andi happy had become his favourite thing to do. His purpose in life, he said. She'd become his muse, when they were making music together in the studio, and when they were making love together at home, so he said. For Andrea, Tommy, her unborn child, Sofia, Hannah and Rosalie were her whole world. Making music again, the way she had for so many years, back with her sister and now her husband, completed the picture of her imperfectly perfect life. She'd never felt happier or more complete.

Tommy's entourage led him into the corridor of VIP fans as his band was already warming up the crowd. Andrea watched on a television monitor as he was hooked up to a microphone stageside, and he closed his eyes, rolled his neck from side to side, then stepped onto the stage, where he was deafened by a packed-full arena.

Tommy the rock star belonged to his fans for two hours, then Tommy Dawson would be all hers again.

* * *

Hannah could tell from Rod's body language that he was batting back wisecracks, no doubt football related, with Billy and Frankie at the small bar that had been set up in the communal dressing room.

'Are you boys talking football?' she asked, leaving the sofa where she had been sitting next to Sofia and crossing the room.

'No, ma'am,' Billy said between swigs of beer as Rod draped an arm around Hannah's shoulders. 'I was relaying a story of a delightful blonde with really big boobs, whom I believe is called Belinda, who threw some very pretty panties at me on stage.'

Hannah laughed. 'You know sex addiction is a real thing, Billy.'

'I've heard it's only a problem when you're not having it,' he countered with a wink, making Hannah laugh harder as she rolled her eyes.

'Could one of you gents do the honours?' asked Rosalie as she appeared in the middle of the group holding a chilled bottle of champagne.

'Give it here,' Rod said.

He popped the cork with too much vigour and the fizz started to bubble out of the top.

'Don't waste that!' Hannah said, thrusting a glass under the falling bubbles.

'That's my girl,' Rod said. 'Not one to waste the good stuff.'

He pinched Hannah's butt, receiving a feisty growl in return and welcoming it, Hannah could tell from his boyish grin.

Armed with a glass of champagne, she walked into his arms, holding his chin firmly between her fingers and wiggling it from side to side, the way she did with the kids.

'Can't you ever behave yourself?' she asked him.

He looked her up and down, unashamedly, scrutinising her legs in unusually high heels and the advantage of her cleavage in the fitted black number she was wearing to take full advantage of a child-free date night.

'When my woman is looking like this? No chance.'

She pouted playfully and wiggled her ass as she went back to the other side of the room with Rosalie, moving to sit on the two leather sofas where Andrea and Sofia were already seated.

Hannah had been right to call Rod out on his flaws last year. Since they finally started to really talk to each other, Rod had been doing everything to show her that he would try to never take her for granted again. He said he wanted her to have more in her life than him and the kids. Whatever made her happy. Because when he saw people failing in marriages around him, he refused to be one of them.

He slipped sometimes. Feet on the furniture, beer bottles on the coffee table and, yeah, sometimes he still forgot to leave the toilet seat the *eff* down.

But Hannah was happy with his progress and happier generally. She was working as a band manager, spending two days a week in the city and three days working from home. The kids were doing great. Luke had even started college and was playing ball.

Her life with Rod was as hot, as entertaining and as good as it ever had been.

Rod was her forever guy and Hannah was his forever girl.

And she smiled at her man as she took her seat among her best friends and their little sister.

Some things would never change, and she didn't ever want them to.

* * *

MORE FROM LAURA CARTER

Another book from Laura Carter, *Table for Three*, is available to order now here:

https://mybook.to/TableforThreeBackAd

ACKNOWLEDGEMENTS

I have to start by thanking my husband, Sam, for being patient with me when I'm lost in the world of my characters and for the hours (even the ones when you're just pretending to listen) spent beach walking and talking (mostly me) about my books. And by thanking Rocky, for being the best writing companion and furbaby I could have ever wished for. I love my boys immensely.

Thank you to:

Little Jenny, for being happy to traipse around Williamsburg with me and for hours spent listening to country music when we're getting ready to go out, whether you want to or not (keep rollin' and strollin').

Jenny P, for sharing our crush on Elvis and for all the giggles in New Orleans, Memphis and Nashville, despite the snow (and for eating as much BBQ food as me without judgement).

Helena, for totally getting my obsession with The Beatles and not moaning about the snail pace at which we walked around The Beatles Story.

Nicola, Katie, Clair, Jen and Jenna, for sharing tales of your children's blunders, and to your gorgeous babies for giving you stories to share with me.

To all the friends and family I haven't mentioned by name, who give words of encouragement, ask about my WIP and show more understanding than I probably deserve when I'm rubbish at keeping dates and replying to messages. I couldn't write about relationships and friendships without having yours.

Geoff at Abbey Road Studios for answering an abundance of questions about music production, and to Howard for putting us in touch.

In This Together wouldn't be a published book without some very important and amazing people in the book world. Huge thanks to my agent, Tanera, who championed this book from the first draft.

I owe a massive thank you to my editor Emily (and all the editors at Boldwood), for giving *In This Together* a new lease of life. To the wider team at Boldwood – designers, marketing, sales and production – thank you so much for completing the *In This Together* jigsaw.

Needless to say, I adore country music, so last but by no means least, thank you to all the country musicians who give blood, sweat and tears to share their stories in music and lyrics, so that I could write mine.

ABOUT THE AUTHOR

Laura Carter is the bestselling author of several rom-coms including the series *Brits in Manhattan* which she is relaunching and expanding with Boldwood. She lives in Jersey.

Sign up to Laura Carter's mailing list for news, competitions and updates on future books.

Visit Laura's website: www.lauracarterauthor.com

Follow Laura on social media:

- facebook.com/LauraCarterAuthor
- x.com/LCarterAuthor
- instagram.com/lauracarterauthor

ALSO BY LAURA CARTER

The Law of Attraction

Two to Tango

Friends With Benefits

Always the Bridesmaid

Fake It 'til You Make It

Stuck in Paradise With You

Table for Three

Catch a Falling Star

In This Together

Boldwood
EVER AFTER
xoxo

JOIN BOLDWOOD'S **ROMANCE COMMUNITY** FOR SWEET AND SPICY BOOK RECS WITH ALL YOUR FAVOURITE TROPES!

SIGN UP TO OUR NEWSLETTER

HTTPS://BIT.LY/BOLDWOODEVERAFTER

Boldwood

Boldwood Books is an award-winning fiction publishing company seeking out the best stories from around the world.

Find out more at www.boldwoodbooks.com

Join our reader community for brilliant books, competitions and offers!

Follow us

@BoldwoodBooks

@TheBoldBookClub

Sign up to our weekly deals newsletter

https://bit.ly/BoldwoodBNewsletter

Printed in Dunstable, United Kingdom